Flash Drive

Books by Jacqueline DeGroot

Climax
The Secret of the Kindred Spirit
What Dreams Are Made Of
Barefot Beaches
For the Love of Amanda
Shipwrecked at Sunset
Worth Any Price
Father Steve's Dilemma
The Widows of Sea Trail—Book One
Catalina of Live Oaks
The Widows of Sea Trail—Book Two
Tessa of Crooked Gulley
The Widows of Sea Trail—Book Three
Vivienne of Sugar Sands
Running into Temptation
with Peggy Grich
Running up the Score
with Peggy Grich
Running into a Brick Wall
with Peggy Grich
Tales of the Silver Coast—A Secret History of
Brunswick County
with Miller Pope
Sunset Beach—A History
with Miller Pope
Flash Drive

Flash Drive

Lost and Found @ Sunset Beach

by

Jacqueline DeGroot

Every time we walk along a beach some ancient urge disturbs us so that we find ourselves shedding shoes and garments or scavenging among seaweed and whitened timbers like the homesick refugees of a long war.

–Loren Eiseley
The Unexpected Universe

The life of a writer, especially a self-published one, is dependent on many people. Without them, I would never be able to turn my stories into books, get them into the stores, and into the hands of people who, with their encouragement, perpetuate the cycle.

My writer's group, Writers Bloc, is a tremendous support and quite possibly the best critiquing partners in the country. We often joke about needing band-aids when we leave the meetings as we pride ourselves on being brutally frank with each other.

I am so grateful to my dedicated proofreaders who give up their time to read through my stories when it is probably least convenient, and with looming deadlines. They are amazing, each and every one. Without them, I cannot imagine how I could ever get this done. It is their encouragement in the final hours that pushes me toward the end produt. I doubt that I will ever truly understand the use of commas, but I do believe I am getting better as time goes on.

Thank you to my proofreaders:

Ray Cullis
Bill DeGroot
Jack Echard
Peggy Grich
Pam McNeel
Sandy Raymond
Barbara Scott-Cannon

A big hug to Miller Pope, for always being willing to drop whatever he's working on to help design my covers and take me to lunch.

Love and affection for Peggy Grich for helping to edit, format, and package the final manuscript—seems I'm always asking her to put her life on hold at the end of May to get a book out for the summer season.

Heartfelt gratitude to my family for being so supportive of a writing career that keeps me very active, and overly focused on a 12 x 9 monitor.

Thank you Anne, Pat, and Suzanne of Pelican Bookstore for giving my books a prominent place on the shelves and for suggesting my books to new readers . . . we all still blush when talking about them, don't we?

There are many places that sell my books but I am especially grateful to Ginny and Debbie at Sunset River Marketplace, all the wonderful people at Silver Coast Winery, Tracy and John Hopgood at Sunset Beach Trading Company, Dave Nelson, Kelly and Andrea at The Sunset Inn, Wanda at How Sweet It Is, Barbara at L. Bookworm, and Clif and Laura at RBR Books.com

Flash Drive

Chapter One

The House in Ocean Ridge Plantation

Laurel

Where the hell was it? Laurel, a petite blonde with the wild green eyes began tossing things out of her purse, scattering them all over the high-glossed table. It was a big purse, too big really—and deep—one of those popular hobo shoulder bags. Standing on tiptoes in her size-six Andres Machado pumps, she strained to see the bottom. She tucked a strand of blonde hair behind her ear so she could see into the dark void. She moved things around, but clearly, her flash drive wasn't there. Panic caused her chest to seize. Afraid her heart had stopped, she put her hand over it and froze until she felt it kick-start.

Not to be deterred, not even by a heart attack, she turned back to her purse and dug deeper. She began tossing everything out. *Where was it? Please don't tell me I've lost it—if I've lost the files containing my fantasy life, I'll die.*

Half an hour later, when it hadn't turned up in any of the sane, as well as insane places it might be, she had to let the thought encroach and settle . . . *I've lost it. Oh. My. God . . .*

The little snack-sized baggie with her 4GB flash drive was missing. *Missing!* The fact that she needed it to back up her computer files before leaving the house was the only

1

reason she even knew it was missing. *Missing!* Someone could be reading her stories right now. Dread sapped the life force out of her.

She was late for her appointment. She was torn about what to do. Her mind raced. When had she last backed up? When had she written something she'd saved? Today was Friday. It had to have been on Wednesday that she'd had that little black and red modern miracle of technology in her hand; she'd inserted it into her laptop, and saved the erotic ramblings of one seriously sex-obsessed woman—namely herself. Into the baggie her libidinous, salacious, priapic thoughts had gone. Then the Ziploc had been tucked into a side pocket of her vintage Gucci Diamante shoulder bag.

She ran around the house dumping sweetgrass baskets, pulling out drawers, opening and closing closet doors, until it became nauseatingly clear that she was not going to find that highly pornographic storage marvel before she had to leave, which really should have been fifteen minutes ago.

She threw all her stuff back into her purse, vowing to dump it all out and start the search all over again when she got back. *It had to be there. It just had to be.* She couldn't comprehend how awful it would be if it weren't. She forced herself not to go there—no, not right now. People were waiting for her.

But thinking of whose hands that not-so-innocent little thing could have fallen into, made her cringe. It held her secrets, all her dirty little secrets. Every single wicked scenario that played out in her mind eventually made it onto that thumb drive.

Laurel was having a really bad morning. And if she didn't find that flash drive, she was going to have a really bad life.

Chapter Two

Village of Sunset Beach

Garrett

Garrett Grayson normally hated grocery shopping, preferring to eat out or order in when snacking on cheese and crackers no longer satisfied. But he was at Sunset Beach now, at his beach house, and it was almost a pleasure to do the domestic duty at the local Food Lion. Everyone was friendly, and if he forgot his MVP card, they always offered to use theirs or to look his up by his phone number. None of the cashiers in the grocery stores in his hometown of Laurel, Maryland would have taken the time.

He piled the reusable canvas bags on the front passenger floorboard of his blue Corvette convertible, grouping the ones with the cans and cartons of juice together so they'd brace up the milk. He stacked the bags of chips and bread on the passenger seat, tucked the cereal and pasta boxes behind the console, and jammed the deodorant and toothbrush into his shirt pocket. It was inconvenient having a two-seater at times, but well worth it for the long trip down 95, especially in late August, when the weather began behaving again and he could drive with the top down.

Mid-August heralded the beginning of the season for the homeowners on the island. With the kids back in school the beaches weren't crowded, favorite restaurants didn't have a crush of people waiting to get in, and the fall festivals were lining up. Until the end of November, and often well into December, it was a glorious time to be at the beach. And he didn't mind grocery shopping—not one single bit.

He pushed the empty cart over to the "buggy" return and shoved it over the bar embedded in the asphalt so that it wouldn't roll out and dent someone's car. He frowned when his eye fell on something red glinting in the sun near the toe of his Bacco Bucci sandal. At first he thought it was a Swiss Army knife, but on closer inspection saw it was a deep burgundy, not the crimson red of the Swiss flag. *A barrette maybe?* He pulled at the denim creasing his thighs to allow for a deep squat. It looked like a flash drive, half in and half out of a snack-sized baggie. He picked up the plastic bag and turned it over. Lexar™ was printed in white type on a black case with the identifying marks: 4GB, Made in China, followed by a long model number and the standard four international communication symbols. The ruby red insertion plug that had drawn his eye was the housing for the USB connection that swung up from the black case. It was a typical flash drive—its bold red accents made it stylish, solid, and intriguing.

Garrett stood and took it out of the baggie and examined it closer. It was small in his big hand, but not all that special—he figured it cost about thirty dollars. It had a ring on one end that could be used to attach it to something. It wasn't scratched, so it didn't appear as if it had ever swung from a set of keys.

He tossed it up and down as he looked around the parking lot. People were coming and going, oblivious to his find. He called out to the only person he saw, a man rearranging things in his trunk. He looked up and listened as Garrett explained what he'd found on the ground, then shook his head "no." It wasn't his.

Garrett tucked the baggie and the flash drive into his

front pocket. He knew from past experience never to get into a 'vette with *anything* in your *back* pocket. He'd learned that the hard way when his had comb gouged the leather seat on his '85. This was an '09 and it was pristine.

He thought he should probably go inside and take the baggie and its surrendered prize to the lost and found. Whoever lost it might backtrack and come looking for it. But what were the odds it was a local person? He decided he might have better luck returning it to its owner than a clerk who would probably just throw it into a drawer and forget about it. He'd take it back to the beach house, plug it in, and see if there was anything on it that would identify the owner. He loved a good mystery and solving puzzles was one of his passions.

He was so intrigued by the challenge that he was distracted and almost drove right past the entrance ramp leading to the new bridge. He smiled and shook his head. That made three times since he'd been here that he'd done that. Old habits were hard to shake, he mused, as he downshifted to make the turn in time. He sped up to crest the summit. The old swing bridge had been quaint, but a detriment for low-slung sports cars as his. Still, he missed its picturesque presence and the hold-the-world-at-bay sentiment it represented.

He took his foot off the gas at the top of the 65-foot span so he could enjoy the view on the way down, and ran his fingers through his thick wind-tousled hair. It was a new vantage point for him and he enjoyed seeing the island spread out before him. He couldn't see his house on the east side of the island because of the rows of houses blocking it, but he could see the beach in front of it, as well as the ocean stretching out like an aquamarine kaleidoscope shimmering in the sun.

The sense of peace this place brought him was worth every dime he'd invested. And then some.

Chapter Three

Laurel

This was the worst day of her life! She couldn't believe she'd lost it—her flash drive—the key to her "secret" life. The one that no one, absolutely no one, was supposed to ever know about—thoughts so prurient, so sinful . . . so shocking.

No one could learn her secret shame. If anyone knew how wicked her thoughts were, how dishonorably she desired to be treated in her fantasies, well, she'd just curl up and die.

Why the heck hadn't she been more careful, at least put one of those address stickers on the bag? Lord knew she had a zillion of them as she'd contributed to every charity that had ever sent her personalized stickers. If she'd only used one, at least her name and address would be handy if anyone wanted to return the stupid thing!

She was sick to her stomach. The flash drive was all she could think about. All day it had been foremost in her mind. She had written down every single place she could remember being since the last time she had absolutely, positively known she'd had it in her possession. Called every one of those places, explaining who she was, what she'd lost, and where she could be contacted if anyone turned it in. She'd left word with her doctor's office, two grocery stores, the bank, and the Mexican restaurant.

That was fun; explaining what she'd lost, in broken high school Spanish. She was sure they thought she'd lost a watch. She finally drove to Las Palmeras and showed the manager a picture of her flash drive, one she'd downloaded from the Internet. He shook his head, nothing like that had been turned in.

Upset as she was, she still had things she had to do, and she couldn't keep leaving her home computer and laptop without backing up the data. She consoled herself by thinking how lucky she was that at least she hadn't lost any of her work. Not a lick. It was all on her laptop and home computer and everything had previously been saved to a disc.

The tragedy that she was dealing with was that she'd lost control of her life. Some total stranger had her life in his hands. He, or she, had access to everything she'd written in the past five years, everything she thought significant or noteworthy. But that wasn't the worse part.

She was fairly certain that her *daytime* thoughts were fairly normal for someone in her late twenties. It was still uncomfortable, knowing her private musings were out there and could be flying around the country if the person who found her flash drive had a mind to pass them on, but it wasn't her daytime thoughts that made this an end-of-the-world catastrophe. It was her *nighttime* thoughts—her "stories." *Bed*time stories to be more explicit, because damned near all of them were about sweet, young heroines in bed with fabulously hunky heroes doing incredibly wicked things to their lovely bodies.

Chapter Four

Garrett

Garrett climbed the steps to his beach house carrying all six bags—he-men never made two trips, no matter that their fingers were still bloodless hours later. The beach house he'd named *Stock Exchange*, was a present to himself after he'd earned his first million on the market, and now, many millions later, he came here whenever he had the chance. He had in fact, structured his life so that he could work from here as much as possible.

Sometimes during the fall, but always after the holidays, during the semester that was in the dead of winter, he was a college professor teaching online classes for the University of Maryland—correcting papers, grading tests, doling out assignments, and offering career advice to students attempting a master's degree in the field of business management. But that was his philanthropic endeavor, it wasn't his moneymaker. It was the job that soothed his conscience and appeased his mother.

His "real" job, the one that paid the bills for his beach house, the Corvettes, the hi-tech toys, and his outlandish Nordstrom account, was day trading. With a laptop and a mouse he could win or lose thousands in seconds, hundreds of thousands actually. He thought of it as winning and losing, not earning and spending. To him it was gambling, pure and simple. Sure, he changed the odds by learning all he could before "rolling the dice," but he was always cognizant of the fact that he was gambling—majorly. He didn't dabble, this was big league stuff. It didn't pay to do it otherwise. And he was damn good at it. Hell, he and the I.R.S. were 60/40 partners now and he often wondered whether it would be worth his while to expatriate and move to Ireland where his grandfather still lived, augmenting his county pension by carving wizards on walking sticks.

After putting the groceries away, he booted up the laptop and used the remote to turn the TV to CNBC for the international business report. In his email there were already ten newsletters queued up to read and he doubted he'd been gone an hour. Because of his job—both of them—he was practically always reading. There was so much to know, especially these days with all the companies merging, changing, going under, starting up, going public, embezzling, lying, falsifying reports, and then reorganizing, that he had come to rely on a myriad of newsletters from financial institutions all over the world. He let the financial pundits and publishers do some of the legwork, and a fair share of the tedious research, while he charted and checked their success rates and read consumer reviews about their products. Ultimately, that was how businesses were made or razed—by customer satisfaction.

He charted how his predictions panned out, short term and long term, on spread sheets. He'd been doing this so long now that he had an amazing statistical analysis model that he updated and maintained. He knew who to listen to, who to hedge with—literally—who to trust with his money, and who to stay away from. Corporate idiots were often his silent gambling partners, and lately there were many who could be counted on to screw up phenomenally. He paid attention to the new whiz kids trying to bring their wares to market because more often than not, he could make hundreds of thousands on their mistakes before they figured things out.

The way the market worked was complicated and quirky for newcomers and he scrupulously monitored the trends of America's youth. They had more expendable income than most and if they liked something, they could make a company an overnight success with their social media skills. Yes, it was a lot of work, but what else was he going to do? He didn't want to teach full time, it was too time consuming and too much damned work.

He muted the TV, read the *Money Matrix* report, pondered for a moment, heeded the advice, and went into his account and sold some stock from his mini-account. Then he moved money from his maxi account and bought more gold. That was his favorite thing to do—buy gold. He felt sure that was the best investment there could be in these uncertain times. But he waited for the right deal before diverting money, because once he bought it, he didn't plan on ever selling it—it had to always be considered part of his set-in-stone investment capital. He had huge reserves and was ready whenever the market fell, had an "adjustment," or announced a failure. He was able to capitalize on doom and get his money into the market fast when volatile times came. He'd done very well with the housing crisis, in essence betting against the country, but he hadn't been as aggressive as he should have been. Who would have thought it would go down so far, and then stay down?

He was good with money because he was well read, diligent, and not at all timid. The rush of a gambler was in his blood, but so was the voice of the professor—the one who made $45,000 a year graduating students who would owe ten times that amount by the time he walked the processional with his colleagues and stood by to watch them receive their degrees. Yet he was a man who knew what it was like to eat beans out of a can, and to hide in his dorm room because he didn't have the money for condoms, nevertheless enough to go Dutch on a date. It had been touch and go those last two years of college and quite honestly, if it hadn't been for the donuts, he'd have never made it.

His dad had died during his junior year leaving his mother a paltry insurance policy and a pension account that the state had severely compromised. He blamed his father for not seeing to his mother's future, but acknowledged that seeing to her welfare had been the driving principle that had fired his ambition. And it had all started with a dozen donuts.

He chuckled as he clicked and made the last transaction, anticipating the close of the market in ten minutes. *Those clods, if they could only see me now.* He shook his head as he made the final click and began the signing off process that would lock his business bank account and keep it secure.

It had been worth it, getting up at 4:30 every morning to high tail it over to the Dunkin' Donuts store to buy six boxes of donuts every morning. He'd turned a cash outlay of $18 and the loss of three hours sleep into $71 every single morning—except Sundays. At a buck a donut, it was a good deal for everyone. It was breakfast—fast, handy, and satisfying for the crusty-eyed jocks who were habitually hung-over, the geeks who stumbled down the stairs after studying all night, and the perpetual dieters who said, "No, I shouldn't," before finally taking one in each hand. The preppies with their doe-eyed and well-tumbled dates were his best customers though, as they often bought a whole box. All-night sex tended to burn the calories in a big way. And of course those little "swimmers" had to be replenished in time for the next nightly bout. His take would have been an even $72, as he always sold out, but he indulged his own sweet tooth, and so ended up with $71. Those dweebs would be amazed to learn that he had parlayed all that donut money into millions.

Chapter Five

Laurel

She could not sleep. She tossed and twisted in the sheets. The angst of not knowing where her flash drive had ended up was keeping her from having a moment's peace. Not a single second of it. She kept visualizing people finding her flash drive, plugging it into their own computers, and then finding out all her dirty secrets. She saw the lecher who drooled over her pornographic prose with his zipper undone, the teenager whose eyes bugged at the scintillating scenes she'd set, the outraged zealot who would want her hauled in front of a tribunal and then burned at the stake. In her nightmares, they each, in turn, sent her stories on—the lecher to the most base websites, the teenager to everyone he knew, the zealot to every righteous supporter, building community outrage. With the cacophony of click, click, click becoming louder and louder, she jolted and cried out in her sleep. Each recipient, in turn, forwarded her files until her most private thoughts circled the world and hordes of people came for her. Crashing through her door, hauling her from her house to strip her, jeer at her, and then finally to flagellate her in the streets. She woke drenched and shaking over and over again until finally, she didn't even try to get back to sleep.

She walked around the house seeing absolutely nothing as she reasoned with herself. *It's not so bad; at least in this country what I've done isn't illegal.* She bumped into a doorjamb because she didn't want the starkness of bright light right now. She knew she already had the deer in the headlights look, she could feel her face taut with it. *We have freedom of speech, freedom to say or write what we want; I can't be arrested for this.*

Then another voice intruded, her skeptical, sarcastic, negative, downer self: *Yeah, but in some countries, what you wrote could get you killed. They would behead you in Iran. Drag your entrails through the streets in Bahrain.*

She put her hands to her head and fisted her hair. *What had she done? She'd ruined her life, that's what she had done!* Think, think, think! Where could that damned thing be?

She'd already gutted her purse, literally ripped the lining out and turned it inside out. Gone over every inch of her car, methodically searched her house, her garage, gone back through the calendar and written down every single place she'd been. There wasn't a minute not accounted for. And she had called or gone to every place she'd been—over and over again. Now the clerks only shook their head when they saw her approach.

She sat down and stared at the spot of light shining on the wooden floor coming from the glow of the nightlight on the icemaker. Then a thought occurred to her. How would they know? How would they know it was hers? Oh . . . was that better, or worse? Some of her best writing was on that drive and now she wouldn't even get credit for it. Couldn't claim it. Well, she could . . . God, what was worse? Everyone in the world knowing she wrote the stories, or having her stories read, talked about, maybe even published and no one knowing they were hers? Is this how *Anonymous* got started? God, could she make up her mind—was she proud of them or ashamed of them? Then it occurred to her that her Quicken files were on that flash drive. *They would know!*

Every single transaction she had with her bank, every

check, every debit card charge, every deposit—it was all there. It would lead to her. She couldn't hide. It told the story of her life. Where she shopped, who her doctors were, how much she paid for her car, her mortgage, her insurance payments. Oh God, this was worse than she thought. Her identity could be stolen! She ran for her checkbook. *Just how bad was this?* What could they know exactly, and would it lead to her? And was that a good or a bad thing? The way she was feeling right now, she'd happily pay a five-thousand dollar reward if someone would just put the damned thing in her hand instead of plugging it into their USB port.

Chapter Six

Garrett

Garrett took his peanut butter and jelly sandwich to the table and dumped a handful of barbequed Fritos between the two halves. Then he twisted the cap off his Michelob Light Lime Cactus and took a hearty swig. Sitting down, he shrugged his shoulders as if readying for battle and picked up the flash drive.

In it went, into the port on his keyboard. He absentmindedly chomped on a few Fritos as he waited for the icon to appear on his desktop. His steely gray eyes focused on the monitor waiting for the first glimpse, and he wondered what the drive had been named. It jumped on screen and sat in the bottom corner as unobtrusive as butter on toast. It was titled "Backups." Boy, that was original. No help there.

Checking to make sure his virus protection was on, he double clicked and watched as files filled the screen. His eyes flared wide as he read some of the names on the files: *The Master's Serf, Debauched Housewives, Take My Wife & Let Me Watch, Dr. BDSM, The Village Blacksmith and the Widowed Lady, Mary's Wedding Night, Surrogate Husband, The Doctor and His Nurse, Forced to Marry My Dead Husband's Brother, The Rake and the Young Innocent, The Dr. and the Corporate Raider, One Climax Too Many, The Professor & His Submissive, Quicken98.*

Unless he missed his guess, the owner of this flash drive was female with kinky sex on her mind. He reached for his beer while deciding what to click on first. He knew he should click on the Quicken file, as it was the one most likely to have the kind of information he needed to track this wild woman down. But the business day was over, he was relaxing, and he was primed for a good story. He was tempted to read about the Professor and his Submissive, but that was a little too close to home, so he chose *Surrogate Husband* and double-clicked to open the file.

Surrogate Husband
Or
The Officer's Submissive Wife

He trusted him with his life, now he would trust him with his wife.

Chapter I

It was all Caliente could do to keep from screaming out her frustration to the night. Alone again, in the oversized bed, and needing his touch so badly her skin was tight, and tingly—itching with a lustful fever that she could not endure. She had a need she could not slake no matter how many times she touched herself. She needed Clint, and she needed him like a feline in heat needed a tom.

But it wasn't going to happen. Clint was still overseas on some damned mission. Six months had come and gone, and she'd been prepared for them, accepting them to some degree. As the last day of the fifth month had been crossed off the calendar, she'd felt her body shift in anticipation, psyching itself up for his return. She remembered the day she began to allow herself to draw the thaw of the long winter into her bones and to let her body melt to the supple readiness that was her true nature. Clint had emailed that all was going according to plan and that soon he would be able to shave off the godforsaken beard he'd had to grow as part of his camouflage for the hills of

Afghanistan. A sniper by profession, but now elevated to the rank of Captain, he was in charge of the special ops team that had captured, and was now holding, a key communications tower for the Army. Her body had sung as she'd zipped through the commissary laying in supplies for his return. *He's coming home, he's coming home!* was the mantra that repeated in her head as she stocked up on rib-eyes, Cocoa Puffs and all his favorite snacks.

When just a week later he had emailed with the news that a lucky shot had hit a propane tank and blew up their shack along with their communication lines and that they were moving on to capture the next tower to repair the lines, she had known that the homecoming she'd been anticipating would not be right around the corner. Two days later he had been officially notified that his tour had been extended another two months. A week after that, he emailed that his best friend, Rand, had been hit and was being sent stateside. No one knew how serious it was, but any gunshot wound was serious when there were no hospitals, surgeons, or antibiotics to fight infection. He said he'd given Rand a letter for her as his gurney had been lifted into the med-evac helicopter. He told her to read it carefully, that it was what he wanted. He didn't say anything else. The following day, he wrote that his team was on the move once more and that he didn't know when he'd be able to contact her again. He said he loved her and that he wanted her happiness more than anything in the world.

She had cried herself to sleep that night, and then, frustrated beyond belief, reached into his nightstand for their toys, selecting the one that would guarantee enough satisfaction to at least allow her to sleep. It hadn't.

Mondays were the worst days, especially here on post where the activities of Ft. Bragg dominated everyone's life. Everyone was back at work, the kids were back in school, and the neighborhood was quiet. There were no parties for her to attend, no socials for her to bake for, no ladies groups to dress up to go to. Nothing to do but cut more coupons, pay a few more bills, and maybe wash Clint's vintage Camaro for the umpteenth time since he'd left.

Clint had asked her not to look for a job when they had married a year ago, hoping to have her all to himself for a few years before she became a bored housewife or busy mother. But the Army had other plans, and instead of spending her days doing his laundry, ironing his dress shirts, cleaning their house on base, and preparing his dinners, she was writing him letters she hoped would find him, and pining for him with every cell in her body.

She didn't know how she was going to make it another two and a half months. She was desperate for his touch, for the feel of his skin on hers, for the fullness of her body as his cock slammed into her.

The doorbell rang and she dropped her dust rag onto the coffee table to answer it. No one on post worried about calling out through the door; if you made it through the gate, you were no threat to the military, and that included their wives and children. She'd never lived in a more secured place.

She opened the door wide to a smiling officer—a very handsome, tall, smiling officer, in full dress as if he'd just come from a military ceremony. There was a funeral at least once a week and any soldier on base not working at the time, was usually obligated to attend. But the grin on this man's face didn't gel with that thought, he was way too happy to have come from burying a friend.

"Callie! I'm Rand Preston, Clint's buddy. He asked me to stop by and see you."

She looked at him closer. She had seen grainy Internet pictures, but they didn't do him justice. No siree, they did not. He was at least six-foot three, likely an inch or two taller. He had sandy brown hair that while thick, was flattened and indented on the sides from the dark green cap with the corded and embellished insignia of the Army that was now tucked ceremoniously under his arm. He had the standard military haircut, short and close-cropped. The men either preferred that, or all of it off—at least when they were stateside. His eyes were a deep brown covered with gold flecks sparkling in the sun. She appraised his long, sooty lashes, well-defined eyebrows, and clean-shaven jaw that was squared off with just the hint of a cleft in the center. Then her eyes fell to his expressive lips, lips that were now quirked up at the corners. God his lips, a little chapped from the Afghan desert, they were full and sensuous and very inviting.

I've been too long without a man, she thought, I shouldn't be taking this man's inventory like this! *This was Clint's best friend for g-d-sake!* Mentally shaking herself, she remembered her manners and pulled the door wider, "Rand, please come in. I thought Clint said you'd been shot."

"I was, in the bicep, but I was really fine by the time they got me stateside. They actually shouldn't have bothered bringing me in. By the time Frankfurt was finished with me, I was ready to be returned. As far as I'm concerned, I'm ready to go back, but my doctor says otherwise. He says to give the muscles and tendons another month to mend."

He strode into the room and typical to his

training, took in everything at once. "Nice place. Clint's lucky; you have a flair for decorating. One would never suspect this is post housing. At least from the inside," he added with a grin. Every house on this street looked identical from the outside—all were two-stories, with wrap-around white porches and terra cotta-styled tiled roofs. The only things that distinguished one from another were the cars in the driveway and the plants on the porch.

"Thank you. I kill time looking through magazines and copying the pros."

"Well it looks great, the colors are very relaxing. Beats the drab olive and tan I'm so used to seeing everywhere."

"Would you like something to drink?"

"Yes, as a matter of fact I would. Clint says he always keeps some special Dewar's on hand, could I have some over ice?"

"Certainly. Anything, anything at all, for one of Clint's comrades," she said with an engaging smile.

He watched her ass as she walked across the room and through the doorway that lead to the kitchen. Clint hadn't lied. She was stunning. Tall and willowy, dressed in black slacks and a gray button-up cashmere sweater, she looked elegant. And the way she wore her hair, loose and long, curling over her shoulders was sexy as hell. But it was her eyes that really grabbed him. A beautiful jade green shot through with silver and black flecks. When she returned, he admired her breasts, high and full, outlined by one of those "put-me-on-the-shelf-and-show-me-off" bras if he wasn't mistaken. A scant half-inch lower and he'd be able to delineate her nipples. Sadly, it was not.

She handed him his drink and he watched as she went over to a carved oriental cabinet and lifted a carafe from the center circle of six wine glasses. She poured a deep burgundy liquid into one of the glasses, stopping when it was barely half full. It appeared the lady was a connoisseur of red wine. He smiled and held his glass high in a toast, "To this bloody war being bloody well over!"

"Amen to that," she breathed and took a seat on the side of an armchair. He placed his hat on an end table and moved to the sofa. Thoughtfully, he took a coaster from a small wooden rack, placed his drink on it, and pulling at the crease just above the knees to keep his dress pants from grabbing at his muscular thighs, he sat gingerly as if the sofa belonged to a child.

"Are you in pain?" she asked with concern.

"No ma'am, just came from a damn medal ceremony where I had to stand for two hours in these new shoes."

She looked down; the black dress shoes were spit shined and clearly brand new. At over six feet tall he had to have big feet. These shoes were probably too small. "Did you get a medal," she asked with a teasing smile.

He grinned back at her, "Of course. That's one thing the new army knows how to do, pin medals on the injured in a very timely fashion. I was just released from Walter Reed two days ago."

"So where are you staying?"

"I'm billeted on post, in the officer's quarters. Not too bad, especially when you consider where I've been sleeping for the past few months—The Flintstones' Hilton—caves on the sides of mountains."

"Well you must stay and have dinner with me."

"You will get no argument from me. I'm already sick of mess hall chow."

"So Chicken Parmesan would work for you?"

"A bowl of Life cereal would work for me, so don't put yourself out."

"I love to cook, so it won't be any trouble. I miss cooking for a man," she said wistfully.

"Uh, that reminds me . . . I have something from Clint for you." He dug into his shirt pocket and pulled out a folded sheet of paper. "He wrote it in a hurry while we were waiting for the chopper and all he could find to write on was the graph paper from the medic's field kit EKG, but here it is. Before you read it, you should know that I know what it says. He told me what he was going to write before he wrote it." His eyes met hers and held.

She thought he was trying to tell her something, but from his sheepish grin, the only message that conveyed was that everything was all right. She took the folded, creased, and sweat-stained paper from him as if it was a treasured piece of Sanskrit and then she took her time unfolding it.

"I can wait outside while you read it if you'd like."

"No, that won't be necessary. I'll take it to the bedroom. You just relax, and enjoy your drink. Help yourself to more scotch, it's on the counter in the kitchen."

She took the paper, and reading it as she walked, she made her way down the hallway to the bedroom.

My Darling Caliente,

How do I say all I want to say to you? I miss you so much and love you so completely. I wish more than anything that we could be together right now. I dream of you nightly, kiss you everywhere, and fuck you tirelessly in both my daydreams and my night dreams. I miss us, I miss our lovemaking, and I miss seeing the pleasure in your eyes as you come for me. Callie, you are what I am living for.

By now you know it could be several more months before I can come home to you and feel your wonderful quivers of delight while you lie under me. During our short marriage I have learned how your body responds to every touch, every lick, every caress, every kiss. And I have learned that you cannot go without sex indefinitely. Since you've never been very proficient at self-pleasuring (and believe me, if I wasn't an expert before, I surely am now), I have a proposition for you. I want you to allow Rand to be my proxy. I know this is a strange request but please hear me out. I want you to allow him to be your substitute husband while I'm away. He is the only man I would ever trust to take my place in your bed, the only man I know worthy enough to fill your body. The only man capable of doing to you the things you need done to you, while being both tender and loving, and reverently respectful of you and your body.

As men in the field do, we've talked about our sex lives and our women extensively. Rand is currently single, having broken ties with his girlfriend before shipping out, but I know how much he cared for her. And after comparing notes, he and I agree that we are both aggressively bent and like to do some of the same things to our women. He has assured me that he will do everything in his power to please you. So . . . please take my best friend to our bed and allow him to ease your lusts. Let him be your surrogate husband. I know by now that you must be strung so high that you're crawling out of your skin. Please know that there will never be any recriminations from this. I sanction this with my whole heart. I give you to him gladly in hopes that you two, my most favorite people in the world, can make some sense of this madness we call war, and satisfy each other's needs. Of course, when I come home, I will expect you to prefer me to him. So, sate yourself for a while, but when you hear that I am on my way back to you, send him away. Now . . .go play.

Your loving husband,

Clint

After carefully refolding the letter and tucking it into her underwear drawer, she walked back down the hallway. Not seeing Rand in the living room, she walked into the kitchen. He was leaning against the counter, his feet crossed at the ankles, his back to the cabinets, looking down at the drink in his hand.

"I didn't realize you guys were *quite* that close," she said.

She had been crying, he could see the tracks of tears on her cheeks and her eyeliner was smudged from wiping her eyes.

"Well, not physically. We both like women— exclusively."

"So . . . my husband wants you to fuck me."

"He didn't say that. At least not to me. Not in that exact way anyway."

"No?"

"No."

"Then what did he say, exactly?" There was a tinge of anger in her voice.

"He said you might be hurting, that you might need someone. That maybe I could help."

"Do other officers do this? Give their wives to their men? Is this a common thing in the new military?"

"I don't know. I don't talk to other men about these issues. Clint is the only one I can talk to about practically anything. As to *officers* giving their wives to *their men,* Clint and I are the same rank; we are equals in that regard. I am not his man, nor is he mine. We are friends—friends who help each other out, no matter the prob. . .task."

"So, I'm a task, some chore to tackle, something to scratch off the to-do list?"

"I was going to say no matter the problem, but looking at you, I can see no problem whatsoever." His eyes roved over her body, drinking her in from head to toe. She could see the appreciation as his eyes skimmed her, focusing and holding an intense heated gaze as his eyes lingered on her sweater-clad breasts and then lower, to the crotch of her slacks. "No, no problem, at least none that I can see—other than your attitude. You don't seem very accepting of this arrangement."

"Well why should I be? Why should I even consider *you* as my husband's replacement?"

"From the many discussions he and I have had—and forgive me for being blunt—but we are of the same mind when it comes to women: we both would rather feast on a woman's cunt than have a toe-curling blowjob; we are both very well endowed; not at all adverse to using toys; wholly into buggery, which I'm told is a favorite with you; and we both fancy ourselves to be Doms, if only in the loosest sense of the word—hence we like submissive women, which by the way, you are not turning out to be. I might add, that we both know how to treat women—diligently, with patience, respect, and finesse. And also with a firm hand when necessary," he added with a wink. "In short, we both adore women. And we have both had years of experience giving women pleasure. There. That's my sexual resume. I'm applying for the position of surrogate husband."

"This is absurd!" She searched the counter tops and then mumbled, "Did you see my wine glass?"

"I believe you left it in the living room."

She spun on her heel and left the kitchen. He followed. Then watched as she snatched up her glass and plopped down onto the sofa. Glaring up at him and sipping her wine, she snapped, "I don't even know you."

"I don't know you either, but I'm willing to get to know you . . . and eager to learn all your secrets," he said, lowering his voice while raising an eyebrow and a corner of his mouth at the same time. It was sexy as all get out.

She tilted her head and frowned at him, "Of course you are."

"Hey, I'm a discriminating guy."

"That's another thing—"

"Your husband already asked me all the safe sex questions. I've been cleared."

"Even thinking about this is lunacy!" She gulped down a hefty portion of wine. "No, I won't. I can't possibly. I love my husband." She took another sip of wine, draining the glass. He walked over, got the carafe and refilled it.

"Love has nothing to do with what he's proposing."

She took another sip while she watched him move around the room as if he owned it, as graceful as a Ninja, which she supposed, he kind of was—the six-foot- five kind. Nothing about this man was short, puny, or undeveloped. God no.

Her eyes followed his movements as he fingered things, picking them up and putting them down, and she felt his touch vibrate through her with each thing he touched. How was that possible? She watched him brush his fingertips over a small stone sculpture of a naked lady reclining on a chaise being hefted by her slaves, and she shivered from his touch. He ran a finger over her smooth breasts and her own nipples stiffened. She had stroked that same piece countless times, it was marble and cold, but the sight of him idly stroking it was heating her blood, boiling it really.

She drained her glass and reached out to put it on the coffee table. She missed and bobbled it. He spun and caught it before it hit the floor. Their eyes met, inches apart, it was the closest they had been to each other and she could smell him. He smelled of spice, scotch, musk, and man. Hungry man. He placed the glass on the table and stood, never taking his eyes from hers.

"I love my husband! And I miss him terribly! I want *him* here with me, not you!"

Then, to her total humiliation, she started sobbing, heart wrenching sobs that came from her chest, bubbling up and causing her to gasp for breath, making her convulse and shake. He gathered her into his arms, lifting her against his chest and then he turned to sit on the sofa. He held her snug against him as she cried into his shirt. He held her for a long time; eventually lifting her higher onto his lap so he could wrap both arms around her as she alternately sobbed, cried softly, and hiccupped into his shoulder.

It was killing him to see her in so much pain. When he could no longer stand it, he gently turned her, laid her with her head on the bolster of the sofa, and began to kiss her collarbone and nibble on her neck. Her smooth skin smelled of jasmine and it drove him wild. He had to taste more of her. As he kissed up her neck to her ear, lingering and listening to her soft mewling whimpers, he began to unbutton her sweater. It had a long row of tiny pearl buttons so she had to be aware of what he was doing, but she didn't stop him. He took his time, giving her every opportunity to stay his hand, to deny him the next button as his lips continued the leisurely foray up and down the side of her neck.

When her sweater was completely unbuttoned, he spread the plackets wide and caressed her soft abdomen. Then he flicked the single button on her slacks and eased her zipper down. Her eyes opened wide and she whispered, "No."

"Yes."

"I miss my husband."

Taking a handkerchief from his pant's pocket he folded it over three times and tied it over her eyes. "I *am* your husband," he whispered in her ear as he blindfolded her. "Pretend I'm Clint. For tonight let me be your husband. Let me love you as he would if he were here. Call me Clint, forget his friend was ever even here." His voice was soft and seductive, his tongue laving the whirls of her ear, masterful, practiced, and reminiscent of the man she loved.

His fingers traced the tears on her face, wiping

them dry, then his palm cupped her cheek and she moved her face into the caress. She was his. For now.

Chapter II

He knew the things she liked, knew the things that would drive her wild. Clint had told him all he needed to know. Men preparing to die bared their souls; they shared an intimacy unlike at any other time in their lives. Two times in six years he and Clint had sat facing each other, surrounded by the enemy and out numbered in spades, and each time they had talked late into the night, telling all manner of secrets to keep the fear at bay. The last time, just a few weeks ago, over the course of three days, he had learned everything there was to know about Callie, her unique desires, and the ways that Clint had found to satisfy them.

Then a few days later as Clint had sat beside Rand talking to him to keep him conscious while they waited for the helicopter, he had given him this sacred mission. He sent him home to care for his young wife. Knowing it was the type of mission they were both used to—covert, dangerous, and terrifying in its on way—he gave his trust to Rand. He was confident that Rand could bring sensual pleasure to the woman he loved, as right now, he was unable to.

Rand stroked Callie's smooth tummy, letting his fingers dip into her slacks and under the edge of her panties until he could lightly caress her soft curls. When she moaned, he backed off. His fingertips moved to trace the crests of her breasts where they delved under the lace cups of her barely-there demi-bra to press and eventually pull a nipple into view.

When the hard nub peaked over the edge of lace and felt the cool air of the air conditioner fanning it, she hissed. He shushed her as he gently flicked it back and forth with the barest tip of his index finger. This time she moaned. He abandoned that breast and did the same to the other. Looking down at her and taking her in, he had to bite his lip to keep from groaning at the sight. With her tits hiked up so that her nipples were displayed over her bra and with her panties pushed down to reveal the beginning triangle of her soft dark curls, she was lust incarnate.

He could have stared at her for hours but knew she would be expecting more from her husband, hence more from him. He reached over and deftly unsnapped the center clasp of her bra. It sprung wide and her breasts spilled out. She sobbed at the sensation and moved to cover herself. He didn't know if she was upset due to the sensuousness of her breasts being exposed or if it was due to the fact that she was allowing a virtual stranger to view her like this, to see her displayed in such a blatant manner. He didn't much care what the reason was, he wasn't stopping now.

He took her hands in his and raised them over her head. Her wineglass was on the coffee table. He lifted it and forced her palms to cup the bowl of the glass. He saw her brows arch over the top of the blindfold when she realized what he had done. There wasn't much left in it, less than an inch, but if she moved, red wine would spill everywhere. She was a meticulous housekeeper; she knew what letting go would mean.

She gasped then blew out a long sigh that indicated either pleasure or acquiescence. He assumed the best scenario and capitalized on her pleasure. He used his fingertips to caress, stroke, and circle her full breasts, careful not to touch the now ultra sensitive tips.

After many minutes spent massaging and exploring the underside of her breasts, he stopped to just admire her. He watched in amazement as her nipples puckered. He smiled, as he knew she was waiting until he'd had his fill of looking at her, drinking in the sight of her. Knowing he was examining her chest, and that he could for as long as he liked, was making her hot—ready—titillated in the truest sense of the word. He could sense it—see it in the arch of her back as she offered herself to him. He bent over her and gave her what he knew she wanted. He gripped a nipple between his thumb and forefinger and pinched, tugging her nipple away from her body. Instantly she arched and keened.

"You like that, I know you do," he whispered, keeping his voice low, no more than a whisper, so she wouldn't place it as one other than her husband's. With his left hand, he did the same to her other nipple, then both at the same time, over and over. Gently twisting, tugging, pulling. Soon she was sobbing and begging, "Please, please . . ."

"Please what?" he breathed into her ear.

"Please fuck me."

"Oh, no. No. We're going to take our time, little one. I *will* fuck you. But first I want to look at you, examine you, make sure you're wet and ready for me." His fingers stopped their delightful tugging. He gently took the wine glass from her hands, offered her the tiny sip that remained, and set the glass back on the table. He tucked her fingers into the lush curls of the long hair that was fanning the bolster, patting them gently to let her know that he meant for her to leave them there.

He shifted her so he could remove her slacks and her panties, then he positioned her lower half on his lap with her head still resting on the arm of the sofa. His hands caressed her long legs, starting with her feet, rubbing her trim ankles, gripping her muscular calves and stroking feather light touches along her inner thighs, forcing her by minute increments to spread her legs for him. All the while he looked at her, the unbelievable treasure that was displayed in his lap, unfolding and opening for him. Trembling and getting wet for him.

"Spread your thighs wider baby," he whispered, "I want you to show me your pretty pussy and your sweet, glistening cunt. Show me everything baby, and I mean everything. It's been so long since I've seen you with your thighs wide, displaying yourself for me."

She moaned and whimpered as if she was reluctant to do his bidding, yet hesitating only slightly, she began to move her legs further apart. Her thighs slowly opened as she timidly spread them for him. He wanted more. He gripped her feet, pressed them together and pushed them up until her knees faced out, creating a diamond shape of her long, shapely legs, her trim bush the focal point at the top. She gasped at the sudden exposure of her womanhood and he watched as her secret creases unfolded to the cool air and moisture coated them.

Her satiny white skin was a stark contrast to his dark green dress pants. With her arms tucked under her head, her full breasts jutting up and out and her dark silky triangle arrowing down, pointing to her gaping cunt, it was a picture as erotic as anything he'd ever seen. If he tilted his head down he could see her pink slit gaping above his lap, in line with his zipper, barely a foot below his eyes. Using his hips, he shifted her slightly so he could look down and see into her opening. His eyes feasted on the sight, taking in the wondrous present she was giving him, an unencumbered view of the entrance to her pearly pink vagina. Dress pants were always uncomfortable, with an engorged cock burgeoning and straining to be free, they were unbearably unyielding.

"Lovely, you are incredibly lovely," he whispered reverently, awed by her beauty. She was creaming like nobody's business. His cock jumped in response to the blatant proof of her desire. He was insane with wanting her, had to fight himself to keep from taking her.

"Clint," she moaned, and he felt her flex, stretching her inner thighs and arching her hips to show him even more. Her keen sense of her wifely duty, to bare herself completely for her husband, as 'he' had just asked, awed him even more. She *was* a trained submissive just as Clint had said, and he'd had his doubts as to whether she could get into the scenario and be the dutiful wife for *him*, but he doubted no more. She was amazing in her sensuality, very open about her needs, and not at all shy with her body.

Despite being blindfolded and allowing herself to be displayed in such a vulgar manner, she was getting wet, very wet. He could clearly see that. Smell it—her musk permeated the air around them, he inhaled it deeply and let the heady essence of her fill his head. He didn't have doubts anymore, no siree. He looked up at her face and neck, saw her skin flush red, the deep crimson color seeping through her skin and warming her chest, throat, and face. She knew where he was looking, had to feel the heat of his gaze as he examined her so intimately. Was she ashamed, humiliated, overcome with desire? Where was she in her head right now? At this point most women were so deep into their fantasy life it would be a mistake to speak and let reality flood back in.

Clint had told him of her one really wicked perversion and how it fed on her at times. How it made her so needy she would either close herself off completely or climb the walls. Left too long in her mind, she was often overcome with a desire to be humiliated, one of the worst submissive perversions to have, and one of the most dangerous. Also one of the hardest to satisfy and gauge, the easiest to misread, and often over compensate for—a psychological time bomb if done wrong. He had no idea if he should continue, back off or bring her into it. Her breathing was labored but not stressed—he decided to participate, but let her work for what she wanted, what she needed.

He had both hands free and he used them to his advantage. The fingers of one hand tentatively insinuated themselves into her slick, puffy folds while the fingers of his other hand spread her labial lips wide. She flinched and gave a little gasp of distress. "Show me your vagina, Callie. Show me your sweet little honey hole, baby. I want to see that smooth velvet sheath that's tucked up inside you. Then I want to put my dick inside it and fuck it."

She whimpered and arched her hips, opening herself even wider to his heated gaze. He smiled. Just as Clint had said, she had a deep-seated desire to have her cunt admired. Clint had told of sessions where he had positioned her and then finished a full bottle of whiskey while studying her and watching her soak the sheets while her hooded clit grew and grew until he finally had to take her.

"That's it sweetheart, you're so beautiful here, so lovely. I can't help but give my fingers free rein." And he did. He diddled her with long, experienced fingers, like a maestro on keyboard he played her and sent tongues of fire to every cell, every fiber of her being. Always stopping just short of letting her have what she wanted, what she needed.

For many minutes he played with her labial lips,

gently pulling at them, tugging them away from her body, clamping them closed and holding them together just to tease her as he listened to her whimpers and groans, gauging her reaction to everything he did to her. He stroked her slit from top to bottom keeping her juices flowing and bringing the excess up to coat her clit over and over again. He inserted his longest finger into her, leaving it there and not moving a muscle until she could catch her breath, before sliding it out and then reinserting it. Another finger joined the first and she lifted off his lap to deepen the thrust. He smiled to himself as he watched her hike her hips even higher trying to get him to touch her clit. Never taking his eyes off her, he shoved three fingers in, cupped her until his palm held tight to her mound, pressed his thumb down on her clit, and reached up to pinch her nipple—hard. The resulting scream, spasm, and set of rhythmic contractions that squeezed his fingers unbelievably firmly was his undoing as well as hers.

He cried out as his cock responded to the undulating crack of her ass gripping him as she came. He had steeled himself to watch her come, even to feel her quiver and soak his fingers, but he was not prepared for her sphincter muscles to gyrate, pulse, and grip his erection while she was in the throes of deep passion. It was too late to stop what she had set in motion. His jaw firmed, his nostrils flared, and his eyes squeezed shut as he threw his head back and hissed her name through his teeth, "Callie . . . Jesus, Callie."

His ejaculate joined the wet spot she had made in his lap, his seed coming from underneath while her wetness dampened it from above, soaking him to the core. He shuddered from the decompression, from his muscles going from steeled tendons to the lax state only sleep or death surpassed.

He opened his eyes and looked down at her. She was still throbbing and clenching his impaled fingers, although now the rhythmic pulsing was tapering off to small shudders. It was a sight to behold. She moaned as he slowly withdrew his hand. He grabbed her outer thighs and drew her legs together, then shifted her so she was sitting up. He brought her hands down to rest in her lap. He reached up and removed her blindfold. When her eyes fluttered open he saw the most languorous, lambent eyes he'd ever beheld. Together with her rosy cheeks and smiling lips he realized that he was staring down at the most stunningly beautiful woman he'd ever seen, a raven-haired beauty that was one amazing, sexy vixen. No wonder Clint had fallen in love with her so quickly and rushed to secure her to him within only days of meeting her. Had she been free to marry at that exact moment he didn't doubt that he'd be dragging her to a priest right this very minute himself.

The heat of passion now past, she became self-conscious and grabbed for her sweater on the floor. He helped her to cover herself as he smiled down at her. When passion waned, modesty took over again. Shame and humiliation were as old as time.

"I knew you weren't Clint," she said after a few moments.

"And yet you allowed me to continue . . ." he said, lifting a finely arched brow, looking smug as he silently perused her long, slender legs.

"Once you touched my nipples, I couldn't have stopped you. Once you touched me," she nodded in the direction of her womanhood, now shielded under the cashmere sweater, "I didn't want to."

"How did you know I wasn't Clint?"

"You never kissed me."

"Clint asked me not to."

"He invited you to touch my breasts, caress my pussy, examine my cunt, insert your fingers inside me, but you are not allowed to kiss me?"

"I was also instructed to fuck you, perform cunnilingus on you, bugger you, and do a myriad of other things he suggested. And I didn't say I wasn't allowed. Just that he asked me not to."

"What if I want you to?" The vixen was back.

"Then you'd better clear it with him first because he trusts me with his wife."

She laughed and it was a delightful sound. "Do you know how absurd this is," she asked, waving her hand over her semi-clad body.

"I just know he wants you happy. And I know that I can make you happy. And now I see why that's so important to him."

"What did he think, that I'm a lose cannon, ready to walk the streets, hit the bars in search of a hard cock?"

"You said it, not me, but I think Clint prefers the devil you know to any Tom, Dick, or Harry."

"Does he really think I would be unfaithful to him?"

"Hey, don't look now . . ." he said with a wave of his own hand.

"I wouldn't have done this except, well except . . . except Clint sanctioned it, and you held me . . . and I was very attracted to you. And then you blindfolded me so I could pretend you were him so I wouldn't have to deal with the guilt. That was very sweet."

"But you knew differently."

"Still, you cared that I might feel guilty."

"Clint cared, the blindfold was his idea. I've never

carried a handkerchief in my life before today."

Her eyes widened and he watched as they filled with tears and then overflowed.

He'd thought of everything, she thought. Her husband had thought of everything to make this work for them. She felt so loved. She shivered and felt tears welling again.

"Hey, he knows you better than anyone, so he coached me, he wants this for you. And you know what?" he said as he lifted a soft chenille sofa throw.

"What?" she asked through her sniffles.

"I want this for *me* now, too."

He reached for the edge of her sweater that was now bunched around her breasts and slowly drew it off her, tossing it to the floor. He stood with her in his arms, covering her loosely with the throw. "I think I need to fuck you now, very badly. Extremely very badly." Effortlessly he carried her down the long hallway and into the master bedroom.

"This is his bed," she said softly as they crossed the threshold.

He hefted her in his arms, "And this is his wife. If he'll share one, I believe he'll share the other."

She looked up at him and met his eyes. "Kiss me first."

"No can do, sweetheart. I have my limits. I gave my word."

She pouted.

"Although I could kiss your other lips. As many times and as thoroughly as you'd like."

She smiled back at him and her twinkling eyes sparkled with mischief. God she was so beautiful. How was he ever going to give her back?

Holy Moly! Garrett blinked his eyes wide as he stared at the bright computer screen. It was the only thing lit in the room. While he'd been reading the sun had gone down and night had cloaked the beach, the inlet, and the waters beyond. A scattering of light from the moon bounced beams of silver on the lapping waves.

He scrolled down until he could see the next chapter heading after the page break. But he doubted he could go on without some relief. He looked down at his lap—at the bulge tenting the fabric of his boxers. He'd had to remove his jeans somewhere around page nine. He could see that the pre-cum from the tip had made a near perfect circle the size of a silver dollar near the top of the opening. This big boy wanted out, he wanted to play.

He stood and removed his boxers, careful to stretch them over his unbelievably hard erection. If there had ever been a day to star in a porn flick with pride, this would definitely have been it.

Leaving the computer to segue into sleep mode, he stalked across the dining room marveling at the lively bounce that lifted his t-shirt. Walking down the hall, he pulled that off, too.

He didn't wait for the water to heat. He stepped into the over-sized shower and palmed himself, gliding his fingers up and down with a practiced hand before brutally tugging himself to a violent, shuddering climax. He rinsed and toweled himself off and went back for Chapter Three.

Chapter III

He tossed her onto the center of the bed, stripped the throw from her and let it drop to the floor so he could look at her as he began to remove his clothes. Looking down at her he felt his chest ache at the sight of her, creamy white skin against the red duvet. She was lovely, her lips curved into a smile, the apples of her cheeks rosy and her eyes delightfully seductive. Her brunette curls fanned around her head while her shapely arms spread themselves on either side of her head, lifting her breasts high into luscious globes with rosy ruched tips. He untied his tie and threw it on a chair. His shirt was next, thrown with impatience toward the same chair. He toed off his shoes and removed his socks, undid his belt and unbuttoned his fly. The zipper slid down a few inches and he let his pants hang on his hips. She wasn't ready for the unveiling—not yet. He was not scaring this woman off, no siree.

Her smooth stomach with its tiny navel was flat with meager shallows delineating her hips, which flared before coming back to emphasize the dark juncture between her thighs. She was perfection, and right now her teasing smile had all the confidence of a woman who knew her allure. She looked up at him invitingly and he watched, bewitched as she slowly slid her hands toward the headboard and spread her thighs wide. That's when he noticed the straps hanging on the curved bamboo posts, both aft and fore. *Clint, you old boy scout, leave it to you to be prepared!*

Could she really want what she was hinting at? Was she asking to be tied up? She certainly was asking for something the way her hips were twitching and her legs were sliding against each other. *Only one way to find out.*

He took one wrist, brought it to his lips and kissed the soft inside. Then he wrapped the velvet cuff around it and pulled the strap taut. He walked to the other side of the bed and did the same. Her head turned and her eyes followed him around the room as he kept his eyes on her face, watching her for signs of distress. There were none. Her breathing had sped up, but she was smiling coyly—she was getting into this. He whipped his belt off and backhanded it toward the chair. It snapped coming out of the loops and again when it hit the chair to fall in a coil on the seat. He was impatient to touch her, to kiss her smooth, warm skin and to have it brush against his.

Lovely, dark chocolate eyes that were giving all the signs of her going under as soon as he'd tied her other hand to the post, beckoned him closer. He saw her thick lashes flutter against her cheeks, and had he not known better he would have thought her drugged and ready to fall asleep. His cock jumped, he couldn't wait to let it have its way. But he was a long way from granting that.

He ran his hand from her hip to her ankle. Her head moved slowly back and forth and her legs shifted against the down comforter as she fought him when he tried to take one ankle to the corner of the bed. It wasn't a valiant effort and he had to chuckle, "Surely you can fight better than that if this isn't what you want?"

His eyes met her glazed ones and he knew that this was exactly what she wanted. "Tell me this is what you want, tell me you want to be tied up," his voice was husky as he gripped her ankle and pulled it far away from the other, "or I won't do it," he added wickedly. He knew she wanted this, and that she wanted it probably more than she wanted to breathe.

"I want you to tie me up," she whispered.

"And?"

"And . . . and then I want you to touch me."

"Touch you how?" his voice had gone hoarse.

"I believe you promised kisses."

"I believe you're right." He brought her foot up and kissed her instep before securing it in the strap he found tucked under the bed skirt. It was plush velour, the finest in S & M restraints. Clint hadn't scrimped; his wife's pleasure was a serious luxury. He kept some slack in the restraints so he would have the freedom to move her legs as he wished them. Walking around to the other side, he removed his T-shirt, jerking it off and letting it drop to the floor by the bed.

She blinked as she took in his bronzed, muscular chest. She knew what it took to be an active soldier, knew how proud they were of their fighting skills and their bodies, but Rand's chest, arms and torso were nothing short of impressive. No wonder he was able to lift her as if she was filled with helium. His muscles rippled as he moved his hand down to his trousers and unzipped them all the way, revealing a sizeable bulge. His pecs flexed as his thumbs, at his waist, pulled his pants down then hooked under the waistband of his desert-sand colored underwear. He pulled the elastic waistband around his protruding member before bending and removing his pants and underwear together. His thick, long, erection jumped and as he walked to the head of the bed it grazed his flat belly and flexed with each bounce.

Her mouth watered. He was divine. Still, she could not believe he was here, and that Clint had sent him, and that he was going to kiss and lick her where she needed a man's mouth most. And then he was going to put that massive rod inside her and fuck her, exactly as her husband had directed.

"You're such a good soldier," she murmured. "Coming all this way to lick the Captain's wife."

He smirked as he slid between her legs and put his big hands under her thighs, lifting her and exposing her to his gaze. "I'm going to do more than lick this pussy. You'd better take a few deep breaths, you're going to need them." And with that, he ducked his head and commenced Frenching her nether lips. One hand stole around to her mound and a long finger pulled at the top of her slit, rubbing tiny circles over her hooded clit until it was hard and prominent. When it was no longer hidden inside her, begging to be included in his tongue's forays, his mouth took over. He teased her by licking all around the plump morsel before sucking it between his lips. Greedily, he sucked her entire vulva into his mouth and then groaned at the shudder that passed through her. She whimpered. A finger from his other hand delved into her welcoming crease and he moved it in and out, setting up an erotic rhythm that matched the movement of her thrusts. Another joined it. His tongue flicked mercilessly over her clit, finally daring to touch the prize it had been so carefully circling.

She moaned, cried out and arched her hips. His teeth grazed the engorged bud and her cries of "Oh, oh, oh!" filled the room. She bucked frantically against his mouth, coating his lips and tongue. He sucked the folds of her labia into his mouth, savoring her as she rode out the spasms that were milking his fingers. When she started to settle, he followed the line of her ass crack and inserted a damp finger just beyond the rim of her tightly puckered rosette and pulsed it. She jerked, convulsed and screamed. He groaned his pleasure into her flesh and drank her juices. She was all but passed out as he cleaned her with his flattened tongue, trying to slowly desensitize her.

Looking up at her face, he smiled. She was still in a state of euphoria, and he intended to keep her that way. He climbed up her body and put the thick head of his shaft at her opening. Her eyes popped open as he thrust home, seating himself fully. For several moments she froze with trepidation, then as her body adjusted to his size she visibly relaxed. "Ohhh," she moaned after her sheath had accepted him, delighting in his size.

He couldn't believe he was inside her. This was his best friend's wife and he was fucking her. His dick was buried deep to her core and he was in heaven.

She couldn't believe Clint's best friend was on top of her thrusting himself into her body, filling her completely and driving her mad. She had known this man less than a few hours, yet here she was, letting him tie her up and fuck her. And it felt wonderful. She was in heaven. The tenseness that had wound her so tight for weeks was gone, her muscles felt lose and limber. She felt alive again. The perpetual wait wasn't foremost in her mind anymore. The smell of this man was. And if she had to give this man's essence a name it would have to be "Sin"—glorious, delicious, dark sin.

He pulled out, teasing her with the head of his cock slapping at her opening before thrusting inside her again. She arched and met his forceful movement pulling him deeper each time he retreated and returned for more. He groaned and pumped into her, angling down to get in even deeper. She followed him, clenching at him, not wanting him to leave her, not by the minutest amount. He pummeled into her—his hands above her shoulders in push-up stance, giving him better leverage. He entered her fast and hard, sending the mattress bouncing to receive and recoil with each penetration. The pace would have killed an ordinary man, but Rand was so driven with lust for this woman that he hardly knew the strain he was placing on his body, had no idea how hard his muscles were quaking under the strain. He only knew that he needed to be deep inside her, needed to feel her squeeze him fist-tight with her climax.

To keep from kissing her—which he desperately

wanted to do—his mouth sought her ear. He ran his tongue inside the swirls, mating with it, sucking on her lobe and biting into the hollow of her neck just below it.

Her hips jerked upward, her clit stretched in its hood and strived to press some elusive, but wholly necessary part of him against it. But the touch was fleeting . . . if only she could have it for a second more. As if reading her mind, a mere moment later, his pelvis complied and the root of his manhood pressed hard against the straining nub, sending her into an intense orgasm. The resulting aftershocks were so strong that he literally felt as if her vagina was milking his cock with a velvet-gloved hand. He was staggered by the intensity and the duration. And so taken off guard that all he could do was let it take him as he cried, "Fuck me! Oh God. Oh God, yes, fuck me!" Petering out to "fuck it . . . fuck it . . . mmm," followed by a shiver that went through them both.

When their bodies tumbled back to earth, he slid out of her and fell to the side. Both were covered with a sheen of sweat and as he lay beside her he reached up and clasped her hand in his. "Give me a minute," he said breathlessly, "and I'll untie you. But damned if I'm letting you go anywhere."

Her breathing was labored as well, but for the first time in many months she was sated. Her nipples were sore, her pussy was sore and her neck where he had bitten her was sore, but she felt wonderful—free, deliciously loose, and well and thoroughly loved.

Her husband had done this for her, arranged this . . . asked this man to be his stand-in, and he had chosen well. Unbelievably, incredibly well.

Garrett held a paper towel to his flaccid penis,

wiping and gathering the surprisingly copious amount of cum from his groin. Not half an hour ago, he'd just done this in the shower. How had he managed to regroup so fast, he wondered as he wadded up the towel and tossed it into the trashcan beside his desk. *Jeez, did he have enough stamina to even attempt another chapter?*

He got up and walked into the kitchen to get something to drink. He stretched his back and his neck as he rummaged around in the fridge for some orange juice, marveling at how whatever it was he wanted was always toward the back. He filled the largest tumbler he had and in one continuous gulp downed it, his throat working feverishly to get the sustaining liquid down. How long had he needed to quench his thirst or get nourishment into his body, he thought as he shook his head in wonder. He'd completely forgotten to eat. He'd gone to the grocery store because he was hungry, with the idea of fixing a meal worthy of kings.

Moments later, like a crack addict, he sat back down at the computer with a Michelob Lime Ultra. He took a hearty swig, shook his head like a champ getting back into the ring and scrolled to Chapter Four.

Whoever this woman was, she was an amazing writer. Her writing was crisp, her characters intriguing, to the point that they drew you in—and her sex scenes, my God, they were . . . he looked down at his penis; the skin was red and chaffed from the abuse, the tip swollen—semi-hard it was amazing that it was still in the game. Well . . . this woman, whoever she was, was going to be sending him back to the store for KY Jelly or some kind of friction reducing lubricant.

Chapter IV

As he stood to untie her she watched his flaccid penis drip a mixture of her cum and his onto the duvet cover. Good thing it was washable she thought as she felt more seep out of her and trickle down her thigh to the bed. She should be ashamed, she thought as he removed first one hand and then the other, but she was not. He was looking at her with palpable interest, taking in every aspect of her body as if this might be his last opportunity with her.

When he went to the bottom of the bed to untie her ankles, his eyes drank in her slick, drenched pussy. His eyes shifted to hers and then he helped her to sit up.

"Never met a woman who got as wet as you. Never met a woman who could take my control away so easily either. You are one incredible fuck. Clint is a very lucky man. And I'm the lucky bastard who got sent home to take care of you for him. I can hardly believe my good fortune that I was shot that day."

He pulled her into his arms and with an arm around her waist he hauled her off the bed. "Come, I'll help you to the shower, then I'll leave."

"Leave? I thought you were staying for dinner?"

He raised an eyebrow. "You still want me to stay for dinner?"

"Well yeah, why wouldn't I?"

"This isn't a date you know. I introduced myself, had a drink, and then fucked you."

"I thought that was your assignment."

"You were. Mission accomplished," he said with a sheepish grin.

"So is your tour of duty over now?"

"He never specified the duration."

"Do you think he left that up to you? Or to me?"

"Uh . . . I don't know, it was never mentioned one way or the other."

"Well, I hardly think one, two, three or even four

orgasms, no matter how wonderful they are can make up for six, seven, or eight months without any. Besides, the letter I read said, you didn't have to give me back until he returned. Didn't you say you had another month stateside?"

"Yeah . . ."

"Well, what are you going to be doing for the next month?"

"What do you suggest?"

"Spend it with me."

"Taking the edge off is one thing, setting up house is another . . . ." Clearly he didn't want to over step his bounds.

"You haven't taken off the edge, you've just primed the pump. Are you going to turn me out on the streets now, send me out to find any Tom, Dick, or Harry?"

"Christ Callie, when Clint told me he wanted me to be his surrogate, I got the impression it was a temporary duty assignment. We didn't talk about a time frame so how do I know he's going to be okay with this?"

They were in the bathroom now and Callie had started the shower to get the water hot.

"Well, we could send him an email and ask him how temporary this tour of duty is supposed to be."

"Oh yeah, and how would that sound if anyone intercepted it? *Hey honey, I just had a marvelous fuck from one of your division commanders, and I wondered if he could stay and fuck me until you get back? Love, Your Caliente.*"

She slammed open the shower door and stomped into it. "You make it sound so sleazy! Go then if that's what you want!"

She slammed the door in his face as he was

about to follow her inside. He watched her soap up and when she had her eyes closed while shampooing her hair, he snuck inside and wrapped his arms around her waist from the back.

"It isn't sleazy, you and I know that. I want to stay. I would love to stay. But Clint is my best friend. You are his *wife*. What would your neighbors say, me being here for one night nevertheless a month, knowing that your husband is away? I don't want to cause trouble for either of you. I love him, and I am becoming very fond of you." His hands slid up her ribcage to her breasts. He kneaded them and squeezed them gently before plucking softly at her beaded nipples.

She moaned and he instantly grew hard. "Shit Callie, look what you've done."

He looked down at his erection; she turned slightly to look over her hip. "Did my husband indicate whether or not it would be alright if I sucked on that monster?"

His sudden intake of breath made her laugh.

"My initials are C.S. E. for Caliente Susanna Edwards, or as Clint likes to say, Cock Sucker Extraordinaire."

Holding onto him she slid down to her knees. His hands fisted in her hair. "Callie . . ." There were no more words. Even though it was his cock filling her mouth, she had effectively silenced him. Moments later, like a Sherman tank, she backed him out of the shower and into the bedroom, following on her knees.

She cupped his swaying sac, gently squeezing the perfectly round balls within and eliciting a long drawn out sigh from him as he stood at the end of the bed. Callie let his steely erection fall from her lips, gave him a sly smile and climbed up onto the bed.

She took her time positioning her body across

the breadth of the bed, laying on her back and letting him view her slick body while he wondered what she was up to. Then with her head hanging over the edge, her long hair trailing to the floor, she beckoned him with the crook of her finger. "C'mere and give me that," she said. As he swaggered close to her face she was able to grab his bobbing cock and pull him to her lips.

A tongue-lashing followed, and again, a long groan of pleasure. Going back to caressing his balls, slowly and gently with her other hand, she guided him between her lips and into her mouth. He was thick and long, but she knew what to do with the excess.

Making sure her head was positioned properly so that the curve of his penis matched the curve of her throat, she deep throated him, taking him all the way in until she was literally swallowing his penis. Since this sealed off her windpipe, she couldn't breathe, so she quickly set the ground rules, namely that she set the pace.

Instinctively, he knew this and while not at all relaxed, he let her take over. No man in his right mind would go against a woman swallowing his dick. She directed each thrust and retreat like a pro, eager to slurp him back inside so he couldn't withdraw completely. But he wasn't going to just stand there and be idle.

His hands grabbed her breasts and began kneading them causing her to arch into his hands and to take him even deeper with the next stroke. When his fingers pinched her nipples, she wanted to moan but couldn't. He did it for them both, ending with "Nnngh, nnngh, ahhh!" as his ejaculate pumped down her throat. His cum had entered her so far down her throat that she had not been able to taste it until he gently withdrew and dribbled some on her tongue.

"Never," he whispered, hoarse with emotion.

"Never have I had a woman suck me down like that. Jesus, Callie. You are phenomenal. That's the best head I've ever had." He collapsed on the bed beside her and fell fast asleep.

Garrett rubbed sore eyes and gingerly stroked his much-abused penis. He hadn't come again, it had been too soon for his body to consider it, but he was mightily aroused again. Fatigue swept over him, he was dog-tired. It had been a long day, and that was before committing an erotic demolition derby on his body. He put the computer to sleep and headed off to dreamland himself.

He could only hope he'd get some sleep—he was groggy with exhaustion. Yet he didn't doubt he'd be back in that computer chair in a few short hours to see what Rand and Callie would be up to next. *Geez, who was this woman who wrote this wonderful trash?* She sure had some amazing insights and a very knowledgeable command of the male anatomy. Not for the first time, it occurred to him that the writer might be a man.

Nah! No way. This was definitely a woman's voice. He was surer of that than he was of his own name. But who was she? Where was she?

It trying to find out who the flash drive belonged to, he'd managed to step into another world—the fantasy world of one hot romance writer, it seemed.

Garrett woke the next morning to a woodpecker attacking the wood siding on his beach house, right outside the French doors leading to the deck. The sound drummed into his head in a noisy staccato that told him no way would he get back to sleep. Didn't the fool know the difference between real wood and hardy plank? His beak would be worn to a nub before getting through the masonry siding. He looked at the alarm clock—6:36. Then he shifted the covers and looked down at his morning reminder of manhood.

Hmmm. It felt hot, burned a bit, and looked abraded in crucial areas. He grimaced. The tip could use a generous slathering of Vaseline or Neosporin.

The erotica he'd just read had been honed to a fine edge, and it touched on fantasies that he well understood. He was fascinated by her story and realized that her erotic fantasies were a counterpart to his and he couldn't help the gnawing in his belly that was making him want, making him need.

He settled into bed and marveled at how he could long for, no, lust for, a woman he'd never met, never even seen. She literally, was becoming the girl of his dreams; fortunately, he was past the age where they were the wet kind.

He had not thought it possible that there was a living, breathing woman who wanted what he wanted—no holes barred, wild, kinky sex play. And it was a given that if he kept this up he'd soon become obsessed with finding her. With only her flash drive, could he cobble together enough clues to find her? Because he definitely wanted to find her. It was as if he'd found a treasure map with G.P.S. coordinates to this woman's orgasms. All he had to do was lock them in. For a man who loved women and appreciated their amazing bodies, he was hyped for the hunt.

He threw the covers aside and got out of bed and made his way to the master bath. Turning the corner he walked into the tiled shower and flipped the levers, allowing his own water to blend with the pelting shards raining down on him. He belonged to the Madonna school of thought, which had now been adopted by so many of the returning war vets. On the battlefield, in lieu of medicine, soldiers often peed on each other or on themselves for the ureic acid that could defeat diseases caused by bacteria that grew in moist, abraded areas. There would be no fungus growing on him, no Athlete's Foot, no Crotch Rot, no Tinnea. Hell, it all went down the drain to the same place, might as well take advantage of nature's health benefits. Of course if he hadn't had a maid coming in weekly he might have felt differently. He liked a clean, fresh smelling bathroom and knew that women did, too.

After a bruising pummeling, he dried off at the edge of the walk-in shower and finger-combed his hair. He heard the programmed coffee maker making his first pot of the day. He wasn't big-time into luxuries, but he liked his showers big, with lots of pulsing heads, and he liked his coffee rich and flavorful. He had a Gevalia coffee maker at both residences and a whole cabinet devoted to a variety of their best seasonal coffees. He'd experimented with a Keurig system but found he preferred having a whole pot at his disposal.

Strolling out to the living area, he pressed down on the space bar to wake up his laptop before continuing on into the kitchen. While the last gurgles and hissing pops heralded the final fragrant cascade, he stooped and rummaged through the cabinets for some lubricating oil—Wesson, peanut, even a can of Crisco—anything to soothe and coat his sore member. He needed something to lessen the friction because no way was he not reading the rest of that story.

Chapter V

Rand helped her make dinner and then later, over dessert and coffee he suggested, "Let's go to Myrtle Beach, it's only a few hours from here. No one will know us there. We can check into a motel right on the ocean; maybe run through a few bondage scenarios," he said with waggling brows, exaggerated à la Groucho Marx. "We can cohabitate—with benefits." They'd shared a bottle of wine and both had a giddy buzz.

Her eyes glazed over and she shuddered at his words. He could tell she was thinking of saying no, but the words that tumbled out instead were, "Yes, let's do that."

"I hear hotels on the beach are giving a patriotic discount for active military and I have back pay just sitting in my account."

"It sounds wonderful. I'd love to go to the beach."

"Say please, and kiss the tip of my cock," he said as he leaned into her and kissed the tip of her nose.

"My pleasure," she purred as she knelt, unzipped him, pulled his erection from his pants and kissed the tip, then bent again to lick the drops that began oozing out. He groaned, dug his fingers through her hair to massage her scalp and direct her away.

"Please," she whispered, when he tried to pull her up. She bent again taking him all the way into her mouth, feeling him nudge the back of her throat. She arched her neck, relaxed her throat and took him deeper, stopping only when her lips met his curls. He hissed, grimaced and let her tug his pants down and then drop them to the floor. She moved her lips up and down his impressive length taking him in until he touched the back of her throat and then she slid back slowly releasing him. When he could stand it no longer, he withdrew, stood above her, wrapped her hair around his fist and lifted his cock out of the way while he fed her his shaved sacs. She flicked her tongue over them enjoying the rough texture when she sucked each testicle into her mouth and gently cupped her lips around it. When he felt his ejaculate ready to explode from him, he pulled her head away using her hair. He wanted her to watch, he wanted her to see what she did to him. He pumped his cock twice and she opened her mouth in supplication. He groaned at the sight and then came on her tongue, her lips . . . her chin.

"Jeezuusss, Callie! Who taught you to suck a dick like that? God woman! You are amazing!"

"If it's worth doing . . . ," she said as he gripped her elbows and pulled her to her feet. She rubbed her face on the line of fur running down his belly. "Come on, let's clean up so we can pack. I can hardly wait to get to the beach!"

Her childish enthusiasm overrode his curiosity about her cocksucking capabilities. He knew Clint watched porn and quite likely it was something they did together. But still . . . she was exceptional and it made him wonder. He helped her clear the dishes then left to go back to the Barracks to get his gear.

When he returned an hour later using the key she had given him, she was asleep on the sofa. He took the time to sit across from her and watch her. She was so beautiful and she looked so peaceful. She reminded him of Snow White with her fair coloring, dark hair and lashes, and rosy red cheeks and lips. She was perfect. He couldn't believe she was going to be his for a month. That he'd have her all to himself. He thought of her mouth and her special talents and shook his head and sighed. *Dear God, there would be nothing left of him.*

He leaned over to kiss her cheek and saw the letter she was clutching in her hand. The way it was folded he could read the words:

... satisfy each other's needs. Of course, when I come home, I will expect you to prefer me to him. So, sate yourself for a while, but when you hear that I am on my way back to you, send him away. Now . . .go play.

Your loving husband,

Clint

He hung his head in his hands, between his knees. Shit! He had all but forgotten she wasn't his, that he was just borrowing her.

He gently lifted her and carried her to the bed then stripped and slid in behind her. He snuggled up to her and tucked his knee between her parted thighs. With his arm around her waist holding her against his chest, he kissed the back of her shoulder. How did a man thank his best friend for a gift such as this?

Chapter VI

They took Clint's old 1978 Camaro Convertible. It was a beautiful aquamarine color with pristine white vinyl seats and a white convertible top, and so clean it could have been parked in an operating room. She let him drive, saying she believed that he should be in charge. He thought it might be code for *I want to be your submissive*; he could pretty much read it in her eyes and in her manner as she deferred to him in all things. Clint had trained her well.

As they prepared for their trip this morning she'd asked a lot of questions. What did he want her to fix for breakfast? How did he want his coffee—regular or decaf? What should she pack? Should she shower now or later? What would they be doing? When he had just looked at her with that all-knowing look, she had smiled and said, "Oh. Of course."

He packed the trunk with their luggage, three small cases for her, a large duffle for him, and a heavy bag that she assumed had liquor in it because it clinked when he carried it. She knew it was heavy because she'd tried to move it aside to make room for her cosmetic case and couldn't budge it. He'd easily lifted it to the side with one arm and she remembered that Clint used to have a flight bag like that. His had contained sex toys. She suspected Rand's might, too. She shivered in anticipation of the things to come as she settled into her seat.

He started the car and asked, "Do you mind if we ride with the top down?"

"No, I would like that. Just give me a moment to secure my hair or it'll look like a rat's nest by the time we get there."

He watched as she sensuously braided the long, shiny tresses into one big fat braid, then wound it around her fingers before pinning it at her nape. The sun made the auburn highlights gleam as he lowered the top.

"Good?" he asked, as he ran the gearshift grid, familiarizing himself with the pattern.

She nodded. He put the car in gear and they were off.

After they left the base and were on Route 17 headed south, he leaned over and stroked her thigh. She was wearing a short spandex skirt and it was easy to move it up further.

"So, tell me what you like," he said with an all-knowing smile and a raised eyebrow to make sure she understood his meaning. "Tell me everything."

"Well, you already know most of what I like. And of course Clint had to have coached you on some others. With the assignment he gave you, I know he would have."

"Well yes, as a matter of fact he did."

"Tell me what he said."

He thought for a moment. *How to phrase it?* Just say it, he told himself. Go for it. Put the cards on the table. "He said you liked to show off your beautiful pussy. And believe me, he groaned mightily when he said that. Then we heard gunfire over the hill and we ran for cover."

"Is it?" she asked. Like all truly beautiful women, she doubted her attraction.

"Is it what? Beautiful?"

He knew what she was asking for, fishing for. She needed his approval, his validation that she was lovely and desirable. Despite the physical evidence he had shown of the immense pleasure he found in her, she was still insecure. Most women were. They required frequent praise of their bodies to allay their fears and to make them feel comfortable; for all her beauty, she was no exception. Clint had said as much, indicating she could actually be shy at times and that she'd often have to be coaxed to exhibit herself. But Clint had reiterated that Callie was one of those rare women who derived insane pleasure from being the object of voyeurism.

"I don't really remember," he said and knew she would know that he was lying. The image of her in his lap yesterday while they were on the sofa was forever burned into his memory. She was delectable. "Slide your panties off and show me."

"I can't do that now!"

"Sure you can. Slip your underwear off, pull up your skirt, turn toward me and then spread your thighs wide. I promise not to wreck."

"People will see me."

"Only a truck would be tall enough to see anything. And if I see one coming I'll give you ample warning. Unless, of course, you wish to share the view." He winked and smiled to encourage her.

Clint had said Callie had this exhibitionist thing

tugging at her, but not at all times, he'd back off if she wasn't receptive. Knowing submissive women as thoroughly as he did, Rand suspected it was more that her acquiescent tendencies were connected to a humiliation thing she had going on. One she probably didn't even know about.

A lot of submissives needed shame—or its related partner—humiliation, to be included in their sexual scenarios. Somehow it was interwoven into their pleasure make-up. And it was the touchiest thing—so easy to misread, and even easier to take too far.

And no woman, at least none he'd ever met, was honest enough or perceptive enough to know just how much was the exact right amount she needed. For a man, it was like showing up without a script to play a part in *The Three Bears*—no one knew upfront what would be too hot or for that matter, too cold. In order to have it "just right" you had to have read every single sign along the way. Every sigh meant something, every shudder, every flinch. Only the best attempted a shame scenario as so much could go wrong so easily. But the rewards for getting it "just right" could set a woman free. Rand knew he was one of the best. Clint knew that, too. He gave her a big smile and nodded his head at her lap. "Come on, you can do it. Show me."

He watched her out of the corner of his eye as she reached up and slowly tugged her tiny thong panties down her legs and then unwrapped them from her ankles. "That's a good girl. Now sit back into the corner and pull your skirt up to your waist." The thought of her obeying him in this was beginning to fill his body with need. Hot surging need.

When she had squirmed into position, he murmured, "Go on, you know what to do next." He kept his voice soft, husky, but gently encouraging. "What lovely long legs. I want to see what's at the top of them. Let me see you."

He was at a stoplight now and no one was around so he turned, put his arm on the back of the seat and watched her as she settled her back into the corner between the seat and the door. She kicked off her sandals and gingerly swung her feet onto the sides of the bucket seat. She looked over at him then, and he arrogantly raised an eyebrow. She needed to know that he expected her to do his bidding. And he needed her to be fearless. She knew what he wanted to see.

He watched as she took a deep breath and closed her eyes. Then she put her feet together against the console and let her thighs open. He about lost it. His penis came to full attention and slammed into the barrier of his zipper, filling the already tight crotch of his O.P. corduroy shorts to the max. He had to reach down and adjust himself, situating the burgeoning length so it shared the opening of his shorts with his leg. Copious amounts of pre-come oozed from the tip, drenching his thigh. He'd have to remember to clean these seats.

"Sweet Mother of God!" he murmured as his left hand gripped the steering wheel. His eyes bore into her, seeing every fold, every crevice, every pink-coated surface as she completely exposed herself in the bright morning sunshine. A honk behind him forced his eyes to the rear view mirror then to the windshield as he shifted the car and eased out the clutch. He thought the sound of a horn behind them would make her close her legs, but it hadn't. Her eyes were half closed, her teeth scraping lightly on her bottom lip. If he didn't know better he'd think she was already going under.

The next time he was able to tear his eyes away from the road and look over at her, she had her hands on either side of her labial lips, pulling them apart. "Is it pretty," she asked, "is my pussy pretty?" Her eyes were glazed over and he saw that she was in a good place, a wanting-to-please and tease place, not an I-need-you-to-humiliate-and-degrade-me place. He'd seen women pushed beyond this barrier before but only because they were the type that required pain or belittling, and substantial amounts of it, to go along with the degradation in order to get off. Callie only needed his approval, he could see it in her eyes. She needed affirmation that she mattered to him; that another woman didn't measure up—to whatever standards he'd decided to impose. For this scenario, she needed to know she was lovely—down there. And by God, she was.

He groaned as she slipped a finger inside her vagina. He stole as many glances as he could while getting up to speed—55 miles per hour was not the best time to be a voyeur with a view such as this just off to his right.

He heard the high-pitched whine of a truck downshifting as he slowly cruised to another stoplight. He looked in his driver side-view mirror and saw a big semi getting ready to pull alongside. "Unless you want this trucker to see your sweet little vagina, you'd better sit up. And fast."

His eyes left her moist center and slick fingers to flick up to her face. He saw a moment's hesitation before she removed her hands, closed her legs and tugged her skirt back into place. But sitting as she was, sideways, facing him with a red face, it was impossible for the trucker not to imagine the show he had just missed. The trucker used his air horn to protest her clothing rearrangement and she saucily blew him a kiss.

"Christ! Are you trying to force me to do hand-to-hand combat here? That guy's likely to run us off the road and demand a show of his own."

"Show's only for you," she said with a coquettish smile.

"Are you sure? Because for a moment there I thought otherwise . . . heard otherwise."

There was a long silence.

"What did he tell you?" her voice was suddenly harsh.

He had made a serious tactical error and he knew it. What a stupid blunder. He bit his lip. Nothing do about it but tell truth he decided, knowing that he was a terrible liar and incapable of a quick rejoinder anyway. Damn! He was mad at himself for he had read her right, absolutely positively right. She was wet and slick for wanting. Another minute and she'd have begged to be fucked—right there on the side of the road. And he'd have found a way to accommodate her.

But he'd blown it, he'd taken her over-the-top desire to please him, and put it right back on her, making her feel cheap—sleazy. A wicked idea struck, a way of softening the blow. "He said you and he often go to bars on the strip where you sit on the counter with your legs splayed showing all the patrons your furry bush; that you love to go bowling on league night with a short skirt and no panties so all the men can see your lovely derriere and juicy cunt; that a walk in the park for you means flashing all the men who walk by, standing with your legs wide apart in case they desire to kneel and see more."

She gasped. "He did not!"

He gripped her hand. It was flailing in midair and he was afraid it would hit him if he didn't. He chuckled, "No, he didn't. He said you were lovely, prettier than any porn star, and *sometimes*, just as uninhibited. And I agree." He brought her hand to his lips and kissed each fingertip. "Your body is far lovelier than any I have ever seen, be it in pictures, on film, or in real life. I have never seen a more gorgeous woman anywhere, ever. I swear it."

He turned slightly and his eyes met hers over the tips of her fingers. There were tears rimming her eyes and her lips were spread in a big, quaking smile. She looked pleased—inordinately pleased. Knowing that she pleased him seemed to make her happy. Yes, she definitely needed affirmation of her loveliness, like most women since Eve. It was such an important and such a needy thing for some. They needed to know they were desirable, and being told that kept them secure in their relationships. Many never got the affirmation they so desperately needed—few got to know they were beautiful where they believed a man cared most for them to be beautiful.

He turned off the highway onto a single lane country road. "We have a long, lonely stretch for the next few miles." He stated in his most commanding, gruff, military voice, "Pull your skirt up and get back into position. I haven't had enough of seeing you. I demand to see more."

Her eyes lit and her smile brightened as she slid sideways on the seat to do his bidding.

God help him, he was never going to survive a month of this. She was too needy in all the right ways. He was curious how this obsession had manifested itself in a woman so lovely. There was no one in his memory, real or imagined, that could compete with the sight being showcased for him right now on this vintage Camaro bucket seat. The sight before him was one most men were never privileged to see, at least not when the woman was as beautiful as Callie.

Truly beautiful women didn't need to go to these extremes, they could afford to be aloof and hold themselves to a higher standard. Someone had to have cultivated this level of submissiveness—coerced it, if he wasn't mistaken, and he wanted to know why. Because a woman this beautiful did not have to do this to earn love and acceptance—not that he wasn't totally enthralled with the view.

Chapter VII

Keeping his eyes on the road he reached over and inserted his middle finger into her. With a quick glance, he was surprised by her adoring look. It occurred to him that the longer she was displayed like this, as she flamed with shame, the wetter she got. Soon he'd have a flood on his hands.

He marveled as he watched and she morphed into a different woman altogether. One so oddly apart from the other—brash instead of shy, forward to the point of whoring herself, going from as angelic as Shirley Temple to as flagrant as Jenna Jameson in mere moments.

He decided he would see if he could pleasure her while she was in this mindset; try to take her back to the world she had somehow slipped into. He wanted to know how she entered the place where what a man thought of her body counted more than what she thought of herself.

Moving his fingers in and out of her as he drove, he listened for changes in her breathing while still watching the road. After a few moments he added his thumb, circling and pressing down on either side of her clit. Her breathing escalated. He ran with a hunch. "Lovely, absolutely stunning. Your pussy is a true delight; I can see why you enjoy showing yourself off, I can't get enough of you, show me more. All of you. Show me all of you."

She arched, spread her thighs impossibly wide and keened loudly. Even though the sound of it was drowned out by the rushing wind, it hit a visceral chord in him. He was as hard as a pikestaff.

He held his hand steady as her orgasm milked his fingers, drenching them and practically forcing them out of her sheath in the process. He pinched her clit and she convulsed all over again, hissing and gritting her teeth. Then he watched as her face fell into a relaxed pose, her eyes closing, her lips going lax, and finally, her legs drawing up and closing. Within moments she was in a fetal position, crying.

He pulled over and attempted to pull her into his arms but she drew away, whimpering as if scared. He gave her the space she seemed to need as he stared down at her, then he pulled back onto the road. He kept an eye on both her and the road, not exactly sure what to expect next. She had been so open, so free, mere moments ago.

He said nothing as he drove with both hands on the wheel until the essence of her on his right hand overpowered him and he had to bring his hand close to his face to draw deeply of her fragrant musk and to lick along his middle finger.

A few minutes later he looked over to see she was sitting upright, her clothes straightened and her skirt pulled back down. He glanced to the floor and saw that her underwear was not on the floor anymore. It was either back in place, or it had blown out of the car. Her head was relaxed against her arm on the windowsill, facing him with her eyes closed. He couldn't imagine it, but she appeared to be asleep, blissfully, and contentedly asleep. And so beautiful it hurt his heart.

Dear God, please don't tell me I'm falling in love with her, he thought. *For God sakes, I only met her yesterday!* A voice in his head whispered, *Yes, but you've been looking for her all your life.*

Half an hour later as he pulled into the parking lot of the motel they had selected, she woke with an eager smile. Who was this woman who appeared to be the proper lady and loyal wife, and at other times, became like Jezebel, who saw it as her duty to whore herself and submit fully to her master's desires?

Chapter Seven

Garrett walked back to his shower with the only oil he'd found, a decorative bottle of olive oil with tarragon leaves and a thyme branch tucked inside. He supposed he should be grateful it wasn't one with hot peppers floating in the oil considering what he intended to do with it.

Ten minutes later as he was toweling off he wondered what he'd have to do to keep his shower from smelling like an Italian trattoria. Realizing he had to take a mental and physical break from the most erotic story he'd ever read, he dressed for a run on the beach. He had a few things he had to figure out and running on the beach always seemed to break things down to the most basic components.

Ratty college t-shirt over jersey shorts, he bent to lace and tie his three-hundred-dollar sneakers. He thought of himself as frugal in most things, but he'd learned long ago that if you took care of your feet they took care of you. If you didn't, it affected almost every arena of your life.

He grabbed a water bottle and the single house key, which he tucked into his inside pocket. He made it all the way down the stairs before running back up for his Maseru sunglasses. Then he sprinted over the access decking to the beach.

It was another glorious day, sunny and hot with a gentle breeze that lifted his hair and his spirits as he set the pace that felt familiar and comfortable. He usually ran five miles a day, but he had a late start today. A quick look at his watch told him that the Japanese markets were down and reporting on the close of business over ten hours ago, so he figured there should've been plenty of time for the reports he needed to be ready. He acknowledged that when he got back he had some work to do before the TSE opened tonight. He could *not* spend the day reading about Callie and Rand. He could not.

He smiled at a group of women who waved at him, dodged a couple pushing a stroller and outran the little poodle nipping at his heels. But he was intrigued. He thought about the woman who owned the flash drive. He fancied he could read her thoughts; feel her anxiety over having lost it along with some very personal thoughts.

Her writing was good, professional caliber if he wasn't mistaken. He reminded himself to Google local authors when he got back, maybe he'd get lucky. He wondered about this writer of passions. She seemed to have a pretty good handle on the pleasures both men and women experienced. She seemed to really know what turned men on . . . what turned him on.

A woman on a bike passed him, heading toward Bird Island, peddling with a purpose. His eyes were drawn to her firm butt wiggling back and forth on the seat with each pump of her legs and the cute soft-looking blonde curls that bobbed in the sun. From the back she looked to be in her twenties, but great legs and a nice backside had fooled him many times. Often the face belonged to a much older woman, at least here at the beach where the women were fanatics about their bodies. He watched her ride away, watched as she waved a jaunty hand to a group of women walkers all in the same turtle watch t-shirt.

He admired her bike as much as he admired her form, a Drifter in pastel green and tan. It was a stunner, too. Her effortless way of peddling while snaking around the tidal pools made riding a bike on the beach look fun. He vowed to get his own bike out of storage and bring it down next time he drove the truck down from Maryland.

Chapter Eight

Laurel waved to the women on the beach, two were neighbors and two she knew from her turtle watch walks, one she'd thought she'd met in church. Gosh there were so many people moving down to the southern end of the county now that it was hard to keep up. But a wave was always polite, so she gave it all she had until she needed that hand to steer the bike.

What a glorious day! She was so glad she had decided to ride her bike on the beach even if she hadn't been able to find her usual parking place at 40th Street. The extra miles biking from the pier wouldn't be a hardship at all today.

The hottie she had just passed, loping effortlessly down the beach, made jogging in the hot sun look not quite as hateful as she knew it to be. It was tempting to turn back to get a peak at his face, because those legs and that ass were damn near perfect. Had to have a nose á la Cyrano de Bergerac, just had to. So why ruin the fantasy?

Ah this was nice, she mused. She was so glad she finally pulled herself away from the house where she was endlessly looking for that damned flash drive. This morning she'd been sitting on the floor of her closet, rummaging through a pile of purses she hadn't used since she'd moved them here three years ago. It couldn't possibly be there. But she wasn't ready to give up. Wasn't ready to admit it was gone forever. Her stories scattered to the winds like the seagulls frantically taking flight in front of her.

When she got to the mailbox she took pen in hand and cried out her frustration to the Kindred Spirit while alternately marveling at the beauty before her and trying to cheer herself. Hey, she did have backups; she hadn't lost the work. Everything was still on her computer. So what was the problem really, she asked herself. The problem was that she felt lost, out of control somehow. The not knowing where years of her time had ended up. Whether whoever found it would try to publish any of it, and how would she feel if they did? Would she fight them, claim the work as hers? It wasn't that she was ashamed of it, exactly, but she was definitely not ready for the world to see her in that light. She didn't want anyone to know her inner thoughts so well, to know *her* so well . . . so intimately.

There was really nothing to do at this point, but find a way to move on. She had to stop obsessing about it. She'd had worse things to deal with in her life: her parents dying in a car wreck, during the holidays, on their way to visit her—for one: the winning lottery ticket found in her father's wallet the following week—for two.

His dream, his whole life, had been to win the lottery, just one time—five, ten, twenty thousand . . . not overly greedy, just enough to make a difference. "Easy Street." he used to say to her every time he bought one. He'd wave it in front of her face and smile his crooked smile as he came back to the car after running into the 7-11 or wherever it was he bought gas. "Easy Street, this is the ticket, baby. Pack up the moving van, we're going to Easy Street."

Well he hadn't made it to Easy Street. He'd never even known he'd won. As his heir, his sole heir, she'd finally cashed the ticket in, six days before it was to expire. Thirty-six million, nineteen thousand and change after taxes and legal fees. She was set. She was on Easy Street. Broken hearted, alone, and aimlessly drifting, but she was on Easy Street.

She remembered going home after meeting with her banker, her lawyer, and an investment counselor. She'd plopped down in her computer chair in her two-bedroom apartment and Googled "Easy Street," searched MapQuest for streets so named. Even flipped through the listings for the county map books she had for Northern Virginia. She'd found a lot of companies, restaurants, songs, and sayings, but no street she could move to . . . there would be no Easy Street for her. Six months later, she'd finally found the courage to walk into her parent's house in Ocean Ridge Plantation at Ocean Isle Beach, North Carolina.

Neighbors had looked after it for her and she'd hired a maid service to go in and clean it once a month and a handyman to maintain it, but she hadn't been able to gather her thoughts enough to actually drive down, put the key in the lock and see all her parent's things. She couldn't stand to think about revisiting the good times they'd had there.

It had taken weeks of mind-numbing drudgery to go through each room and sort things out. Storing what she couldn't bear to deal with yet, like her mother's clothes, and the kitchenware and cookbooks that were such a huge part of their family celebrations, donating her father's clothes, his golf clubs, the pool table, and the furniture from his den, selling his gun and record collections—then repainting, papering, and decorating to make the house uniquely hers. This was not Easy Street; her first months here had been anything but easy. And while Ocean Ridge Plantation had drives, circles, places, notches, lanes, ways, and courts, it had no streets, at least none she could find. So Castlebury Way would just have to do. She was young, not even thirty yet, so she would never have picked a retirement community like this to live in if she had not inherited it, but she felt safe here with the lingering touches of her parents all around her. So she dug deep, pushed aside her reservations and ensconced herself in her new home and began to write.

She made friends, joined groups and wrote several hours every day. It had helped with the grieving process. And now everything she'd poured her heart into was out there—in the hands of a stranger.

She ended her anguished missive to the Kindred Spirit with:

So you see, Kindred Spirit, I am lost and floundering. Whether I will ever see that #$*&@ flash drive again is anybody's guess. But for now I guess I have to let it go. Try to put it out of my head until one of my stories stares back at me from the pages of a book. Then I'll deal with it. Then I'll decide whether to "own" my secret thoughts and hidden fantasies or assign them to another. I guess it wouldn't hurt my feelings any if something I wrote became a bestseller. But that in itself is another can of worms. I don't need the money, but I sure would hate someone calling my child theirs when they hadn't given birth or thought to it. Until next time, thanks for listening, sorry I'm so self-absorbed in sorrow today. I'm going to go find five shells, spit my vituperate soul into them and fling them far into the ocean, never to be seen or heard from ever again! Oh to wash away this feeling of despair.

She stood and replaced the notebook and pen. Out there, she thought as she scanned the horizon, seeing the great ocean and envisioning the world on the other side. For all she knew, the name Anonymous could be appearing under one of her stories this very minute. What with the emergence of self-publishing, and e-books like the Kindle and Nook, she could be published right now and not even know it.

She got on her bike, threw her shoulders back and faced the wind. It would be harder riding back but she'd had it tough before, she'd manage. She always did.

Chapter Nine

Garrett sat on his deck in a wooden Adirondack chair, slumped with one leg crossed over the other, sipping a beer and staring out at the ocean. He was fighting it. Oh, he wanted to go back in and read more; but first, he had some work to do. Then he promised himself he'd make an attempt to establish who the owner of the disk was. He'd at least check out the other files to see if he could glean anything from them. The Quicken file could easily yield something useful. Then, and only then, would he'd treat himself to another chapter.

After his run, he'd checked his portfolios, made a few trades and grabbed a sandwich. Then he'd headed to the shower with the intention of cleaning himself, that was all, nothing else. That bottle of olive oil was getting down to the dregs and his right hand smelled like pizza.

He pulled himself up, grabbed his cell and called a few traders to talk things over. Then he set up a few meetings with investors for when he got back to Washington, ordered some computer equipment online, and finally pressed the number for Christopher's Pizza. He ordered a large pepperoni and sausage pizza—the smell of his hand so near his face had finally won him over.

Chapter VIII

Holding her open to what she thought was a wide bay window, he murmured to her, telling her how naughty she was showing so many strange men her naked pussy. Indeed, he wished the windows with the drapes drawn over them was a mirror so he could see what he was holding open to the imaginary men reflect back to him. "There's a young boy, maybe sixteen with his nose to the window, stroking his cock. I'm going to hold your cute lips open so he can see into your vagina. Would you like me to remove your blindfold so you can see the lust in his eyes?"

"No! Please don't!"

He knew she'd say that. He knew she couldn't handle that final degradation of actually seeing a strange man's eyes feasting on her. And thank God for that, as all she would see was the intricate pattern of the drapery that was shielding her from the late-night carousers walking just outside their window.

Recalling what had happened last night on the bed in front of the window, he tried to convince himself it had just been a dream. In the light of day, he knew that it hadn't been.

He'd carried her over the threshold early yesterday afternoon and started making love to her before they could get their luggage inside the door and lock it. Then he'd taken them both to heights he'd never fathomed. They'd slept, tangled limbs entwined, her heart beating against his. His world was bliss.

He'd woken to her restless thrashing, watched her as she shifted on the sheets and positioned herself feet forward facing the window. Dropping her knees wide, she thrashed her head back and forth while she begged invisible captors, not to display her in such a wicked way. Clearly, she was setting this scene herself, for no one was forcing her to do anything.

Rand had looked down into her anguished face and saw that she was still asleep, deep in the throes of some captive slave fantasy. Her tight dark nipples, her glistening slash, and her heaving chest, told him she was enjoying being the center of attention in a sexual fantasy far removed from what she would allow in real life. He'd jumped in to play the role of her captor and tormentor. And after bringing her to a keening orgasm that he was pretty sure she slept through, he deposited copious amounts of sperm onto her belly before collapsing back to the bed.

When he awoke to shards of sunlight coming through the outer edges of the drapes, he realized that he hadn't moved since falling back to the bed after their second bout. His hand still gripped the base of his cock and everything in the vicinity was wet to the point of being chilly in that arena. He shifted onto his side, looked at Callie, feet still facing the drapes but her legs shifted off to the side with her hands tucked under her cheek. *God she was beautiful.*

In slow increments he raised himself and lifted off the bed. *Housekeeping was going to talk about this room for days.* He made his way to the bathroom where he coaxed his hard-on to face the porcelain before sliding back the wavy glass door and stepping into the shower. Cold, hot, then cold again, he did it all while using the tiny sliver of soap to wash up. Stepping out, he dried his massive chest, all dark curls and muscle, before stooping to dry his hairy legs from the ankles up. It was a form of toe touches for him and the way he limbered up for the day, stretching out his back and forcing his hamstrings and calves to go taut.

Then he sat out on the small patio sipping orange juice and watching some college girls playing volleyball. It was just after ten and the sun was working its away toward full and high. How they played in such skimpy bikinis without losing them, he never knew. But he enjoyed the prospect of that very thing happening to the busty one in the orange Speedo. He wondered if she liked to take it in that bubble of a rear. His eyes roved over the others, and he imagined them, each in turn: sucking his cock; on all fours at the end of a bed; and tied to a whipping pole at his old SM club in San Diego.

He'd left that life a few years back, taking with him years of experience in bringing both pleasure and pain—and a wealth of knowledge about a woman's body, and of course a collection of some very inventive tools to make sex play ever so much better for both partners. A few of them he planned on using on Caliente in the upcoming days if she'd go for it. And after the scene they'd run through last night, he was pretty sure she'd be amenable. More so than he'd first imagined when he'd grabbed his bag of toys for this trip.

His thoughts reverted to the woman he left sleeping soundly on the bed behind him. He recalled last night and her overwhelming desire to exhibit herself. He had an extensive background in psychology and had even taken some classes given by a world-renowned sex therapist. Living in southern California and attending Stanford for a few years had certainly broadened his knowledge about women and sexuality in general. So had the Tantric Sex courses at UCLA. But how could he use that knowledge to help this woman—this very responsive, dichotomy of a woman?

On the outside she seemed cool, calm and

dignified. But once you got her passions up she became a wanton, careless strumpet. It would be so easy for someone to abuse her, or for her to abuse herself. He tapped his fingers against the icy glass. She definitely had something going on there with her desire to display herself. The facing-the-window-and-showing-it all-to-anyone-who-cared-to-look thing she had going on last night was over the top, that was for sure.

From his experience and from what he'd read about exhibitionism, it usually stemmed from one event—one traumatic, impressionable, life-changing event. For most women, the way they were approached or treated during adolescence set the tone for the type of sex they wanted, needed, or could not tolerate. But often, the memories came from an earlier time. Little girl babies could even be affected by the way their daddies or an older brother changed their diapers.

He could see how easily that scenario could have happened with Callie. A precocious, but clearly adorable little two-year-old squirming on a changer, a father holding her open while wiping her, coating her with a layer of Desitin, stopping to admire and whisper how happy a young man was going to be with her sweet pussy when she grew up. All initially innocent—or possibly not—but getting stuck in a mind that consciously could not even remember the moment. Unconsciously, the moment had the power to shape things for years to come. That was basically what human sexuality was all about, experiences—the good and the bad, built up over the formative years.

He wondered if Caliente had a brother. Older brothers could be wicked. He knew this firsthand. In college he'd heard tales of sisters abused by older brothers; siblings made to entertain friends, cousins, or teachers; mentally challenged innocents being drugged and then sold on Saturday nights to the highest bidders just so a stepbrother could have some extra spending money. He didn't have any siblings, but had missed having them so much that he knew he would have cherished a little sister, even a little brother.

Funny, now that he thought of it though, he had never imagined himself as the younger sibling. He took another swig of his orange juice and focused again on the heated game in front of him. He would have to ask Callie about her family, see if there were any clues there.

The ball was spiked high then slammed down with such force that it ricocheted off an elbow and made its way toward him. One handedly he grabbed for it and caught it in a firm grip. One of the girls looked over at him and then ran toward him. It was the one in the orange suit. *God is good.*

As she drew close she gave him a coy smile and asked, "What do I have to do to get my ball back?"

He couldn't resist. "Show me your tits and it's all yours."

As if it was the most natural thing in the world to her, she pulled her top down and let him look at her bountiful breasts. After the initial shock of her actually doing it, he stared, mouth agape for a few moments before tossing her the ball. She turned, tossed it back into play and then faced him again. Walking backward ever so slowly, she drew her straps to her shoulders. "If there's something else you'd like to see, you just let me know." Then she turned and ran back onto the beach, her little butt puckering as she ran back to her team.

Maybe Callie's issues with displaying herself so graphically weren't as bad as he thought. That young woman had had absolutely no qualms about displaying her charms to a complete stranger.

He heard a noise behind him and looked over his shoulder. "Hey sunshine, you're up."

"And not a moment too soon I see. I was about to get kicked out of bed and replaced."

He stood up and took her into his arms, loving the feel of her in her plush robe, "Never, she was too young. I prefer my women to have a bit more experience. And although her tits were nice, they were a bit too big, don't you think?" He gave her a lopsided grin that only served to make him more devilish looking.

"I thought where you guys were concerned, there was no such thing as tits too big."

"When they smack you in the face when she's on top, they're too big."

She laughed and snuggled into his chest.

"Ready for some breakfast?" he asked.

"Yeah, I'm starving."

He spun her around and smacked her on her bottom, "Well get yourself showered and dressed and I'll feed you."

She saw that he was already shaved and dressed in shorts and a tank top. "How long have you been up?"

"A few hours. I don't sleep much these days. Got used to not getting much sleep overseas," he said, then he winked at her, "you play havoc on my sleep cycle too." He had kept her up late into the night finding all her pleasure zones and exploiting them. When he had gathered her up beside him, her back to his chest, and dozed off it had been well after two.

He drove to the International House of Pancakes on the mainland, and over breakfast began asking her questions about her family.

"So you were an only child, like me?"

"Yup. Momma said they broke the mold with me.

But I think by the time I came along, she thought she was too old for any more."

"How old was she?"

"Thirty-eight, my dad was forty."

"That's not so old. So where are they now?"

"My mom lives in Aberdeen, not too far from the base. At least she did last time I saw her, she's been known to move around a bit. My dad died when I was nineteen."

A wave of sadness clouded her eyes, but at the same time he saw something else, was it shame? Could he have possibly called this one right with his out-in-left-field idiotic imagination?

"How'd he die?"

"I disappointed him, and he didn't take it well. Look, I don't want to talk about it, okay?"

"Yeah, sure. So when's the last time you saw your mom?"

"Christmas, two years ago."

"She didn't come to your wedding?"

"We aren't close. And it was a quick ceremony on post. Clint was scheduled to deploy in a few weeks."

"So, did you ever in your wildest dreams think you'd be an army wife?" he asked as he forked a bite of pancakes into his mouth.

"No, I didn't. I thought I'd be a spinster librarian." She took a swipe of the whipped cream from the pancake platter that had just been put in front of her then licked the thick cream off her finger.

Rand felt every muscle harden. He cleared his throat. Suddenly it was dry. He reached for his juice. "Why spinster?"

"None of my relationships ever seemed to last. I think I scared them away with my neediness."

"I haven't seen anything I can't handle," he said

with a grin.

"I suspect you're already into or have at least tried some of the things I tried to get my boyfriends to consider."

"Oh, I cannot wait to see this list. Finish up, I'm ready for a nice long walk on the beach."

"I need to shave first, I didn't get a chance earlier."

"I'll shave you."

"I don't mean my legs."

"I know."

He grabbed the check, stood and put his hand out to pull her from the booth. With his hand on the small of her back, he bent and whispered in her ear, "I may do a more thorough job than your husband would like, but I want you naked there. I want to be able to see, touch, and taste everything."

He felt a shiver go up her spine and he smiled to himself. *Oh yes, he'd make them both very happy in that arena. Clint be damned.*

Chapter Ten

Before either his hand or his penis became chapped, Garrett clicked out of the file he had previously copied to his hard drive and inserted the flash drive he'd found. He navigated to a file he remembered seeing, an older version of Quicken, and double clicked on the icon. If there was going to be any personal information on this little magic wonder, it would be in the financials. And he was a master at reading financials.

He clicked from page to page, digging deeper into subcategories and extrapolating information from the entries. There was only one account set up in the program. It appeared to be a checking account combined with a debit card. It had been initiated as Nations Bank and was maintained through to the present—the last entry July 12th of this year. Scrolling through he noted that there was no break in the service so he had to assume whoever it was had kept the same bank account. He knew that Nations bank had merged and was now Bank of America. Could it be any harder? Just about the largest bank in the country. *Great!*

There was no personal information listed, not even the account number in the appropriate place. *Of course not, that would have been too easy.*

The beginning balance in 1999 had been $2,324. The ending balance on July 12th, was a whopping $97,812—a tidy little sum for an account that seemed to be more of a household account than anything else.

Painstakingly, he read each entry, going from the bottom up. After two hours he had these "clues" noted on the pad beside his laptop:

Prefers Food Lion to Lowe's/ Wal-Mart and Harris Teeter only occasionally

Costco over Sam's Club

Is not at all particular about where she gets her gas

Is definitely a she, no man spends this much money on shoes at the Reebok Outlet, The Shoe Store, The Sandal Shop, and FootSmart

Spends less than $100 annually on booze—either she's a teetotaler or she's into beer or wine and buys it while grocery shopping

Favorite restaurants are: Grapevine, Purple Onion, Provision Company, Osaka, El Cerro Grande, Applebee's, La Cucina, anything with Pizza in the name

Shops at Belk, Dillards, Coldwater Creek, Amazon, FootSmart, and occasionally The Dollar Store

Goes to Holden Brothers or Annie Gray's Fruit Stand every other week or so

Frequents Dr. Pam Owens in sporadic intervals—no way to plot a date for future visits

Ditto Totally Chic for hair where she always has "cut/color" on the memo line

Averages $350/month to BEMC for electricity, which would indicate a larger home, at least in this county, $120 or more for water at BCPU, so she probably has sewer, not septic and waters her lawn fairly frequently

No entries for car repairs. So she either has a late model car still under warranty, has a maintenance plan, or she just doesn't drive

No purchase over twelve years and no payments, so the money comes from another account, or again, she just doesn't drive

Odds and Ends:

Buys nice sheets at Linens and Things $380 noted as just sheets indicates premium quality, large quantity or improperly categorized
Paid someone a hefty amount for olive oil—$280, name on check just initials (S.R.) Must have come directly from Italy in huge tins, someone traveling? Ahh . . . a hint at age. Tampons/Costco—$40 worth. Did the woman really drive all the way to Myrtle Beach for just tampons? If not driving by herself saw an amazing value and couldn't resist?
 No prescriptions noted anywhere
 No medical payments
 Either she has amazing insurance or she gets a discount for cash
 There are many ATM withdrawals for cash usually in $100 increments sometimes $50

Chapter IX

The days sped by as they did all the naughty things usually only teenagers were known for. They dragged a blanket into the dunes and made love under a full moon. Beneath a pier, hidden in the late evening shadows, in the pouring down rain, he hoisted her against him, and using only the back of his hands to protect her smooth skin against the rough creosote piling, he pressed into her—rubbed and grinded until they both came despite their suits remaining in place. At dawn he took her on a bench built into a wooden beach access. The dunes shielded them but the idea that anyone at any window in the hotel facing the ocean could look down on them, excited Callie so much that she trembled with desire.

When Rand teased her by breathing into her ear that he thought he saw the glint of binoculars in one of the rose-tinted windows, she came so violently and so loudly that he had to gag her with the bikini top he had just taken off. As "punishment," for misbehaving, he made her walk back to their room, down the access, through the deserted alley and empty parking lot, topless, her gorgeous tits bouncing as she hurried along. He smacked her butt as he jogged alongside her causing her to shriek, knowing discovery would flood her and make her eager to come again. The curtains in one window fluttered and an old woman peered out. Her eyes went wide as they ran past, Rand waving Callie's top like a trophy.

A long nap had ensued followed by a hearty breakfast at the pancake house. When they looked at each other everything around them seemed to disappear. A few times the waitress had to tap Rand on his shoulder to get his attention as he was so mesmerized by the woman sitting across from him. Her smile alone delighted him to his core, her laughter made him lightheaded. He was gone on her, and he knew it. Every waitress in the place was pretty sure of it, too. They would have looked on Callie with the worst kind of envy if it hadn't appeared that they were privy to a fairytale unfolding. There isn't a woman alive who doesn't swoon when she witnesses a love story having its happily-ever-after right in front of them.

On the way back to the room they decided the weather was too perfect to waste so as soon as they closed the motel door behind them they began stripping with the idea of putting on their swimsuits. Rand couldn't resist and had to grope her as she dropped her dress and shimmied out of her panties. It was touch and go whether they'd actually make it the beach before being tempted back to the bed before the sight of Callie's furry bush reminded him that he had a little grooming chore to perform on her.

He picked her up and tossed her over his shoulder as if she weighed nothing and then charged into the bathroom. She giggled and protested while playfully slapping his shoulders as he placed her on the edge of the tub, her feet inside.

Still naked himself, he stepped into the tub and faced her. His hands parted her thighs and as he admired the view, he sloshed warm water on her lush mound. Shaving cream was next, slathered so thick you couldn't see the black curls covering her. Then he squatted in front of her, his massive thighs used to holding his weight in a deep crouch for long periods of time.

The first swipes were the most telling, as rinsing

the razor in the flowing stream, thick rich curls were washed by the handful down the drain. Concentrating, he made many downward strokes before ducking his head and paying particular attention to the soft folds and creases. Her hands on the side of the tub, she was forced to lean back and watch as he meticulously removed all traces of her pubic hair. Alternately rinsing and running his fingers over her denuded flesh, he murmured his pleasure at the sight. When he was satisfied she was clean-shaven and smooth, he leaned in and kissed her with an openmouthed kiss that searched and explored, reveling in her naked pussy. Then he stood, lifted her over the rim and toweled her off.

"I want to eat you and fuck you, run my fingers all over you, and then take the whole day to just gaze at you, but I know you're anxious to get to the beach, so I'll give you a one-minute head start to get your suit on and grab your beach bag before I put my agenda before yours."

"I kind of like your agenda," she said with a coy smile, "but I know if I play my cards right, I can have both today—a day lying on the sand and a night lying under you in bed."

"You heard my ultimatum." He looked at his watch, "you've only got forty-five seconds left."

She squealed and grabbed the towel from his hand and ran for the bedroom. The drawer was pulled open and a bathing suit bottom and top were tossed onto the bed along with her beach bag. She turned and stepped into the bikini bottom and threw the string bikini top over her head not bothering to tie the side strings. Grabbing the bag and the towel she raced for the door. At the door she slipped into her flip-flops. As he advanced on her she opened the door and slipped out. Juggling everything, she managed to wrap the towel around her torso to cover the portion of her breasts that weren't yet tucked behind flimsy triangles.

She smiled back at him as she closed the door behind her, "See you on the beach!"

The door clicked closed and she could hear his boisterous laugh. Then moments later he joined her, lying beside her on the pristine sand. As he settled beside her, both on their stomachs, he lifted himself to his elbows and reached over to untie the knot and to pull the string she had just finally managed to get tied.

"I wouldn't mind if you tanned topless."

"Well, I'm sure that lifeguard over there might."

"No, I'm pretty sure he wouldn't mind a bit," he said with a roguish grin.

"Forget it. This is a family beach. Besides, I sure don't need a burn there."

"That's true, since I plan on mauling those puppies later, it would be best if they weren't overly sensitive." He bent over her and kissed her bare shoulder blade.

"I brought something," he said as he moved a cooler into view. He slid the handle back and lifted out a sipper cup with a tall straw attached. He made sure little drops of ice cold water dripped onto her warm back. She shrieked and he bent and licked them off as he handed it to her.

"What is it?"

"Something that will assure me I will be able to have my way with you."

She gave him a sideways quirk of an eyebrow. "As if that wasn't a sure thing . . . what's in this?"

"Screwdriver."

She took a tentative sip and shuddered from the strong alcohol-laced drink. "There's a lot more screw than driver in this."

"I'm all the driver you need, trust me. Looking at you, being here like this . . . I am as hard as a pile driver. You just worry about being the screwee."

She took another healthy swallow and smiled. "A woman could get used to this life. Sun, sand, sex."

"You soak it all up, as soon as I put some sunscreen on your back and legs I'm going to get some sleep so I can be ready for the all-night marathon."

"All night?"

His sunscreen-coated hand slipped between her thighs. "All night. There isn't anything I want to leave untried by morning."

"Making up for the time lost you spent overseas?"

"Maybe. Mostly making good use of the time I still have left. I expect it's only a matter of time before your husband comes to collect you." With that, he laid his cheek on his crossed hands and closed his eyes.

Callie looked at his handsome profile while she sipped the very potent screwdriver.

An hour later Rand opened his eyes to a clearly snookered Callie. If the dazed look in her eyes wasn't a clear indication, the fact that she had completely removed her top and was lying on her side facing him surely was.

He sat up and looked around. Thankfully, their little area was many yards away from the nearest group of sunbathers, all facing the shoreline and not aware of the couple close to the dunes.

He draped his t-shirt over her breasts and kissed her pinkening nose. "One would think you were proud of these," he said as a finger delved below the white cotton tee and grazed a pebbled tip. "Do you like showing these off? How does it make you feel when a man looks at your breasts with lust in his eyes? Lust, full and throbbing, palpable in waves like those roaring just a few feet away?" His voice was low and lyrical and his lips soft as he kissed around her ear.

He should have felt badly that he was using hypnotherapy techniques he had honed in school while plying her with alcohol, but he didn't. He had a burning desire to know what was going on inside this beautiful woman's head. He felt an overwhelming need to know how anyone with her beauty could end up so insecure, so needy that she would actually remove her bathing suit and show herself to complete strangers.

"Tell me how you met Clint."

"Oh, I worked at the library—"

"The truth. I hear you met at a party."

Her eyes opened in shock, "Did he tell you that? I didn't think he'd ever tell anyone the truth about that night."

"Never mind what he told me. I'm asking you to tell me. Here, have some champagne, it'll loosen your tongue." He opened a small split and filled a plastic flute. Tucking the empty bottle back into the cooler, he put the sparkling wine in her hand. He sat, one arm draped over a raised knee and said, "I'm listening," in his most commanding officer's voice.

Callie took a big sip as if to fortify herself and began. "It was one of those bachelor things I sometimes worked. Nine of us were hired out as a team; some were flagrant—strippers really. Others like me were more conservative and we just mingled. The company policy was that the girls only had to take off what they wanted to take off, and no one was ever allowed to touch them. I was one who never took everything off. I was the classy one, usually in a low-cut gown with a long slit showcasing my legs.

"Before we came into the room someone had to

read the policy card of 'I'm Your Babe,' the company we worked for. We wore any number of costumes: nurses, teachers, schoolgirls, French maids, policewomen, even nuns, whatever was arranged when the party was booked. The night I met Clint I was a French maid— short black dress, ruffled petticoat underneath, skimpy pinafore covering breasts propped high in a bustier, all topped with a cute hat over hair curled every which way. Vampy, but classy, if you know what I mean."

Clint nodded and opened another split for her.

"We always got a lot of catcalls, especially on the way up to the apartments. The minute I was announced and stepped into the room I knew there was going to be something different about this party. Although it looked typical, something felt wrong. Twenty military guys, all in uniform—or mostly at least. Some were half-dressed. There were a few other women there, wives or girlfriends, and some of the guys had their shirts and shoes off. A few had their pants unzipped. Two of the girlfriends were running around topless and everyone was feeling them up as they passed out drinks.

"This one guy sat at the end of the sofa, his arm draped on the armrest with a drink dangling from his hand. He looked like he'd just come from a dress parade compared to others. He was taking it all in, a cynical smile on his lips."

"Clint."

"As you say—Clint. His eyes met mine and held. We had that meeting across the room with your eyes kind of thing the whole time the host was reading the rules about how we were to be treated. Then the bump and grind music one of our girls carried started and broke the spell.

"But this guy's eyes didn't move far from mine, they dropped to my chest and he waited. He waited until I had used my feather duster on every man's chin, smiled into all their blood-shot eyes, and turned to swish my bustle-clad derriere in their faces. I unbuttoned the pinafore straps and let my top fall exposing the tops of my pushed-up breasts. His eyes burned into me, I could actually feel the heat as he looked at me. I had a set of much-used silver sequined pasties on and I remembered hoping I had used enough glue to keep them on in case a nipple happened to pop up over the edge of the bustier. My contract didn't call for me going topless; I didn't get paid the extra fee for doing it, and I simply didn't do it. Everyone knew that.

"Still, I felt dirty and ashamed; it was the first time I had felt that way in all the months I had been doing this. I remember I had to force myself to prance around the room, smile and shimmy my shoulders to make my tits jiggle. Then things went bad.

"The groom-to-be grabbed my breasts, pulled them free and squeezed them hard. I screamed, and as a reaction to the pain, I slapped him. That made him angry and he hit me, sending me into another guy who pawed at the dangling ruffled top of my pinafore as I tried to get away. He ripped my dress clean off. Then more hands grabbed at me from behind and not being able to pinch my nipples for the pasties that I was wearing, they tore them both off. It hurt real bad.

"I was topless and wearing only a skimpy pair of bikini panties. And I was stunned and mortified. I remember trying to cover myself, screaming 'Stop! Don't!' and then as tears were streaming down my face two guys in camo started tugging me down the hall toward the bedrooms."

"I don't suppose our chivalrous Clint allowed that."

"No, he did not. He stood, pushed several guys

out of the way, punched the guy in the face who was dragging me down the hall, Judo-kicked his friend, and then he bent and picked me up and tossed me over his shoulder. I remember bouncing against his shoulder as he ran down the outside steps with me, and then I was in his car, on the front seat hugging myself and sobbing while he screeched out of the parking lot and drove off.

"'I need my costume,' I cried, rocking myself back and forth as he drove through the worst part of town.

"'Fuck the costume! What the fuck were you thinking? Those guys are animals! Most of them haven't had a woman in months!'

"I looked over at him and saw that he was staring at my breasts instead of looking at the road. 'I needed the money! And you're not much better! Where are you taking me?'

"'I am not unaffected by your nakedness, but I'm not about to rape you.'

"He asked me where I lived and despite the fact that I had been admonished never to give a client my home address, I gave it to him. I wanted to get home. I needed my clothes. It was only a few blocks away and I thought I'd be safer there than where I was, practically naked.

"He wrapped me in his shirt and carried me upstairs when we got to my apartment. He set me on the mat outside my door and shoved three one hundred dollar bills in my hand. Then with that stern look he has he said, 'You will strip for no one else but me, from now on.'

"I didn't know what he meant by that until the next night when my boss came to my apartment. She told me to get dressed and took me to a downtown hotel. As ordered, I was dressed like a schoolteacher. I thought the other girls were already inside the room and that my boss had come to personally escort me to the job when I hadn't bothered to show up for work. When she knocked on the door and Clint answered I was stunned. A fistful of cash was crammed into my boss' hand and she left. He pulled me inside.

"'We sat on a tiny sofa watching old movies and eating pizza. He didn't ask me to take anything off. Every night for a month he paid me three hundred dollars to meet him at a different hotel. After the second week he asked me if I would go topless for him, but he didn't touch me, he just looked at me.

"While I ate whatever carryout food he'd brought in, and watched late night TV, he looked at me. He watched me as if memorizing me. After a while I was desperate for him to touch me and he knew it. One night I was asked to take everything else off while I sat beside him watching Larry King. During the last week he asked me to lie down on the bed and spread my legs for him.

"He sat with his head between my thighs staring until I finally begged him to touch me. 'I thought you'd never ask,' he said, looking up at me with the biggest grin on his face.

"That night he gave me pleasure, pleasure I had never known before. When he paid me that night he said he had to go overseas in a few weeks. And that he didn't want anyone else to see me without my clothes on so he wanted me to marry him. He told me if I married him he could cut out the middleman, not have to arrange all this with the escort company. That I could pocket all the money he was paying for me instead of splitting it with the company I worked for. He said I'd have a house to live in that wouldn't cost me a dime. He never said he loved me, just that he wanted to protect me.

"And he said he wanted to have a beneficiary for his government life insurance. I was already in love with him, so I said yes. We were married the next day by the post chaplain and on our way to the Bahamas for a quick honeymoon before noontime."

Callie had drained her second glass and was sitting up staring off into the distance. She was now wearing Rand's t-shirt and he could see the outline of her breasts with their tightly puckered nipples.

He sensed there was something about that honeymoon she was going to gloss over so he lied. "I heard there was something special that happened there."

"Good Gosh, is nothing sacred? I can't believe he told you that!"

"As I said before, two guys in a bunker, shells exploding all around . . . a good time to talk all night because you sure can't sleep." *Clint was going to kill him for this.*

"Well, he found out something I wish I had been able to keep secret a little while longer."

"Such as?"

"I thought he told you?"

"I want you to hear it in your own words." He refilled her glass for the third time and lifted it to her lips. He was starting to feel guilty about plying her with alcohol. But he wanted to know all there was to know about her. To him the end justified the means.

"Well, we were celebrating. And I suppose I had one too many rum punch drinks. I don't do well with alcohol. It definitely does relax my inhibitions. I started stripping out of my clothes before we even got to our beachfront room, and so we practically fell into the room making out and groping each other. Clint went to the blinds to close them and I told him not to. In fact, I begged him not to, pleading with him to leave the drapes open.

"And so he did. Soon we had an audience, a group of college kids out for a night on the town. They had stopped at our window, seen what we were doing inside on the bed, and they were whooping and hollering about what they could see. Both of us were naked and Clint was taking me doggie-style in the middle of the bed. I don't know what came over me, but I begged him to let them see where he was entering me. I remember pleading for him to pull out and to let them look at my cunt.

"When he finally turned me to face them, my legs splayed wide, I asked him to not only let them look at me but for him to use his hands and spread me open for them. He said no. I whimpered and cried, begging him to show them my vagina, and then reveling when he finally did. Through the glass I could hear all the lewd comments about my pussy, my cunt. How it was, 'such a cock stiffening sight,' 'fucking beautiful,' 'and can you believe this shit, he's showing us his wife's pussy!' I started to come and he helped it along and then tripled the effect by smacking my ass hard and whispering in my ear, 'Naughty girl, you're showing them your cunt, *my* cunt. What a bad girl you are.' I came and came and came, drenching his fingers and the covers below us. He flipped me over, stepped behind me and fucked me so hard I had to grip the mattress through the covers to stay on the bed. I'll never forget the sounds he made when he came, like an animal keening in the night. When he was finished shuddering and quaking, he pulled me down beside him, drew me close, and reached over to turn off the light, effectively shutting out the outside world and the leering boys with it.

"He knew now, if he hadn't before, that the reason I had been skirting the lifestyle of an exotic dancer was because I had a secret desire to exhibit myself—that I had an overwhelming desire to show off my body, particularly my pussy. I had fought it for as long as I could. I had hidden it from myself as much as anyone could hide something so deviant in their nature from themselves. I was so ashamed.

"I cried and I cried that night as he held me. I told him I was so sorry and he shushed me. Some things are fantasy, they're never meant to happen, they're only meant to tantalize and titillate—they're never meant to be more that what's in a woman's head. This event, while powerful and wicked while in the moment, was pure evil and horror in the hours and days after. It was a perversion I didn't want—that I couldn't stand to think came from inside me. The thought that it could conceivably happen again threatened to shut my mind off from everything. But Clint made it okay, said he wasn't ashamed of me, and that he'd see to it that I was never vulnerable in that way again.

"I wondered how he could possibly love me after that. Lord, I had *insisted—begged* him to display me, *forced* him to allow complete strangers to examine my genitals, allowed them to see me spasm and shudder in orgasm. And I had reveled in it. I was afraid he would be disgusted with me and send me away. Instead he held me and soothed me and told me how much he loved me. And when I asked him to please forget this, to never discuss it again, he simply stroked my hair and said. 'Okay.'

"So we forgot it. Our wedding night . . . we simply erased it from our memories, pretended it never happened. But it had. And the fear of those desires still peeps through from time to time, scaring me with its intensity. Making me wonder what the hell is wrong with me. What could possibly have possessed me to do that—to have actually begged Clint to share me like that?

"The only solace was that it was been far from home, in front of men—hell they were only boys really—who I'd never see again. I'd never have to confront them in the grocery store or be served by them at the corner diner.

"We left Nassau early the next morning so I wouldn't have to face anyone, and spent the rest of our time away in the Cayman Islands. I never knew what had come over me that night, but every once in a while I still have to stifle the urge to do something outlandishly vulgar—enticed by some kind of intoxicating sense of shame that washes over me and beckons. It's scary. And it's the only thing that keeps me from being truly happy—the only thing I'm afraid will rise up and take control of my sensibilities—override the protective boundaries I've learned to trust and swamp me with that horrible need to be shamed, to be humiliated, to be degraded by leering, dreamy-eyed men."

After a moment of silence, Rand said, "Hmmm. So here you are, drinking on the beach again. Am I going to have a problem with you tonight?" He gave her a rakish smile. "I should warn you, I'm not fond of sharing."

She leaned over and kissed his chin. "Don't look now, but you are sharing. I am another man's wife, remember?"

A serious look came over his features as he toyed idly with a lock of her hair. "Not just any man's. My best friend's."

He pulled her to him and tucked her face into his

neck. "How am I ever going to give you up?"

They sat in silence, holding onto each other for many minutes. Then Rand said, "C'mon, let's go get showered. I'm going to take you out to dinner, we're going to find the biggest steak in the county."

He helped her gather their things and they walked arm-in-arm through the sand to the access leading to the back of the hotel. Walking across the dunes Rand asked her a question that had been on his mind all afternoon. "Callie, have you ever had anal intercourse?"

She looked up at him and shook her head. But there was a spark of interest in her eyes.

"Would you like to?"

Her eyes met his and they held—each feeling out the other by the glints growing in their irises and the desire darkening their pupils.

"I think with the right man, I might like to try it."

"Am I the right man?"

"Why don't we see?"

His groin hardened, heat cruised through him and he felt his penis begin to swell. "How do you think Clint will react to me taking your cherry there? I assume he was going to get to it eventually. Any idea why he hasn't?"

"I was afraid. He's so big. And we hadn't known each other all that long."

"So you're no longer afraid? Is it because I'm smaller?"

"No, actually you're a bit larger."

He couldn't help but puff with pride. As with all best friends, especially in wartime, he'd seen Clint's penis many times, but never engorged and ready for sex play, only when peeing or being washed. He remembered it as pretty impressive in its normal state.

"So why the change of heart?"

"Curiosity. And such a deep fondness for you that I want to please you—in all the ways there are. For some strange reason, I don't want you to find me lacking."

He stopped on the wooden access and pulled her to him. Sighing heavily he breathed into her neck, "I could so easily love you."

To himself, he admitted that he already did.

Chapter X

Dinner at TBonz was more a love fest for food than anything else. While Callie sipped a raspberry-scented merlot, picked at her baked potato and nibbled on her rib eye, Rand downed a slice of prime rib that would have done Henry the VIII proud. His baked potato was loaded; his salad plate piled high, and he seemed to have a particular fondness for the Texas-styled toast.

They ate in relative quiet even though it was a noisy place filled with happy and robust vacationers.

When he looked over at Callie and saw her idly turning her wine glass in a circle on the table, staring into the burgundy liquid, he had the odd feeling that she was someplace else. Still, he tried to make the best of it.

"Uh oh, I may have fed you too much, you look like you're not far from being out for the count."

"A day in the sun does that sometimes. Of course, the wine isn't helping. But I don't want to spoil our plans for later."

"You couldn't possibly spoil any of my plans, unless you've decided not to come back to the room with me."

"I was so hoping we could . . . well, you know . . ."

"There's always tomorrow and the day after that. We don't have a time schedule you know."

"But we don't have all the time in the world either."

There it was—out in the open, dumped on the table, so to speak—their time was limited. Clint would be coming back; and he would have to report back to duty soon. This idyllic time together was a one-time event, never to be repeated, never to be even mentioned, and they both knew it. It was a sobering thought, but it affected them both in the opposite manner. She reached for her wine glass. He reached for his tumbler of whiskey. Neither said anything as they sipped and looked over the rims at each other.

"I want you now more than I ever did before, but it's a raw need and I'm afraid I'll hurt you," he said as his bright eyes met hers. He conveyed the depths of his desire solely with those fathomless eyes.

"You're only going to hurt me when you go away." The look on her beautiful face was one of timeless sadness. She could have been a Victorian lady sitting by her window and watching her husband leave for war, instead of a modern day woman staring at the soldier sent to occupy her husband's place in her bed.

"I'm sure Clint wasn't counting on me developing these feelings," she said as she finished her wine and placed the empty glass back on the table.

He had just finished signing the check and tucking his charge card back into his wallet. But he hadn't missed the look of acceptance that crossed her face. Yes she was wistful, so was he. But she belonged to Clint and they both knew it.

Tonight was not the night to experiment, to try rough things, to be demanding, possessive, or animalistic, even though his body was now roaring with the desire to take her in the basest of ways. He stood and gently lifted her to her feet, then tucked her under his arm and held her close as he walked her out to their car. Tonight was meant for gentleness, soft caresses, caring and tentative touches, and snuggling up close—a night to slowly slip inside her and feel her come apart in his arms. It was a night to make love while avoiding any issuance of the word from their lips. He loved her, but he couldn't keep her, and he had known this going in.

Chapter Eleven

Laurel met her friends, Vivienne, Tessa, and Catalina at the Silver Coast Winery. It was the best place to meet for a quiet afternoon of wine, chitchat and gift shopping. They were sitting at an outside table listening to birds chirping and following the erratic flight plan of hundreds of butterflies glinting in the late afternoon sunshine, and sipping white wine from "the blue bottle."

Life didn't get any better than this—unless you had a randy lover waiting for you at home. Which they all did . . . all except for Laurel. Friends of her mother's, these three women had been her support group through the worst days of her life. Now, despite being almost two generations older, they were her best friends. And over the last two years she had seen each one fall in love and remarry—to men who absolutely adored them.

"Well it's not like I really wanted to publish them. But that's not the point. I'm not as worried about someone stealing them and publishing them as their own as I am my name being attached to the stories. I think one day I might attempt to publish, but I don't think I'll want to use my real name."

"Is your real name on anything on that flash drive?" Tessa asked.

That one simple question floored her. She sat back on her chair and blinked. Her mind flitted back, rummaging through all the files and what might be on them. "I'm not sure."

After a few more moments of mentally ticking things off on her fingers, she turned to look at Tessa. God she was so lovely, quite a few years older than herself, as they all were, she positively shone. Marriage to Roman had made her a new woman, confident and sassy.

"You know I don't think there is anything with my name on it. My email files aren't on that particular stick. It's mostly my stories, some plot ideas, and my Quicken file.

"Quicken, you still using that old '98 software?" Cat asked.

"Sure, why not? Anything more complicated than my checking account and my debit card goes to the accountant. I don't need anything more up-to-date and I sure don't want to have to learn new software if I don't have to. I just barely got Word figured out. I don't like having to relearn things I already know, especially on the computer. And besides, I'd never be able to merge the files. You're talking about an awful lot of work just to be able to do pretty much the same thing I'm already doing now." Laurel sipped her glass of Seyval Blanc, commonly called *The Blue Bottle* by locals. It was crisp and fruity. She nodded her approval to Al as he walked by.

"So if your name's not on anything, how is whoever found it supposed to return it?" Viv asked.

"Good question." Laurel sat silently sipping. "I guess they can't, can they?"

"Not unless you advertise, offer a reward or something." This from Cat who was flipping back and forth, looking at the wine selections. She never left the winery without a case of something to replenish her wine cooler.

"Has anybody ever read your writing?" asked Viv.

"Not since high school, and believe me I wasn't writing like this back then."

"When are you going to let us read some of it?" Cat asked.

"You three are the last ones who need to read the smut I write! Good God, let's see a show of hands. Raise your hand if you haven't had sex today," Laurel said, then jokingly raised hers. She was surprised when Cat raised hers, too.

With a sheepish expression Cat said, "What can I say, Matt's out of town."

"Yeah, well . . . I still say you are the last ones who need more stimulation in that department."

"So the answer's no?" Viv prodded.

"No one reads my stuff, I'm not ready yet. Might never be."

"Well, you'd better make yourself ready, because someone's probably reading it right this very minute wondering where the hot chick is who writes such wonderful porn," Cat said.

"That sounds like an oxymoron, is there such a thing as wonderful porn?" asked Laurel.

"Hell yeah, Roman reads it to me all the time," Tessa said.

"Well then, let's lift our glasses to Laurel getting her good porn back," Cat said.

Everyone seconded it with a "Hear! Hear!"

"Laurel's porn, please come home!" was added emphatically by Viv.

Al walked by and they all heard him mutter, "That wins the award for the strangest toast I've ever heard." And they all laughed.

Back at home Laurel marveled at the support she got from her friends. They had come running as soon as she had called, listened to her woes, and managed to minimize them in her mind. And they were right, in the whole scheme of things, how much did this really matter? Except that it still kind of did. But not in the gut churning, itchy hives, need to hide under the covers way that it had.

They had called every week after her parents had passed, which was impressive, as they had each recently dealt with their own heartbreak after losing their husbands. Then, after moving in, they had insisted she go with the trio while volunteering with the local oyster recycling program. They hit it off right away despite her being so much younger. They all liked to drink wine, talk about men and sex, and experiment with food. She'd learned a lot about Asian food from Tessa, and had even been coaxed into trying octopus by Roman.

God, Roman . . . if only God had made a man like that for every woman. Of course Philip was nothing to sneeze at, and Matt, the way his eyes lingered with blatant hunger . . . and his warm and ready smile that made you feel as if you were the only one in the room, wasn't hateful either. Her friends had been very lucky, finding new mates and new lives at a time when most people were content to plop their butts in a rocking chair and knit their way to heaven.

Laurel went out to the garage to get her gardening tools. Nothing calmed her like pulling weeds. With any luck she'd be able to get in front of the computer this evening and "get back on the horse." It would be nice to settle back into writing again. Losing that flash drive had distracted her and kept her from her stories. She could only hope it hadn't staunched her muse.

Chapter Twelve

All told, he had spoken to sixteen local writers; no one had a clue who he was describing. A few spoke of romance writers living locally and he called each one only to be told they hadn't lost their flash drive, and that no, no one else writing erotic romance came to mind. The library in Shallotte and the library in Calabash added to the list of names he could try, but he struck out with all of them.

He was beginning to wonder if he should expand his search—maybe she wasn't all that local—when he remembered the buying habits he'd gleaned from her Quicken file. She bought groceries at Food Lion, Lowe's, Bi-Lo, Wal-Mart, and occasionally Kroger. That smacked of southern, so did the gas stations that were noted. The amounts were small chunks, bi-weekly, at places like Market Express, Citgo, Kangaroo, and Quick Mart, so there was no long distance driving, but that didn't negate flying—except that there were no entries for airlines or travel services. Of course she could be using a separate card for those. He certainly did—it paid to rack up those frequent flier points on certain cards. But the Quicken file didn't show any other accounts. Of course, that didn't mean she didn't have them. Maybe she only tracked this one debit card and checking account.

But he didn't see any evidence of travel, no big ticket gas entries, no restaurant or bar bills from anyplace outside a hundred-mile perimeter. From Wilmington to Murrell's Inlet she seemed to have no partiality, her tastes were eclectic. And no stomping ground frequented enough or visited on a regular basis for him to bother staking out. Plus, a listing of her utility bills indicated consistent use. Adjusting for the seasonal fluctuations, he compared them to his and it didn't look as if she went anywhere or was gone for long—if she was out of town at all. The clincher was the newspaper subscription entry, $201.16 for a year of *The Wilmington Star News.* He'd gone online to check it out. The amount listed was a year's subscription, weekdays and Sundays. If you didn't live here, you wouldn't get the daily paper delivered, he reasoned. She also received *The Brunswick Beacon,* paying $30 a year for the local paper that was mailed out every Wednesday.

Scrolling through the previous year's entries, he felt it in his gut that she was a local woman, at least now—probably not all along. Likely she was a newcomer of sorts, much as he was. Her style of writing, her phrasing didn't have that "southern bent"—sassy, witty, and either degrading or syrupy sweet.

In fact, he'd have bet money she was from the northeast, and as his portfolio attested, he didn't usually bet on something he wasn't fairly certain about. But, God, he wasn't certain about anything with this woman, except that she was sexier than all get out, and that if she'd patterned herself after Callie in any way, than he had to meet her . . . seduce her . . . pleasure her. She was just asking for it with these kinds of stories, wasn't she?

What kind of woman wrote like this if she didn't want to live like this? Or had lived like this? Hell, could this be a memoir? Was he chomping at the bit for a woman in her dotage reliving her past?

He didn't think so. Too many things spoke of her youth. And that war, it was still ongoing. Rand, Clint, and

Callie were all contemporary characters, living modern hi-tech lives. They emailed for God's sake. No she wasn't some old biddie. In his mind she was young and vibrant and had a mouth that enticed, kissable and hungry. . . ready to wrap around his—

The phone rang and pulled him out of his reverie. The Caller I.D. was one of the numbers he had dialed and left a message for. Another dead end. It was a repeat of a call he'd had earlier. He was told there was a Joey Hill who wrote erotic romance and had once lived around the Southport area. He'd already checked that out. Joey Hill was not the owner of the flash drive he'd found.

He'd already spent a few hours Googling random phrases from the files and hadn't had a hit, so he was fairly certain "his writer" wasn't published. Either that or she was very obscure and not on any Internet media.

He washed four Ibuprofen pills down with a swig of Guinness and walked out onto his deck to look at the ocean. Slumping in the wooden Adirondack chair, he stared out at the sea and got lost in his thoughts. She had to be somewhere. And he had no doubt that he'd find her.

He looked over at the empty chair beside him. What he wouldn't give for her to be sitting there, beside him, enjoying this breeze.

Chapter XI

The days were idyllic. They slept late, walked on the beach, had picnic lunches they fed to each other, and lazed in the afternoon sun, disappearing to the seclusion beyond a dune with a blanket when the urge to mate was overwhelming.

And each night they experimented with something new and titillating from Rand's bag of sex toys, discovering she liked nipple clamps as long as they dangled like jewelry when she was a good girl, and spreader bars and paddles when she was naughty. Rand had talked her into wearing an anal plug to stretch her so she could accommodate his size more readily. And he was counting the days until he could claim her ass.

After they had been at the beach for three weeks, Rand promised her a shopping trip to Coastal Grand Mall, provided she wear the next largest size, one only slightly smaller than his dick, while they shopped. He secured it with a crisscross of elastic straps that overlapped the flange that held it in. It was a day of secret looks and embarrassing cringes whenever she had to sit, stand or climb steps. His knowing look and wicked smile made her hot all over—hot and wet. While she had been dreading this before, she was now eager for his possession of her in such a base and totally male way.

She got her wish as soon as they arrived back to their room. She had no sooner dropped her packages on the bed than he came alongside her and swept them to the floor. Her skirt was lifted, her panties pulled to the tops of her thighs and with a hand on her back he bent her over the bed and removed the self-fashioned harness and plug. He wadded it up in a tissue on the nightstand, his hand coming back with a tube of lube from the drawer.

"Unless you relax, the first time isn't going to be all that great, so try to work with me here. Bear down when I say to and try not to let your sphincter go tight. We're going to take it slow and easy, by half-inch increments if we have to. Just remember one thing."

"What's that?" Her voice had a slight tremor to it and it made him smile.

"Don't be embarrassed, because I'm going to be having the time of my life. Loving every single stroke between these beautiful globes." He caressed them both then pulled them apart and used his thumbs to anoint her small bud with the lube.

He shifted her so they were long ways on the bed and she could watch him penetrate her in the mirror. Then he reached under her and unbuttoned her blouse and unsnapped her bra letting them both fall forward and open, grazing the arms that propped her up.

He kissed the back of her neck, whispering about all the naughty things he was going to do to her while his fingers tugged on her nipples, stretching them and pinching them until she cried for release. One hand alternately cupped and squeezed her swaying breasts as the other found her cleft and slicked her juices from front to back. More of the cool lubricant was added to both her opening and to his thick penis that had already been burrowing between her ass cheeks.

"Ready, baby?"

"Mmmm humm," she moaned, delirious with the friction he was causing both with her breasts and with the anxious battering ram sliding in and out of her crease.

He kissed the side of her neck and down her spine, moving back on the bed until he was standing on the floor. He gripped her hips and dragged her back to him, bringing her splayed feet to the edge of the bed. The fingers of one hand held her checks apart while he placed the lubed tip of his cock at her bud opening. Gentle nudges placed it up against the tight ring and with one quick jab he shoved it past the tight band of the puckered rim.

They both moaned, albeit for two different reasons, she because she finally realized what was happening, what this was really going to mean, and he, because he was on his way to paradise. Slowly over many minutes, he gently rocked against her, incrementally working his way inside, agonizing with each inch disappearing inside her as he was fighting to hold back from his greatest desire—to fuck the hell out of this sweet, tight ass that was wagging back and forth in front of him.

Sweat was pouring from his temples and popping like tiny beads from her pores when he had finally seated himself, his balls snug up against her.

"Dear God, this feels incredible. I never want to leave; I want to fuck you like this forever. Are you okay?" he asked as he bent forward to turn her face back. "Am I hurting you . . . badly I mean. I know I'm hurting you."

She closed her eyes and sighed. "I've never felt anything like this. I feel . . . I feel . . . like you own me."

The words, combined with her devastating beauty, and the needy look on her face, spiked his passion making him pull out and thrust back into her. They both groaned and when he saw her face in the mirror, this time it was undeniably rapturous with pleasure. "Damn straight!"

He smacked her ass cheeks. Hard. Making them

crimson and heightening her pleasure as he told her what a bad girl she was, his bad girl. With his fingers digging into her ass cheeks and using his thumbs to hold her cleft wide he watched his prick entering and retreating. He began to take long, slow strokes. Watching his long, thick cock disappearing between her crack and then into her hole was the most erotic sight he had ever seen. His whole body shook with the pleasure.

She groaned and his fingers moved to caress her needy clit. He felt it plump as her pleasure built and then with one loud sob, she shook with delicious abandon and screamed, "I'm coming! Oh good God, I'm coming!" He watched her face contort in the mirror as she climbed to her peak. While his fingers milked her clit, he jabbed into her hard and fast, fucking her ass and sending her over the edge to oblivion. Her pussy spasmed against his hand and he let loose the last vestige of his sanity. He groaned as his release tightened every muscle in his body. Clenching his jaw and closing his eyes tight, he threw back his head and bellowed. Every nerve shuddered as his semen spurted deep in her ass, causing the tight hole gripping him to flutter in response. Her strained muscles clamped around him and pulled him back inside as he shoved against her and flattened them both on the bed. His cheek rested on her back and he actually dozed for a scant few moments before turning his head to kiss her shoulder blade.

He had never experienced a climax like that. With his ejaculation had come a sense of happiness, elation he had never even imagined possible. He was completely satisfied with everything in his world; relaxed in a way he didn't know he could be. It was almost spiritual the way his orgasm was so cleansing—

which was ironic, he thought, as he lifted off of her and pulled his flaccid member from her, because he was anything but clean right now.

Coming back from washing up, he smacked her on her tender bottom. "Hey Angel, don't go to sleep on me. It's only five o'clock."

She mumbled something that sounded like, "gars sleep do, g'way."

He laughed, "If you're saying you want to sleep, go away, nothing doing. I'm starving." Good sex always did that; great sex like this gave him the shakes as he was so depleted.

She lifted herself up on her arms, turned her head to look at him and then collapsed again. "Room service," was all she could manage to say.

"Well, I'll tell you what little lady, since you were so *accommodating*, I will get dressed and like the big game hunter I am, I will go out into the world and bring back food. What would you like?"

"Pizza," she said into the pillow she had dragged down from the top of the bed.

"Pizza is not big game food, but if that's your fondest wish, I will bring it forthwith." With that he shoved his long legs into the jeans he picked up from the floor and pulled on a tank top he found in the chair. A few moments later she heard the door click behind him.

Leveraging herself up she tried twice to get up but finally just ended up rolling until she fell off the bed. Falling to the floor with a loud thwack as her butt hit the floor, she squeaked in protest. Her bottom was on fire; places that had never made themselves known before now felt raw and abused. Nerve endings that had been quietly dormant were not just screaming, they were sending heat throughout her system. Pulling up on the bedspread to get to her feet, she managed to get to the bathroom where she turned the taps on full over the tub. She felt like she had to go to the bathroom, but ten minutes on the toilet convinced her that she didn't know that part of her body anymore, at least not right now.

Sliding down into the tub was both soothing and irritating. She was, after all, sitting on her sore bottom. Rand had been a bit overzealous with his spanking. She smiled at the memory. She loved it when he lost control like that, it made her feel powerful to be able to run his lust up so high. To get him so far gone he'd do anything for the pleasure, including spank her and drive into her like a mindless madman. She loved it when she could turn him into the male animal he was, despite his desire to temper the beast seeking so hungrily to mate.

Ten minutes later she almost felt normal again. She had mixed feelings about Rand's possession of her there and wondered how women managed with men the size of Clint and Rand shoving their dicks into that fragile cavity on a regular basis. By the time she got out of the tub and dried herself off, she had to admit, she didn't hurt anymore, and she actually felt a bit hollow—empty in a way she'd never felt before. Maybe with time, you got used to it, she thought as she heard Rand open the outside door. She heard it close a few minutes later, then the bathroom door opened and he walked in.

She was holding a towel to her breasts, drying them, and it was high enough that her shaven pussy was clearly visible. Watching his eyes, she realized that he could also see her red bottom reflected off the mirror. He was taking it all in, front and back. "You must have been a pretty bad girl, looks like somebody spanked you, but good."

"Uh huh, and I plan on being bad again, but not until somebody feeds me."

He gathered her into his arms and pulled her close. "No problem." Gazing down into her smiling face he realized that he was happier than he'd been in his entire life. Even his best day to-date, graduating from West Point, couldn't touch this one. He bent his head and brushed his lips over hers then insinuated his tongue and busied it with hers so he wouldn't blurt out that he was in love with her.

He poured his heart into that kiss and when they finally broke away, she stared up at him, a questioning look in her bright eyes. He had finally kissed her. Something had changed between them and she wasn't sure if it was in a good way. She caressed his cheek then ran her thumb over his bottom lip. "About that pizza . . . my body needs fuel for the next . . . uh, combat situation. Maybe it's your turn to be punished for insubordination this time." As she separated from him she brushed her hand along the length of his zipper and squeezed.

He groaned and stepped back to release her, watching her sweet fanny in the mirror as she stooped to retrieve her towel.

They ate at the tiny dinette with her dressed in one of his oxford shirts, the sleeves rolled to her elbows. Unconsciously, she toyed with the buttons on the placket and it positively drove him insane. They had ice cream for dessert and he managed to convince her to eat it topless for him.

After dinner they walked hand-in-hand on the beach, looking at the turtle nests tucked up against the dunes and helping several older gentlemen fill in a huge crater some kids had left. Then they settled in the sand a few feet from the encroaching tide to watch the sunset and play chicken with the tide, scooting up and back and laughing like children. They talked about life, memories of their childhood vacations to the beach, and the man they both loved, who was still so far away.

When darkness settled over the island, they raced each other to the room, stripped off their soggy jogging togs, and jumped in the shower to wash the sand off their bodies.

Callie began teasing Rand by stroking her breasts, plucking at her nipples and running her hands up and down her soapy body. When she slid a finger inside herself, he bent and knelt on one knee to open her legs wider so he could watch.

She made him so hot he couldn't stand it. His cock, perpetually at full mast around her, was jumping in its eagerness to be inside her. When she shoved two fingers into her sheath, he leaned forward, uncovered her clit with his thumbs and sucked it between his lips. When she came mere seconds later, flooding his mouth with taste sensations that drove him wild, and pulsing contractions beckoning him deeper, he groaned more from her pleasure than from his. Still, he reached between his legs and jerked roughly on his penis. Her hand covered his and then took over. Soon she was kneeling and taking him into her mouth and sucking the corona with long tugs, then keeping him between her lips and sliding up and down the length of his erection, sucking even harder, letting the loud slurping noises that were echoing over the tiles arouse him even more.

Suddenly he gripped her head with both hands, forced her away and in a swift motion that was only accomplished because of his superb muscle tone and innate power, he lifted her against the wall, kicked her feet apart, and shoved his cock home. He fucked her hard and fast, pummeling her and sending her inching up the slick wall with each forceful thrust. Finally, he gripped her shoulders from the back to hold her in place and piston fucked her, he was so far into his lust that he didn't even realize moments later that he'd taken her completely into his arms and was holding her independent of the wall, supporting her solely in his arms, yet still keeping up his frantic pace. She cried out his name as she came—joining it with long, plangent wails that brought jolts of pleasure to him as she screamed his name over and over again. With one final thrust that he buried deep in her core, he gave a choked cry of his own as his body jerked and shuddered, expelling his seed. This mating had been primal and he felt it to his toes as every muscle in his body quivered with weakness. He staggered the few steps necessary to lean her back against the tile wall. He was kissing her neck and moaning her name when he heard the bathroom door click open. Despite his sensual fog, all senses came alert and he caged her body with his.

Clint opened the door and stepped into the steamy room. He was in camo fatigues; his posture rigid as he kept his hand on the doorknob as if that alone could keep him in check. From his initial assessing glance, Rand could tell that he was livid. Rand felt stupid standing there with his cock in his friend's wife's pussy. Water was running down every surface so it was pretty obvious that they'd been at this for quite a while. He reached down and with one hand he hit the faux crystal knob that turned the water off.

Callie, her head tucked down and facing the opposite direction knew something was up by the sudden tensing of Rand's body. Every muscle was hard, except the one that now slithered out of her. She lethargically turned her head to the door and over Rand's shoulder she saw the hat of a man in uniform. She moved so that she could see around Rand's shoulder to the man who stood there watching them.

"Clint," she breathed. Rand almost chuckled, how she managed to throw so many emotions into that one word, he'd never know. But it was apparent that she was pleased, scared, awed, on guard, and feeling a bit guilty.

"I came to take you home, Callie," he said in a soft, quiet whisper. To Rand he said, "Soldier, you're relieved of duty. I'm here for my wife. Stand aside and return her to me."

Rand stepped away, no longer feeling the protective need to block Callie's body from view. He helped Callie out of the shower enclosure. And then, not just in a figurative sense, he handed her off to her husband.

Clint took Callie's hand, raised it to his lips and kissed it tenderly. Then he pulled her close, mindless of her wet state, and his eyes took in every aspect of her face before he kissed her in a most demanding and possessive way. Using both hands cupped over her jaw he plundered her mouth and fed on her lips. He'd dreamed of nothing but this moment for days, his mouth was desperate for the taste of her.

Rand grabbed a towel from the rack and inched his way around them to the bedroom.

After a few moments he heard Clint's gruff voice coming from the other side of the door, raised so that Rand could hear it, "Who's the bastard whose been manhandling my wife?"

Rand, the towel wrapped around his hips, leaned in and peaked through the opening. He saw his best friend running his fingers over the red handprints on his wife's otherwise lovely ass. He watched as Clint's hand switched to the front and cupped her mound. When she jerked upright, he saw from her expression that Clint had just shoved a finger into the vagina he had just vacated. He looked at the face of the woman he had just made incredible love to and felt his heart being torn from his chest. It was time to leave her now, but no way did he want to.

But before he could walk out the door he needed to know how she was handling this impromptu reunion with her husband. He knew his presence was keeping her from being herself right now, keeping her reaction to the returning soldier subdued when she probably wanted to devour him whole. But damn! What about him? What now? Was he supposed to just get dressed and leave? Like a ship going out of commission, a weapon being outdated, he was being discarded as useless fluff. He was lost. Should he leave? Should he go?

Clint answered the question for him. "Help me take off my clothes, sweetheart. I haven't had a shower in three days. I was lucky to have found a toothbrush and some mouthwash." With his boot, Clint kicked the door shut behind them, in Rand's face.

As Rand dressed, he listened to the sounds of clothing being undone, heavy fabric finding its way to the floor, elastic being pulled and then released, boots thudding on the tile. The shower was turned back on and he heard the sound of the curtain being drawn. After a few moments of staring at the closed door he turned away. He assumed she was in the shower with him. Lathering him up, cleansing him from his long trip . . . getting him hard.

He clenched his hands at his sides. He'd known

this day would come. He'd known she was only on loan. But shit, he hadn't known he was going to fall in fucking love with her. Now what?

He alternated pulling on clothes with throwing things into his duffle. How had he been so stupid? He'd sheltered his heart for years; never let a woman get under his skin. Now look at him! He was a mess. Jealousy churned through him as he heard Clint's laugh over the sound of the water, irritation burned in his gut when he heard Callie's teasing chuckle, and rage just about overtook him when he heard the steady slap of skin on skin against that fucking wall—again!

He felt tears burn his eyes and had to remind himself that he was a soldier, one of America's best. He'd seen his buddies die, one right after the other, sweated many nights out fearing he'd meet his maker before sunrise. And now look at him, a tiny slip of a woman had come into his life and he was putty. A total goner. He shoved shorts and t-shirts into the cavernous bag; mindless of the disheveled state he was putting them in. He was sitting on the bed putting his shoes on when the bathroom door opened. He was afraid to look up, but couldn't help himself.

Callie was snuggled under Clint's arm; both were wrapped in the bathrobes that had been hanging on the back of the door. Clint was wearing his robe, one he had bought at the mall when they had arrived here. Despite loving this man like a brother, his jaw bunched and his teeth gritted at the sight, but he kept his head low so only he knew how much this all mattered. While he finished lacing his running shoes he faced the fact that she was Clint's, that he knew going in that this had only been temporary. He had to be a man about this, the good soldier. And it was time to decamp. Resolved, he stood, and with an air of nonchalance that he did not feel, he reached out and shook Clint's hand, "Good to have you home, Captain. You're back sooner than expected."

"Finally found the damn bunker, practically blew out the whole damn mountain just to be sure we knocked out all the surveillance, and then high-tailed it back. They had a plane just finished being repaired and I hopped on." He squeezed Callie around the shoulders, "Other than the manhandling that was caused by what Callie assures me was wholly inspired by her, I see, and of course I *heard*, ahem . . . that you've been taking very good care of my most prized possession."

She was not a possession, Rand thought, certainly not if she couldn't be *his* possession, but he didn't say anything along those lines. It was pointless. She *was* Clint's wife, not his. The agreement had been to help out, not to take over. He felt as if a knife was stabbing repeatedly into his chest, he had to get out of there before he broke down or tore the place up. He reached for his bag and began stuffing things from the nightstand into his pockets.

Clint took Callie's hand and led her over to the only armchair in the suite. He sat and then patted his knee as he pulled her down. For a fleeting second her robe flapped open and Rand saw the tops of her thighs. He was hard in an instant. God, was this woman always going to affect him like this?

"Not sure I appreciate you shaving her pussy though, but she seems to like it. Time will tell if it will grow on me, but I guess I'll have to give it a go until she grows it back." The dominant part of him was coming out now, the one Callie must have responded so well to. "Right, Sugar?" he asked as he patted her thigh. She looked at him and smiled then she looked over at

Rand and winked.

His heart melted. God he loved her so much. How the fuck had this happened? He had to get out of there. Now. Before he made a fool of himself in front of his best friend and the only woman he'd ever loved.

"Can I borrow the car?"

"It's yours. Keep it. Consider it payment for services rendered."

Now that did it! "I do not need to be paid for fucking your wife!"

Clint's eyes went wide; Callie shrank against her husband's chest. "I'm not paying you for *services rendered*," Clint said his voice steely. "I'm giving you a gift because you did me a great favor, and Callie, a wonderful honor by being her surrogate husband while I was away."

"Well I'm glad you see it that way. I saw it as payment . . . sort of like stud fees."

Clint put Callie aside and stood. "Rand, I know this must be hard for you. But let's not say things that could ruin our friendship. Take the car. If after a few days you still won't accept it as a gift, let me know and I'll arrange to come get it. Meanwhile, I suggest you take a few days and mull things over. Hang out with the guys, go to a few clubs, play some roundball. Before you know it, it'll be time for us both to deploy again. So just chill . . . go play while I get reacquainted with my wife." His hand stole around her waist and she dutifully leaned into him.

Rand focused his eyes on Callie's trying to see if there was a message for him there. There was no message, at least not one he could read. She looked elegant, reserved, and so beautiful it broke his heart. She looked just as she had the first time she'd opened the door to him. And he'd fallen into her trap. Her sexy, gotta-have-her womanly trap.

He turned and grabbed the car keys off the dresser. "How'd you find us anyway?" he asked, curious now as his system calmed.

"Not too many '78 Camaros in the motel parking lots. And everyone seemed to know the young couple *on their honeymoon.* I went to the office and a young impressionable ROTC cadet was on the desk. In uniform, you and I look enough alike that I just asked for another key, said I lost mine on the beach last night. He wasn't about to buck a Captain."

"So you *wanted* to walk in on us?"

Clearly losing patience, Clint said, "I knocked for five minutes. I could hear water running. I wanted to be sure everything was all right. To be honest, I felt like a fool standing at the door, everyone looking up at me from the pool while I was pretty sure you were in there fucking the bejesus out of my wife. Not that I hadn't asked you to, mind you. It's just different in reality."

"Let me just ask you a question."

"Go ahead."

"If you had to do it over again, would you do the same thing?"

"You mean Operation Surrogate Husband?"

"Yeah, that's exactly what I mean."

"Yeah, I would. And you were the perfect man for the job. Now, you're relieved of duty. Go find the boys and have some fun."

"What the fuck are you going to do next time you deploy *Captain*?" Rand said as he grabbed his duffle and stormed out of the room, slamming the door behind him.

Jaw set and eyes furious, Rand crossed the parking lot and unlocked the car. He threw his duffle into the back and slid into the driver's seat. He didn't doubt that everyone on Kings Highway heard him as he burned rubber peeling out of the parking lot and onto the highway. Jesus! How had he fucked up his life this badly in such a short amount of time? He wished he could just drive to the base hangar, steal a fighter jet and head back to Afghanistan. Instead he drove to the nearest bar.

Chapter Thirteen

Garrett sat back in his chair and rubbed the back of his neck. He wasn't used to doing this much sitting. Idly he scrolled through the document to see how much there was left to read. He was torn between wanting to know what was going to happen between these three and not wanting it to end. His stomach growled and he realized he needed to get something to eat. Then he had work to do, and he really should take a run on the beach today, as tomorrow they were calling for rain.

He looked out the window and caught sight of a line of pelicans winging their way south. He stood and watched them soar and dip, and then one fell out of formation in time to swoop into a wave and come up with a fish, that quickly disappeared down his gullet, before he rose on the wind to rejoin his comrades. Too pretty a day to spend it inside, no matter how tempting it was to finish what he figured was only two or three chapters. Later, he promised himself as he stepped around his makeshift desk and strolled into the kitchen. It would be his reward for a good sweaty run.

Head ducked under his arm, he foraged in the refrigerator and finally came up with some leftover black beans and some rice, a pear and a bag of pre-washed spinach. Food Lion had certainly improved their food selection, and while it was no Trader Joe's, they had a nice selection of international foods. He'd been able to get a ready-made pouch of Spanish rice, to which he'd added a can of black beans and a can of spicy Rotel. Served with a spinach salad and pear slices nuked for twenty seconds and drizzled with raspberry vinaigrette, it made a great lunch. He took everything outside to the deck and ate at the table he'd had made to match his Adirondack chairs. From the deck, he alternated shoveling food, flipping through *GovMint News, Stansberry and Associates,* and *Gold Stock Advisor* newsletters while taking in the sights on the beach below.

His beach house was in an area that was fairly secluded beach-wise. It was toward the east end and not too many day-trippers set up that far down. There was no place to park, for one thing, and it was not convenient to the pier, where the bathrooms and gazebo showers were.

People staying on this stretch liked to be away from the action. While not remote, it was peaceful and not quite so restrictive. You weren't likely to have to deal with gulls being fed crackers just a few feet away, or someone blaring country music and being just drunk enough to think they could line dance to it in front of you.

He liked it here. He could work, play, and entertain ladies from time to time without causing anyone to shift their attention to him. He wasn't a loner, he thought as he speared a pear slice and dunked it in a pool of dressing. He was just busy, and when he was here, he considered this his hideaway.

He rarely told anyone he knew here at the beach when he was coming down. Friends on the island saw him come and go, and a slight wave was all that was required to stay connected—everyone had their own gig, and he appreciated that. Except for the holidays. They were special times, and he usually had more invitations than he could accept. He smiled as he thought of Miriam Marks and her daughters Mimi and Jackie in *Plum Nelly*, a few houses down from his. He never turned down an invitation to one of their spirited gatherings.

Then he frowned as he remembered a disastrous party he'd attended across the street last year. It was as if he'd been *The Batchelor* among a bevy of wanna-be brides. Pulled from one overly made up face to another and gripped by his coat sleeve to busty bosoms, he was passed around like a prize. One brazen vixen in a fuzzy Santa Claus hat had actually licked his ear and said she wanted to taste him . . . everywhere. Another tucked a note in his coat pocket after advertising her *special* Christmas tradition—licking the red stripe off a "big ol' candy cane"—until there was nothing left. The note had her phone number, written in red and encircled by a lipstick stained kiss print, also in bold, seductive red. There was apparently a shortage of available "big ol' candy canes" on Sunset Beach during winter break.

The homeowners who'd been here before 179 became a route number on the map, often made a special point of trying to get him around their grandnieces and granddaughters. Somebody was always introducing him to a sweet young thing from either Clemson or Duke. Or there was a daughter in banking from Charlotte, a daughter of a friend who was a single mother from Cary. Once, a whole group of teachers was brought to his table and he was asked to guess the subject they taught by the drink they held in their hand—Margarita for the Spanish teacher, Appletini for Physics (Isaac Newton), Poinsettia for the Botany Major, a mulled cider drink called a Wastrel for the Music teacher, and so on, ad nauseum. And while the sports medicine prof was very hot (Red Bull and Grey Goose), he didn't see himself making trips to Tallahassee on a regular basis.

Sometimes he took the bait, and went off for a late night walk on the beach with the bubbly co-ed or budding HR manager, but most of the time he deferred. He didn't need issues with his neighbors. They didn't need to know that the sweet young things they were offering to set him up with weren't all that sweet. And if they were, he didn't want to be thought of as the big bad wolf with the love 'em and leave 'em attitude.

A pattern he'd noticed, and actually charted one time, showed that the younger the college student, the more adventurous she was in bed, and the more independent she preferred to be so she wasn't tied to any guy. The closer to graduating she was, the more traditional she became and fun-loving and independence gave way to desperation as she was soon going to be sent out to into the world of natural selection—where each year she was unattached put her farther from the goal. While he never dated his own students, he became partial to juniors or those with aspirations for a Masters degree. But lately, they all seemed a tad on the young side and he found he wanted to talk before getting between the sheets.

Moving off campus and teaching online got him away from ambitious teacher's aides. He was always conscious of the threat of harassment suits and moral's charges that could be brought from students who wanted better grades with less work. Even young men, thinking they might have a chance with him because he knew how to dress and liked to ride his bike to class had become a problem.

A young thing in a yellow bikini setting up a chair and applying sunscreen snagged his eye. He watched as she put ear buds in her ears and attached her iPod to an arm holder. He checked her out as she put her sunglasses on and began walking toward Tubbs Inlet. She was blonde with a dark tan. He couldn't see her from the front, but her tiny backside swished back and forth as she strolled and waved her hand to the music. Hmm . . . he thought, might be time to take that run on the beach now. Check out the sights, fore and aft. Possibly offer a sip of something cool to the little woman, as it was a very warm day.

The sound of his cell phone ringing in the other room erased those thoughts as he realized it was time for the conference call with a group of investors. He gave the woman with the swishing cheeks one last perusal before heading inside to hear what a new generation of tech nerds from M.I.T. had to say.

Chapter Fourteen

Twenty minutes later he ran down the steps of the beach house and headed east, getting to Tubbs Inlet just in time to make the turn and pass the little blonde on her return trip. What had looked so fine from one angle, didn't hold the same appeal when he was front and center. What was it about women who Botoxed the hell out of their lips? She did smile and wave, or at least he thought it was a smile—her lips didn't seem to be able to turn up much. Then he saw that the mounds behind her tiny top didn't so much as shimmy with each footfall, those puppies are high and tight . . . forever, he thought. He waved back but was careful not to make eye contact.

Why did women feel the need to improve on nature? He'd have preferred her with a light cinnamon tan, instead of one so dark it cast a black silhouette on her slight frame, natural, soft breasts that jiggled and moved to fill your hand when you kneaded and caressed them, and lips, that even thin, were soft, pliable and capable of feeling so much more. He shook his head as he ran. Ruefully, he realized he was looking for someone like Callie. Callie, or the woman who had created her.

As his sneaker-clad feet thudded on the hard-packed sand at the water's edge, he went over the things he could do to try to find her. There had to be a way to track her down. With each footfall he processed a thought and then discarded it. At the pier, he slumped against a piling to catch his breath for the return trip. An odd thought occurred to him and he laughed out loud causing a few people to turn and stare. He put his head back against the wood and closed his eyes, blocking out the sun so he could just listen to the lyrics of the beach. He smiled to himself as he thought about his absurd idea to rent a billboard on Route 17, emblazoned with:

If you know who Callie, Rand and Clint are,
call: 910-572-1456.

Yeah like she'd answer and ad like that. He wondered how many calls he'd get from the curious, the bored, or the intrepid reporters. Laura Lewis with *The Brunswick Beacon* had an interesting bent on things. He loved reading her articles and could tell a lot of her ideas for columns came from her keen sense of curiosity. What would she have to say about a billboard like that? He could hear her now, "Now Garrett, did you really think this would work, that your mystery woman would see this and just call you?"

He forced himself upright and after walking a hundred yards, worked himself back into a gentle loping jog. Sweat was pouring down his back where he could feel the sun beating on it. His hair, loose and free at the start of his run was thick and plastered to his head from the salt and dampness. He had to run around a series of sandcastles and avoid a few tide pools. Out on the horizon, shrimp boats were making their way back toward the jetty and Little River Inlet. The waves, curling and foaming as they made their way to shore brought a never-ending rhythm that he knew was as steady as his heartbeat. The day was so damn beautiful he had to stop, hands on hips, and just stare out to sea.

It was primal and thrilling and so constant you could bank on it, bet on it. He knew that the waves would roll in and touch the shore twenty-six times a minute, no matter what the weather. And no matter who died or lived, that they would never cease. As long as he stood here, they would never let him down.

A different kind of wave came over him, one of nostalgia, combined with loneliness, and he knew in that moment what was missing from his life. He wanted someone to share this with. He didn't want to go back to his beach house to shower and prepare to go to Myrtle Beach so he could find a woman to talk to. He wanted to go back to his beach house and have her already there waiting for him.

He caught the sweat dripping from his eyes with the hem of his t-shirt. Then he began jogging again. At a fast clip—anxious to get there. He was going to read the rest of that story, then every story on that disc until he figured out who the woman was who wrote those stories. Because somehow he knew, he just knew she was writing to his soul. And he had to find her.

Chapter XII

While Clint and Callie got reacquainted with each other, Rand caroused the bars, punished his body at the base gym, and brooded. Masterfully. He was quick to feel the unfairness of finally, *finally*, falling in love with a woman. Why did it have to be with his best friend's wife? Why was the only woman he had ever managed to fall in love with already taken?

It took some M.P.s at a bar one night to help him back to reality. Picking fights because he wanted to feel the pain of a bashing instead of the pain blooming in his chest was not a career advancement tactic. Fortunately, he knew one of the military's finest chief warrant officers and he used his influence to keep the highly aggressive harassment he'd doled out to two sailors off the record. So he'd had his wake-up call. Get over it.

But nothing he tried seemed to keep his thoughts of her at bay. And his body, yearning for her touch, was driving him insane. Yet he wasn't ready to be "unfaithful," as ridiculous as that sounded. No matter how drunk he got he remembered how much she meant to him, how much he wanted her. He knew no other woman could take her place in his heart, and he wasn't about to surrender his body just for the mechanics of it.

In a desperate attempt to find a way to be close to her, if only peripherally, he gave in to an all-consuming curiosity to find out more about the woman he loved, so he tracked down Callie's mother.

He felt he had to find a way to stay connected to Callie, and as traitorous and foolish as it was, he felt he'd be closer to Callie if he could talk to someone about her who knew her. He remembered she'd told him her maiden name was Donalty and that her mom lived in Aberdeen, not far from the base. It hadn't taken long to find her, and late one afternoon he'd knocked on Mrs. Donalty's door. Irma was happy to have company, and over a bottle of Jack Daniel's they purged their memories . . . one following the other, as if trying to one-up the other on Callie trivia.

"Her daddy made her go to finishin' school ya know. Cost a pretty penny we didn't have. Nobody I ever knew went to a la-de-da charm school—but her daddy insisted she go. He wanted her to look like a lady, act like a lady—be all elegant and regal like a damned princess. He thought she was about as fine as spun sugar, and twice as sweet."

"She is, and I won't have you saying otherwise," Rand muttered as he toyed with the half empty shot glass, spinning it between his hands on the old scarred up pine table.

"Well it's damn funny then that after all the fancy teachin' that she ends up being unfaithful to her man and having two men puttin' it to her."

"Now I won't have you talkin' about her like that. I mean it."

"I just can't get over the irony, her Daddy's vestal virgin doin' two men at the same time. If'n he weren't already dead, this surely would kill him. Do ya'll watch each other gettin' it on?"

He stood and had to rein in his temper, his fists were like grenades, ready to explode. Then he saw her tears falling on the table. He moved to kneel beside her. Gripping both shoulders he made her look him in the eye.

"It's not like that. We both love her. Adore her."

She snorted, "Trust me, I know about men loving

her, adoring her, wanting to have her . . . as a wee baby she stole my husband's heart and from the moment she called him papa I was never able to get a single piece of it back."

"I got another bottle in the car. I think I'm about drunk enough to hear this."

She smiled sardonically and lifted her glass, "And I think I'm about drunk enough to tell it."

They heard a scraping noise around the corner when the ancient refrigerator stopped the loud humming when the compressor kicked off. They both turned to see Callie leaning on the doorjamb, her purse sliding to the floor by her feet.

"No Momma, let me. I can tell it so much better than you. I lived it, remember?" There was no mistaking the coldness in her eyes or the firm set of her chin. She was not happy that Rand was here. The steely look she gave him told him that she was going to give him the story he came to hear, and that she was going to make sure he heard every blistering detail.

She slung a chair around and plopped into it, seemingly heedless that her legs were splayed and that her skirt was high on her thighs.

Her mother spluttered at the sight.

"I don't always sit like a lady Momma, just because I know how to."

Rand covered her hand with his, "I'm sorry, I shouldn't have come here. And I never should have told your momma about the three of us."

She pulled her hand from under his, "No, you shouldn't have. But as you did, here's your sordid story . . . every disgusting, distasteful, filthy part of it." She took what was left of the drink in Rand's shot glass and downed it.

"My father worked at night, he was a bank auditor.

And for as long as I can remember, he would kiss me on the forehead at 6:30 when he left for work. Then when he came home just before dawn, he would lift the covers, pull up my nightshirt and kiss me . . . there. I didn't think you knew this momma. But I found out differently the night of my father's funeral." She gave her mother a hard stare.

"After everyone had left and we'd made some semblance of showing our respect, honoring him, and crying over his sudden death, you told me how you heard him come in the front door every night, make his way to my room and whisper things to me while I slept. What kind of things I asked you, remember? God you were hateful that day.

"You told me you saw him stroke me and tell me how pretty I was, how lovely my *genitalia* was, because he wouldn't say pussy, although I know that's the exact word he used years later when I was a teenager. If he saw I was awake when he came in, he smiled up at me and kissed me harder, and longer. Sometimes he put a finger inside me, but always he told me how lovely I was."

She looked over at Rand, her eyes defiant but he could see the hurt in her eyes. She took a cigarette from her mother's pack on the table. He'd never seen her smoke, but she tamped it, put to her lips and lit it like a pro. She took a deep drag and let it out, reminding him of Eva Gardner or Elizabeth Taylor in one of the old black and white movies. But it obviously didn't appeal to her no matter how good she looked doing it as she crushed it out in the ashtray after only one puff.

"I wasn't allowed to date for the longest time, and always before going out I was taken aside by him and told not to let my date touch me, especially there. No matter what the boy said, or how I felt. And then after I got home, and he got home, he would come to my room to see if I had done anything I shouldn't have. I never knew how he knew, except that I didn't do anything wrong, so I knew he could never say that I had. Maybe that had been his plan all along.

"When I went away to college, I'm not sure who the separation was harder on, him or me. Despite the nights that I dreaded, we always had fun together all the other times. We played video games, cooked, went to the movies, ball games, fishing . . . he even made doing laundry less tedious. I came to think of it as his due to be able to examine me every night. After all, I was his daughter; he had made me. And when he started referring to the area down there as '*his* pussy,' it kind of solidified those feelings. He did own me. He told me that pretty damned often.

"He always said that it was all right if other men wanted me, but that they could never have what he had. That I was his. That I belonged to him.

"He came to visit me at college once, without Mom. I was surprised to see him when I opened the door. When I said hi and asked why he was there, he said, 'You know why,' and he barged right in. 'Show me what's mine,' were his next words, and I panicked. I was no longer a virgin and I was sure he'd know it as soon as he looked at me. Plus, my boyfriend and I had taken a razor and neatened things up down there—quite drastically.

"So for the first time ever I argued with him and said I didn't want him to look at me there. He got furious, dragged me to the bed and ripped my panties off. As soon as he saw the narrow little triangle my boyfriend and I had left as my sole claim to pubes, he began spanking me, and calling me names. He spanked my pussy—hard, really hard, with his open hand, and I cried at him that I wasn't a slut, and that I hadn't let anyone violate me. When I lied and said I was still a virgin, he finally stopped. Then, when the area between my legs was on fire and as hot as it had ever felt, he spread my legs wide and kissed me. He kept kissing me. He was crying and kissing me at the same time. I don't know how it happened, but I came. And I cried some more. Then he spanked me again. God it hurt. I can still feel it sometimes, that raw, tingling feeling. It hurt so badly, and I was sore for days.

"I had to tell my boyfriend my period came early because I was so red and ugly and swollen. I didn't want him to see me; he would have had a lot of questions I didn't know how to answer. I knew this wasn't normal, at least not for everyone else, but it was normal for me. It's all I ever knew. It had always been this way—ever since I could remember, it had been this way.

"This was in September. The end of November I brought my boyfriend home for Thanksgiving and at the beginning of the meal when we toasted, we announced that we would be getting married in the spring. My dad stood up so fast that his chair tipped over, and I saw his face go red in anger, he looked at Todd, my boyfriend, and asked, 'Have you already fucked her?'

"When Todd didn't answer, he yelled at him, 'Answer me!'"

"'Uh, yes sir. I have sir,' he said.

"My dad spun on his heel and headed for the bedroom. My mom jumped up and followed him screaming, 'No! No! Don't! Don't!' I had no idea what was going on.

"Then I heard the shot. My mother had just gotten to the doorway when his brains flew through the air and splattered onto their bed. He had killed himself."

There was silence in the room for several

moments. Callie lifted her chin from her chest and stared at her mother, but clearly she was talking to Rand when she said, "And that's why she and I were never close. She knew he loved me more than her. That he desired me, and not her.

"After his funeral, it all just fell apart. Todd decided I wasn't the right one for him after all; Mom wouldn't stop drinking and blaming me for Daddy's death, telling me over and over again, that my being a bad girl and 'fucking the first man who came along,' had killed him. Hell, I hadn't even finished my first semester in college. I didn't know what I was going to do, but I couldn't go home. My mother had made it very clear that she did not want me.

"One of my teachers, Mr. Edwards, helped me get a student loan and I moved in with a group of girls who were renting a house. I managed to get a degree majoring in English with Library Sciences as my minor so I could become a librarian. And as soon as I graduated, I was hired at the local library in a junior position. It wasn't enough money to make ends meet and after the student loan money ran out, I started looking for ways to make some extra money.

"I had a boyfriend at the time who thought it would be a hoot if I entertained his friends at a bachelor party. He worked on me for weeks before finally wearing me down. I finally agreed to go topless for them as I desperately needed the money. He said that they'd each pay a hundred dollars to see my breasts. The scenario I would play out was one of a topless bartender and cocktail waitress. He even bought me a skimpy outfit, something between playboy bunny and saucy Lolita. Then he liquored me up to make sure I'd go through with it.

"We arrived at the party and he removed my

overcoat. Underneath I was topless. I remember I had a black velvet collar with a small heart charm dangling at my throat, a white skirt with frothy crinolines underneath, and a lacy white thong. A white garter belt with white fishnet stockings and black stiletto pumps completed the look. As I stood there in front of twenty-eight men, mostly college students, some with their dads, some profs, and one man who I think was a reverend, I remember them praising my breasts. Saying things like, 'Lovely,' 'Spectacular,' 'Great tits,' 'Jay, you lucky dog!' It went on and on. They were effusive with applause, especially two men who had been my teachers. I was red with shame while my boyfriend was multiplying $100 times twenty-eight.

"And he just lapped it all up as he came up behind me, grabbed my breasts from underneath, lifted them high and shoved them together as if offering them up. He thumbed my nipples, and I admit it did amazing things to me. Then he let go and humiliated me by making them jiggle lewdly. While everyone was oohing and aahing and being mesmerized by the size of my breasts, he pinched my nipples—hard. I remember it was harder than he had ever pinched them before. Then the talk was all about my long nipples and how much they'd pay to suck on them."

Rand put his hand out, gripping her arm to stop her. "You don't have to say anymore."

"Yes, I do. It's been years; I have to get this all out. You wanted to know, now you're just going to have to sit there and listen." She glared at her mother, who glared back at her. "And you, too, Momma. My shame is your shame." She took a long breath and continued.

"A long line formed and each man had his turn to touch me until everyone began clamoring for drinks, then I had to do the job I was hired for, and serve them. With each drink I gave out, a hand reached out to pinch, tug, squeeze or slap at one or both of my breasts. Every time I passed by my boyfriend, he stopped me and kissed me with long sloppy kisses and then pinched my nipples incredibly hard. It hurt. Others were pinching my nipples, too, but he was getting some heightened pleasure from my pain. I could see his eyes glazing when I gasped, winced or cried out. But he didn't stop, if anything he pinched even harder. For three hours my breasts were squeezed, caressed, fondled, thumped, pressed, licked, sucked, pulled, and slapped. I was alternately needy or repulsed. After the party really got going and everyone was getting very drunk, it was decided that it would be a really good idea to get my panties off, too. Jay was sent to take care of that—it was decided that, as my boyfriend, it would be his job to dispense with the rest of my clothing. They all chipped in and gave him five hundred dollars to get me totally naked. Of course, I didn't know this at the time or I'd have bolted straightaway.

"Acting all amorous, he took me into a bedroom, leaned me up against a wall, and began making out with me, covering my breasts with kisses, sliding his hands under my skirt and under the elastic of my thong so he could insert his fingers into me. I was hot and needy and soon I was ready for him to fuck me. But instead, he slowly and painstakingly undressed me. I was so hot and so horny I would have let him do anything to me at that point and he knew it. In minutes I was completely naked, propped against a wall, my clothes thrown all over the bed. Then he grabbed me by the hand and pulled me back to the living room, and with a bow and a flourish, announced, 'Gentlemen, my beautiful Callie, in all her naked glory. Isn't she lovely?'

"I was naked in front of forty men as the party

had grown considerably since it had begun. And as I was the only naked female in attendance, I was the center of attention. As I stood stunned, Jay began to caress me in front of them, pulling on my nipples and running his hands over my body. Then he walked me over to one of his teachers and said, 'Mr. Johnson, would you like to feel my girlfriend's cunt? I could sure use a better grade.' They all laughed as Mr. Johnson reached his hand down, grabbed my mound and squeezed it in his large hand. He slid his rough hand between my legs and his thick fingers played with my labial lips. I remember him saying in astonishment, 'God, is she ever wet, I never felt a cunt so wet! Callie, you were always one of my favorite students, so this is a wet dream come true.'

"One finger went inside me, then two, and then he began frigging me like a jackhammer. Jay laughed as the others gathered around to watch and to wait their turn. I was mortified and tried to get away but Jay held me in place. Then someone stood up saying they had an idea and a bucket was passed around and money was dropped into it. Everyone wrote their name on a twenty and soon the bucket was filled and a name was drawn. One of the geeky grad students who had been my lab partner during my sophomore year won the right to take me into the back bedroom and fuck me. He was told he had to leave the door open so they could all watch. I don't remember much about that part; it seemed rather short-lived. I don't think he had a girlfriend and of course he was quite excited to have won me. Jay made him wear a condom, and all the others were envious because he was quite large.

"After he was done, Mr. Edwards, the teacher who had helped me get a student loan and kept me in school, covered me with a sheet and led me out.

Before I left they took all the money from Jay and gave it to me. I had earned $3,490.

"On the way to the library, where I'd left my car, Mr. Edwards offered me $300 to suck his cock in the parking lot. I thought, 'in for a penny . . .'

"He gave me a $200 tip. I made almost $4,000 that night and began my career as a stripper for stag parties. I never saw Jay again. He finally stopped calling after a month or so.

"Then one night I saw Clint looking at me across the room and wanted it to be all over. By the end of the night, it was. Until you showed up he's had exclusive rights to my body."

Rand stood, put his hand out and pulled her to her feet. He pulled her into his side and she sagged against his body. "C'mon, I'll take you home."

She nodded, bent to retrieve her purse from the table, and looked over at her mother. "Momma, I'm sorry you lost your husband. But if you'd done your job and been the mother you should have been, maybe none of this would have happened. Maybe Daddy'd still be alive, maybe he'd have kept loving you instead of obsessing over me. I've finally come to terms with this. And so has Clint. I didn't do anything wrong! I was a good girl!" She broke down in sobs as Rand bent and lifted her into his arms. He carried her out of the kitchen toward the front door and was surprised when he saw Clint sitting in the dark in a chair close to where they'd been talking.

"What are you doing here?"

"I brought her here. We were looking for you. Again, the car is a damn giveaway, you might as well wear a target."

"What did you want me for?"

"Seems that girl you've got in your arms can't

live without you."

Rand's face lit up, "Really?"

Clint smiled and patted him on the back. "Yeah, really. Let's go home."

"As in our home, the three of us?" Rand asked.

"That's what she says she wants. I told her I could live with that if you could."

"I'd shake your hand but they're a little busy right now," Rand said as he shifted Callie higher in his arms.

Clint opened the door for Rand and Callie then followed behind them to the car.

"How'd you two get here?"

"Base taxi. Give me the keys, I'll drive. You and Callie have some making up to do."

"Yeah, I suppose we do," Rand said as he smiled down at the woman in his arms, "I suppose we do."

"And you seem to have had a fair amount of alcohol . . ."

"You know how it is Captain, when you're trying to get information out of a hostile witness, sometimes you have to loosen the tongue a bit."

As Rand settled into the back seat with Callie, he reflected on the talk he'd had with her mother. He was stunned that he had come so close to his initial assessment. He could not believe he had linked her sexual issues to her father, and that they had all started with diaper changing. Maybe she'd been too young to understand her father's words of praise, but she would have been able to tell by his cajoling tone, his big grin, and the twinkle in his eyes—that he was pleased with her.

Her innate sense would tell her the reason why when she saw where his eyes were focused, where he touched her, where he may even have even kissed her. As a baby, when she saw him focus on the area where her legs joined her body, she would remember how she had gotten into that position, how he had pushed her knees up almost to her chest, held them wide apart and tenderly wiped her, patted her dry—smoothed powder over her bottom and genitalia.

Logically, she would want to make him happy like that again. Eventually, to win his approval she would do this for him any time he wished her to. Daughters did that. He shook his head as he watched the woman he loved smile up at him and he hated the man who had dared to call himself her father.

During the initial weeks of bonding with his daughter, things had taken as bad a turn as possible, setting the tone for their relationship for years to come. It had determined her sex life in her later years; it was why she was still seeking approval from men in a similar manner, for she would have adored her father inasmuch as he worshipped her, while he touched her and toyed with her, while she unwittingly became his focus, his single-most driving obsession.

His arm wrapped around Callie's shoulder and he bent and kissed her on the temple. Ironically, she was now his obsession—his focus . . . his whole world.

And poor sweet Callie, she was still trying to please men in the only way she knew, the way her father had taught her, by displaying her body, objectifying herself, and allowing herself to be debased, shamed, and humiliated. Had she never seen the thread in her logic that should have lead her to the conclusion that hers was an emotional response caused by parental abuse? If she had ever thought it all out or even talked it over with someone, surely she would have realized that the last thing her sick father would have wanted was for her to share her body with a man other than himself. But that was exactly what he had driven her to.

Rand bit back a chuckle; he was better at this psychobabble than he thought. Now the nagging idea of becoming a family counselor after the war was over no longer overwhelmed him. It enticed him. The fact that he could grasp these early development concepts and see how they played out in later years was intriguing. Like a mystery unraveled, he had zoomed in, taken a snapshot of her life, and figured out Callie's exhibitionist issues. It had only taken diligence, caring and detective work.

He could see where her father's approval had meant everything to her, and her guilt afterward must have been horrendous, after all her father had killed himself because she had given herself to another man. Was she punishing herself with the humiliation and suffering the guilt by doing what she thought he would want?

Where did they go from here? This was the scary part. He could easily make things worse, for the obsession that was her father's had now become hers. When she became passionate, she moved into the grip of a fanatical need—an almost overwhelming craving to be told how desirable she was, to be assured by the man in her bed that he saw her as the most seductive creature he'd ever seen. And in truth, she was—at least to him. He imagined that for the men who had been privileged to see her naked and spread-eagled, that she was probably the closest thing to the airbrushed pictures in *Hustler* or *Maxim* they'd jerked off to as teenagers.

Clint pulled up to a stoplight and made a left turn, and while subconsciously, Rand knew he should question the change in direction; he was lost in his thoughts. His brow was furrowed as his fingers idly traced a pattern on Callie's shoulder. All this was well and good, he'd figured out the mystery of her psychosis. Now what? How did he make it so that she didn't crave every man on the planet telling her how lovely her cunt was? Could he keep her to himself—and to Clint of course. Could they fix her? Should they fix her? And how could they be sure they didn't break something else in the process? God, if he fixed this problem, but made her shy away from anal sex, he'd die! And Clint would probably kill him. He might still.

Clint had only given him a sketchy idea of Callie's problems, sugar-coated them really during one of their long sieges in the mountains of Afghanistan . . . had showed little concern about them at the time. Maybe that was because he was new to the marriage, or maybe it was because Clint *enjoyed* showing his wife off—hell, for all he knew, maybe he *liked* the idea of other men viewing her. Could he have downplayed her exhibitionism because he was the kind of man who got off watching another man having sex with his wife? A lot of men who were married to porn stars allowed the cameras to see it all. But he just couldn't picture Clint presenting his wife's vulva for all the world to see. Yet, Clint had hooked *him* up with his wife, knew she'd display herself for him.

So how was all this going to play out? He thought of all the porn movies he had watched and smiled inwardly. Callie's problems with exhibiting her body paled in comparison. He felt his penis jerk as the thought occurred to him that he would love to have some pictures of her. He looked over at her as she touched up her makeup, using her pinky to smear lip-gloss over those pouty full lips. His cocked jerked again, then he felt the telltale thud of his heart as all systems worked to redirect his blood flow for engagement.

For a few seconds he debated getting those

pictures before he "cured" her, but then he shook his head, he wasn't going to be the one to immortalize her slick, wet, welcoming little twat. Idly, he wondered if Clint already had.

"Why are you shaking your head? It's as if you're having an argument with yourself," Callie said.

He tugged her head to his shoulder and she rested it there. In the rearview mirror he could see Clint staring at him. He stared back. They had issues to discuss, parameters to define. What was this new relationship going to be? How would it affect their friendship? He could tell by the look in his friend's eyes that he had the same questions.

Then he redirected his thoughts and looked around. They had just turned onto a one-lane dirt road and were winding their way into a dense forest.

"Where are we going?"

"After watching Callie mope around and pine for your ugly old ass, we sat down and had a heart-to-heart about what we both wanted. Seems you were in the picture whether I wanted you to be or not—fortunately, I wanted you to be. The lifestyle we're talking about is one that would be frowned upon on base, so we went house hunting."

Chapter XIII

Clint pulled up in front of a sprawling rustic log cabin that was all decks and chimneys and as far from primitive as could be. He leaned his arm over the front seat and grinned.

"Welcome to our new home. Callie and I talked things over and if you're of a mind to try a plural marriage, so are we. I know you've had some threesomes in the past, but this is not going to work if you think of it as just a casual affair. This has to be a committed relationship—on everyone's part. And one of the things that had to change, if we wanted this to have the best chance, was to buy a house in the country where everyone doesn't know our business.

"I know you love Callie; I can see it in your eyes. And I know she loves you. She's told me so. Not that she could've kept it a secret, she's been miserable without you these two weeks. So what do you say? Are we husband, husband, and wife? Can we do this and not lose the friendship?"

Rand looked into the mirror and smiled at his friend. "As long as I don't have to kiss you to seal the vows, I'm in."

"Good. Now let's go fuck our wife."

"Was afraid you'd never ask," Rand said with a grin as he slid Callie across the seat and then scooped her off the vinyl and carried her up the path and over the threshold and into their new home.

Moments later they were in the huge master bedroom stripping their clothes off as if there was a race to be the first one naked. Callie and Clint had a head start as Rand had been in a business suit, so when he finally shucked his underwear and turned to face them, he was surprised to see Clint standing behind Callie, his hands cupping her full breasts from the bottom and holding them out as if offering them to him.

He groaned, not only from the sensual gesture, but also by what it meant. He didn't have to be asked twice. His tongue laved her nipple, pebbling it. He lightly grazed it with his teeth and then sucked it between his lips, tugging and pulling, hollowing his cheeks with the effort.

Callie moaned and gripped his head to her chest, begging and pleading him not to stop. Clint knelt at her feet and ran his tongue over the back of her thighs while his fingers dove between her legs and plunged into her. He rasped, "Good God she's wet," as he kissed along her inner thigh, sucking a particularly sweet patch of skin between his lips and humming his pleasure.

As if on cue, they both lifted her and gently placed her in the center of the bed. They positioned her for viewing and then walked around the bed, admiring her from all angles as they stroked their engorged cocks and suggestively cupped their heavy sacs. Her eyes were liquid with desire, the want in them tangible. They stalked the bed, fondling the hair on their chests, stroking their long hard cocks, pumping lewdly as they circled the bed, scenting her. They were the hunters, she was the prey—they had captured her and now they were ready for the feast.

Clint leaned over the bed and sucked her pussy into his mouth at the same time that Rand bent and drove his tongue into her mouth. They fused and mated and she sobbed as pleasure overtook her. She peaked when Rand kissed her ear and whispered, "He's sucking the prettiest pussy in the world." She keened and whimpered as her body convulsed and quivered.

"I got dibs on her ass," Rand stated.

"And I'm going to plow this lovely furrow and plant my seed, maybe even give her a baby," Clint breathed against her slick opening.

"What do I get?" she whispered, still in a stupor.

"Don't worry we won't forget about you. We're going to take this nice and slow. And then we're going to switch sides and start all over again; because I've never had that pretty little ass and it's about time I got to savor that sweet pleasure."

She moaned at Clint's words as Rand covered her nipple with his mouth. He sucked and teased it then bit the tip lightly. He lifted her and placed her on her hands and knees while Clint got the lube from the nightstand drawer. It was tossed to him and Rand caught it one-handed. He looked at it and read the label, "'Giant Economy Size,' I like the sound of that."

He squeezed out a generous amount and smeared it over the head of his penis then he spread her ass cheeks and massaged the remainder around the tiny opening that was puckering in anticipation.

She fell to her elbows and put her forehead on the bed offering her pretty little ass with a suggestive wiggle. "What are you waiting for?" she asked in a sultry voice.

Rand smacked her playfully on the ass. "Cheeky lady, let's just take our time with this. It's still pretty new to you. And believe me, I'm more than content to just stand here caressing these ultra fine globes until I can get myself squeezed in. Mmm, mmm. What a view." His fingers dipped lower to toy with her sleek moist folds. "Hmmm . . . maybe I should avail myself of this first?"

"I did an extra deep enema this morning, please don't waste the effort."

"What the lady wants . . ." Rand's fingers moved to her crack, pried her buttocks apart and poked at her small, puckering cinnamon bud.

"Well, turns out that's what the gentleman wants, too," he said with a heartfelt sigh. "Lovely, simply lovely. God I'm hard as a poker. Let's see how this goes, shall we?" He placed the crown of his penis at her tiny opening and began to push.

Clint knelt on the bed beside her facing Rand

and helped hold her cheeks apart and encouraged her to bear down as Rand pushed his cock head past the tight rim. "That's it baby, let him in. Take his dick in your ass. Damn, this is so fucking hot!"

It took several tries before he could inch his way inside her. His forehead was beaded with sweat as he was using all his control to keep from ramming his steely member up into her, driving home in a possessive need such as he'd never experienced before. *His wife.* God, could he really be so lucky? He was harder than he'd ever been as he carefully forged forward into her tight channel.

"Easy," Clint breathed, "you almost got it. Just a little more to go." Using his fingers he pulled her cheeks even further apart trying to stretch her to accommodate his friend's thick penis. He looked over at Callie who was looking over her shoulder.

"You okay?" he asked, the concern evident in his voice.

Her breathing was labored, her jaw clenched and her teeth clamped together as she hissed, "Yes, oh God, yes! Take me Rand, take me! Give it all to me!"

"Fuck yeah," Rand muttered and drove home.

She screamed from the pleasure-pain and Clint added a nuance to the mix by tugging on the nipple of one of her dangling tits, milking the hard nipple and pinching it tightly before treating the other one to the same pleasure.

He knew she loved the edges of pain, the erotic sensations that only came from jacking things up to the wild and ragged side of the unmentionable, unthinkable, and forbidden. Her eyes closed, her throat elongated and she arched her body. She was in the throes of one of the most powerful orgasms she'd ever had; yet still, she needed more. "More, for God's sake, don't stop.

God no, don't stop, give me more—I need more!"

"Clint, C'mon man, get on, let's do this."

Rand carefully pulled her back with him as he arranged himself into a half kneeling, half sitting position against the headboard. He pulled Callie back against his chest, keeping her high on his lap, her knees pulled wide as he invited Clint to, "Climb on man, we're ready to blow!"

Clint climbed up from the end of the bed and knelt between Callie's splayed legs. He positioned his cock at her opening and wedged it in. "Fuck, she's tight, God Rand I can feel your cock right up against mine. Is there even room for me?"

He shoved inside keeping his thrust almost vertical. He groaned his pleasure and felt goose bumps line his arms and legs. This was heaven. A physical bliss like he'd never known.

"Pretty awesome huh?" Rand said through a series of rough pants.

"Fucking yeah," Clint groaned. And then when Rand lifted her a little higher, allowing Clint more access to slide fully into to her slick channel, he grinned, "This is fucking wild!"

"Yeah," Rand grinned back. "Now pull back a little and feel this."

Clint pulled back and Rand's cock was sucked into the void, and so it began, one in, one out, never leaving her empty, filling her more than she had ever been filled before. All the while, Rand plucked on her nipples while Clint made circles with his thumb on her pearly clit. When she trembled and came, squeezing them both, in turn, it catapulted them all over the edge— Rand groaning and crying out while his cock throbbed and pumped his cum deep into Callie's ass, still trying to get more of him into her as he closed his eyes and rocketed to heaven. Clint, moaning in agony, but loving every second of his hot spurting release going deep inside her slippery channel like a heat seeking missile. Callie never feeling more complete in her life as the men she loved spilled their seed into her while she shuddered through one climax after another. Moments later, when Rand fell back, she fell against him, Clint followed. They were stacked like pancakes.

It took several minutes for them to collectively catch their breath. Then Callie whispered, "I love you."

"Who you talking to?" Rand asked.

"Both of you," she answered.

"I love you, too," Rand whispered.

"And who are you talking to?" Clint asked.

"Both of you," Rand replied, with a sheepish grin.

"I suppose it's my turn," Clint said, "and since I don't normally do this on a first date, this must be love."

They all laughed, joked about their ridiculous positions and passed around a few lingering caresses as they worked on untangling their bodies.

"I don't know about you, but I could use a drink," Rand said as he moved from the bed to the bathroom.

"Ditto," Clint said as he shoved his legs into his trousers. "We've a fully stocked bar and kitchen."

"I'm for food. How about I make some omelets?" Callie said.

"A woman after my own heart," Rand murmured as he came back from the bathroom with a towel wrapped around his torso.

"I hope I already have it."

He bent and kissed her neck as he cupped her breast. "You do. You definitely do. I love you Callie, have from that first day."

Clint came alongside and nuzzled the other side of her neck. "You've had my heart from the first day, too—from the moment I laid eyes on you."

"Wasn't I topless at the time?"

"I didn't say where I was looking."

He turned her so he could kiss her, "Callie," he breathed, "you are one amazing woman. Look at us," he motioned to the three of them, standing in various stages of undress in their bedroom. How many women would put up with this? A man bringing his best friend home and sharing her, in their bedroom?"

"Only every woman who has the chance—and the stamina."

"I want you two to have a ceremony. Even though it won't be legal, I want to watch you both say vows and pledge yourselves to each other," Clint said.

"I want that, too," Rand said as he cupped her ass. "I want to marry you Callie, and hear you say you're going to love, honor and obey until death do us part."

"And I want you to think about having a baby," Clint said. Then added, "Our baby."

He looked over at Rand who nodded his agreement. "We won't care whose it is, we'll both love it and provide for it. Callie, I hope that's what you want, too."

"I want . . . a nice long honeymoon, with lots and lots of sex."

"We'll take care of it," both men said simultaneously. Then they vigorously shook hands, sealing their bargain to love, honor, and cherish this woman who was their wife.

Chapter Fifteen

Garrett managed to toss his laptop to a safe place on the floor before he groaned from exhaustion. His back hurt, his neck was stiff and his right hand was in a perpetual working-the-mouse grip. He flipped over and plowed his head into one of the pillows on his king-sized bed. He was tired, for the moment sated sexually, and both happy and sad. It had been a perfect ending as far as he was concerned, there couldn't have been one better; but he was sad that the story had ended, the characters on their happily-ever-after lives while he was left alone in this big ol' bed. Humping the mattress. Okay, so maybe he wasn't as sated as he thought. That last scene, so vividly told, was still conjuring images in his mind. But really, he was beat. If he had any chance of zeroing in on the woman who was writing this stupendous fiction, he knew he had to get some rest. His body, his mind, and his penis needed some R & R. He glanced over at the alarm clock on the nightstand. 3 A.M.

Most nights he'd be checking the foreign markets after having slept four or five hours. But today, whatever was going on in Australia, Greece, or China, was the last thing on his mind. Was she blonde? Redheaded? Brunette? Was his mystery woman even close to his age or was she a seventy-year-old woman dabbling in a second career. The image of a sweet gray-haired lady, librarian by day, romance writer by night, swept through his mind.

Nah. Her writing was too fresh, too contemporary. Her style was more in line with the new chick-lit generation. Her ideas and her way of writing dialogue spoke of a woman in her twenties or thirties. He didn't know this, he just felt it. There seemed to be a bond pulling him to her, and at times he could feel it. And without anything to back up his wayward thoughts, he knew she was starved for sex. Or at least she wasn't getting her jollies off the way she wanted to.

This woman was earthly, sensual, free-spirited . . . and not afraid of anything that could go on between a man and a woman. In his mind he saw her as having dark hair, a cute spiky hairdo, legs encased in boots that went over the knee and smooth, long thighs, with eyes so green and clear they took your breath away. Damn he was hard again just trying to conjure her up. He groaned, rolled out of bed, and went in search of some Ambien. He *had* to get some sleep.

Chapter Sixteen

Laurel was having one of those days, the melancholy ones that brought her low and reminded her of all the things she didn't have anymore, instead of all the things she did have.

Facing the mirror, she was distressed that her hair wouldn't behave, and that her skin was lined where her pillow had creased it. To top it all off, she felt bloated—face, arms, legs, you name it—even her eyebrows looked puffy this morning.

And her normal breakfast of hazelnut coffee and a cup of blueberry Chobani, followed by an apple, wasn't sitting right on her stomach. The Gevalia coffee that she was so enamored of, felt as if was burning a hole in her gut. If she hadn't known better, she would have sworn she'd been on a bender last night instead of at home watching a Lifetime movie.

Showering helped the physical ailments but not her mood. Dressing in an uninspired tunic top, and not even bothering to match her shirt to her standby jeans, she grabbed the vacuum from the closet and rolled it onto the carpeted area for its weekly cleaning. Even having her iPod shuffling through her favorite songs couldn't dispel her gloom. And the vacuum—never cooperative—constantly ran over its cord, got stuck on thresholds, and smashed her big toe.

Her household chores, normally fulfilling and

satisfying to tick off her to-do list, were just dragging her down more. And of course, the sunshine streaming in through the tall Cathedral-type windows in the family room was inviting her out to play. Although Eric on Channel 6 predicted rain, it didn't look as if that was going to happen. Which meant watering the flowerpots this evening was added to her list of things to do today. After forcing herself to empty the dishwasher and put away the folded laundry, she said *screw it* and grabbed her car keys. The keys to the fun car—the car she'd had since college, the vintage Firebird Convertible that had seen her through the good times as well as the bad.

The gentle rumble of the V-8 engine, amplified as it bounced off the walls of the garage, did something to brighten her mood and lit a spark inside her. The fact that a warm sunny day waited beyond the open carriage-style doors helped too.

With no destination in mind, she was surprised that the screaming yellow Pontiac headed directly toward Sunset Beach. She hadn't been on the island for a week or better and agreed that maybe the fresh breezes over the ocean were exactly what she needed to sweep out the cobwebs and cleanse her head.

As always, the view from the top of the new bridge made her sigh. It was so lovely here, the view in either direction heartwarming and so picturesque you couldn't help but sigh with contentedness. *No bad moods allowed,* she intoned to herself as she goosed the pedal to crest the top of the bridge and then eased off to coast down to the curving bottom.

The causeway was perhaps her most favorite place in the world. A little over half a mile, it was like driving through a travel brochure of the south—pristine, meandering marsh grasses occasioned by the token heron, wood stork or crane—and all within spitting distance from her car. It was like being on a safari where all the wildlife surrounded her car, questioning her arrival on the scene. Only here, there was no tour guide, everything was free, and nothing, absolutely nothing was staged. All the pictures she saw in the galleries were here, live, in front of her. She began singing, "Nothing could be finer than to be in Carolina in the moooorrrning." And stopped with a scowl on her face when she heard the booming rap music coming from the gleaming black car behind her drowning her out.

She was tempted to flash her brakes to stop his tailgating, but instead resorted to a lighthearted revenge. She pushed the button that sprayed her windshield knowing full well that he was within range. He surely was, and his frantically waving hands indicated he was not happy. It cheered her to see him back off a little.

Parking on the beach, always chancy after 8:30, was never a problem for Ocean Ridge residents as they had their own Beach Club, a magnificent beach house right next to the pier. Grabbing her bottle of water, Laurel made her way to the beach access and walked west until she realized that the tiny flies that were sometimes a nuisance were out in spades today. And some were in a biting mood. Naturally. She took it as a sign that the day was not going to do a total about face and miraculously improve for her.

Walking back to her car, she smiled at the mother washing her baby in the outside shower. The outside shower door was unlatched and blowing open in the breeze. Both mother and child were naked and not at all self-conscious. The crooning and patter in German explained the lax attitude. But nothing explained the hideous tattoo covering most of the mother's chest when she turned to face her. Why would anyone who had decent breasts detract from them that way, she mused as she climbed back into the Firebird and left the island. Had that actually been a devil, complete with a forked-tongue serpent snaking between her breasts?

Looking down at her own chest, she snorted. As if anyone had taken the time to look at hers lately. God, how long had it been since a man had seen her breasts, touched them, kissed them? Her mind flew back through the days, months, hell years . . . and stopped at a time in her life that was four years gone now. She could see the scene as if it were yesterday—her hand cupping a man's head to her chest as he suckled, her fingers entwined in his dark brown hair. What was his name? Oh yeah, Jonathan. Jonathan of the dashing smile and dimpled chin, from Clyde's, where she and her friends had often hung out on Friday nights after work.

She'd been sitting at a Trivia machine, stumped by a question when he had leaned over her shoulder and whispered the answer in her ear. She had arranged to be there every night after that, and so had he. Two Friday nights later she had taken him home to see if he was as smart about a woman's body as he was about random trivia. Turned out he was adequate when he put his mind to it, which he stopped doing six Friday nights later when his wife knocked on her apartment door.

She shook her head and came back to the present just in time to see the most striking man running toward her up the steep incline. He was in the bicycle lane as she approached the summit. Gaaaawd, what she'd do to have that man's lips plastered around her nipple!

She had just enough time to take a second glance at the tall runner as she crested the top and began the downward coast to the curved slope that led off the bridge. Their eyes met for a fraction of a second and held. Instantly she knew that this man would be more than adequate, much more than adequate.

She regretted that she had to drag her eyes back to the road. He was all hunk, but not worth sideswiping her car over. No man was, she said resolutely. The devil and the snake were beginning to make sense. Temptation could easily make you drive off a bridge.

Chapter Seventeen

Typical of people used to the old bridge, she turned the wrong way coming off the lower ramp and ended up heading in the wrong direction. But because of it, she saw the sign the Town of Sunset had erected at the new park. Gosh, what a controversy that had been. But not having been a resident of Sunset Beach, she had been able to sit on the sidelines and read each letter to the editor in *The Brunswick Beacon* with a prejudiced view. In favor of the park, as many non-residents were, she thought it was a wonderful idea. People like her, who lived outside the town limits wouldn't have to pay for the enjoyment of it.

The park wasn't developed yet, but since the Town owned the land, it was now proudly proclaiming the area as belonging to its residents. She saw a dirt road to the left of the sign and debated driving back to see the space that was now slated for the new park and boat ramp. If she'd had a 4-wheel drive truck she might have ventured, but knowing how low-slung her Firebird was she chose instead to pull into the parking lot of the coffee shop on the corner. It, too, hadn't been there all that long. When she'd moved here, the ABC Store had owned that corner, now *Mavericks* was posted above the door.

Laurel decided it might be nice to get a latte and then saunter over to the park to enjoy it. She'd always enjoyed scouting out new businesses and cheering them on. A coffee shop during the season would have no problems—off-season, well that was a different story—the locals had to carry the banner for retail businesses, and well she knew it.

In the three years she'd lived here she'd seen many nice restaurants and shops fold for not being able to make it from one season to the next. Ten weeks is an awfully short time to make the income one would normally generate in a year.

She was greeted by a sweet young woman, who Laurel learned was one of the owners. Jen was her name and she was more than accommodating, as Laurel dictated her preferences: large, extra hot, skinny, sugar-free hazelnut, no whip—with a straw please. They chatted about where they both were from, and how they ended up here at Sunset Beach, as Jen went through the tedious production of making the latte.

Then Laurel strolled around the store sipping her latte and admiring the wines on display and promising to come back for a tasting. She was pleased to see the vintage Wurlitzer jukebox, and was fascinated with Zoltar, the fortune-telling machine in the corner. Jen plugged it in for her and she got a fortune printed on a bright yellow ticket.

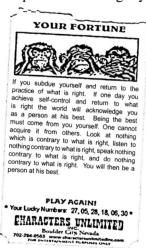

YOUR FORTUNE

If you subdue yourself and return to the practice of what is right. If one day you achieve self-control and return to what is right the world will acknowledge you as a person at his best. Being the best must come from you yourself. One cannot acquire it from others. Look at nothing which is contrary to what is right, listen to nothing contrary to what is right, speak nothing contrary to what is right, and do nothing contrary to what is right. You will then be a person at his best.

PLAY AGAIN!

* Your Lucky Numbers: 27, 05, 28, 18, 06, 30 *

CHARACTERS UNLIMITED
INC
Boulder City, Nevada
702-294-0563 www.charactersunlimitedinc.com
FOR ENTERTAINMENT PURPOSES ONLY

She would have loved being able to focus on, "Being the best must come from you yourself. One cannot acquire it from others." And that her lucky numbers were: "27,05,28,06, & 30." But instead her mind jumped around from one "right" to the next. "Look at nothing which is contrary to what is right, listen to nothing contrary to what is right, speak nothing contrary to what is right, and do nothing contrary to what is right." If it had said, "Write nothing contrary to what is right," it could not have fit her situation more perfectly.

Taking her latte with her, she crossed the parking lot and the street, then made her way to the park, stepping over a rope barrier. Despite the lovely day, the majestic live oaks, and the amazing views of the waterway, she slipped back into her melancholy mood. "Being the best?" What did that mean exactly?

Thoughts of her parents crowded her mind and as she walked along a seawall that held back the marsh. She lamented the fact that they could not see the beauty of this place, that they could not enjoy this glorious summer day. That they could not lean against this solid and imposing tree that had stood here for so many generations. Or marvel at the air plants known as Spanish moss that draped and cascaded from practically every limb like lacy netting. Laurel had been on a tour once where they talked about the gray fuzzy plants that were mistakenly thought to leach the life out of trees.

She'd learned that they actually absorbed water from the humidity in the air and sent life-giving nutrients in the form of dust particles with every breeze. And that the silvery scales on the feathery leaves were designed to capture water and minerals, and with enough rain, that they could actually cast a green shadow because of the plant's own chlorophyll. She was told that the moss, soft as horsehair, was as strong as cotton and was once used in the Deep South to make fishing nets. Looking up at it, she smiled as she recalled that the shabby drapery fed the tiny denizens of the forest and made a fine nesting material for squirrels and bats, and as a side benefit to her, was used as decorative bedding by florists. Walking around the tree she stroked a long silky vine and said aloud, "So contrary to popular belief, you don't kill the trees you grace with your draping tresses, you just make them look mysterious and romantic."

She'd seen pictures of her mom and dad when they were newlyweds, posing under trees as majestic as these, adorned with the tangled dark fibers that are a symbol of southern grace and tranquility.

Back to thoughts of romance, she leaned into the tree and closed her eyes as she envisioned an eager young man pressing into a soft and yielding woman as he caged her body against the very same tree, telling her that he wanted to make love to her mouth. Her sultry reply, given with a winsome smile, "So what's stopping you?" would have made his blood heat just before his head lowered and his lips crushed hers.

God, why was she always writing love scenes, creating sinful dialogue between a man and a woman? Why did it never stop, this constant playing out of lurid love scenes? Was she a pervert or what? Over three years she had written many wicked sex scenes, and experienced vicariously more sensual escapades than most women experienced in a lifetime.

And now she had lost them, every single one. They were out there . . . every romantic scene she had ever written. Her missing flash drive became the catalyst to her next thoughts, those of shame—her shame.

Zoltar was right, she had done what was contrary to right, and now she was ashamed because of it. Tears fell from her eyes as she stared unseeingly at the sailboats drifting under the new bridge. After a few minutes of the salty freefall she sniffed and realized that she had actually let a machine dictate her emotions. She laughed out loud at herself. Zoltar had made her ashamed of herself.

She came to with a start as it occurred to her that there was no one in the whole world that would be embarrassed or humiliated by her when this became known, that there was no one left who would be tainted by her immoral thoughts, her depraved writing.

She started to cry again. This time her tears were joined by a light drizzle followed within seconds by the sky opening up. Lightning flashed. Thunder boomed. The temperature dropped ten degrees. Perfect.

Laurel turned and looked across the street at her Firebird in Maverick's parking lot. The top was down. "Perfect" was the last word on her lips as she made a mad dash up the hill and across the street. *Fucking perfect.*

Chapter Eighteen

Garrett made it up the steps and in the door just as lightning flashed and the first boom shattered the silence. Clouds clustered above and the heavens darkened in a matter of minutes. The world below was shadowed in sepia tones broken only by the bright jagged lights that moved like giants stalking the edge of the ocean as he leaned back against the door and pulled off his sweat-soaked tank and running shorts.

Toeing off his running shoes he bent to tug off his damp socks. He'd made it just in time. The next boom vibrated the door against his back and he jumped away from it. He walked naked to the large picture window to watch Mother Nature's show. There was absolutely no chance there was anyone on the beach, not in this downpour.

He stood there, hands on trim hips, in his impressive glory, staring out as thunder crashed all around him. Lights flashed on the horizon in an uncanny sequence. Knowing the timing of the performance was mathematically predestined made it even more magnificent. He felt like a god. He didn't worry about being seen from the beach; anyone down there in this storm deserved what they got. But he had to admit, it was erotic as hell envisioning a certain writer turned voyeur as he raised his arms and stood before a grand orchestra and played at being maestro for this dark, impromptu summer symphony. He remembered the eyes of a stunning blonde staring at him over the hood of an old yellow Firebird. It didn't surprise him when he finally turned and made his way to the shower that he was as hard as a steel pike.

Damn that woman, where the hell was she! She consumed his thoughts. Even running he hadn't been able to wipe her sex scenes from his mind. And it wasn't just the sex he had realized about halfway through his run—it was the interaction of her characters. She made them real; she made them flawed, and human in every way when it came to their desires. He felt like he knew them—as if he could look Rand, Clint, and Callie up in the Fayetteville phone book and go knock on their door. They were people he wanted to know. He supposed that's why he wanted to know their creator so badly. If she was anything like Callie, she could wring him dry anytime.

He stepped out of the shower and toweled off, more determined than ever to find her. He had purposefully kept his hands away from that part of his anatomy, knowing from experience that if he kept that erotic edge, it would hone him into the hunter mode. Predator to prey . . . he was going to find this lady. And then he was going to fuck the living daylights out of her.

Still naked, he slid onto the seat at the table in front of his laptop and began opening her files in a random pattern, mostly bottom to top, right to left—figuring they'd be the latest saved. Choosing the smaller files, he found documents that were compiled notes, plot outlines, to-do lists, random thoughts, first chapters that apparently hadn't worked out, and recipes . . . tons of recipes. The lady had to be a freakish cook—there was everything from breakfast couscous to Delmarva crepes.

He read a few and after awhile he noticed that there was no meat in any of them. Some had seafood, mostly shrimp, lobster and crab. He scanned another group of recipes, but there was definitely no meat—no steak, no chicken, no bacon, sausage, or pork. *Ye gods, the woman of his dreams was a vegetarian!*

Chapter Nineteen

Soaking wet, Laurel climbed into her car and put the top up. Then she sat in the darkened interior sobbing so hard her shoulders bounced. So did her boobs, she noticed, when she looked down at the piece of Spanish moss she held in her lap.

Pull yourself together Laurel Ashleigh Leighton, they've been gone a long time, being alone is par for the course after all this time. Others have had it worse. A lot of people didn't even have parents they could stand nonetheless adored as you did yours.

She resolved right then that she would give this depressing mood fifteen more minutes then she'd be done with it. *Fini*. She'd shake off the doldrums and get things back to their proper perspective. Meanwhile . . . she needed groceries. And since she was already soaked, she might as well run into the Food Lion, grab some Chobani yogurt, some salad fixin's, and a bottle of Ménage à Trois to wash away her sorrows and ensure a decent night's sleep.

Maybe it was even time to make mother's Ultimate Mac and Cheese and let the comfort of warm pasta and cheese fill the hollows of her soul. Yeah, tonight was a night for excess. She put the car in reverse and pulled out to the right to make the U-turn to head back the opposite way.

At the grocery store, she grabbed what she needed and

as a tribute to her mother, she purposely displaced an item to ensure someone's job. She laughed as she remembered her mom doing this on every single shopping excursion they'd ever been on.

Anything picked up and then later deemed unnecessary was never taken back to the appropriate shelf; instead it was purposefully left, glaringly out of place for the "gleaners" to find and reshelf in the proper location.

Her mom had a cousin named Ellen who was once a "gleaner" at an A & P in a Baltimore suburb, and she had drilled it into everyone in her family that if people always put things they decided they didn't want back on the proper shelf, that she'd soon be out of a job. Ellen was learning disabled and the job was perfect for her. She loved returning items to the shelves and learning about new foods. Finding the right place for each thing was like solving a puzzle. And she was the only person who could direct someone to kumquats, yum yum sauce, or capers. She couldn't wait to get up each day and go to work to find misplaced cans of tuna among the charcoal bags.

Just to make sure Ellen never lost her job, Laurel's mom did her part whenever they shopped in Ellen's store, laughingly leaving Tampons in the cereal aisle, mustard next to the eggs, and an assortment of spices invariably ended up tucked here and there. She had wanted to do her part to help Ellen keep her job.

Laurel laughed out loud at the memory as she grabbed two of the biggest boxes of ribbed macaroni she could find. She left one next to the popcorn in the snack aisle. It made her feel good to celebrate the tiny little traditions her mother had shared with her. Stupid though they were.

Pulling out of the parking lot, she had to wait for a pretty blue Corvette to drive past. She couldn't help but notice the man behind the wheel as his window was down and his hand was tapping out a rhythm on the outside of his door. At first, she was only able to see his profile but she sensed immediately that there was something familiar about him. Then he turned and their eyes met for a fraction of a second and she knew that if she'd ever met him she wouldn't have any trouble placing him. She knew without a doubt that she'd remember every single detail of their meeting; he would have his own memory card imbedded in her frontal lobe, much like her digital camera card held her photo files. She would have taken notice of everything about him, and she would not have to go hunting for the memory—it would scream at her. He was her bridge guy. Oh well . . . he was probably taken, she thought. All the remarkable ones were.

She swung her car into the intersection and followed the sleek sexy car until it turned onto Georgetown Road. Watching the car in her rear view mirror as she continued through the intersection, she saw it speed up and head toward Calabash.

Damn! She thought with a chuckle. If she'd only thought to rear end him, she might have been able to fill that memory card with enough sensory material to write another story.

That thought led her back to the saga of her missing flash drive. Ugh! Would the dread of that be with her forever?

Forcing her mind back to her mom's Ultimate Mac and Cheese, she mentally went through the ingredients to make sure she hadn't missed getting something that she'd need. This batch would have to be identical to her Mom's in order to squelch this funk.

Chapter Twenty

Garrett got back from having an early dinner at Beck's, and after finishing up the work he had to do, clicked on the icon that had his mystery woman's files. He sat as if in a trance and stared at all the files listed.

Clues. He needed a really good clue if he was going to find her. He pulled the flash drive out of his pocket and rubbed it as if trying to divine something by holding it in his hand. It had unknowingly become his talisman, and he often found himself rubbing it between his fingers. After all, it was his only link to the woman he had a desperate and heady desire to meet.

If he could just go through the files, concentrating on the ones that weren't stories, the ones that gave a glimmer of her day-to-day life instead of the ones that let him into her psyche by way of her bedroom, maybe he'd find something.

Determined to find the clue he needed, he opened one file after another, scanning her copious recipes, checking out her music files, reading articles that appeared to have been written for women's magazines. Most of the articles were short, only one or two pages, related to gardening, eating healthy, game playing, antique shopping, or using the web to help with specialized collections. They had titles like: *The Art of Scrabble Playing, The Benefits of Wii Exercising for the Busy Woman, Find that Elusive Boyd's Bear, Improving your mind with Kakuro*—whatever the hell that was—and a humorous piece that had him laughing out loud about jigsaw puzzles and ghosts who visited to steal pieces.

He had to admit she was a good non-fiction writer as well as a superb novelist. She wrote with clarity of purpose. Choosing words carefully, so she could be concise, but giving the true flavor of the moment and putting the reader in the story.

But damned if she left much to go on to track her down. He'd been at this for days now and was no closer to his goal.

Nibbling on a ham and cheese sandwich with one hand while maneuvering the scroll button on the mouse with other, he suddenly sat bolt upright. Leaning forward as if his eyes were peering inside the screen, he blinked twice and sat back with a triumphant, "Aha!"

Tucked into an article on coastal gardening, was a personal reference to her backyard, more specifically her back deck.

"I have a flower box herb garden, several in fact, that are attached to the rails on the back of my deck. It's just a few wooden boxes that I painted a light sage green to match the trim on my house. And every year, I let the chives go to flower because the tiny balls of white petals are so pretty against the pastel green of the boxes. It's a waste of time to try to harvest chives because you can always buy the giant economy-sized container of freeze-dried chives at Costo for four bucks and they actually taste like something—I have never tasted a fresh chive that tasted like anything other than grass. So don't let anyone guilt you out for not cutting them back. Chive flowers are one of the best deals going, they come back year after year.

The golfers looking for their out-of-bounds golf balls often comment on the wonderful fragrances wafting over to them from my herb boxes. It's often because they've actually brushed up against the rosemary bushes that mark my property line, but sometimes, it's the peppermint or the lemon balm. For added color during the summer I add lavender because it goes so well with the paper white chive flowers and the green boxes, and of course, I sprinkle some marigolds seeds around to help keep the bugs at bay."

The article continued, explaining how to select the proper wood to make the boxes; how to use color, texture, height and form to enhance the impact; pointers to choose bushy, upright and trailing vines for variety, adding to the haphazard appeal of having the thrown together look; installing a lining; drilling drainage holes or using screening, and advising a balanced plant mix with equal parts compost, topsoil, sand, and vermiculite, followed by a layer of sphagnum moss. Feeding and watering were detailed as well as mulching and deadheading, but Garrett was focused solely on the part about the green boxes, the green house trim, and the rosemary border bushes. And the fact that her house was on a golf course, so close to the course that golfers had to traipse through her yard to get their balls. He scratched his own balls. *Soon. He'd have her in his sights.*

With that snippet of information he felt certain he could find her house. All he needed to do was play a little golf, and pay a lot of attention to the backsides of the houses along the course. He hadn't played for a while, but he had his Pings downstairs in the storage area, and a pair of binoculars on his bookshelf.

Which course should he start with? The word lavender drew his attention and made him think British, which made his mind go to The Thistle Golf Course. Off of Georgetown Road, it was one of the premier golf course developments in the area. And if he wasn't mistaken, last time he'd played it, there had been about ten houses scattered around 27 holes. Which meant he might have to play 18 first, then ask for a replay for the other nine. Unless he was lucky and spotted those window boxes right away. Adrenaline pumped through him and he had to stand and pace as he thought all this through. Yes, this could work.

After Googling to get the phone number of the pro shop, he picked up his cell and was connected to Ed who arranged a tee time for the next morning. After giving him his credit card information, he hung up and rummaged through the kitchen junk drawer for the key to the storage unit under the beach house. Within minutes he was lugging his big club bag upstairs so he could polish up his clubs and wipe off the custom-made bag. Discovering his shoes were a bit grungy looking and that he only had four good balls, he grabbed his keys and headed out to Martin's to get some new golf gear. On the way, he decided a new visor, glove, and a few new shirts and sweaters were in order. He was excited in a way he hadn't been in months.

Not for the game, as he could take it or leave it on his best days, but because he was going to find *her*. He just knew it. Her files had given him the clue he needed, he just had to be diligent and check each course until he found the house with the flower box herb gardens in the pastel shade of light sage green.

It occurred to him that he should stop at a paint store, just to make sure he had the right idea of the color. And he'd stop by a nursery, check out the chives, sniff some lavender and peppermint—see what rosemary bushes looked like.

Now that he had something to go on, he decided

to reward himself. Tonight, after he got everything ready for his golf outing in the morning, he'd allow himself the supreme pleasure of reading another one of her erotic stories. The titles of quite a few had appealed to him, but there was one file he'd been particularly anxious to open since reading the title, *The Rake and the Young Innocent*. Not that he was all that hepped up on virgins, but this one had shown great promise when he'd briefly scanned the first chapter a few days ago. The storyline had been playing out in his mind ever since. It was a historical romance, which would be a major departure for him as he usually only read contemporary thrillers.

He could not wait to get his chores done so he could grab a glass of wine and settle into bed with his laptop. With any luck, maybe soon he'd be able to settle into bed with a soft, sexy, spirited young writer. Coming off the entrance ramp of Route 9, he shoved the shifter into 6th gear and sped south on 31, enjoying the smooth throaty sound of the 'Vette as the car purred with unleashed power. Looking at the empty seat beside him he gauged the floorboard area, wondering if he had enough room to get his golf bag in. Hell . . . he'd better consider getting a smaller carry bag, 'cause he certainly wasn't getting rid of this car.

Chapter Twenty-one

After having had a double helping of Mac and Cheese, Laurel was surprised that just an hour later she had the *knoshies,* so she fixed a plate of Trader Joe's Bite-sized Everything Crackers with some thinly sliced Dubliner cheese and took it to the room that doubled as her den and office. She had determined that tonight was the night she was going to get back to the business of writing. She was going to forget that damned flash drive and get back "in the saddle."

Several of her stories needed endings and she was beginning to get a niggling feeling that if she waited much longer to face her computer she'd get the dreaded block so many authors feared. Personally, she'd never had it. Words seemed to flow from her fingers to the keys when she was disciplined enough to let them.

Forty minutes later, she shook her head as a reprimand; she now knew the distraction that came from being a writer afraid to face the blank screen. So far she'd opened a package of post-its—each pad in a twenty-four pack was now unwrapped; clicked back and forth from her email to her iTunes account; re-arranged the icons on her desktop, and taken the empty plate all the way to the kitchen on the other side of the house just to leave it in the sink.

She walked over to the built-in bar and removed a bottle of wine from the custom wine rack and decided a nice deep robust cabernet was exactly what she needed. Rabbit in hand, she uncorked the bottle effortlessly and filled a Reidel stemless wine glass half way. Then she walked slowly back to the desk.

Three glasses later, she admitted she had a problem. Not a block she hoped, but definitely she was troubled. She plopped into the leather sleeper chair that she'd fell in love with at G & M Interiors and pulled her booted feet to rest on the matching ottoman. She'd never felt leather so supple and warm. Buttery soft like the finest kid glove, she'd bought the floor model, afraid if she ordered one that it wouldn't feel the same. Burnt sienna wasn't one of her favorite colors, but the chair with the gooseneck lamp behind it, had quickly become the focal point of her study and her first choice for a place to read and edit. Now she pulled the cashmere throw over her legs and melted into the chair.

What the hell did she need to do to move on? She thought about calling Tessa . . . or Viv . . . Cat she knew was out of town. A big smile widened as it occurred to her exactly what she needed to do to get closure on that damned flash drive. She sat bolt upright and let out a gusty sigh. In her excitement she sloshed wine over the rim of the glass and had to lick the side of the glass to keep it from running down her arm. Dripping onto the light Berber carpet was not an option so she hurriedly finished what was left in the glass and put it on the marble-topped side table.

She remembered that Cat, Tess, and Viv had each had a matchmaking-type ceremony, something witchy and crazy involving a big ol' tree on the Maples Course in Sea Trail. Within days they'd each met their future mates. All of them attributed their newfound love to the ritual they had performed as they had chanted to some deity that was supposed to be living in the tree. The name Merlin seemed to float in her memory.

Would something like that work for her, could she get

closure on this dumb flash drive by having a stupid symbolic ceremony? She wasn't superstitious and she certainly didn't believe in magic, but she prided herself on being open-minded. She needed to forget the flash drive and get on with her life. There was nothing more certain than that right now. Nothing. Well, if the ceremony worked for them, maybe it would work for her?

She thought about it as she reached for her wineglass, just to find it empty. Thought some more as she climbed out of the chair, tripped over the throw, and half walked, half crawled over to the bottle on the counter by the desk to refill it. She came to the conclusion, when she only found a few drops left, that she had to try something. Had to make an effort—if only symbolic, so she could move on for Criminy's sake!

She stumbled over to the computer and Googled "Pagan ceremonies." After the first screen loaded, she watched, her eyes agog, as video after video showed a man and a woman marrying in the buff before a fully clothed, solemn celebrant. Panning out, she saw the wedding couples standing before completely dressed crowds of witnesses, as if this was the most normal thing they'd done in their lives.

It was the oddest thing, and it reminded her of her short story, *The Rake and the Young Innocent*. She smiled dreamily as she remembered the hero and heroine in that story and all the things Julia had been indoctrinated to before . . . before . . . Lauren fell asleep sitting on the floor, her head resting on the ottoman.

When the Westminster chimes on the mantel dinged the last of twelve tones she lifted her fuzzy head. Her calves were cramped from sitting on one hip with her legs curled beneath her. Stretching, and listening to her joints pop, she blinked as she realized she was horny, unbelievably horny. Her nipples tingled as thoughts of her dream came back to her and she knew she was wet under her jeans. *I wonder if*

I'm ever going to find the man who's right for me? A man who's dreamy and strong, handsome and gruff, yet sensual— with an insanely wicked tendency toward kink to match my own?

Chapter Twenty-two

Idly shuffling one of her Tangram puzzle pieces around, Laurel sighed. She'd been up most of the night nursing her headache and trying to come up with a way to purge the emotions that were destroying her thoughts, keeping her from not only her writing, but her gardening, and golf . . . even shopping had no appeal. She glanced at the clock on the mantel as she sat on the floor playing with her beloved puzzles. The same ones she and her dad had played with on this exact same coffee table so many years ago. Tangrams were one of her passions now; they were a way of remembering a simpler time, when life wasn't so uncertain or disappointing.

Thought to be a game women played with their children in ancient China, and handed down by the river traders, Tangrams ended up in the western hemisphere when sailors traded opium in the brothels. "The Chinese Puzzle" found its way to Europe and then to America in the 19th century, and amused all who shuffled the colorful *tans*. Soon there were books and picture card sets, puzzles made of wood or fired clay, then later more elaborate examples were carved from jade, some inlaid with ivory, some dressed with gold. It became addictive to some—especially those with a mathematical bent. The 1,942 proven convex designs were often inspirations for quilts, appliqué projects, and imaginative storytelling. Laurel's father, a wiz at geometry and ratios, taught complex math principles to his young daughter as she played with the silhouettes and unwittingly learned about Sam Loyd and his colossal spoof with the publication of *The Eighth Book of Tan*, and the complex idea of paradoxes. The wonderful hours she spent playing with the firm, smooth pieces and listening to his low, melodic murmurs were what she knew of fatherhood, and at times she couldn't breathe for the grief that moved through her. But still she kept every puzzle they had collected, polishing the pieces and adding to the sets of seven until she had to have a case built to house them.

It was just before nine. She wondered if it was too early to call her friends. Tentatively she picked up the phone, stared at it, and with each name that came to her mind she wondered if she'd be making a husband angry by calling at what easily could be warming the sheets time for either Matt, Roman, or Philip.

She put the phone down. She picked it up. Then jumped out of her skin and tossed it into the air when it rang. For the few seconds it took her to realize what had happened, it continued to shrill from the carpet on the other side of the table. Finally, she crawled around to it and hit the talk button as she put the phone to her ear.

"Hello?"

"Hey there, Cat just got back in town and Viv and I wondered if you'd like to meet us at the Bagel Dock for a late breakfast or early lunch."

"You are a lifesaver, I really need to talk to you guys."

"Okay. How soon can you be ready?"

"Give me ten minutes and I'll be on my way."

"Great! The girls will be thrilled you can make it."

"I'm the one who's thrilled, I really need your help."

"Do tell. Everything alright?"

"It will be. I feel sure you're going to be able to help me out."

"Well, we'll certainly try."

Twenty minutes later, she was pulling into the Bagel Dock, eager to chat with her friends, share her dilemma and solicit their help. As they carried their food to a table by the window, Laurel confessed she'd about lost it last night, describing her stilted attempt to write and her cabernet-based hangover, she bemoaned her missing flash drive and described the angst that not knowing its whereabouts was causing her, ending with, "So I thought I could have a . . . well . . . you know, a Ya-Ya type ceremony to banish it from my thoughts, but I just don't have any idea how to go about it."

"Well that's easy," Cat said as she waved a chunk of her sesame flat bagel in the air. The melted butter was about to drip down her hand but she popped it into her mouth just in time.

"Yeah," Tessa said as she slathered her own bagel with a thick layer of cream cheese. "We can't have our favorite writer sidelined. It's ridiculously easy. We're practically experts." Then, as if remembering she really knew nothing about witchcraft, she looked over at Cat with an arched brow. "How easy?"

Cat had a tendency to get them into trouble, and Viv always went along for the ride, but Tessa was learning to look before leaping. Roman encouraged her friendships with her zany friends, but she'd about had enough of his chiding her over bailing her out from their misadventures.

"Like lighting-a-match easy. Come on baby, light my fire," Cat crooned.

"Really?" Laurel said, her eyes twinkling with excitement. Finally she could get back to her life and forget that stupid lost flash drive. She'd do whatever it took. Well . . . within reason.

"Really. All you have to do is write down all the

reasons you need to get this out of your system—all the things that are scaring you and causing you so much stress. Just write them down. Then we'll burn them and bury them by our tree."

"Seriously, that's all it's going to take?"

Viv piped up for the first time. "Well it's going to be harder than you think. You have to be truthful, confront each issue, dissect every feeling you're having about it and get it all down on paper. If you forget one single facet, it may not work. You'll still have something left over to deal with if you forget anything. You're going to have to be very thorough." The voice of experience, Laurel turned to see Viv nodding her head with mock seriousness. Everyone knew Viv's mother, who fancied herself to be a witch, and Viv, while sure she herself had not been gifted, had grown up in a world full of caldrons and potions. But she was far from a believer. As far as Viv was concerned, Philip was the only thing magic had brought into her life.

But Laurel was already pulling out a notepad from her purse. Her earnestness brightly illuminating her face, she blurted, "I won't forget a thing. How do I start?"

They all laughed.

Chapter Twenty-three

Clubs polished and ready, collared Columbia shirt ironed and pleated Dockers in lieu of jeans, Garrett waited at the Thistle bag drop for his cart to be brought around. It was 7:30 and one of the few bustling places in Brunswick County on this early Thursday morning. He'd been partnered with an older man from Charlotte who'd seemed less than pleased to be riding with a "youngster" as he'd dubbed him. At thirty-two, Garrett didn't think of himself as being young, but I guess when you were seventy-some, age was relative, he mused.

By the second hole Garrett had dazzled the old geezer with his knowledge of stocks, complex banking issues within the man's own city, and expounded with authority on biotech stocks, showing his expertise in the world of finance. Having been a medical administrator for one of the larger medical centers in Charlotte, the man had been pleasantly impressed. So he'd won the old coot over and kept him chatting long enough to scope out the homes along the cart path. He paid particular attention to the homes with O.B. markers, as his mystery woman had said that:

"The golfers looking for their out-of-bound golf balls often comment on the wonderful fragrances wafting over to them from my herb boxes. It's

often because they've actually brushed up against the rosemary bushes that mark my property line, but sometimes, it's the peppermint or the lemon balm. For added color during the summer I add lavender because it goes so well with the paper white chive flowers and the green boxes, and of course, I sprinkle some marigolds seeds around to help keep the bugs at bay."

But by hole fourteen he was disheartened, both by his game and by the absence of window boxes, rosemary bushes, and any flower remotely resembling lavender. He would have called the game if his real purpose hadn't been so clearly defined. Despite the fact that he was twelve over par, he was still beating ol' Henry from Charlotte. He stood to make a nice tidy profit of $9 from their wagers, despite treating him to hot dogs for lunch. Still, it bothered him immensely that he hadn't found "his woman's" abode.

Finishing up, he shook Henry's hand, pocketed eight damp dollar bills and watched as two cart guys loaded his bag into the front seat of his car. Instead of getting in the car, he went up to the bag drop area where the guys were hanging around, ostensibly to tip the bag boy who'd helped him stock the cooler with water and ice, but instead, sidled up to one of the rangers and asked about the houses on the course. *Window boxes? Nah. Rosemary bushes? Hmmm, nope, don't think so. Lavender? Is that like heather?*

He gave all four men at the bag drop a sizeable tip and thanked them for their help, then strode to his 'vette and folded himself in. He was a tall man and he had to bend his knees at an angle before he could stretch them out toward the pedals. Normally that wasn't a problem, but today, after standing on the sides of hills to take his shots, his muscles were protesting.

A soak in his hot tub was on the agenda after he reviewed the stock market. Then he'd arrange a tee time at the next course on his list. After that he'd be free to take a nap and dream of the woman who eluded him so completely. If time provided, there were more stories to read . . . more chances to delve into the love lives *she* created. He felt as if he'd unwittingly come across a Black Widow Spider spinning its web, and now she was luring him in.

Chapter Twenty-four

The next day the four women texted back and forth, questioning what Laurel had added to her list and offering their thoughts—refining the list so that when the deed was done, all her negative feelings would be too.

Cat sent a text suggesting they meet one last time at Tiger's Eye Restaurant to go over the plan. They met on the back deck, enjoying the view of the tenth tee box and the eighteenth green. From that meeting Laurel was able to add her final and true concerns to the list: that maybe her flash drive had been found, and that while possibly in discrete and careful hands, that she'd never know whose. That for all the years she had yet to live, she'd have to wonder if the person in line at the grocery store or at the post office or sitting across from her at a restaurant knew more about her than she cared for them to. That while acting prim and proper, they might secretly be reveling in all they knew about her wicked thoughts while she was totally unaware.

She pictured herself as having a soiled soul . . . running and trying to hide it from everyone in the universe like a bad girl covering a stain on her dress . . . running and turning away from leering eyes and condescending faces. In a particularly vivid nightmare she was Alice going down the hole with people watching and pointing as she zigzagged back and forth down the tunnel—only for her there would be no rabbit or mad hatter at the bottom of the chute, just scornful people wagging a familiar looking flash drive in her face.

Cat was the one who brought everything full circle for her. "So why do you care? What difference does make if everyone knows you write erotica? Why not just step up to the plate and be proud of it instead of hiding from the knowledge that one elusive person knows and might tell all. Let everyone know and be done with it."

"Yeah. Instead of fearing the worst, just let it happen," Tessa murmured her assent.

"You mean go public? Publish?" Laurel said her eyes wide at the thought.

"Yeah," they all said at once. Every one of them smiled, their eyes bright with glee. The idea sank in and took hold and clearly it pleased them very much, as they were all grinning broadly. "Yeah," they chorused again with more enthusiasm.

Viv nodded, her short curls bouncing softly against her cheek, "Yeah, that way you kill two birds with one stone. You erase the fear of being outed, and also the one about someone beating you to the punch and publishing your stuff as theirs."

They sat and stared at her as all their thoughts jumbled, aligned, and jelled in her head. Then Laurel huffed out a breath of air and smiled, "Yes, I suppose I could do that. I could get the stories together, work on the ones that aren't finished, and put together an anthology. I could be anonymous."

"You'd use a pseudonym?" asked Tess.

"Of course. I might be willing to consider publishing, but I am *not* considering publishing as *me*. I don't think Ocean Ridge is ready for that yet."

"You'd be surprised, your neighbors aren't all angels you know. *None* of us older women are. We've lived through too much. If there's an innocent among us she's either faking it or has old-timers and has forgotten the heady days. No, judging from the women I've seen hootin' and hollerin' at all the parties, we're certainly not angels."

"I know you three aren't," Laurel said with a laugh.

"Now how would you know that?" Cat asked, flipping her hair as if affronted.

"For God's sake, look at your husbands, they all look like *fallen* angels. Hell, if I call Tess and Roman answers the phone, I leave a puddle on the floor just hearing his voice. *Laurel Darlin', and just how is my bonny lass today?* And Philip, if he even touches my elbow, images of all the women he's been with before flash in my head like scenes out of one of his porn movies. And oh God, Matt, those eyes—he eats you up with them, devours you with one singeing glance. So I know you guys aren't angels because I know Matt and Philip and Roman—three of the lustiest men living—were running like wild mustangs until you three figured out how to corral them. So, add me into the mix and there are certainly no angels here. Nuh uh. Not at this table."

"Angel or not, I still think you should use your real name. You're not Lucifer," said Viv.

"No, I'm Venus, baring her soul," Laurel said with a jaunty wave of her hand.

"I haven't read your stuff, so would you say you're on par with say, Jackie Collins?" asked Cat.

Laurel gestured with her palm up, as if keeping a balloon in the air, indicating something on a higher scale. "Worse, keep going."

"Anais Nin, Bram Stoker, Casanova. Lady Chatterly . . .?" offered Tess. Laurel gestured for her to go higher still.

"*The Story of O? Nunnery Tales, The Pearl?*"

"Now you're getting somewhere," Laurel said, "And all written by Anonymous, mind you."

"Hmmm," from Viv. Then she added, "Those were

different times. *The Story of O* was 1930s or 40s wasn't it?"

"Outed in 1954 actually. In France. No one knows for sure when it was written. He or she used a name of no one living at the time. Mine are more contemporary, and more over the top."

"Well then I definitely think you need to publish," Cat nodded emphatically, eyes bright, and they all laughed at the caricature she made as her long ponytail swished and her sunglasses bobbled on her head.

"So, your material—where do you get it? Do you do like . . . research?" asked Viv.

"I read a lot. And I have a very vivid imagination for fantasy. And yes, I know you're dying to ask . . . I do have a copy of Philip's last masterpiece, *Elizabeth's Initiation.*"

Viv went scarlet to her roots and washed down the flush with a big swig of her tea. "I'll never get over that sensation . . . knowing that my best friends have seen my husband naked and fucking everything in sight."

"I don't think of him as your husband when I watch it, he's Drago, defiler of innocents, and God was he prime." Laurel fanned her hand in front of her face.

Before Viv married Philip, they'd all gotten together to watch some of his videos. Philip had insisted on it, knowing that if there was going to be a stumbling block to their marriage, that this would be it. His videos, although thirty years old now, were still out there as collector's items and available through many Internet sources, so he knew it was only a matter of time before Viv would to have deal with issues of his previous life as a once celebrated porn star.

Viv had gotten drunk that night, in fact they all had while they watched the man Viv loved, taking one woman after another in several of the movies Philip had provided. The odd thing was that while they had developed an appreciation for his *talents,* they had also seen the masterful yet caring side of him—he loved women and it showed. Surprisingly, they had enjoyed the involved plot lines and appreciated the upscale directing, scenery, and quality of acting. Philip had directed as well as starred in the movies and they had all seen the superb job he'd done bringing upscale porn to the marketplace, while making millions. So while they'd sat sipping wine and mindlessly chomping down popcorn and Chex-Mix, they had gotten quite tipsy and incredibly turned on.

When their men came to fetch them after having indulged in their own enlightening movie fest, showing Philip's heretofore prowess and attributes, they scooped up their wives and took them home to delve into the images still superimposed on their minds, and to explore nuances of technique that had peaked their interest. Clearly, they all benefited from Philip's interesting perspectives and expertise, and with time, they were all able to talk with him and joke with him without everyone going six shades of red. Philip had been right, get it out in the open, so to speak, and confront the elephant in the room, or in this case, the anaconda.

They were all amazingly good friends now, and maybe it was because they didn't harbor any secrets. Everyone had a past. Not all were proud. But it was what it was. Philip had been a struggling attorney, had seen the opportunity in doing upscale and hygienically safe movies, amassed a fortune and, as a result, became very wealthy in banking. Sadly, he had destroyed his young wife in the process, but he'd come to terms with that, and had finally overcome his grief and his guilt. He now loved Viv to distraction. The three couples, and now Laurel, were very close. No one ever thought of Philip naked and ready for action when he came into a room in a custom Brioni suit. Well . . . hardly ever.

"So, back to the research you do and the writing . . . do you get all . . . hot and bothered when you're writing?" asked Cat.

"Yeah, do you get horny . . . and have to, you know . . . do the deed by yourself?" asked Viv.

Laurel laughed, "I will admit, sometimes the re-writing and editing process have me wishing I had a man hanging around the house." She leaned her elbow on the table and stuck her chin on her fist. A wistful look came into her eyes as she stared off into the distance, looking at the eighteenth hole and beyond, but seeing nothing of the gorgeous landscape. "It sure would be nice to have someone help me choreograph some of the more energetic sex scenes. In fact, in one of the stories I just finished it would have been helpful having two someones!" She thought of Rand and Clint and heat coursed through her, zinging all the right places. She was always amazed when the heroes she made up in her head created such a raging need in her body.

Tessa's eyes went wide and she clasped both palms to her face. She was leaning on both elbows staring off too, "Roman and I are adventurous but he's definitively not into sharing."

"Nah, Philip either. Although he sure used to be," Viv said, adding, "as we can all attest to," she forced out a big sigh. "He was wild. I'm not sure I could have handled him back then."

All three women smiled over at her. Cat was the first one to be able to put words together. "It wasn't your time to be with him then."

"Suppose not." She had a funny look on her face.

"Viv, what's wrong?" Tessa asked.

Viv looked over at her and sniffed. "I never told you this, I've never even told him this. But I saw him once, all those years ago. I walked into the wrong room at a party when I was in college and there he was, big as life, fucking Cassandra."

Tessa's eyes went wide and her arms fell to the table with a thud. Her shock was palatable.

Cat had an identical expression, clearly agog with the implications.

"Oh no!" Cat said.

"What?" Laurel said as she watched their little gabfest go somber. "Who's Cassandra? Why's everyone so shocked?"

"Cassandra was his wife at the time," Viv toyed with a straw as if it was the most normal thing in the world to say she'd seen vintage porn of her husband with his first wife.

"I remember thinking how perfect they looked together and I remember stopping in the doorway and watching the intensity in his eyes as he took her. And I mean took her, because the look in hers was anything but adoring. Her eyes haunted me for years and so did everything else about him . . . his broad shoulders, his amazing chest and arm muscles, his taut torso, long legs and his very impressive erection. I masturbated to that image all through exam week."

"How did you know that the woman was Cassandra?" asked Cat.

"I found pictures he'd kept of her—in the Charlotte house, under a window seat in his den."

"Wow. That must have been tough," said Tessa.

"Yeah."

Clearly this hadn't been a good moment for her, Laurel thought, judging by the misery she saw in Viv's eyes. But then she watched as the woman transformed in front of her. The grin on her face that grew was almost comical. "But I also found more videos." She waggled her brows.

"That's good?" laughed Cat.

"Let's just say the man was in his prime in the 60s, and 70s, and so were his *friends*."

"I wanna see 'em," Tessa leaned in and then whispered, "You gotta share."

"No way. This was his very first one. Very different from the later ones."

"Fine. I'll go online. It should be easy to scare up my own copy," said Cat.

"And what are you going to say to Matt when he comes home and sees you sitting on the couch watching his best friend being carnal with a slew of nuns?"

"Really? Nuns?" said Tess.

"Not real ones!" Viv gave Tess a glare. "He's not that bad." She turned back to Cat, "So what are you going to say to him, huh?"

Cat shrugged. "I can't imagine there'll be a lot of talking going on with Philip as inspiration."

"No, me neither," Tessa said. "It boggles the mind just thinking of it. And Roman . . . that sounds like something he'd be very into. Hey, I wonder . . . you think they've watched that one together? Philip's not beyond a little boasting, and there were six nuns."

Laurel shook her head in disbelief. "This is the strangest conversation."

"Well, you have to admit, the situation is unique. How many women even know a former porn star nonetheless wind up married to one?" Tessa commented.

"Come to think of it, ya'll make me look pretty normal," Laurel said.

They all laughed until they cried.

"So you might as well use your real name if you publish," said Tess.

"We'll see. There's still a lot of work to do before the decision of a *nom de plume* has to be made." Taking a pen out of her purse Laurel added an item to her list and then smiled, waving the sheet. "All fears, thoughts, angst, and emotions are now down on paper."

"Then we have a ceremony to perform," said Cat.

"All done?" Tessa confirmed, gripping Laurel's hand.

"Completely. Burn baby burn!"

"Cool. Tonight at midnight," said Cat.

"Midnight?" Viv breathed out with exasperation. "Why does it have to be midnight?"

"It just does. Tonight at seven just sounds so . . ."

"Early," quipped Viv.

"Not mystic," countered Cat.

"How about ten, can we agree on ten?" piped up Tess. There was a meeting of eyes around the table. Everyone nodded.

"Okay, ten it is!" Laurel said with a smile. "I've done some research and I think I might have found just the right tree to use."

"Do tell," Cat said and they all propped their elbows back on the table to listen.

Laurel described the majestic tree she'd seen just around the corner by the old Brooks cemetery. All eyes lit as they made their wacky plans and giggled like schoolgirls. Then they gathered up their things and said goodbye, promising to meet that night at Laurel's house, so they could drive over to the tree she had selected for her "purging" ceremony.

Chapter Twenty-five

The next day Garrett and one of his neighbors hooked up to play Sandpiper Bay, and although it was an enjoyable round, it didn't yield any flower boxes. The houses were only slightly set back from the course, but it was hard to see up close to the homes. He thought about coming back with binoculars but there weren't any likely candidates. There were no out of bounds markers combined with flower boxes that he could see with the naked eye. And although he was willing to sacrifice a hole by purposely hitting in the rough to get closer to a house, none struck him as likely.

That afternoon he went back out and played Oyster Bay. Following the cart path back to the clubhouse after playing only fifteen holes as the sun was setting over the marshes, he checked out the decks of the remaining houses on the course. Nada. He was beginning to get frustrated. He'd thought he'd had a good plan, but it was not turning out that way.

He got back to the beach house just as the sun was bestowing its last glimmer over Bird Island. Stowing his golf bag in the ground level storage room, he muttered to himself and rubbed his hand over his face. He needed a new plan. He was tired. He was hungry. And although he had enjoyed playing golf, he'd dallied with it about as long as he cared to. He had to get back to his investment portfolio, and his body was crying out for a good hard run. But not tonight, he thought as he trudged up the steps. Definitely not tonight.

A big pile of mail awaited him in the center of his dining room table, left there, he supposed, by Judy, his bi-weekly housekeeper. Two big packages had arrived, one containing a thick prospectus he'd requested, the other with mail forwarded from up north. The mailman must have brought it to the door for him. He loved the hometown feel and the caring nature of the local people. His neighbors often rolled his trashcan back up the drive to its niche under the house to spare him the fifty-dollar fee for leaving it out over the twenty-four hour limit. And the mailman, who was actually a woman, was always bringing bulky packages right up to the door for him. Up north, he'd usually find packages crammed into the box, or resting at the base of the post, suffering the weather, and tempting any passerby to investigate the contents.

He quickly scanned the mail, tossing the majority of it in the trash. Then he picked up the phone and speed dialed Christopher's Pizza. He was starved and felt as if he could devour a whole New Yorker Pie. He added an order for the house salad to salve his health-oriented conscience, and then checked his watch against the time. He had enough time to shower before the delivery man got there, so he made his way to the bathroom and to his man-sized, tiled-in, state-of-the-art steam shower—an indulgence that made all his hard work worth it. As far as he was concerned some luxuries were necessities. This was one of them.

Forty minutes later he was sitting at the table, his fourth slice of pizza in hand as he read the Sports section of *The Brunswick Beacon*. An article by Elsa Bonstein caught his eye, and he laughed at her Golf Groaner joke at the end. He'd met her once at a First Tee charity golf tournament at St. James Plantation and had liked her right away. Energetic and full of praise for the program, she had impressed him. He had left a sizeable check in her hand for the kids.

She's a good writer, he thought as he scanned a section of the article that had interested him most, a listing of local courses and golf directors' comments on the quality of the greens this summer. He'd read some of her articles before, and was impressed with her writing. That, and the fact that she seemed quite knowledgeable about the game and well connected in the golfing community. On a whim he decided to email her.

Elsa, I met you a few months back at a First Tee tournament. I doubt that you remember me, but I was the one you talked into outbidding that obnoxious idiot who thought he could get four tee times for Lion's Paw for $25 by hiding the silent auction sheet under his hors d'oeuvre plate and blocking it for an hour. If you recall, he wasn't happy when I changed his bid to $250 at the last moment as he'd already told his friends to call the pro shop and a book tee time, on him. Best laugh I had all day was when he called *me* a cheater as his friends gathered round and thanked him for paying for the next day's golf outing.

Anyway, I wonder if you could take a moment to answer an odd question for me. Digging deep into your vast knowledge of the local courses, do you remember ever seeing a house with a big rosemary bush close to out of bound markers? Supposedly it also has flower boxes on the deck with lavender.

He reread it, typed in Elsa's email address at The Beacon, and pressed send. It was probably going to be fruitless. What were the odds? But he was getting desperate.

When he got back from taking the pizza box out to the trash, he was surprised that he already had an answer.

Of course I remember you. You making that guy spit and sputter, paired with a $5,000 contribution makes you pretty hard to forget. That, plus all the young women asking me who you were all day . . .
Re: the house you're asking about. Seems to me there's something like that on Panther's Run at Ocean Ridge, somewhere around the 3rd or 4th hole, not sure exactly about that though, but I vaguely remember losing a ball in the rough and then getting back into the cart and wanting a big ol' plate of spaghetti. Hope this helps! Would love to see you at the next benefit if you're going to be in town. Elsa.

Garrett smiled. Ocean Ridge. Why hadn't he thought of that? Of course. The Food Lion at the Village of Sunset would be the closest grocery store for an Ocean Ridge resident since the Piggly Wiggly, which then became the Lowe's, had shut down. And the upscale houses that were Ocean Ridge would certainly suit what he knew of *his* woman's personality.

Invigorated now, he decided he'd manage to muster himself up for one more round of golf this week. He went to bed after clearing out some shows on his DVR—reruns of *Justified, Castle, Whitney,* and *The Mentalist* that he'd missed. Then he set the alarm for seven. It wasn't likely he'd get an early tee time in the morning, but unless he called by eight, he probably wouldn't get one at all.

On his way back from the bathroom, his laptop beckoned from the dining room table, it was as if one of her stories was calling to him. There were sections of the last one about the lady doctor he'd scanned and now he really wanted to read the whole story. He wanted to experience that surge he got, that spark that charged his whole body with energy when he read certain passages. He had to admit that her sex scenes were amazing, and he had to wonder just how much was experience and how much was imagination. He knew that some would call her graphic in her descriptions, maybe overly so from the little he knew about writing—gleaned from a creative writing course he'd taken in college. He did remember one professor suggesting that writers leave some things to the imagination of the reader. However in this case, he thought of her as being merely thorough, and completely honest in relating all the titillating facts by filling in the blanks with detail that could only be firsthand. Plus, in erotica, maybe the genius was in the details.

It was those details, that grit, that drew him in the middle of the night to the flashing beacon on his sleeping laptop—that dark hunger that drew him in. Like a siren on a rock, she called to him, and like Pepe LePew with his nose in the air, he scented her, and followed. *The Master's Serf* was trying to draw him in, but he really did need to get some sleep if he was going to play golf tomorrow morning.

Chapter Twenty-six

Laughing and stumbling up the small rise, the four women finally made their way in their totally unsuitable heels to the tree Laurel had deemed worthy. The tree was in a small plot of land off Dartmoor, just before a bridge that was right out of a fairytale, the castle and princess kind. They'd had to park at the Tiger's Eye Clubhouse and walk to the cemetery, as the approach didn't allow for parking on the road. They each carried a small flashlight that pinpointed their progress. From a distance it appeared as if tiny white dots were bouncing erratically and making their way up toward the dark sky.

Majestic, with spreading branches reaching to the slow moving silver-infused clouds, the tree was the focal point of the tiny cemetery. There was no doubt where Laurel was heading as they progressed through the headstones. The tree's canopy overshadowed the marked gravesites.

The sound of the breeze rustling the leaves reminded Laurel of layers upon layers of crinolines brushing against satin as a woman's hips swayed while she walked. That made her think of Miss Havisham of Great Expectations. Ghostly . . . otherworldly . . . all alone—as she was. That made her remember why they were here. At this point in her life, she could not afford for all her secrets to be known. She wanted to find a man, settle down and experience something of the life her heroines enjoyed before being ostracized.

Ten feet away from the gnarly trunk she stopped and turned, "Perfect, huh?"

"Perfect," they said in unison.

Each placed the bag they had carried at their feet and tucked their flashlights inside. Cat's tote held a small ceramic effusion lamp with green and gold Asian graphics, Tessa's held the fire "wand" she took from Roman's grill, Viv had a bottle of *Unforgettable* she'd bought at Belk's, and Laurel held the list she'd been working on, along with a bottle of Ménage à Trois already opened and capped with a dichromatic glass styled stopper. Each had a party-sized acrylic wine glass tucked into the pocket of their long, flowing cardigans. For security purposes, they had decided to wear black. After all, it was a cemetery and one had to be respectful. *And* Ocean Ridge had a security team that was ever vigilant for vandals.

The effect of the all-black draping, for the dog walker approaching the eerily lit hill shrouded in sepia tones, was that of four witches sans the pointed hats. Make that four sexy witches—as the moon drifted overhead the silhouettes on the rise were showcased. Balancing on toned legs in spiked heels and revealing curvy bodies with each breeze that whipped their dresses, they were anything but old crones.

Laurel's long blond ponytail shone like a curved banana against the back of her head in the dark. Viv's silvery mop caught the moonlight and reflected like polished pewter. And Tessa's light curls bobbed and glowed in the gusting evening breeze. A glimpse of Cat's rich honey-amber tresses swinging back and forth as she bent to put the effusion lamp at the base of the tree, would have convinced anyone who chanced to be around that there were teenaged hooligans at work here.

"Okay, here's the chant," Cat said as she handed small strips of paper to each woman. On them were words, she whispered, that said in harmony as the tree was circled, would do their magic for Laurel. Cat, always the drama queen, was full into the imaginary world she'd dreamed up. Viv, whose mother truly believed she was a modern day witch, scoffed. None of this impressed her, or at least it shouldn't have. Except that in a very similar ceremonial rite, not too long ago, the fates had deemed her worthy and called forth Philip, whom she now loved to distraction. Still . . . she couldn't let them believe she went in for this kind of stuff. "Yada, yada, get on with it, would ya?"

Each woman looked down at her strip of paper and followed as Cat read what she had typed out: "Wicked though wicked be . . . close thy mind to dreams of he. He who finds will no evil do . . . and words now lost, are safe with you."

"Then Laurel, you read this," Cat continued, "'Oh Merlin of this magnificent tree, bring my words back to me.' You say this three times as you walk around the tree, and be careful of those roots. Whose bright idea was it to wear heels up here anyway?"

They all turned as one and gave Tessa the evil eye. She lifted her palms up and shrugged a shoulder, "Just thought it would be appropriate to dress the part. And you have to admit, we look wicked hot."

"We look crazy," Viv said.

"That too," agreed Tessa.

"Let's do it," said Laurel, she grinned and whipped out her list.

The effusion lamp was opened, the notepaper rolled into a tight curl and lit by Tessa's wand. It was dropped into the base of the lamp and left to burn until only ashes remained, while the women chanted the words written on the strips of paper. Viv spritzed *Unforgettable* into the air and three times they intoned, "Wicked though wicked be . . . close thy mind to dreams of he. He who finds will no evil do . . . and words now lost, are safe with you."

Cat poured the special patchouli scented oil into

the ashes, shook the mixture to blend it, then added the intricately worked caged top and lit the special igniter. She blew and coaxed the fuse to catch and then they all lifted their faces and watched as spiral after spiral of the fragrant incense rolled out and wisped up into the moonlit night.

Cat nodded to Laurel and she began walking around the tree while murmuring, "Oh Merlin of this magnificent tree, bring my words back to me . . . Oh Merlin of this magnificent tree, bring my words back to me . . . Oh Merlin of this magnificent tree, bring my words back to me." She ended where she began and Cat handed her the lamp with its curling wisps rolling out like waves of spun silver. The old tree creaked as overhead branches swayed and somewhere in the distance an owl hooted. It was creepily spooky enough to make Laurel shiver.

At Tessa's signal they pulled their wine glasses from their cardigans and Viv poured wine into each woman's glass. They raised them in a toast and sipped as they watched the smoke billow and rise, mesmerized by its unwavering frequency as it puffed and curled out of the fancy top.

When each glass was emptied Viv wiped them out with a handi-wipe she pulled from her sleeve, and each was tucked back into a pocket. Cat picked up the bag she had left at the base of the tree and Viv grabbed the empty wine bottle. Each woman reclaimed her flashlight and flicked it on. Then Laurel turned and walked down the hill, picking her route carefully as the procession of witchy women followed—all somber and seriousness until they reached the bottom of the hill where they simultaneously peeled off and burst into raucous laughter around their still grinning friend. Laurel looked happier than they'd seen her in a long time. A weight had been lifted off her and it showed in her dimpled cheeks and twinkling eyes as she wiped at the tears leaking from her eyes.

"That was just plain crazy," Tessa shrieked as she fell

on Viv's arm.

"We've done stranger things," said Viv, her tone blasé as she recovered from being unbalanced by Tessa. Grabbing onto Laurel, she reached out and brought Cat into the circle with her free arm. The four women huddled around the lamp and smiled at each other over the plume of smoke still rising to the heavens.

"Your words are on their way back to you, I can feel it," Cat said.

"Yeah, your stories are safe now, I feel it too," said Tessa.

"I only feel foolish, and kinda chilly," said Viv as she hiccupped and rubbed her open palms against her upper arms. For emphasis she stomped her feet. "Let's take our wine glasses back to Laurel's house for a refill, shall we?"

"Hear! Hear!"

"Motioned carried."

"What do I do with this," Laurel asked, holding up the lamp.

"That's some really nice oil," said Cat, "it'll eventually go out on its own, until then it'll make your house smell real pretty. I want you to keep the effusion lamp as a memento of our Ya-Ya night together. This was special."

"Yeah, it was," said Laurel and she kissed each woman on the cheek. "Thanks. I feel so much better. You guys are amazing. Just knowing you care enough to dream up this dumb stuff on my behalf makes me feel better."

Affronted, Cat feigned falling back in outrage. "Not dumb stuff. Ask Matt, Roman and Philip how dumb it is. They'll all tell you they believe in Merlin's magic."

"Because it worked for them," Laurel replied.

"Because it worked for all of us," Tessa said with a faraway look in her eyes. "Yes indeed. Merlin certainly did his magic for us."

"Well then maybe he'll do it for me too," Laurel said.

"You only need to believe. Let him do the rest," Cat whispered in her ear as she pulled her close for a hug.

"What have I got to lose?" Laurel said as she hugged her back.

"The idea was to find what you already lost," reminded Tessa.

"Oh yeah. C'mon Merlin, do your stuff!"

They made their way back to Laurel's where she put the decorative effusion lamp in a place of honor on the mantel in the family room. A new bottle of wine was opened and quickly dispatched, along with a wedge of brie and some apple slices, and then Viv and Tessa climbed into Cat's Lexus and rode back to Sea Trail with Cat.

Laurel stood and stared at the lamp for what seemed like forever before making her way to her bedroom, where she kicked off her heels and discarded her clothes in a heap by her bed. Neglecting her flossing regimen, she crawled between the covers, where she had her first good night's sleep in weeks. Life was good again.

Chapter Twenty-seven

He didn't even wait to call first, he just got his gear ready and headed over to the course. The pros were busy checking several groups in so he patiently waited until they were free to inquire about a tee time. Although unusual to come to the course without first booking a tee time, it wasn't unheard of.

As a single, he was assured they could work him in. And so at the pro's suggestion, he headed over to the driving range to hit some practice balls. Twenty minutes later a ranger came over to let him know they had placed him with a group from Raleigh. Their fourth was under the weather from too many shooters the night before, and they were happy to accommodate a single.

He had to check himself to keep from racing over to the cart where the foursome was getting "saddled up." He was so close to his quarry, he could hardly stand the excitement. By the time this round of golf was over he would likely know who his mystery woman was. It was all he could do to focus on the introductions and the preemptory what-do-you-dos that followed. He was paired with Gregory, a middle-aged finance manager for a Volvo dealer.

The first hole he was so nervous he couldn't even follow the flight path of his ball and was surprised to find it near a tree not twenty feet from the green. But putting had never been his strong suit, so while they kept his first shot for Captain's choice, his putt didn't help them out at all.

The second hole came up short and they used another man's tee shot.

On the third hole he tried to hit it out of bounds, as he knew that's where he was going to need to be to check out the houses along the course, but intentionally shooting into the rough wasn't the guaranteed shot he thought it would be. It took two more shots to get into the tall grass and by then, he thought it was pretty obvious that was what he'd been trying to do.

"Hey, what was up with that last shot? You weren't even addressing the ball—your stance was way off," Greg said.

"Trying something new. Hip's been giving me a fit, so I thought I'd face it out. Didn't work, as you can see . . ." Garrett mumbled.

"No, I'll say it didn't." In a huff, Greg turned and rooted through the clubs in his bag before jerkily pulling a head cover off one of his woods.

Garrett took his seven-iron and whacked around in the tall grass as if looking for his ball when he knew exactly where it had landed. He studied the out of bounds markers and scanned the abutting properties. Then he saw her.

The moment she stepped out onto her deck every cell in his body reacted. His system went on full alert and he knew without a doubt that she was the woman he was looking for. His pulse jolted and he sucked in a harsh breath as his eyes made the connection to her petite body and then to her lovely face. In that moment he could not have forced his eyes from her if his life had depended on it. She was stunning.

Gold shot hair was pulled back into a braid, intricately woven against the back of her head. It spoke of elegance. Shapely tanned legs set off against white shorts drew his eye to trim ankles and canvas slip-ons. A sleeveless polo showed off sleek arms and when she turned in profile he saw that it jutted out in the front, emphasizing nice breasts.

"Your ball's over there," Greg pointed as he brought the golf cart around, close to where he stood staring, clearly in another world. She turned at the sound and he was able to see her face. Lovely. And sweet. Something unexpected. Yet vaguely familiar.

"Uh, yeah. Thanks. I see it now," he managed as he forced his gaze away long enough to acknowledge the other man's presence. "Hey can you give me a minute?"

"You can't piss on the course. You'll get fined; they're real serious about protecting the homeowners here. There's a restroom after the next hole."

"It's not that. I just need a minute, okay?"

"Yeah, sure. We're not using your shot anyway. I'll go ahead and shoot."

"I'll catch up." Garrett swung his head back just in time to see the woman go back inside the house through a set of white French doors. *Fuck.*

He scanned the windows but couldn't see anything. His eyes returned to the deck and he spotted two long window boxes. They hung over the side of the deck rail and they were painted a pale green that matched the trim on the house. One had long green stalks waving in the wind, the tops covered with white pod-type flowers. He recognized them as the chives he'd researched. The other box, front and center, was a mass of purple flowers that he now knew to be lavender. His heart leapt and he damn near cried from overwhelming joy. He had found her.

Forcing himself to get back into the game for fear he'd appear to be casing the house instead of being moony-eyed over its inhabitant, he meandered over to his ball and took a devil-may-care swing to part the tall grass before bending to pick up his ball. The back of his club hit a low bush and the smell of rosemary carried on the breeze. He'd found the rosemary bush that was familiar to many a poor golfer.

Chapter Twenty-eight

Laurel turned back from closing the French doors in time to see a tall man bend and pinch off a piece of her rosemary bush. Usually something like that would put her in a bad humor, but then the way he held it to his nose and sniffed as if it were the most fragrant of roses, made her smile. She reached over to move the sheer panel away so she could see him better but he moved out of her line of vision behind a tree. Her next glimpse of him was about thirty yards away and he was tucking the fragrant sprig into his shirt pocket. He fanned a clump of liriope with a golf club and tossed a golf ball into the air as he walked. He looked younger than most of the players she usually saw on this course, younger and tantalizingly male. And somehow familiar. He was wearing long gray pants that were cuffed, black and white shoes and a white polo shirt that was tucked into a trim waistline. Thick dark curls ruffled in the wind, and she noted with a smile, that he had a great butt.

She watched him until he climbed into a golf cart driven by another man who sped off as soon as he was seated. She dropped her hand and the sheer curtain fluttered back in place. For a few seconds she paused and allowed herself to wonder what it would be like to have a man like that close his eyes and drink in the essence of her as if there was nothing sweeter, as he had with the rosemary branch. Then she checked her watch and mentally shook herself, she'd better get a move on or she'd be late for the charity luncheon and fashion show at Twin Lakes Restaurant.

The Old Bridge Preservation Society was hosting it and she'd promised Ann, Chris, and Karen that she'd come early to help check in some last minute silent auction items. She went into her bedroom to change and fix her makeup. Fifteen minutes later she was ready to go.

On her way out the door she stopped to check herself in the full-length mirror in the hall. In her lime green Chico capris and matching sleeveless cropped gingham top, she took a moment to assess herself. From the Lucite heeled sandals with the feathery pom, to the jeweled studded barrette cinching the bottom of her French braid, she was stylishly chic. Fashion conscious women would approve . . . but would a man? A man like the one who'd had a penchant for her rosemary? She wondered if he was single. She wondered if they passed on the street if he'd give her a second glance. And decided that maybe he would.

She'd lost that haunted look she'd had the last few years, the one that warned others away as she'd crawled into a protective shell to deal with the pain of her parents' death. In its place was a smattering of freckles over her nose, sun-kissed cheeks and eyes challenging the world again. Yes, she agreed, he definitely would look twice; she'd wink at him and see to it.

The fashion show and lunch was well attended, and by the time she left to go home her head was spinning with all the names and faces. It never failed to amaze her how many civic-minded people turned out for these events. There were so many good causes to support and the Old Bridge Preservation Society and Communities in Schools were among her favorites. And both committees appreciated her willingness to volunteer her time as well as her generous donations, but there was just something special about

Karen, Chris, and Ann. She smiled as she drove through the impressive gates leading into Ocean Ridge. She'd had such a good time. And the chopped Cobb salad had been excellent.

She looked over at the hand-painted birdhouse on the passenger seat. She'd won the bid on it and of course paid too much. But she couldn't neglect her garden. Mentally placing it amid her ball gazer and whimsical "spilled flower pot" just off the lower terrace, instantly brought the star struck golfer to mind. How she'd love to have someone like that to come home to. Someone to grill chicken on the deck with, to hold hands with while admiring their garden as the sun set, someone who would smile knowingly at her as he locked them inside their little Shangri-La for an evening of pleasure between the sheets . . . on the couch . . . on the bar . . . against the shower tiles . . . going up the plush carpeted stairs. Hmm . . . all had possibilities. She laughed out loud at her wicked thoughts and then realized with dawning awe that her urge to write had returned. The ceremony had worked! She no longer worried about that damned flash drive.

As she watched the coffered garage door go up, she mentally rearranged her afternoon and evening. She had to take advantage of this sudden compulsion to sit in front of the computer and see what her muse was working on today. The gardening could wait, so could the laundry. She didn't have anything to do until five when she was supposed to ride with the Sunset Cyclists. That would give her three and a half hours to write. By then she'd need to get up and get the kinks out. She could hardly wait to get inside the house and get started.

She didn't notice the Corvette that drove past as she got out of the car with her new birdhouse held like a prize in front of her. Didn't notice when it slowed to a crawl at the end of the drive just as the garage door was settling back down. But she did feel a strange pull as she looked over her shoulder at the now closed door. The low rumble of a sports car pricked her ears but by the time she got inside and looked out the front window there was nothing there.

Chapter Twenty-nine

Garrett stopped in front of the house for a few seconds. He simply had to. There she was getting out of a shiny new CRV, grinning as she held a tall birdhouse in her hands. Every nerve ending came to life, and he wanted to jump out of the car and run over to her. Now. He wanted to meet her now. It was everything he could do to force the car forward as the garage door slid down. Despite the air conditioning being on full blast, he felt sweat beading at his temples. He was panting like a dog in heat. He had to get control of himself. And he had to get away before she spotted him.

At least now he had her address. From that he could go online to the county website and get her name. He didn't doubt that with a few clicks and access to the right links, his fantasy woman would come to life before his eyes. He'd know all the pertinent information about her five minutes after booting up his laptop. And after calling his researcher, a private investigator he frequently used to check out corporate structures, he'd have the inside story. With luck, by this time tomorrow.

He drove through town whistling "On the Street Where She Lives," from *My Fair Lady*, and laughing at himself. He parked under the beach house and ran up the steps, hardly acknowledging the tempestuous waves that were crashing on shore. A storm was coming in, he'd heard that on the radio, but he didn't have time to worry about that now.

While his computer came back to life, he grabbed a beer from the fridge and some Swiss cheese slices. He needed a shower, he could feel the sweat drying on his body, but the smell of rosemary coming from his pocket pervaded his senses and gave him purpose. He sat just as the MSN home page appeared. Mere moments later, he sat back and sighed. Laurel. Laurel Ashleigh Leighton. Perfect. He loved her name.

What a coincidence that her name was Laurel. He was from a town named Laurel. Like a favorable horoscope, he saw it as a good sign. The more ominous prognostications, he always ignored.

He Googled her name. Nothing. Hmmm. She was a writer; surely there must be something. He tried Bing. Wiki. Who's Who. Facebook. LinkedIn. Nothing. *Who was she? Why wasn't she coming up?*

Of course! She probably used a pseudonym. He'd need a hometown to go any further. On a whim he went to Amazon and started typing in random passages he copied and pasted from her books. Sometimes certain lines or character names came up in a search and linked them to a particular book. No such luck. It dawned on him, not for the first time, that maybe she just wasn't published.

He went to *The Brunswick Beacon* site and typed her name in the search field. A picture with a caption and a small blurb came up. She was standing with five other women presenting a check to the South Brunswick Islands Woman's Club to be used for the Fully Belly Project. The woman's club website wouldn't let him access a roster. He thought about calling the president and asking about her, but couldn't figure out an angle that was believable. Plus, he needed to stay in the wind on this.

But more than anything, right now he needed to know if she was married. According to the Register of Deeds, the house was deeded in her name only, so that was encouraging. He Google Mapped her, then looked her phone number up as well as the neighbors on both sides. He could call them . . . come up with some excuse. Hell, he could just call *her*. And explain everything.

But he wanted better odds than that. He wanted this woman. And for that he was going to have to have more information. He'd learned long ago not to lead with his emotions. Plod steadily. Learn all you could before jumping in. He pulled out his cell phone and called his researcher, offered him double to drop whatever he was doing and work on this now.

Five minutes later Paul, his P.I., called back, "She's single."

His face flushed with pleasure. "Okay, how the hell did you get that so fast?"

"I called the pro shop, she plays golf. Golf pros know the lowdown on their members. She's an 18 handicap, got a beautiful swing and a lovely ass. Nice lady, always tips the cart guy three bucks and a baggie of homemade snicker doodles. They fight over her when they see her coming. Everybody likes her. She inherited the house when her parents died a few years ago. Drives a gold Honda CRV, and helps collect golf clubs for First Tee. No boyfriend that anyone knows of. Plays with the woman's group on Wednesdays and sometimes on Sunday with three women from Sea Trail. Oh, and she likes to sunbathe behind a screen on her deck—topless."

"What?" The idea that she was exposing her breasts where others could see filled him with a jealous rage.

"Yeah, apparently she's not familiar with Google Earth. But take it easy; whatever they've got loaded is grainy and low resolution. I checked. Seems she's got a deck off to the side that she thinks is private. Hey, you sound angry, she must be something special."

"Yeah. Working on it. You got anything else?" he asked as he typed her address into Google Earth. He had to see for himself. Yeah, grainy . . . and too far away. No nipple action, but she clearly did not have a top on.

"Yeah, County's got a record of a 1969 Firebird convertible being taxed each year. Nominal amount—14 and change. Curious thing is the account carries a credit balance. Two hundred and some."

"Nuisance bill. She must have paid it in advance knowing she's never going to sell it. I do that sometimes. Did you say Firebird convertible?"

"Yeah."

"Does it list the color?" The yellow Firebird convertible he'd seen on the bridge came to mind. A blonde in Jackie O. sunglasses had been behind the wheel.

"Nah. No color showing."

"Anything else?"

"Nah. Got some calls to make for some hometown stuff, I'll check in tomorrow,"

"Right."

"Thanks for the bonus."

"You earned it with the news that she's single."

"Go get 'er, tiger."

"Gotta meet her first. I feel like a stalker."

"Technically you are."

"Thanks."

"You want me to send Lou or Mike to chat up the neighbors?"

"No. Let's not spook her. Just get some background for me."

"Will do."

He ended the call and took a long pull on his beer. *Hot damn. Single. And hot.*

He got up and made his way to the walk-in shower, peeling off his clothes as he went. God, just the thought of that elegant braid and that petite, tight body was making him hard. He had to remember to go back and print that picture from the Beacon. She had lovely green eyes and full curving lips that smiled as if she had a secret. And she did. He smiled. *Yes she did. And he knew them all.*

Chapter Thirty

He couldn't help himself. He was embarrassed by the pull she had on him. Like a magnet drawn to steel, the attraction was overwhelming. But he drove back to Ocean Ridge to the Panther's Run Pro Shop anyway. Made up a dumb excuse about having lost a club on the course, and asking to borrow a cart so he could search the greens. Carts were coming in and being lined up at the bag drop to be cleaned and put away, as they were getting ready to close the course for the day, plus it looked like a storm was brewing. He gave the cart guy a ten-dollar bill and promised not to be long then he jumped in the cart and made his way around the course to the back of Laurel's house where he sat and just drank it all in.

A light sandstone colored brick, it rose three stories from the ground. It had a full deck running the length of the house, and a flagged patio below that led out to an impressive garden, with walkways sectioning off areas for a double swing, a colorful hammock, a small fountain, an outdoor kitchen, and an entertainment area where contemporary wrought iron furniture covered with brightly striped pads wrapped around a glass-topped table. The landscaping was inspired and appeared professionally done, either that or she was one hell of a gifted gardener.

His eyes were drawn to the large, arched windows, but the drapes were drawn and he couldn't see inside the huge panes that were now reflecting the late afternoon sun. With its multi-pitched roof, stacked-stone chimney, tiled roofing with cooper accents, and over-sized shutters, it was easily a $750,000 house. Done in the French style with a side turret, it could have been on a hillside in Rouen instead of in this golf community in the lower Brunswick Islands.

He sat scanning, memorizing every detail of the house and yard until he felt like an intruder, and reluctantly began to turn around and head back. Swinging off the path and into the rough to reverse direction he heard a door opening and he looked back in time to see her cross the deck with a pair of scissors in her hand. He managed to maneuver the cart around a tree as he turned back to watch her. She was wearing a sparkly purple bicycle helmet, a bright yellow t-shirt, black athletic cropped yoga pants, and strappy black Crocs, if he wasn't mistaken. If it hadn't been for the distinctive long blonde ponytail trailing down the center of her back he wouldn't have been sure it was her. Except that his heartbeat had accelerated and now outraced his panicked mind as his eyes tracked her over to a group of ceramic pots overflowing with colorful blossoms. He stared enthralled as she snipped and gathered until she had a full bouquet in one hand. Then she turned, looked over at her neighbor's house and waved at her neighbor who was watering her plants. When she turned back to go into the house he recognized the logo and distinctive lettering on the back of her t-shirt. *Sunset Cyclists.* An idea formed and then gelled as he put the pedal to the floor and raced back to the clubhouse.

That night he went online and found the website for the newly formed bike club he'd read about in the paper. Then he emailed the leaders, Charlene and Allen. He asked for the particulars on the next group event and found out that on Saturday they were meeting at the Sea Trail east entrance gate to drive to Southport so they could catch the ferry to Bald Head Island, where they would spend the day biking the trails and sightseeing. He couldn't have planned a more perfect first date. He signed up even though he had no way of knowing whether she would be riding or not. He knew he couldn't tip his hand by asking. He'd just have to go and see. It would be incredibly rude for her to be a no-show for their first outing. He smiled as he continued to make plans. The idea that he might actually get to meet her, talk to her . . . watch her cute little butt shift up and down all day gave him more happiness than he could have imagined.

The next day he went to Island Hoppers on Route 17, across from McDonald's, and picked out a new Sun Drifter. He outfitted it with three gears, a white mesh basket, and a gel seat. He left Steve to get it ready for him while he drove to Shallotte to the Ford dealership, where he purchased a new Edge Limited SUV. Wal-Mart was next. He found the exact kind of bike rack he needed, specifically one capable of carrying two bikes—as he was confident that one day soon he'd be transporting hers, too. Then he spent fifteen minutes trying on helmets. He finally selected one he thought matched hers. If nothing else, he figured it would be a conversation starter. Then he was off to the Tanger's Outlet in North Myrtle Beach for new shoes and riding pants. She could ogle his muscular thighs and calves while he kept his eye on that lovely rear of hers.

By the time he got back to the beach house he had just enough time to catch up with the trades he needed to make that day and take a run on the beach. He knew he was sexually charged and that he had to burn off some of the pent up energy. He couldn't be an agitated man on the prowl, he had to appear laid back and as if just out for a bike ride—a newbie to the club, just trying to stay fit and enjoy the day in the sun. For the first time in years, he prayed for the weather. Instead of praying for a snow day to stay home from school, he prayed for a perfect sunny day, breezy enough so he wasn't sweating from every pore, yet nice and sunny so they could sit in the sun on the ferry and maybe get to know each other before their morning ride.

He couldn't remember the last time he was this excited, the last time he had something this special to look forward to. He added another prayer: that she was making her own plans to spend the day riding with the cycling group on the island. He wouldn't know until they were boarding the ferry, as he'd been told that some of the riders would be meeting them there, and at that point, he'd be committed. With or without her, he was going to be touring Bald Head.

He'd just finished his run when the heavy clouds unloaded on him. The sky was streaking with white jagged lines as he ran up the access and took shelter under the beach house. He stood, hands on hips, and watched the grand display as he caught his breath. There was nothing so magnificent as an angry storm on the beach at sunset, and Mother Nature was showing all her colors as the sky darkened and thunderbolts lit up the horizon. It was raw, beautiful, and enervating. He loved this time, and only wished he had his arm draped over a woman's shoulders. A certain blonde-headed, green-eyed woman.

After a few minutes, he went inside to continue watching from the windows. He noticed a red light flashing behind him reflecting in the darkened window. He turned and saw it came from his answering machine. He walked over and hit the button. Then took a beer out of the fridge and opened it as he listened.

"I'm not sure you're not gonna be happy about this. But your mystery woman has no verifiable income. No job, no income, no debts, only a VISA debit card, balance kept close to zero, no car payment, no mortgage, no visible means of support. It's as if she was plunked here with a shitload of cash five years ago. She's awfully young for the community she lives in. Is it possible she could be a hooker or a stripper? Maybe keeping house for a rich sugar daddy who lives out of town?"

Garrett spurted out a stream of beer at Paul's suggestion. He swiped at his chin with the back of his hand and cursed. It took only a few moments to get Paul on the phone.

"That's all you've got?" he barked.

"She's not spending any money, not using any credit in any way."

"She inherited, remember?" he said sarcastically.

"Yeah, but court records show there was a mortgage at the time, and that the estate she inherited was worth less than fifty grand. And *now* there's no mortgage."

"There's any number of explanations, so I'd prefer if you didn't call her a whore."

"Testy, aren't we? I'm just giving you the facts and calling it as I see it. Myrtle Beach is a huge market for high-end escorts."

"She's not like that!"

"How can you be sure?"

There was silence on both ends then Garrett clipped out, "That's what I pay you for."

"Then I need to get some eyes on her. I can have someone there in 48 hours."

More silence.

"No. Let's wait on that."

He thought about the stories, the way she told them . . . her curious but otherwise healthy attitude toward men. "My gut tells me otherwise. Although I can see why a man would pay a small fortune to keep her, I don't see her as being kept. Let's just hang back for a while. I'll let you know if I want her watched."

"You're the boss."

"You're giving me things to think about. Things that I don't like."

"It's my job."

"Well stop doing it so fucking well!" He pushed the disconnect button and sat on a barstool staring out at the churning ocean. No. She wasn't a whore. His instincts couldn't be that far off. But Callie, and her character from the first story he'd read, came to mind. And she tanned topless. Damn, she'd better not be a stripper either.

Chapter Thirty-one

The day was exceptional, Laurel thought, as she watered her plants before leaving for her ride with the group. She'd awakened eager and excited about seeing Bald Head Island. She'd never been there and had heard so many wonderful things. The fact that the day was breaking so beautifully was a bonus, as it had stormed the last two evenings. But God, how she'd loved storms. Both nights she'd stood in front of her windows watching the show unfold, jumping back twice when the green behind her house lit up like daylight.

She picked up her scissors and grabbed the fistful of flowers she'd cut. She loved to have fresh flowers in the house, but always brought them inside and put them in water in the laundry room first so she could use the misting sprayer to wash off any bugs. Right now she was anxious to get started, she didn't want to be late as she promised Sandy that she'd pick her and her bike up. They often rode together on these excursions and carpooling gave them time to catch up.

Sandy was a good friend, but working in the non-profit field and managing the ins and outs of fund raising kept her on the road a lot. They often ate out when she was in town, laughing and drinking wine while rating the men they saw in the bars. Sandy was more outgoing, so they often had friends overflowing their tables, but Laurel didn't even try to keep up with her. Sandy was a girl on fire and could not stand to sit in one position long. She was often reminded of her own career and the long workdays she'd put in. And she could honestly say she didn't miss that life. She just missed the part about not having a family. Not having anyone to come home to, not having a special someone who knew whether she came home or not.

And as usual, when she got to Sandy's house, she was rushing around doing six things at once. A master multi-tasker, Laurel watched as Sandy fed her cats, bagged up her recycling for them to drop off, loaded her bike onto Laurel's bike rack, packed some snacks and answered four text messages.

"Good God, Sandy, do you ever just do one thing?" Laurel had watched movies with Sandy at her house and she'd be a blur of movement as she answered her phone, poured wine, fixed popcorn, washed fruit, set out crackers and cheese, talked, listened with full on intensity, and tried to figure out the cable remote. Only with a glass of wine under her belt was she finally able to relax and melt into her buttery soft leather sofa and slow down. For both of them, a nice cabernet was a signal for the day to be done and the winding down of night to begin.

Today was going to be different though, she could tell as Sandy looked down at her Blackberry and read the message on the screen. "Oh Laurel, I got the contract I've been working on! They want to sign today. I have to conference call my team. I am so sorry. Do you mind going on your own? This is just too important to put off. This contract is going to make my year!"

Laurel smiled and hugged her. "Of course not. Congratulations! That's wonderful news. I know you've been worried about this deal for weeks. We can ride another time. Here, help me get your bike off, then you can go do what you have to. I'll be fine—there's plenty of people riding today, I'm sure I can find someone to partner with."

"Laurel, you're always so understanding when my plans change or when I just pop in on you."

"I understand you're a working woman and that many people have constraints on your time, so don't give it another thought. I only hate that you're going to be stuck inside while I'm out enjoying this beautiful day."

Sandy laughed, "Well that's the beautiful thing about conference calling from my Blackberry, I can do it anywhere. I just might seal this deal on my deck!"

The bike was unstrapped and lifted off, and after another hug, Laurel got back in her CRV and pulled out of Sandy's driveway. She was tempted to scrap the bike ride and go to the pool or just hang out at the house, and was actually very close to pulling back into the plantation as she passed the gates, but she thought of her mother and father and of all the wonderful times they'd had as a family biking together. So she continued on, driving to Southport to the ferry station while she listened to her favorite Il Divo CD.

Chapter Thirty-two

As was his habit, he was early arriving at Deep Point Marina in Southport. His whole life he'd only been late a handful of times. He prided himself on his organizational skills and the fact that he had the uncanny ability to wake before the alarm if he had something scheduled. He couldn't take credit for that this morning though. He'd been so excited about meeting Laurel, about having the opportunity to actually talk to her and see her up close that he'd hardly slept. At four he'd given up. He'd gotten up to shower and to do a test ride around the island in the predawn light just to make sure his new bike was in working order. It would be lame for a tire to go flat or for a chain to slip. He wanted everything to be perfect today. So despite his confidence in Steve from Island Hoppers, he rode the perimeter of the island, enjoying the sunrise from many aspects, and stopping to absorb the serenity he was sharing with the egrets foraging at the edge of the marshes.

At the port, he bought his ticket and put his bike in the corralled section for the nine o'clock ferry. Then he found a railing near the entrance to lean against and watched as both people and bikes were offloaded, while also watching the parking lot fill up. His eyes flicked back and forth, checking out each new arrival. He was looking for a particular Honda, a gold CRV. Courtesy of his researcher, he had her license plate memorized should there be more than one.

People clad in the requisite bike gear along with the bumblebee yellow t-shirt symbolic of the club, piled out of several vehicles, and he was approached by Charlene and her husband, Allen. She had told him when they had talked on the phone that she'd bring him a shirt, both for the camaraderie and spirit of being part of the group, and for safety. No one was going to miss seeing a swarm of bright yellow t-shirts moving down the road.

Pleasantries were exchanged and he was introduced to ten people, all of them already paired up. He went to the men's room and changed shirts, and as he came out and rejoined the group, he heard someone say that Laurel and Sandy should be on the way. All hope of being partnered with her was dashed and he wanted to scream. Pragmatically, he rationalized that one-on-one time while bicycling the island together would have been too much to count on. He shouldn't have banked on that.

"There she is. That's her Honda," someone said, and he turned in time to see her pull into a parking space.

Trying to appear unaffected, he watched as she got out of her truck. There was no one with her. His spirits lifted. Maybe they'd be partners after all.

While she could have taken the bike off herself, three men from the group hurried out to meet her and helped her lift it off the rack. He watched as she smiled at each man, and was hugged by one of them. Garrett's hackles rose, and as he registered the nature of the feeling, he had to blink hard behind his sunglasses to tamp down the hot emotion. She wasn't his yet, he told himself. He had no right to jealous feelings. Hell, he couldn't remember the last time he'd felt possessive about a woman—high school maybe? Regardless, what he felt was out of line. He had no right to be jealous of any man, no right to be concerned over how she reacted to any man. But knowing it, didn't change how he felt.

Laurel wheeled her bike up as she chatted to the men

accompanying her and Garrett drank in her petite figure, clad in black capris and the ubiquitous yellow tee. She had on cute little black ballet-type crocs on her tiny feet and a black visor advertising Tiger's Eye framed her face. Despite knowing her exact age, and her date of birth along with it, she appeared to him as an adorable teenager striding to the platform. He removed his polarized sunglasses; he didn't want his first person-to-person appraisal of her to be filtered in any way.

She didn't disappoint, in the bright sunshine she was radiant, and her vibrant energy sparkled through amazing green eyes. Her bright gleaming smile showed off flawlessly white teeth. He wanted to kiss those soft lips and stroke the edges of her smooth teeth with the tip of his tongue.

She called out a cheery greeting to several individuals and he was so mesmerized by her soft lilting voice that at first it didn't register with him what she was saying.

"Anyway, she couldn't make it. The contract had to come first. Right now her life is her business."

"Well, we're sorry she can't make it today but as we've got a new member, you won't have to ride around the island on your own. This is Garrett, Garrett Grayson. Garrett . . . Laurel Leighton," said Charlene as she motioned him to come forward. He sensed one of the men in her little circle of admirers bristling from that news.

He forced himself to count to five before straightening up from the rail where he'd been leaning. He didn't want to come off as eager. He walked over and leaned in to shake her free hand, and as they touched, their eyes met. He was considerably taller than she was and with her visor angled toward his chin he couldn't see her eyes until she lifted them to his—until summer green met vivid blue and locked.

He'd never seen eyes so green; he sank into them, searching their beckoning depths. And he fell into them.

He'd always heard that at moments like this time

stood still. For him it sped up. He saw images of her flash through his head. Not the erotic type he'd had plastered there for weeks, but the placid bucolic scenes of a confident woman laughing, conversing over a dinner table, seductively smiling over her shoulder while cooking at the stove, walking and swinging hands on a deserted beach. He managed to appear outwardly in control while inside his emotions were rioting. *Could this be what love at first sight felt like or was he really becoming an insidious, tedious stalker for God's sake?*

Her broad smile was genuine and while he was sure she was thinking thoughts about the day ahead, he was picturing those full pink lips yielding under his on a blanket by the dunes. He derailed the thoughts that were piling up in his head and gave himself a mental slap. He eased his hand away and gave her his most devastating smile.

"Here, let me take your bike while you get settled and get your ticket."

He would have bought her the damned ferry at that moment if she'd asked him to, but he knew it was too soon to even offer to buy her passage to Bald Head. *Go slow, you idiot, go slow.* But he couldn't help winking at her as he took her bike from her and rolled it over to the bullpen with the others. The bikes were being loaded now, and just like a kid at Christmas, he was ready for the adventures to begin. He had high hopes for the day. If he could just concentrate on de-emphasizing the consequence of all this, maybe he wouldn't have a heart attack. It's just a bike ride, he told himself, a day in the sun, some exercise, a chance to relax and make new friends. Like hell. He already knew the significance of this day. It resounded in every fiber of his being. If he didn't have this woman, he would die. It was as simple as that. If ever there was a mate assigned in a pre-creation phase, she had been set aside as his.

His inner voice agreed, and said it was more than

desire that he was feeling. *It's gotta be more, even though you desire this woman like nobody's business.* The hardest part for him today was going to be keeping his "hardest part" out of the picture . . . while biking of all things. Because even though he prided himself on his control, physically, she leveled him. He was as randy as he'd ever been.

He looked down at the bike he was passing off and something clicked in his mind's eye. The bike he was pushing was a drifter in pastel green and light tan. He remembered seeing one on the beach, was it just a few weeks ago? Hadn't a blonde been riding it? Hadn't he thought they were both stunning, her and the bike? He shook his head as he relinquished the bike to the ferry employee. Could he have been that close to the owner of the flash drive so soon after finding it? His mind reeled. Life had a way of unraveling in such a weird way, he thought.

He rejoined the group, passing the claim ticket for the bike over to Laurel via her hugging buddy. It would be best if he didn't touch her again. There was something about that creamy sun-freckled skin that drew him in, he wanted to stroke and caress it, satisfy his curiosity—could it be as smooth and soft as it looked . . . so toned and firm? He just couldn't chance touching her again. Maybe he'd touch her later. Just how much later would depend on her. You didn't rush things that were important. And already she was as vital to him as breathing.

Chapter Thirty-three

Laurel had to force herself not to blink her eyes wide. Dear God, where had *he* come from? Widows, singles, even stolid yet randy wives had unique sonar in the south, and good-looking men like this just did not get overlooked. She knew she'd never heard his name before. But gall-darn—if she hadn't drawn her ideal man, as if he'd been pulled from a magician's hat. He was not so much as a hair's breath outside the chalk line of the fantasy men she dreamed about. Thick brown hair, so dark it was almost black, well-defined slashes of brows that arched over ocean-blue eyes, and lips . . . well she knew she couldn't focus on them now—already she was wetting hers and thinking lewd thoughts.

Irreverently, he hadn't shaved and was sporting a sexy, dark shadowed beard. She wanted to run her palm over his face to hear the scratchy bristles. She wanted to run her thumbs over his lips. He looked a little familiar . . . could he have been the man on the bridge? The man in the Corvette?

Well, today would certainly be an interesting one. Thank God I wore my new Athleta lotus capris with the waist cinching Branwyn top instead of the skuzzy cutoffs and halter I'd been planning on wearing.

She was glad she'd taken the extra minutes to brush her SPF 15 mineral make-up over her face and shoulders instead of waiting until she got here to use the white stuff in the tube.

She smiled and took his hand when he offered it. And didn't want to let it go. *What was wrong with her?* It was sunny and bright out, so why was she getting that delicious shiver tingling through her insides? Deliciously alternating between fire and ice, it finally warmed and settled as a melting fuse in what her mother would have called her hoochie koochie. If she didn't know any better, this attraction she felt presaged infatuation. But that was absurd. She knew only one thing about this man and that was his name. Okay two: he was drop dead gorgeous. With a tit-for-tat brazen appraisal, she acknowledged the physical effect he was having on her. His intense gaze caused a wild array of delicious responses, but no way would she let on that she was bathed in his intoxicating aura. This was like something out of one of her stories.

He murmured something she couldn't make out and then stepped closer and took her bike from her. Loretta, one of the members of their group, turned her and pointed her toward the ticket booth, and, as if in a trance she walked over and purchased her fare. Then she walked back to where he stood talking to the group.

Gotta put yourself together. He's going to think you're an idiot. Just relax, smile, and for God's sake don't fall off the bike ogling him. But God, those wide shoulders, the outline of those broad chest muscles filling out that tee shirt, those long, hair-dusted legs. He had to have an ass that was worth watching all damn daylong. She wasn't sure if that was such a good thing.

She sidled back into the group, and as her claim ticket for the bike was handed over to her, he did the oddest thing. He winked at her.

Ah, well at least they were on the same page. Boy meets girl. She smiled and slid her sunglasses down from where they'd been perched on her visor. Eyes—windows to the soul . . . she couldn't afford to broadcast her every thought at this point. Mostly because they involved things she should not be thinking about doing with a man she had just met.

Chapter Thirty-four

"So where are you originally from?" Laurel asked. They were on the bow end of the ferry and they had to practically shout to be heard as the ferry got up to speed and began crossing the channel.

"Laurel. Laurel, Maryland. Just like your name. Ever heard of it?"

"Sure, who hasn't?"

He grimaced. "We're a lot more than the place where Wallace got shot."

"My dad used to have appointments in Ft. Meade. He used to take me to the racetrack on Saturdays when we visited there, so I'm a little familiar with the area. "

"Sorry. We're sensitive to the event that put us on the map."

"No problem. Who's Wallace?"

He gave a delighted, full-throated laugh and his hand covered hers on the seat between them. They both looked down. He wrapped the small hand with his large one and gave it a squeeze before releasing it. It was way too soon for the boyfriend/girlfriend stuff, so he had to pretend it meant nothing.

"He was the governor of Alabama—macho, racist type who kept blacks from going to school and getting a coveted white education. Maybe you heard of two black students, Vivian Malone Jones, James Hood, and the

University of Alabama?"

"Oh, that Wallace."

He grinned at her. "Yeah, that Wallace. There was a little shopping center incident that involved a gun. George Wallace was shot and ended up in a wheelchair because of it."

"Not a good legacy."

"No. His stance was popular to some at the time. But our generation sure wouldn't have pegged him as a hero."

"The south certainly has evolved, look at us now." Her arms lifted and spread wide as if encompassing the churning ocean appearing in front of them. "This is where blockade runners once ran the blockade. Also over white and black issues," she added with a meaningful nod.

"Yeah. Blacks weren't even allowed to learn how to read, nonetheless go to college. Thankfully, the days of the southern plantation are over."

"That's funny, I live on a plantation. I never took the time to absorb the meaning of the word with regard to the community I live in."

"Where do you live?" He could have bitten his tongue. *So this is how it's going to be? You're not only going to lie to her by omission, you're going to act the fool so you can never get out of this and be honest with her?*

"I live in Ocean Ridge Plantation, it's considered Ocean Isle Beach, but it's on 17, at 904 near Grissettown. Have you heard of it?"

Ah, a chance to get back to a semblance of honesty. "Yeah, I have. In fact, I play golf there whenever I get a chance."

"That's interesting. Were you playing there last week? I saw someone who looked like you on the course."

He dodged that one with a wry smile, "Oh, what did he look like? Handsome, athletic, an accomplished golfer the likes of a young Greg Norman?"

She smiled back. "Hardly. You're not blonde, and

when this man was in the rough looking for his golf ball, he swiped some of my rosemary."

He remembered the moment vividly but didn't know if he should cop to it. He needed to steer this conversation to safer shores. "So you're a gardener?" Again, he was painting himself in a corner for the time when he needed to come clean.

"Avid. My friends say I'm obsessive. I've even taken the Master Gardener classes in Bolivia. Working in my garden is therapy for me."

"Therapy?"

"My parents died in a car accident a few years ago. I lost my focus. Kinda thought my mind, too . . . for a while. But I'm better now."

"Wow. I'm sorry. Were you an only child?"

"Yeah. Still kind of feel like an orphan." There was silence between them for a few seconds before she asked, "How about you? You have family?"

"Yeah, on the eastern shore. Dad's gone but Mom's doing well. She still teaches, almost forty years now and still going strong. She has a boyfriend who takes her to church and to the movies on Sundays. She insists it's only for companionship, but I know better. I found a box of condoms in her medicine cabinet last time I was there. Stood and stared at those suckers as if I'd never seen one before. Must've been five minutes before I could put 'em back. What a shock that was. I went back into the kitchen without the band-aid I'd gone in there to get. Some things you're ready for. That sure wasn't one of them."

"I know what you mean. Well at least you know she's having safe sex."

He threw back his head and laughed, "Yeah, too bad. I always wanted a brother."

She laughed along with him and he delighted in it. *God she was lovely.* He was having a helluva time reconciling her to the woman who wrote those incredibly erotic stories. She looked so young, so innocent . . . waifish, but in a very classy way. A woman who would gasp if a man even suggested she suck on his penis, not one who could give a play-by-play as if she'd done it a hundred times. Not for the first time he wondered if he could have mistaken her identity. Maybe it wasn't Laurel who had lost the flash drive.

The wind whipped their hair around their heads, and although it had been warm back on the dock in the sun, it was a bit chilly out on the water, and she reached for the Bhakti hoodie she had in her backpack. He helped her put it on, reveling in the feel of her hair cascading over his fingers. Purposefully he brushed his fingers across her neck as he settled the collar in place and flipped the hood forward. He watched as she shivered from the innocent caress and he felt his loins throb and his cock jump. Before it grew hard and drove him to distraction, he jumped up to get his camera.

He would need a picture of her to keep him company on the days he had to force himself to stay away. If this wasn't love, he didn't know what else it could be. He wanted her deep in his core, more than he'd ever wanted anything. It actually hurt not being able to secure her, to bind her to him . . . to make her his. For all time. *Whoa! Where had that come from?*

Now all the stories and poems he'd ever read about love and devotion made sense. Overnight, he had moved into the realm of a need that eclipsed lust. It eclipsed everything.

Chapter Thirty-five

After retrieving their bikes from the holding pen, the group donned their helmets and set off, following the leaders onto the island streets. For two and a half hours they rode around the island sightseeing and stopping to gather for mini-tours at places of interest. Bald Head was the perfect place to nature watch, everywhere you looked, the environment came into play, minimally developed with conservation foremost, the residents were proud of having a low human footprint.

They learned that turtles were a special interest here, and had been since the early 80s. Nationally known for high numbers when it came to tracking sea turtle nesting, it was one of North Carolina Marine Fisheries Service's index beaches. At Turtle Central, they were all about educating and displaying coastal life. Garrett was all about watching her interact with the group and watching her coo over the tiny creatures in the touch tank.

As a group, they did a beachcombing walk and listened to a man talk about what it was like to go crabbing, kayaking, birding and cast netting. Eventually, Garrett found himself staring down one particularly solicitous man from their group. He looked like he was old enough to be her father; did he really think he had a chance with her? It was to her credit that she was nice to everyone, but surely she could see past the old geezer's intentions and see his motive. He didn't like this jealous demon that kept lifting its head at the oddest times. He'd never been tempted to lay a man low for a woman, but he sure was now. He forced himself back on his bike and focused on the ocean glistening in the distance.

Gas powered vehicles were not allowed on the island so everyone had a golf cart or a bike. Cyclists had to keep their eyes on the narrow roads because the locals with golf carts weren't always fond of sharing. You could ride but you had to be diligent.

The main road wound around the island with many streets intersecting it, so traffic was heavy at times, especially around the lighthouse and the marina. There were a few opportunities to ride side-by-side, but for the most part Garrett followed Laurel's lead and enjoyed the view.

When an elderly man coming from the opposite direction fell off his bike, Laurel was the first one off hers and racing to him. After checking him over and asking him if he was all right, she insisted he rest for a few minutes with his head in her lap. That was the moment Garrett fell headlong and completely in love with her. He came to the realization that this was no longer about anticipating the great sex or the wonderful chemistry they had going on, but something deeper, stronger—something that made him feel as if living the next thirty-odd years was going to be so much more rewarding than his first thirty. And up to now, he'd had a pretty awesome life, so that was saying something.

In the tower of Old Baldy, the lighthouse that was the main attraction, Garrett was able to touch her as he guided her up the unevenly spaced wooden steps, and then again as she practically fell down from a section of the step staircase. Fortunately he had preceded her down and turned at her gasp just in time to catch her as she tumbled into his arms.

Once the shock of her plunge and subsequent safe harbor registered, she settled comfortably against his more than capable chest, and looking up, their eyes met. For a moment he was sorely tempted to kiss her soft, parted lips. Open, in a perfect circle from surprise, they were the most tempting sight, and the scent from the Werther's caramel candy she had been sucking on earlier made her breath all that more enticing. He loved caramel.

But reason returned and he remembered his directive to go slowly, just as the group turned as one at the bottom to look up at them.

"Laurel, you okay?" Charlene asked.

"Yeah, Garrett broke my fall. I'm fine." She looked back at Garrett, "Thank you," she whispered. Sex personified. He felt his penis jerk.

"You're welcome, anytime," he breathed into her ear as he righted her on the stair above him.

He forced himself to turn back around and descend the remaining steps. The others were waiting at the bottom, all faces focused in concern. He could only hope they weren't looking any lower. He had a raging hard on, but thankfully his tight biking shorts were helping to rein him in.

"She's fine," he reiterated. "Just misstepped on the oddly spaced steps."

That man stared at him with hard eyes, for quite a bit longer than Garret thought he should have and he fought against meeting the challenge in his eyes. Who the hell was he to be warning me off, he thought. What was he to her?

Then he took a good look at the man, and reasoned that if he lost Laurel to the likes of him, he wasn't worth his salt. Older, with thinning silver hair circling a bald pate that was shiny from his exertions, and gray stubble accentuating the daredevil scars on his chin, he no doubt thought he looked rakish, as he was fit for his age. And if his mannerisms were anything to go by, he was still pumping out testosterone just fine. Clearly he wasn't endeared to the woman he had been paired with though. Widowed, and riding in a sixties-style knit pantsuit, she seemed asthmatic and somewhat of a novice to riding, but she made up for it by being cheerful and eager for the experience of joining the group on this trip.

Maybe it was due to the fact that he and his partner seemed so mismatched that Testosterone Man was developing a proprietary air toward Laurel. He guessed that based on their skill level that they had ridden together before. But clearly, he was overstepping his bounds. With animosity coming off him in waves, the man appeared to be stopping just short of calling him out.

The man waited until both he and Laurel had descended the steps, then he used his body to separate them. He was obviously concerned for more than just Laurel's safety. Garrett thought he had done an admirable job coming to her rescue, but no way was this man going to acknowledge that.

"Laurel, you could have been hurt! You have to take your time on these old steps, and for god's sake hold onto the rail. You could have broken something."

"Thankfully I didn't. Luckily Garrett was there to break my fall."

"Well let's not count on luck anymore. And next time *I'll* be there." With a nod to Garrett, he took Laurel's arm and led her down the stone stairs at the entrance.

Laurel looked over her shoulder and shrugged at Garrett, giving him a bright smile. He raised a fine eyebrow to her as a salute to her much in demand charms.

Lunch was next on the agenda, and much as he wanted to elbow his way into the group and steal her attentions, he opted to back off and observe her from outside her circle of adoring friends. He mounted with everyone else, then waited as they all filed by, leaving him to take up the rear. He rode at a brisk pace admiring the sights, drinking in the tang of the sea air, and peddling in one of the lower gears. He told himself that he needed to assuage his own raging hormones and he reminded himself that he didn't want to come off as being domineering. But caveman instincts were warring inside him and although his right fist was gripping the handlebar, clenching and readying itself for battle, he admitted it was one he could not have. He'd overpower this opponent. It would not be a fair fight. Still, somewhere back in his head a voice was screaming that she was his. No one else in the world knew it yet, not even her. But dammit, she *was* his.

He hopped off his bike at Ebb and Flo's Steam Bar and propped his bike alongside a fence while he waited for the others to stow theirs. Then he purposely took the lone seat left at the end of a long picnic table. He needed distance. And she needed a chance to have some dewy-eyed wonder about him.

He ordered a Corona and sat back to watch the traffic flowing in and out of the marina. When he heard her voice call out a greeting to the group as she and Testosterone Man settled into an adjoining table, it was everything he could do not to turn and search her out, and snatch her away from the idiot who thought he could have her.

The cold beer soothed his parched throat and because of that, he didn't give it a chance to warm in the sun. He ordered another, along with a burger all the way, declining the raw onions. *Just in case. A precautionary move at best.*

Chapter Thirty-six

The iced tea went down cold and smooth and the cheeseburger Laurel ordered was cooked to perfection. Picking at her fries as she idly dipped them in a pool of ketchup, she watched Garrett's back. He was enjoying a second beer and bantering with both the waitress and one of the more avid cycle club members, a man retired from an insurance company. They obviously had a lot in common as they were both nodding their heads and talking with their hands when they weren't using them to eat.

How had she gotten stuck eating lunch with the same man she always sat with? The man who had been everywhere and done everything. The last half hour had been one travelogue after another, while the man across from her tried to prove how young he still was by recalling last year's white water rafting trip, his windsailing adventure in St. Kitts, snow skiing with a backpack in Pennsylvania, and mountain climbing in Japan. Now he was detailing why he felt it necessary to spend $6,000 on the new fiberglass kayak he'd just ordered.

Why wasn't Garrett looking at her? Was he purposely ignoring her? Or was he really having a good time chatting with the other members, as it seemed? She excused herself to go to the ladies room and on the way back noticed her lunch partner had vacated his spot. Ah . . . maybe she would order dessert after all.

A few minutes after settling back onto the seat, she was gently nudged to the side as Garrett straddled the bench beside her. He hefted a plate and raised a fork toward her face. "You have to try this cheesecake, it's amazing."

She smiled, clearly delighted to see him, and opened her mouth to receive the forkful of cheesecake he was offering. Her lips closed around the confection and as he pulled the fork away from her lips, the morsel of cheesecake disappeared. He watched as she let it linger on her tongue before she slowly chewed.

"Oh yeah . . . that's superb."

He was entranced by her mouth. "More?"

"Um hmm," she said and closed her eyes while opening her mouth. His breath hitched. *This was so intimate . . . so carnal.*

To an outsider approaching, the scene in front of them was as sensual as the feast from *Tom Jones.* The fork became the connection between the two hungry mouths. Ardently moaning, they were playing it up for fun.

Mountain Man was none too thrilled to return to their side to see the woman he thought of as his lunch date, engrossed in a food fest with his rival.

"Oh, do you want your seat back?" Garrett asked solicitously as he stood, plate and fork in hand.

"Yes, yes I would," the man snapped out. Militarily, he stood aside to give Garrett room to move out of the way.

To his dismay, Laurel stood with Garrett. "Oh no you don't, I go where that plate goes," she said with a devilish grin and she followed him over to a railing that overlooked the marina, where she wrapped her hand over his and practically took the fork out of his hand as a sign that he hadn't been feeding her fast enough.

His nostrils flared wide and his breathing hitched as he watched her over expressive eyes. Her eager tongue tantalized him. It was magical, the way she teased him and had needs tearing through him. *God, she was sexy.*

"Do you think we should get another piece?" he asked, a huge grin on his face as he watched her scrape the plate with the side of the fork. He couldn't believe the immense pleasure he felt over such a silly thing.

"Can't afford it," she said as she slid the last crumbs off the fork with her fingers and fed them to herself. He watched her every movement, imagining his tongue licking the graham cracker crumbs off her bottom lip.

"I'll pay," he stated, biting back a groan at the sight of her tongue licking at the corner of her mouth.

"Oh it's not the money. I can't afford the calories."

He made a show of looking her up and down. "You can afford the whole cake, you look terrific."

"Yeah, well . . . many more lunches of burgers, fries, *and* cheesecake and I won't. I'm going to have to have a salad for dinner tonight, for sure."

Hmmm . . . so, not a vegetarian after all. He visibly let out a breath of relief. "Speaking of dinner tonight, any chance of me providing that salad? I know this place that makes great a really great ginger salad."

"Are you asking me out?" She smiled broadly as she challenged him.

"I am."

"Tonight?"

"Or tomorrow night if you're too tired once we get back."

"I think I'd like that. Tomorrow would be nice."

"Because of the cheesecake today?"

She smiled and nodded, a blonde tendril breaking free from the brim of her visor. She was adorable. He didn't know how he'd wait until tomorrow.

Charlene called out that it was time to get back to the ferry. The dock was only a block away, and from where they were, you could see that the ship was filling up fast. Unless they wanted to wait for the next one, they needed to leave now.

Mountain Man came to walk her back to her bike and Garrett graciously let her go. He could afford to be magnanimous. Tomorrow he would wine and dine her. And with any luck, he might even seduce her. Then he wouldn't have to worry about another man sniffing around her anymore.

If there was anything he was justifiably confident about, it was his skill with women. He would not leave her wanting. He knew her secrets. He knew what she desired. He'd be Casanova with a playbook. She didn't have a chance.

Coming up the stairs to the top deck after checking his bike and using the restroom, he watched Laurel settle in beside her friends on the bow end of the ferry. Timidly she looked over at him and waved with the tips of her fingers. *No, he was not going to come at her urging. And he was not going to fight for a seat next to her like a kid in junior high. As Scarlett O'Hara once said, "After all, tomorrow is another day." He had accomplished what he'd set out to do. He'd met her. It was a bonus that she'd already agreed to meet him again. One step at a time, dangle the carrot and step back he reminded himself.*

He winked at her, then sat back and pulled a book out of his backpack. Max Tucker's latest. As he flipped from page to page he wondered why the young women hitting the bars didn't read his books. It was like being inside the head of the enemy. Even with his latest machinations, he couldn't compete with Tucker's debauched depravity, but his antics sure made for great reading.

Twenty-five minutes later, when the ferry docked, he waited to retrieve his bike, and then he rode it over to Laurel's CRV. Mountain man was attempting to help her lift her bike onto the rack. With one hand, Garrett reached between them, and gripping the frame under the seat, he notched it into place.

When she turned to face him, her nose grazed his chin and she jerked back. He reached out to steady her. Their eyes met and lingered as they each tried to see through the dark lenses of their sunglasses. The late afternoon sun glinted off them obscuring everything behind them. For him it didn't matter, he was solely focused on her lips and suspected she was being equally enticed by his. Her tongue darted out to swipe at her bottom lip. He held back the groan that surfaced but gave into a low "Mmm," as a sigh of approval.

Mountain Man hadn't missed the exchange. And finally getting the message, he stalked off. Garrett had to force himself not to chuckle at the man's haughty displeasure. How could he have even thought he had a chance with someone as sublime, as beautiful, as breathtaking, as Laurel?

He turned back to face Laurel. "So tomorrow then, Asian salads?" he asked, sliding his sunglasses down his nose and looking over them. It was his professor look and he knew without a doubt that it slayed female students.

"Umm yes, I'd like that very much."

"Just tell me what time and I'll pick you up." He hadn't mentioned needing her address and she noted that with an arch of her brow.

"I could meet you there," she hedged.

"I already know where you live, remember?"

She removed her glasses, tucking them into the neckband of her top. A puzzled expression swept over her face as she tilted her head up and met his. "Ahh, so it *was* you taking leave of my rosemary bush."

His reached his hand up and grazed his thumb alongside her jaw. He watched her tremble and felt as if he owned the universe. Every muscle in his body tensed. In that moment he felt as if he could swing from the trees like Tarzan. He forced himself to lower his hand and step back. "Your garden enchanted me, and now it seems so has its owner." He forced levity in their exchange by playfully touching the tip of her nose. "Seven?"

"Sure."

"See you then." Before he could fall at her feet and beg her to take him home, he spun on his heel, got on his bike and rode over to his new truck. Knowing full well that she was following him with her eyes, he grabbed the cross bar of his bike and lifted it onto the rack with one hand. *Let's see Mountain Man do that.*

Chapter Thirty-seven

He drove home singing an old favorite that he had on his iPod. Belting out *Lay Lady Lay*, he congratulated himself on the fact that he had found her. He'd systematically examined each clue, pieced the mystery together and he'd found her—solved the most amazing puzzle of his life. And God, was she ever beautiful.

And yes, he felt like a stalker. The fact that he'd hired a private investigator and because of it, now knew way more than he should at this point in their relationship, made him feel like a snake. But it couldn't be helped. She'd lost something, he'd found it, and he'd made plans to do everything in his power to return it to her. By God, didn't he deserve a little something out of this? But then it dawned on him . . . at this point he really couldn't return it, could he? Not without showing his hand. This could turn out to be a problem down the road, but he didn't want to think about that now.

He wanted to see where this would go. He wanted to woo the woman using the secrets he'd gleaned by reading stories based on her fantasies. He wanted to be the ultimate lover, all knowing, like Mel Gibson in *What Women Want*. He wanted to lead her to the pleasure troth, and to do that he had to bide his time . . . strategize . . . and wait to return her flash drive when it was advantageous for him to show his hand. He had to smile at himself. Would that day need to come? Because really, why ruin a good thing?

As soon as he got out of the shower he made a BLT on toast, filled the edges of his plate with BBQ chips and followed it with a huge glass of milk. Which naturally called for a few Oreos. By eight he was ensconced in his king-sized bed, propped against the teak headboard, his laptop in his lap. He was tired but determined that he was not going to go to sleep without his "bedtime story." Not tonight, not after meeting the gorgeous writer of bedtime stories that literally were meant for the bed.

He opened the file he'd copied from the flash drive and scrolled through the story titles—to the one that had intrigued him earlier. But *The Rake and the Young Innocent*, didn't appeal as much to him now as it had earlier. Now he was in the mood for something contemporary and not quite so long. He clicked on the document file for *The Doctor and the Corporate Raider*. The description of the file length at 15,800 words indicated he could easily read the whole story in one night. And now that he'd cleared his agenda for the evening . . . he was anxious to have a "date' with his writer. The document opened and as he sipped on a robust Cabernet he read.

THE DR. AND THE CORPORATE RAIDER

When Dr. Mallory Greene walked into examining room three, there he was. He was sitting on the end of the examining table, his muscular legs dangling over the side, what was left of the paper skirting they'd given him, crumbled into a ball in his lap.

She was instantly mesmerized by his extraordinary good looks and couldn't help staring for a few seconds at his impressive body, spattered generously in places with thick, curling, dark hair. His nipples were all but completely obliterated beneath the bounty of black hairs fanning out over his chest. What was it about a man with a fan of chest hair over great pecs? She felt that telltale tingle of arousal. Damn hormones.

Taking a deep breath, she forced her eyes upward to his hard planed, yet handsome face and was stunned to see the intense interest she found flashing out of blue eyes framed with thick lashes. A sculptured brow raised in inquiry told her that her presence surprised and intrigued him as much as his did hers.

Forcing calm where there was none, she took a deep breath and crossed the room. "I'm Dr. Mallory Greene, Mr. Ravencross, and I'll be giving you your physical," she said as she approached him and extended her hand. He looked at it for a moment then slowly took his out of the wad of paper and shook it. She could feel the energy in him, the spastic energy that he was so well known for. It was sparking all around him like an invisible curtain of power and she sensed it was suppressed only if he intended it to be.

"Dr. Greene," he said, a tad too formally.

How uncomfortable it must be for him to be at such a disadvantage, sitting semi-naked in front of her for their introduction, she thought.

"I understand we're doing a complete physical, EEG, EKG, all the necessary blood work, a thorough check for any possible melanomas, and a colonoscopy."

"It's a condition of the insurance company representing the company I'm taking over. They insist that their new CEO have a thorough medical exam. I think they're just putting the screws to me because this has been a difficult negotiation. But since this is their last demand, my attorneys insisted that it would be easier if I just complied. But I've never heard of someone having a routine colonoscopy at the age of thirty-eight."

She gave a slight smile as she looked down at his chart. "No, that's not a routine test done for insurance physicals. I guess they just want to be extra sure that their new boss is going to live a long, healthy life."

His guffaw told her that he didn't believe that for a single moment.

"Well, it looks like you've already had all your blood tests, the urine analysis and the EKG and EEG have been done, and only the cancer screening and the colonoscopy are left. I've been assigned to do them both."

"Wonderful," he sighed.

"You can request another physician if you're uncomfortable with a woman Mr. Ravencross. Believe me, I'll understand."

"No. It's all right. Let's just get this over with."

"Okay. First, I'll check your face, then your back, your extremities and finally your torso. I will need you to stand for some of this."

"Fine," he said resignedly and started to get up.

"Not just yet," her hand on his thigh stayed him. She felt a tingle go up her arm from the contact. She placed her clipboard on the counter by the sink while she washed her hands.

He watched her from the back, admiring the long blonde ponytail that was gathered at her nape. It fell nearly to her waist and he was tempted to reach over and run his fingers thorough the silky strands. She turned back to him and he met her startling green eyes with his steely blues ones. She wasn't trying to intimidate, and neither was he, but there it was, both of them simultaneously on the defense and offense as they faced the intimacies that they both knew were coming.

She walked over to him and gently took his face in both hands. The warmth of his chiseled jaw surprised her; she had half expected to feel the chill of marble. She turned his head first one way and then another, trying to get the light to work for her as she minutely examined his face. She was aware of his scent, a combination she drew deeply into her nostrils. It was the perfect melding of spicy pine mixed with the pungent musk of sweat that screamed all male. It emanated from the strong, freshly-shaven jaw she held between her palms. Involuntarily, her thumbs stroked it as her eyes focused on his defining brows, straight nose, high cheekbones, and chiseled, squared-off chin. His lips were soft and full, and if she didn't know any better, she could almost imagine that they were parted in welcome. There was a small scar on his right temple and her finger traced it as she asked him about it.

"Never let a woman with too many rings slap you, one's bound to be facing the wrong way."

"What'd she slap you for?" she asked tentatively, knowing it was none of her business.

"Breech of promise, I think she said. Sadly, I don't even remember if she was right. It was a very long time ago."

"Ah, the vagrancies of youth."

"Something like that."

Using her fingers, she pushed his thick hair back from his hairline as she examined his forehead and scalp. It was very hard to see through hair as thick and lustrous as his. He wore it fairly short, so the best she could do was part it in small sections as she ran her fingers through it.

"I'll give you all day to stop," he murmured huskily and she chuckled.

"You have nice hair," she commented.

"You have nice hands," he replied.

She moved her hands down to his neck, and moving behind him, she felt the back of it. Then her hands splayed out as she ran them over the entire surface of his broad back. His skin was warm to her touch and she could feel the small bristly hairs sprinkled over his shoulders. "A few moles, but nothing I see should be of any concern." She went over to a drawer and took out a small metal ruler with very fine gradations. "I'm going to measure the ones I think we should monitor and note the measurements on your chart. A year from now, we'll see if there are any changes."

For the next few minutes, he felt her press her fingers lightly against each mole to feel if it was raised, then he felt the cold press of the small steel ruler against his skin as she measured in fractions of millimeters.

She finished his back, ending just above the separation of his buttocks. But he knew she'd be getting to them sooner or later and he grimaced at the thought.

He was actually starting to enjoy these minute inspections by this beautiful, young woman. His body was starting to respond to her light touches and he purposefully pressed down on the crumbled wad of paper still sitting in his lap.

She came back around to face him and lifted his right arm. Starting with his fingers she examined his hand, then his forearm and finally his well-defined biceps. "You work out," she murmured.

"When I can. It helps when I'm frustrated."

"Is that often?"

"Depends on my attorneys. Let's just say I should have bought a gym before I started on this particular venture."

"Tough business, huh?"

"It can be, if you let it. I try to stay immune to the emotional parts of it, but sometimes that's just not possible."

"What do you mean?" she asked as she lifted his arm high and gently probed his underarm.

Why the hell did that feel good, he asked himself as he tried to remember what they had been talking about. Oh, yes, the emotional involvements. "When you buy out big companies, people lose their jobs. Lots of people, sometimes."

"And that bothers you."

"Of course it bothers me. It bothers me greatly."

"That's not the impression I get from reading the newspapers."

He sneered, "Of course not. They never get it right. All they think I do is make money every time I put my name on a company."

"But that's not true?"

"Sometimes. But more often than not, when I buy a company, I've saved it from bankruptcy and the loss of every single job there was."

She continued to press into his hairy armpit, searching for lumps. "I'm going to check your breasts now. Could you put your hands on your hips and sit up nice and tall?"

"Check my breasts?" he said with some shock.

"Sure, men get breast cancer too, you know."

Then she was standing back, waiting for him to do as she asked. "Sit straighter and expand your chest for me."

She put her hands on her hips as an example, and took in a deep breath. Her breasts lifted as she tried to show him what she expected of him. What she was showing him was that she had nice, full breasts.

He shook his head, but did as she asked, feeling like Mr. Clean, only with hair and without the earring. She marveled at the totally masculine pose that showed off his expansive chest. He was a god and she was impressed as she took one slightly raised, hairy muscle in her hand and began to knead it. She could hear his breathing change and then his sudden gasp as she rotated the flat areola, grazing the small nipple with her fingertips before moving to the other side of his chest to do the same there.

"Your chest is so hairy that it's pretty hard to say definitively that there are no worrisome moles, but I don't feel any abnormalities, nothing prominent, no raised or non symmetrical ones that I can see. But you know your own body, every once in awhile, when you're in the shower and you can see through the hair, look for any changes in them. You don't have that many, so you must use a good sun block."

"I never miss the chance to have a woman slather me with lotion," he said provocatively.

She cleared her throat, "Well, that's good. Good. Keep it up."

He watched as she visibly cringed at the double entendre and he quirked his lips in response.

She moved to his other arm, examining it, and probing the underarm as she had done to the first. Then she moved back in front of him, stooped, and took one of his dangling legs in her hands. She examined his foot, his shin and his thigh, asking him to spread his legs a little wider please, before doing the same to the other one.

It was time for the rest and they both knew it.

"You'll need to stand up now so I can check the rest of you."

He smiled crookedly and gave a small snort of compliance as he recognized the inevitability of what was coming next.

Not one to be bashful, and not wanting to stand there holding that stupid, insignificant wad of paper to his groin, he got to his feet and left it on the table. And there he stood in all his naked glory. And the splendor of the man did not escape her notice. How could it?

That he was well hung would have been an understatement, he was bordering on massive in his semi-flaccid state and she hoped to God that she didn't do anything to make him expand anymore than he already had.

Quickly, she went around to his backside and admired, uh, examined his smooth, firm cheeks. She'd seen marble statues in museums that didn't look this good, this firm. His cheeks were white compared to the tan he had elsewhere and there were no moles or marks for her to investigate, but her fingers were itching nonetheless to press against the springy flesh that met her eyes. No, that would not be professional; there was absolutely no medical reason to touch him there. She bent to examine the backs of his hard thighs and touched a tiny mole she found there. He jumped forward slightly and she apologized for shocking him. Walking back around to his front, she picked up the chart.

"Sorry, hernia test," she said matter of factly as she pulled on a glove.

He started coughing immediately, well before she reached her hand down and cupped his large sacs.

"Cough once or twice," she instructed and he easily complied, since he'd already been coughing from the very moment he'd seen her put on the glove.

As she gently pushed up and into his scrotum,

she watched his penis jump. Now he was fully engorged and it was all she could do to force herself to avert her eyes. He was magnificent.

Oh, how embarrassing for both of them, she thought, but even so, she was having a hard time keeping her eyes off of him. She cringed when she heard him say, "Okay, I've shown you mine, how about showing me yours?"

She quickly looked up into his face and saw the intense heat in his eyes. Stammering, she replied, "I . . . I think everything looks just fine. If all the tests come back negative, you'll get a clean bill of health. The only thing left is the digital exam and the colonoscopy. They can be done at the same time. I can set that up for two days from now."

He moved to the chair to get his pants, and slipping them on without his underwear, he quickly zipped them up. "I believe I've changed my mind, if it's all the same to you, I'd just as soon have somebody else do those tests."

"Sure. Sure. No problem. I completely understand."

"No, I don't think you do," he said as he walked over to where she stood. There was appreciation in his eyes and something else as he removed the clipboard from her hand and placed it on the counter. He wrapped his large hand around her jaw, extending his fingers so that he cupped her head behind her ear. Ever so slowly, he bent his head and took her parted lips with his. As he savored the feel of her soft, pliant lips against his, his other arm snaked out, encircled her waist and pulled her tightly into his chest. The plundering began in earnest as his lips molded themselves to hers and his tongue continued to delve into her soft, moist velvety mouth, tasting and taking her essence with a fevered passion.

She wasn't going to allow this! This was highly unprofessional. She pushed against his chest, but he wouldn't allow any separation. He held her even tighter and she realized that she had no choice. He was going to take this kiss to the limit whether she wanted him to or not. And now, the soft, warm press of his lips against hers was making her unsure of what it was she truly wanted. His tongue, possessive and sure, traced every nuance of her mouth as his warm, hard chest pressed against her soft, yielding breasts. His manhood fought against the pressure of his zipper to pulse and probe her belly. He didn't bother to rein in the hard ridge that was throbbing and earnestly seeking a place for relief. Her low moan attested to the fact that she had absolutely no control of this situation. He could have lifted her up, placed her on the table and climbed on top of her and she would have been unable to stop him, he had so affected her senses. It occurred to her that this was the type of dream that often woke her at night.

Fortunately, he had more decorum than she did at the moment and he pulled away to stare at her wet, pink lips. "I don't know if you know it or not, but you've been teasing me with your oh-so-light touches and oh-so-gentle probing since the moment we met. I just thought you needed some retribution."

"Well, if I deserved that, then I guess, I can't fault you," she stammered.

"You deserve that and much, much more," he said as he deftly peeled open the collar of her white doctor's coat and revealed her throat and the tops of ample breasts as they strained against the simple, low-cut tank top she always wore underneath. He ran his fingertips across the tops of her breasts and she felt goose bumps break out all over her arms as she shivered. He gave a low chuckle and swooped to kiss a swollen mound of the plumped flesh.

"You've seen all of me, I'd like to see a little more of you. How about dinner tonight?"

"I'm sorry, I can't."

"Are you married?" he asked with sudden apprehension.

"No, involved."

"Yes, you are involved. Tell whomever it was you were going to see, that now you're involved with me," he said as he possessively grabbed her by her buttocks and pressed her up against his hardness. "I'm not going to let you get away with this without some payback," he whispered against her neck.

"I don't understand what you mean, I was just doing my job," she breathed, her eyes focused on his bare chest and then on his neck. The flow of blood advancing into his jugular told her how hard his heart was pumping and she was sure that hers was outpacing his.

"I don't think so. I think you were enjoying your job too much, you took way too many liberties."

"I didn't really."

"Tell it to your attorney, honey."

"What!" she said as she pushed against his chest and jumped back, "I didn't do anything wrong!"

"That's not the way I see it or the way your patients will see it when this becomes public."

"This is blackmail!"

"This is how I do business. Only *leverage* is what I call it. All I'm asking is a simple dinner and I'll consider letting bygones be bygones. No smirches on your reputation, no digs at your professionalism."

"Fine. I'll go to dinner with you! Once, just once."

"Fair enough. I'll send my limo for you at seven.

I'll need your address."

She spun around and wrote it on a prescription pad. She was sorely tempted to give him a bogus one, but somehow she knew that it wouldn't be a good idea to make him angry.

As she handed the paper to him, she retorted, "I'll set up your colonoscopy with Dr. Farrell for two days from now. Here's the prescription for the medicine you'll need to drink the day before and a pamphlet telling you all about the procedure, I suggest you read the entire thing before tomorrow."

"Somehow I can't help sensing you're getting some kind of perverse pleasure out of this."

"Believe it, I am," she hissed.

"Tonight at seven," he crooned softly as he bent to taste her lips once more. She turned her head and pushed away before she stormed out of the examining room, leaving him to finish dressing.

Later that evening as she was getting ready, she was torn between wanting to look her best and wanting to look her worst. What he'd done to coerce her into this a date wasn't very nice, but still, there was an attraction she couldn't deny, and those kisses . . . she had never been kissed like that before. She had never felt a man kiss the tops of her breasts. When he was kissing her, she felt his kisses all the way down to her toes. They went to the very core of her body where her musky wetness was manufactured and sent out in huge tidal waves.

She decided to be big about this and accept this man's attentions with the clinical detachment of the medical professional she was, one who marveled at the body and its many wonderful components. It was curious that she'd never had these feelings before. She was practically engaged to Dr. Sorbing, yet she'd never had an awareness of her body's carnal needs like this before.

Well, she'd have a nice dinner, maybe another lovely kiss or two and then she'd be off, begging an early night due to the surgeries she was scheduled to perform tomorrow. He didn't need to know that they weren't until late in the afternoon.

She slipped into a soft cashmere dress with a stretchy shawl collar that could be worn tight to her throat or off the shoulder, as she preferred. She pulled it up primly to cover her collarbones. The dress had been a gift from her parents on her graduation day from medical school, and even though that had been over three years ago, it was still her favorite. She loved the way it felt against her bare skin. She knew the way it clung to her was revealing, yet she didn't dare spoil the effect with lines from a bra; her panties, the thong type, would cover the essentials, or they would as soon as they came out of the dryer.

The dress was a beautiful vivid blue that set off her complexion and light blonde hair making her feel ultra feminine. She put on a light application of mascara, some pink blush, and slicked her lips with gloss. Then she brushed her hair until it climbed into the air from its own with static electricity, framing her face and giving her an angelic look. There were advantages to being a natural blonde with fair skin, she had that soft, ethereal look.

She was beautiful and she knew it, but she was tired of being singled out for her looks. She wanted people to see the whole package, a woman with a brain and an independent attitude, a woman to be reckoned with, not just someone to stare at over a dinner table.

Unfortunately, most of the men she had dated had been so enthralled by her beauty that that's all they ever did—drool over her and parade her around. When they refused to talk, to really talk to her as if she was a grown up with complex and deep thoughts, she refused to see them again.

Even though she looked the part of a sexy, kittenish plaything, she was not, and she wouldn't be treated that way by anybody. One would have thought that by adding "Dr." in front of her name that things would have been different, but apparently as long as she had long blonde hair and soft blue eyes, they wouldn't be. Men still saw her as something they wanted to play with and they never meant chess. All except for one.

Dr. Jonathan Sorbing didn't treat her like a brainless ball of fluff. He treated her with respect, discussing everything with her so clinically that often it was a detriment to their relationship. He ignored her romantic overtures and didn't press the advantages he might have been entitled to. By seeing her more as a colleague than as a woman, he'd earned her respect though. It was better this way, she thought. At least she knew that he liked her for her mind and not her body. Bodies changed, you couldn't count on them forever.

At seven o'clock her doorbell rang, and still looking in the mirror, she frowned and tugged the shawl collar of her dress down to her shoulders. She'd make him suffer.

Stewart Ravencross, dressed in a designer suit, loomed in her doorway when she opened the door. Too late, she remembered that her panties were still tumbling in the dryer.

"Well hello, princess. My, don't you look divine. I wasn't sure you'd go to the trouble."

"I almost didn't," she said as she grabbed her

small beaded purse and the light cape from the back of the sofa.

He quickly looked around her living room, taking in the tasteful furnishings and the tidiness of the moderately priced apartment. "Nice place," he commented.

"It's home, for now."

"What's that mean?"

"I probably won't be living here a year from now."

"Why not?"

"I'm practically engaged. Remember, I told you that I was involved? Well, I wasn't kidding, I am."

"And how's he handling all this?" With his hand he motioned to the air between them.

"I haven't told him. And I don't intend to. He wouldn't understand. And I'm not sure you do," she snapped. "I'm only accompanying you because I value my medical practice!"

He smiled at her and nodded, not at all convinced, as he ushered her out and closed the door behind her. *Engaged, huh? Hmmm. Shame.*

He followed her to the elevator, tilting his head slightly as he admired her firm derriere so enticingly encased in her shoulder-to-calf sheath. Very nice hips, very nicely rounded bottom—definitely must be a thong, he thought with a smile, though he couldn't see any lines at her hips at all.

As soon as she'd opened the door he'd noted her generous breasts that were not only outlined by the clingy material, but the delineation was defined, as the tips of her nipples prominently pointed themselves as high, hard buds on her chest. He felt himself harden as he watched the sweet sway of her hips while he walked a few feet behind her. He'd had no idea what her shape was this afternoon under that starchy and oversized doctor's coat. But now, now he could clearly see that she would have been any man's dream fulfilled as a stripper, on a stage, with a pole sliding between her legs instead of the prim, intellectual woman who had chosen to become a doctor.

He pushed the elevator button and they waited for the car in silence, each appraising the other out of the corner of their eyes.

Damn! He looked incredible in that black suit with the crisp, stark-white shirt and the crimson and black paisley tie. His dark hair had been combed back from his forehead and she could see his sinister-looking widow's peak. It seemed to enhance his appearance, and she wondered if he might have a penchant toward the dark side. His strong profile with the lips quirked in humor did nothing to tone down his virility. He was definitely a man who was comfortable in his surroundings, she realized as he stood there, his hands in his front pockets as he unnervingly appraised her with his sideways looks.

She smiled at that thought. He had even seemed pretty much at ease this afternoon as he stood naked in front of her, daring her to drink him in. From the hype of the media, she knew of his appeal and how he wielded that sensual power over women, and even if she hadn't, she found out when they reached the lobby of her apartment building. As usual there were several groups of people in the lobby waiting to join their parties.

Almost as one, female heads turned to openly admire the tall, impossibly handsome man escorting the very lovely doctor who was their prim and proper neighbor. Great. This gave them yet another reason to be jealous. Not only was she blessed with terrific looks and enough money to follow her career dreams, now look at her, stepping out on the town with the most attractive man they'd ever set eyes on. They watched as their neighbor was ushered into the waiting limousine and they burned with envy.

"Well, this certainly is traveling in style," she said as she seated herself in the middle of the back seat, forcing him to take the one facing her.

"I never drive in the city anymore. I have a few cars in my garage at my farm in Connecticut, but when I'm in New York, I'm never very far from my chauffeur, too much traffic and too many distractions. It certainly would have been impossible for me to drive tonight with you sitting beside me."

She blushed and gave him a small smile, "Thank you."

"You're welcome. Do you think it might be possible for me to sit beside you, I really don't like riding backward." He put his hand to his stomach. It didn't occur to her that this could be a ploy.

"Oh, sure," she said, immediately accommodating him by sliding over on the leather seat. "I'm sorry, I didn't think about that."

"That's okay," he said as he moved to sit beside her. She didn't see the self-satisfied smirk lifting the corners of his lips.

She noticed that he sat very close, so close that their knees were touching.

"So, anything dramatic happen after I left? Any code blues or emergency appendectomies?" he asked with a grin.

She smiled back at him, "No, just the run of the mill things. I assisted on an in-vitro surgery. We removed a tumor from a five-month old fetus, resected a bowel for a middle-aged man, and set the arm of a battered spouse. Other than that, my day was fairly normal—life in a city hospital."

"Wow, I'm impressed."

"What about you? Make any big mergers?"

"No. But I'm working on one now," he said with a wink.

"Mr. Ravencross . . ."

"Stewart. You can call me Stewart. You've seen me in the all together, I think we can use our first names, Mallory."

"Stewart, then. This is only dinner. I've already told you that I'm obligated to someone else, so as soon as I finish my dessert, I expect you to take me right home."

He put his hand on her knee and patted it, "Whatever you say, Mallory."

He was patronizing her and she knew it. The man had gall, lots of it. They pulled up under the porte cochere of a very large hotel and the driver stopped the car and opened the door for them.

"You're taking me to a hotel for dinner? Let me guess, this is the hotel you're staying in?"

"Well, yes, I do stay here whenever I'm in town. It's my hotel. I own it. So when I'm in the city, it makes sense to save money and stay here, don't you think?"

"You own it?" she asked as she stepped out of the car and looked up, up, up to the top floors.

"It was one of my first acquisitions. I liked the view from the penthouse. C'mon," he said taking her hand in his and pulling her after him, "I'll show you."

They walked through the lobby, garnering a fair share of stares from both the male and female population assembled there, and Mallory noticed that the clerks at the registration desks visibly straightened as they recognized their boss. He led her over to the banks of elevators and took the open one on the far right. When it reached the 65th floor and stopped, he put a key in the control panel and the elevator continued up more two floors.

The bell dinged and a doorman greeted them as they stepped out onto the carpeted hallway. The doorman rushed to open the huge double doors directly ahead of them and smiled as they went inside the suite.

Once inside, she turned to admire first, the impressive foyer, and then the magnificent view out the far windows. She touched his arm, realizing that he, too, was wearing cashmere, and whispered, "You have someone waiting out there all the time just to open the door for you?"

His delighted laugh warmed her with its sincerity. "No, honey, he oversees the running of my households. He travels with me and makes sure everything runs smoothly. My driver alerted him that we were on our way up. Tonight, he's making sure our dinner is served promptly and efficiently, and then he will see to it that all the staff is dismissed, and then he too will discretely disappear."

"We're eating here?" she asked, suddenly even more nervous than before.

"Why not? The view is unparalleled; we can watch the sun set on the city, and my chef is one of the best in the country, if I do say so myself. Does it bother you that we're here?"

"I just thought there'd be other people around."

"Safety in numbers?"

"Something like that."

"Well, I knew I only had one shot, that I'd have to impress you the very first time out of the gate."

"I'm impressed," she said as she stared out at the lights of the city. "But I'm also a little uncomfortable being alone with you, in your home. We just met today."

"Yeah, well, you've read about me and surely you know a lot more about me than I know about you. I'm the one who should be a little leery," he said with a slight nod, "you could do any number of things to me while we're up here all alone."

She laughed at his serious put-on and then bogus expression of worry, and he thought he'd never heard a more charming sound. He took her wrap off her arm and her purse out of her hand and placed them on a burled mahogany table that was elegantly positioned behind a large curving leather sofa. "Come have a seat, I have some champagne chilling for us."

"Oh, I can't drink. I have several surgeries tomorrow."

"Just one," he said as he popped the cork and poured them each a tall fluted glassful of the sparkling golden liquid.

He carried the flutes over to her and waited for her to accept hers before lifting his in toast, "To us, and to a night to remember."

"Stewart . . ."

"It's poor form not to acknowledge a toast," he admonished with a seriously lifted brow.

"To us," was as much as she'd say.

They sipped their champagne as he pointed out the sights of the city below them. A few minutes later they were called to dinner.

They dined in the formal dining room, both of them seated at the same end of a very long table. They regaled each other throughout the meal—he with misadventures in his business travels, her with her days at med school and then with her residency in Boston. They both loved Boston and spent most of the time over the final courses talking about all their favorite places.

They had a simple dinner that consisted of a small spinach salad followed by herb-roasted chicken breasts and asparagus served with a delicious mango chutney sauce. For dessert they had a tiramisu that was made with the lightest and creamiest mocha filling Mallory had ever tasted. She refused the after dinner drink in favor of a cinnamon-flavored cup of coffee. And noted that she was sad that their dinner date was coming to a close.

"This has been very nice Stewart and I thank you very much for having me," she said as she stood up. He rose and walked her back to the other side of the suite to the living room. Soft, low music was playing and he took her hands in his, "Dance with me."

He looked down into her eyes and as they bored into hers, their hypnotizing effect caused her to say, "Yes." She simply nodded and without breaking eye contact, he led her over to the wall of windows to a section of hardwood flooring.

He gently drew her into his arms, putting one hand around her waist while the other held her hand clasped against his on his shoulder. She leaned into him and together they swayed to the strains of the Sinatra's *Come Fly with Me*. Increasingly, he pulled her closer, fitting her hips snugly into his while his hand moved to softly tangle in her hair.

"Your hair is so beautiful, and you can tell it's natural, it fits your coloring so perfectly."

"My mother is Swedish and my father's family is of German heritage."

"It's a nice combination," he said as he brushed his lips against her temple.

She was melting and she knew this could mean trouble. She was so enjoying his touch and the feel of being in his strong arms. The champagne and the glass of wine with dinner were having a telling effect. "I think I should be going now, it's getting late."

He stopped dancing and lifted her chin with his fingertips. "I don't want you to go," he said simply. And then he spun her world as he captured her lips with his and didn't let her go. His hand came up to hold her head to his as he ended one kiss only to realign his lips to take another. After torturous moments of languorously moving his lips over hers, she finally allowed his tongue to breach the barrier of her teeth. He probed for her tongue, twining in and out, chasing it while he alternately sucked and nibbled on her bottom lip.

"Mallory," he breathed against her lips, "I don't know what you're doing to me, but I can't seem to get enough of you. Just the taste of you is driving me wild."

His words were heating her skin and dampening her in secret places. She felt the heat of their embrace, the desire pooling in her center, and she shyly touched her tongue to his. Opening her mouth against his, her tongue timidly sought out his, causing him to groan as if in pain.

His lips seared into hers and his tongue parlayed with hers and then he dropped his head and kissed the long column of her neck, showering her with one hot, burning sensation after another. When his lips found their way to her bare shoulder, he used the palm of his hand to ease the soft knit off her shoulder all the way to her elbow, exposing her breast to his waiting hand. His palm curved and he cupped the soft fullness of her, hefting the weight of her fleshy mound in his hand while his thumb grazed the peaked nipple. It was her turn to groan and he thought he would die from the sheer pleasure of hearing it. He bent to take her nipple in his mouth and she swooned against him, unable to support herself from the sudden buckling of her knees and the collapse of her legs. He caught her in his arms, lifted her, and carried her to his bedroom, never once taking his mouth from her breast.

As tenderly as he could, he placed her on the soft linens of his turned down bed. He kicked off his shoes and followed his body down to hers. As he stretched out beside her, he heard her mumble something, and desperate not to have her deny him, he covered her mouth with his.

He plundered her mouth with his unfurled tongue thrusting and retreating until the rhythm was so compelling that she finally had to reach her hands up to hold his head to hers so she could follow his lead. He had one hand under her shoulders holding her to him, while with the other he stripped her dress down past her knees. When he felt, more than heard her gasp against his mouth, he slid his hand up along her outer thigh, grazing her hip and hugging her waist before caressing her breast again.

Instinct took over as he subtly read every nuance of her body as it responded to his. He kept one step ahead of her as he imparted pleasures she was not accustomed to, forcing her body to feel and luxuriate in the primitive urges a woman was designed for.

He sighed with pleasure as his hand roamed over her chest; a woman with breasts this large and responsive was every man's dream, and as she moaned to every type of caress he used on them, his body grew hard and demanding. Moving his lips from one fully distended nipple to the other, he used his hand to caress her waist, her flat abdomen and then to delve into the region between her legs.

He cupped her as his middle finger fluttered against her smooth labial lips, beckoning them to open to his touch. They blossomed like the full ripe petals they were and he groaned at the silky slickness. "You are so wet," he murmured into the cleft between her breasts. He licked her cleavage and the underside of her breasts, enjoying her sweet floral fragrance and her ripe, young flesh as he drew his tongue down her body. That he had a definite target in mind should not have surprised her, but at this point, her mind was mush.

When his mouth grazed her soft blonde mound, he felt her hands reach out to stop him. He knew he had to act quickly or all would be lost. She couldn't come to her senses now; he couldn't stand the agony of it if she did. His lips joined his fingers where they were opening her wide for him and he licked and sucked on her feminine lips while lower on the bed, he insinuated his body between her legs. Her dress had slid to her ankles and it only required a flick of his wrist to send it to the floor so he could lift her legs to his shoulders. Had he known during dinner that she'd had no underwear on, he would never have been able to sit still; he'd thought she was at least wearing thong panties. Oh, she was being naughty—naughty for him. The thought made him shiver. His tongue darted into her as his hands gripped and stroked her thighs keeping her legs spread wide for him.

"Stewart, no. We mustn't . . ." Too late, he had her completely open, her knees bent, her feet on his back, his arms holding her thighs wide as he licked and kissed and lapped at her. Running his tongue up and down inside her slit, he reveled in her juices, enjoying the musky taste and slick feel of her against his tongue and lips.

Expertly, he tongued and fingered her, inching back with some regularity to examine her glistening, gaping opening. Greedily, he went back for more, each time concentrating a little longer on the top of her slit where a hard bud had emerged, trembling and throbbing. Mercifully, he finally gave in to her soft, mewling pleas and took the small, full nub between his lips and sucked. As he felt it contract, and her body respond with an answering shudder, he grasped her buttocks to pull her even closer, giving him unlimited access to fuck her with his tongue. Fast. Hard. Deep. He felt her convulse against his lips, heard her cry of ecstasy as it echoed around the room and he delighted in the sheer satisfaction of giving her such unbridled pleasure that it caused him to feel the urgency of his own release.

He quickly reached down and undid his pants, pushing them down around his knees. He fished for a condom in one of the front pockets, tore it open with his teeth, pulled it out and with nimble fingers rolled it onto his throbbing erection. While she was in a post climactic daze, he mounted her, positioned himself at her opening and entered her. He hadn't gone far when he met resistance. Thinking he was improperly aimed, he pulled out and entered her again, this time more forcefully. And suddenly, without a single doubt in his mind, he knew that he had just broken through her hymen.

Too late to undo anything, he took a moment to revel in the incredible sensation of feeling of her tight sheath surrounding him. Then, totally taken with her and full of a heady lust such as he'd never before experienced, he thrust forward, pinning her to the bed and filling her completely. Sliding his hand between their bodies, he used his thumb to worry her clit as he drove in and out of her. When she shattered for him with a loud, harsh sob, the sound reverberated throughout his body and he moaned. It wasn't surprising that he was only good for a few short thrusts and one deep, soul-jarring kiss before he was so consumed with passion and his incredible desire to possess her that he couldn't control himself. Gripping her buttocks, he fully seated himself in her and exploded with the most incredible orgasm he'd ever had in his life. It left him weak and completely drained as his head fell alongside hers on the pillow. After a moment to recover, he propped himself up on his elbows to keep the bulk of his weight off of her, and he gasped, "Jesus, Mallory! Why didn't you tell me you were a virgin?"

"I don't remember the subject coming up. The last thing I remember saying was, 'Stewart, we mustn't . . .'"

Between huge gulps of air he managed to get out, "Why *are* you a virgin, for God's sake?" If truth were told, he actually sounded angry about it.

"I wanted to save myself for my husband."

As her words sunk in, he groaned. His forehead met hers and his eyes closed. "Oh, Mallory, I'm so sorry."

But deep down, in his true heart, he wasn't. A part of him was thrilled that he had been the first and now the only with this incredibly beautiful and sexy woman. But he was sad that he had taken something from her that maybe she hadn't been ready to give.

"That's not exactly what a woman wants to hear a man say when she's just given herself to him."

"You didn't give yourself to me, I took you. I used every trick in the book to keep you senseless and I took you. I am so sorry."

"I wish you'd stop saying that. Couldn't you just tell me you couldn't help yourself because you wanted me so much, and that it was the most wonderful feeling you've ever had? That would at least make me feel like my virginity wasn't completely wasted."

"Oh, Mallory, it wasn't wasted, trust me. And it goes without saying that I wanted you. I've wanted you since the moment you walked in and said, 'Hi, I'm Dr. Mallory Greene and I'm here to give you your physical.' Mallory, that was the most incredible climax I've ever had. It's never been this good, ever. No darling, it wasn't wasted," he said as he smoothed a strand of hair off her cheek.

"Well, that's much better. And, you did toast to a night to remember," she said with a sheepish grin.

"Mallory, I will always remember tonight. I would have even if you hadn't been a virgin. You are a beautiful woman and your body is so responsive, you're absolutely incredible."

"That's funny. It never has been before. I don't think I've ever been so turned on. As much as it pains me to say it, I wanted you badly, very badly."

"Why does it pain you to say it?"

"Because I'm spoken for, remember? I'm not supposed to be here in your bed, with you."

He grinned down at her, "Yeah, but now that you are . . . how about an encore?" he said mischievously. He pressed into her and she felt his burgeoning thickness filling her. Instinctively, she pushed back and he groaned his pleasure at the reciprocal movement. "Wait, I have to get a new condom."

He slid out of her, stood and shucked off his pants, shirt and socks before opening the nightstand drawer and taking a foil packet from the box inside. Only when he removed the one he had on and saw it stained with blood did he think to ask how she was and to reconsider whether a repeat performance was prudent. By no means had he been gentle with her.

Assured that she felt fine, he came to stand

beside her. She had pulled up the duvet and used it to cover herself. Her creamy white shoulders were a stark contrast to the crimson red satin. She saw him looming over her and she knew without a doubt that what they were getting ready to do, yet again, was wrong and unconscionable. But one look at the desire burning in his eyes and the powerful, furred chest that she had so carefully examined today, and she melted with her own desire. She watched him put the condom on his long, thick penis and then he was on top of her, positioning himself as his head ducked to capture a long hard nipple in his mouth.

Her fingers delved into the thick mat covering his chest and found his nipples. His low moan ended with a growl. This time he took it nice and slow, letting her feel the power of his thrusts and the dizzying sense of completeness as he filled her again and again. Just when she was convinced nothing could ever feel as good, he pinned her to the bed by gripping her wrists together above her head while pumping like a crazed ramrod into her.

Fast, quick jabs that stroked her right where her body needed to be stroked, and then she was gone, gone into an oblivion she could never have imagined, a place where every kind of color burst into the velvety blackness as she traveled away from earth and everything rocked out of place. She vaguely remembered hearing Stewart cry out, "Oh God," before he groaned her name and bit the side of her neck. He collapsed, so relaxed and so drained that he felt he had left his body.

A few minutes later, she tapped him on the shoulder and said, "I want to thank you for dinner, but I really must go now. I have surgery tomorrow."

He mumbled something unintelligible and then

eased out of her. "Can't you spend the night? I can have my driver take you home early in the morning."

She sat up and held the sheet against her chest. She looked so adorable with her rosy cheeks and her fair complexion. She had little red marks in all the places he had kissed her last, her skin being so sensitive they easily showed, and there were teeth marks where he had nipped her. Her blonde hair was mussed and draped over her shoulders, and she looked infinitely lovely. He wanted her all over again.

"Stewart. I can't do this. This was not supposed to happen. I'm your doctor. I could get into big trouble over this."

"How? I seduced you, remember?"

"Is that what this was?"

"No! Of course not! I don't want you to go. I want you to stay here with me. In my bed."

"I can't. I have to go."

"Fine!" he said angrily as he stood and gathered up his clothes. "I'll take you home." He picked up the phone by the bed and punched in two numbers. "I'll need my car and driver downstairs in twenty minutes." He hung up the phone. This was a man who always got what he wanted and it didn't seem that he even needed to say please.

"I want to see you again."

"Impossible. I'm practically promised."

"Then get unpromised. I want to see you again."

"No, Stewart. I can't do that."

"Friday night, I'll pick you up at eight."

"Friday night I will be at the Heart Ball with Dr. Sorbing."

"Is that your beau?" he asked sarcastically.

"He's my intended, if that's what you mean."

"How's he going to feel about all this?"

"I don't intend to tell him."

"Did he know you were a virgin?"

"He knew definitively that I was a virgin."

"What's that mean?"

"He's an OB/GYN."

He spun around and stared at her, his eyes wide with shock and disbelief, "You let him *examine* you?" He said the word examine as if it meant something incredibly filthy.

"Well, I needed an exam. It was purely clinical."

He walked over to her, gripped her by her arms, and held them to her side as he challenged her, "You mean you laid on a table, spread your legs as wide as they could possibly go and let a man examine you, one whom you're romantically involved with, but not sexually involved with?" He made it sound like something sick. And he also sounded somehow possessive, as if her almost fiancé didn't have the same rights that he had just taken.

She broke out of his hold, "It was purely clinical! Doctors do those kinds of things all the time for each other."

He put his hands on her shoulders and turned her back to him. He looked deeply into her eyes. "If any man, who's thinking of making you his wife, can see you displayed like that and not have the overwhelming desire to take you and make you his, he is not going to make you happy. I may not know a lot about you, but I think I do know a little about your sexual nature, and this Dr. Sorbing, isn't the man for you. Did he do a breast exam, too?" More sarcasm.

She looked up into his piercing blue eyes and simply nodded.

"And that was completely clinical, also?"

Again, she just nodded, this time adding a raised

brow in defiance.

"Honey," he said as he took her balled up dress from in front of her, "I can't see how any man could look at you clinically." He looked down at her breasts as she stood naked before him. "If this man had the opportunity to see and touch these delicious mounds and was not overcome with desire to suckle them and caress them lovingly, then he can't possibly be in love with you. In fact, he's probably gay."

She smiled up at him as she gently took her dress back from him. "He loves me, and he's not gay."

"So what are you going to tell him on your wedding night, when he finds out that you're no longer a virgin?"

"I'll think of something—stretched my legs too far in Yoga class or something." She slipped into her dress, tossed her hair over her shoulder and started looking for her shoes. "Now I really must go," she said as she found them under his shirt and started to put them on.

He took the shirt from her hand and put it on. As he buttoned it, he appraised her, "There's a brush over there on the dresser you can use, you look a little loved."

"Thank you," she said as she walked over to his dresser and used the brush to smooth her hair.

He ran his fingers through his hair as he watched her in the mirror, "Damn it, I'm not letting you go this easily."

"Stewart, you have no say in the matter."

"The hell I don't! I'm the man who took your virginity!"

"And I will always be grateful that you did it so nicely. I have never had an orgasm I hadn't orchestrated and tonight, you pleased me in so many ways." She gave him a big smile in the mirror and then got a faraway look in her eyes. "I will miss that if Jonathan isn't as good as you are in the bedroom."

He slapped his hand flat against the doorframe, making a startlingly loud noise as he cursed. "I can guarantee you that he's not even close." Then he stalked out of the bedroom to wait for her by the front door.

They rode down the elevator in silence and when the doorman opened the door for them, he waited for her to precede him before following her out. Always the gentleman, she thought. Jonathan didn't know all the intricacies of being a gentleman. He probably would have bolted in front of her as soon as the doorman had opened the door, his sense of sexual equality being what it was. Then she chided herself; it wasn't fair to compare him to this man. They were on opposite ends of the spectrum, from two totally different worlds. Their lifestyles were as different as night and day. Jonathan ate a bagel for breakfast in the hospital cafeteria; Stewart probably had a complete kitchen staff fix him a full-blown buffet. And she knew she'd have a lot more in common down the road with a doctor as her husband than with some spoiled millionaire—a playboy financier who wasn't even the marrying sort to begin with.

When they were both in the back seat of the limo, he pulled her over to him and tucked her under his arm. He softly kissed the hair at her temple as he whispered to her, "It goes without saying that I had a wonderful time tonight."

She looked up at him and smiled, and it was that smile that broke his heart.

"I did, too. Although, I still don't think I did anything wrong today while I was examining you. Oh, by the way, I forgot to tell you that Dr. Farrell's on vacation, he can't do your colonoscopy. It'll have to be me. Or maybe, I can get Jonathan to do it. He can unknowingly vindicate himself for you taking his wife's virginity," she said with a huge satisfying grin.

He looked down at her and shook his head, "No thank you. Never mind, I'll get my attorneys to get that part of the exam stricken from the insurance clause, either that or I'll have it done by my own doctor when I'm in Connecticut next week."

"That would probably be better."

"Yeah," he said as he bent to kiss her on the temple. Followed by one on her lips.

What started out as a little love peck, turned into a passionate kiss that grew into full-fledged desire and soon, he had her pulled onto his lap.

His hand slipped under her dress and she stiffened. "The driver . . . don't," she said as she stopped his hand from going any higher.

"Honey, he can't see a thing. Nobody can. It's one-way glass all around."

His hand resumed its upward journey. "If I have to say good bye to you forever, I'd like to make love to you one more time."

"Here?" she squeaked.

"Honey, I swear to you, he can't see a thing. Here, I'll prove it." He pressed a button on a console in front of him and spoke to the driver, "Tony, if you can tell me how many fingers I've got up, I'll give you a thousand dollars." He put three fingers up and they heard Tony over the intercom say, "Five." He and Tony played this game all the time. Stewart always held up three fingers and Tony always said five and no one was the wiser. But, you really couldn't see through the glass, much to Tony's chagrin.

"Can't we just go up to my place?"

"No," he said firmly. "Here." He laid her back against the leather as he slid her dress up to her waist. "I have to tell you, I was shocked to find you had no underwear on tonight, it just didn't seem like you. No bra, no panties . . . so accessible," he murmured as he bent and kissed her flat tummy. "Hell of way to dress for a first date."

"You have to wear thong underwear with this dress or all you can see is panty lines. And I only have one pair of thong underwear. I had just washed them out by hand and they were in the dryer when you came to the door. I didn't think it would be appropriate to ask you to wait while I put my panties on, so I just left without them." She was suddenly conscious that she was rambling like a nervous schoolgirl.

He hooted with laughter, "Well, I didn't mind you not having any," he said as he took a condom out of a side console. "Here, this time you put it on, I want to feel you touch me," he said in a deep, husky voice, "without gloves," he added. With his other hand he held down the intercom button, "Tony, how about a nice, long drive around the park?"

"Yes sir."

He released the button and simultaneously groaned as her hand delved into his opened zipper and found its reward.

The next day, twelve pairs of designer thong underwear with matching bras and two-dozen red roses were delivered to her apartment. The note attached to the box of underwear said: "I would love to see you in these, Stewart."

She looked at the sizes and realized he had gotten them exactly right. This was a man who knew women.

On Friday, she got the shock of her life when someone cut in on her and Jonathan while they were dancing at the Heart Ball. Jonathan graciously stepped aside and Stewart gathered her firmly into his arms as he murmured into her ear, "He doesn't seem the type to put his head between your legs and get a soft, curly blonde hair stuck between his teeth for two days."

In her shock, her eyes went wide and she pushed back from his chest as he led her effortlessly around the ballroom. Their eyes met and held. "It's quite all right. I finally got it out this afternoon. Your hairs down there are very thin and silky, had a devil of a time with it, but I bought this extra fine floss, and voila, it was out. So I'm ready for the next time."

"Stewart, we've had this out already. There will be no next time. And thank you very much for the roses and the underwear."

"I want to see them on you," he said huskily, his warm breath fanning her neck as he leaned down to whisper into her ear.

"Well, I'll see if Jonathan will mind an audience during our honeymoon."

"You're not going to marry him."

"That's where you're wrong."

"Can you honestly tell me that you're in love with him, Mallory? Because if you can, I'll waltz you right over to him and deposit you into his arms."

Slowly her eyes met his and he had his answer. "I thought not. So what's the big deal with marrying him? You could do a lot better." He looked over at Jonathan who was talking to a fellow physician. "He's already getting a paunch, or hadn't you noticed?" His lips moved close to her ear again and he whispered, "The bite mark I gave you has faded, I'll have to give you another."

"He's stable and we'll have a lot to talk about. Stimulating conversation is very important in a marriage."

"So, talking about someone's hernia, bypass, kidney stones, hysterectomy, or gall bladder is exciting to you?"

"You make it sound so awful."

"How about if I tell you what I'd like to be doing to you right now, in medical terms? How exciting would it be to know that I want my testicles slapping your luscious vulva with each reinsertion of my erection as we achieve coitus? Intercourse, if you will—my hard penis separating your silky labia and us copulating as I fill your nice warm vagina? I would like to feel your throbbing clitoris clench against my genitals as you achieve orgasm and I ejaculate my semen deep inside your vaginal cavity, this, while suckling on your areola, nibbling on your nipple, and gently stroking your sphincter muscle."

The flow of her whole body seemed to have altered with his words and she felt an incredible surge of wetness at the juncture between her legs. Just then Jonathan strode across the floor to reclaim her.

"Uh oh, lover boy's coming back. Listen, I have to leave town tomorrow, tell me what time I can come see you tonight."

"You can't."

"I'm going to, so either give me a time that's safe, or I'll come whenever I want. I'll be waiting when lover boy drops you off. I wouldn't mind him knowing there's some competition, and by the way, I love your hair like that." He was referring to the elegant chignon that was twisted and pinned to the back of her head and to the soft curls piled on top.

"You wouldn't dare!"

"Give me a time," he said firmly.

"Midnight."

"Isn't that a bit late?"

"We have a party after this one and I'm not exactly sure what time I'll be home. I know I'll definitely be home, alone, by midnight."

"Midnight it is," he said as he leaned down to whisper in her ear: "Wear some of the new underwear for me."

Then he was gone. He completely vanished into the crowd. She couldn't prevent the blush that crept up her cheeks and when Jonathan asked her who that man was, she was sure it deepened. "Stewart Ravencross," she murmured as her hand went to the spot below her ear that had just been kissed.

"Where'd you meet him?"

"At work. He was a patient."

"Really? What's the matter with him?"

In her mind she thought, nothing, absolutely nothing, but aloud she said, "Can't discuss it, doctor-patient privilege, you know."

"Yes, yes. I understand. Do you want to get some more punch, it's not as sweet as it was last year, but it's still very good."

"Sure, lead on," she said as her eyes scanned the room.

From the balcony several floors above, Stewart Ravencross gazed down on her as she searched for him. All was not lost. He'd have her again.

Shortly after midnight, Mallory answered the soft knock on her door. Stewart, sporting a big grin greeted her. He was dressed in casual city clothes, a far cry from the formal tuxedo she'd seen him in just a few hours earlier.

"Hi babe," he said in a sexy, cocksure voice. He was leaning on the doorjamb and he pushed off of it to take her into his arms. Her hair was down now, the curls lying haphazardly over her shoulder. She was wearing a thick velour robe and as soon as the door swung shut behind him, his hands untied the belt and spread the lapels. His hands, moving to her bare shoulders parted it wide so he could see that she was wearing a purple, low cut demi-bra with the skimpiest underwear to match.

"I knew you'd wear them for me. Come here," he said as he let the robe fall off her shoulders. He gathered her into his arms and hugged her tightly to him as his lips sought hers and he kissed her thoroughly, a kiss she felt reverberating throughout her body. He bent, put his arms behind her knees and picked her up before carrying her into the bedroom.

"Stewart, we can't," she pleaded as he laid her down on her already rumpled bed.

"Oh, don't tease me Dr. Greene. Why can't we?" he asked, a big smile on his face as he settled his body on the bed beside hers.

He was still smiling at her fledgling attempt to deny them what they both wanted when she lifted her hand and flashed it in front of his face and he saw the diamond on her finger that was sparkling in the soft bedroom lighting. He grabbed her hand to still it and backed away so he could see it.

"He gave you this tonight?"

She nodded.

"And you accepted?"

She nodded again.

"Why?" he asked and the tone of his voice conveyed some of the pain and annoyance that he was feeling.

"It's been in the works for a long time. We met during our residency and it's been sort of assumed all along that this would eventually happen."

"Wait a minute, you've known this guy for at least four years, he does your gynecological exams, yet you've never been intimate. We know each other one day and end up in bed. Mallory, doesn't something seem a little off kilter here?"

"He's known all along that I wanted to wait until our wedding night."

"Okay, so for four years you hold him off, yet in one day, I meet and bed you. Doesn't that strike you as being a little odd?"

"He doesn't have the way that you have with women. He doesn't have your touch."

He stroked the tops of her breasts, provocatively pushed up and peeking out of the scalloped edges of her lacy bra. "And you're willing to settle for that?"

She looked into his face and he could see tears forming in her eyes but he wasn't about to let her off the hook.

"Let me remind you one more time of what you're going to be missing," he said as he slipped the strap down off her shoulder, exposing the hardened peak just aching for his touch. He wrapped his lips around it and then he let his teeth nip at it before squeezing the hard, wet nub between his fingertips. Her soft moans of pleasure were all the encouragement he needed. He reached behind her and with one practiced touch popped her bra open. He loved her breasts, they were perfect, and he showed her just how much he adored them by paying homage to them as he caressed, kneaded, and tweaked her hard nipples between his fingers. He pulled her over on top of him so that the luscious mounds fell into his mouth and he suckled her until she couldn't stand the sweet pleasure any longer and begged him to take her.

"Why don't you try mounting *me* tonight?" he asked as he moved the small strip of cloth down off her hips.

"I don't know how."

"I'll show you," he said as he unzipped his pants and shimmied them down past his thighs. "Here," he said as he handed her a condom. "Remember what you're supposed to do with that?"

"Umm hmm," she said taking the condom out of the wrapper and placing it on the tip of his swollen member. Slowly she slid the soft membrane on, letting her hand follow it down until she was caressing the base of his penis. His sharp gasp caused her to look into his face in alarm, "Did I hurt you?"

"Ahh . . . no. But you'd better hurry and get on this thing. I'm not sure how long I'm going to last. You rob me of control. You manage to diminish my capabilities with your sweet, yet unbelievably erotic innocence." He lifted her by her hips and slowly impaled her, amazed at how wet she was and more than a little pleased by how very tight she was.

"Straddle my thighs. Now take me all the way inside you, lean forward a little if you can. Ahhh. Yes. Just like that. God, I don't know if I can stand this. You feel too . . . unnhh . . . too wonderful for words." He ran his hands around her bottom and caressed her smooth cheeks, but soon he put them firmly back on her hips so he could guide her. He lifted her and then eased her down. "Ride me, sweetheart. Lift yourself up using your knees and then slide down, but be careful not to come all the way up or you'll dislodge me."

She did exactly as he said and soon the slapping of flesh echoed throughout the room. She enjoyed being in control and soon increased the tempo and intensity and was rewarded with a soul-rending moan of delight. His hand reached out, cupped her neck, and brought her face down to meet his. His lips sought hers and he frenziedly plunged his tongue in and out of her as she straddled him and rode him hard. His other hand reached out and fondled her breast and then it delved to the juncture where their bodies were joined and he sought her pleasure spot with his fingers. He massaged her as she continued to rock up and down on him and then suddenly she arched her back, threw back her head and with a most rewarding guttural sound escaping her lips, she came against his stiff member and his circling fingers. He arched his body off the bed and gripped her hips as he repeatedly rammed up into her. An anguished cry joined hers as he shuddered and careened off into a dark, sweet haven while each pulse pumped essence from his body.

Sensations of an eerie weightlessness accompanied his body as it drifted back to hers and to the reality of the soft bed covers under him and the warm, soft body on top of him.

The word "spent" came to mind, and it held a totally new meaning; he couldn't even hold his hands up to stroke her. Sweat-covered and sated, they folded into each other, holding hands as if they were lifelines on the edge of the world.

After a few minutes, where all you could hear was their breathing settling back into even patterns, he reached over and moved a strand of hair that was covering her eyes.

"Are you sure you should be doing this with me on the night you became engaged to somebody else?" he teased as he stroked the length of her backside.

She didn't answer; she just lay curled into his

body, her fingers exploring the rigid muscles of his chest as she tried to catch her breath.

She was the first to fall asleep and as he lay there watching her, he couldn't remember a time when he had ever been so content. The only thing that spoiled it was the knowledge that she belonged to someone else.

He snuggled up to her spoon fashion and wrapped his hand around one full breast, the other reclined on her hip as he breathed in her gentle fragrance of gardenias. He fell asleep wondering when he had ever been happier.

When she awoke the next morning, he was already out of bed, making coffee for them in her kitchen. "I got up early so I could shower and get out of your hair so you could get ready for work," he said as he came into the room carrying a tray with coffee and chocolate croissants.

"Where'd you get them?" she asked, pointing to the French pastries.

"I sent Tony."

"That poor man had to sleep in the limo all night?"

"It wouldn't be the first time, and the limo's back seat is really pretty comfortable, I've spent quite a few nights there myself."

"Forget to pay your rent?" she teased as she took a big bite out of the croissant.

"No," he said as he swatted her backside when she walked across the room to the bathroom, "sometimes I have to travel from one place to another at night, it's not as comfortable as a hotel room, but I get where I have to be on time. And speaking of travel," he said as he watched her brush her hair, "I'm leaving this morning for two weeks."

"Where are you going?" she asked, trying to

keep the disappointment out of her voice.

"San Francisco, Seattle, Minneapolis-St. Paul, Boston, and then back to Connecticut and New York."

"Phew, do you always travel so much?"

"Not usually for so long. I wrote down some numbers for you, the hotels that I plan to be staying in and my personal assistant's number. She always knows exactly where I am—she can find me anywhere."

"Does she know where you are right now?" she asked with a grin.

"Well, not exactly. But she could have me on the phone in less than five minutes."

"Really?"

"Yeah, there's a phone in the limo and Tony knows where I am."

"Amazing."

"Hey, you won't be married by the time I get back will you?" he asked suddenly very worried.

"Not hardly. Jonathan and I have yet to set a date, and I doubt that it will be before the end of the year. It takes almost a year these days to plan a big wedding, but he wants to do it in six months or less."

"Finally getting impatient?" he teased as he lifted a strand of her hair away from the chocolate on her lips.

"No, he's just a task master."

"Do you want a big wedding?"

"No, not really. But his mother does and I don't object. My parents won't be thrilled about the money it'll cost since they're still helping me pay off my student loans, but I'm going to do everything I can to keep it simple and inexpensive for them."

"What a good daughter."

"I don't feel so good, in fact I feel like I've been pretty naughty lately."

He came up behind her and wrapped his arms

around her middle. "You have indeed and I've enjoyed every minute of it."

Their eyes met in the mirror and they wordlessly communicated something to their souls that even their conscious minds couldn't quite grasp. He started kissing the back of her neck as he told her that he was going to call her every night and that he expected her to clear her schedule and make herself available the day he came back into town.

Rather than argue a point that would undoubtedly come up later, she simply nodded her head as he enfolded her in his arms. "I have to go now, I have a plane to catch, but I'll call you tonight. Is ten o'clock all right?"

"Yes," she said as she lifted her face for his kiss. She knew that it would be their last and she tried to melt his soul into hers with it.

"Wow, I can't wait to get back. I can feel my *toes* tingling," he said with a smile and a sexy wink, and then he was gone.

An incredible sadness washed over her as she showered and dressed for work, a bereft feeling as if she was suddenly all alone in the world.

At ten o'clock that night, she was sitting on the sofa waiting for the phone to ring. At ten fifteen it finally did. Breathlessly, she answered the phone, "Hello?

"Hi Mal. I was just thinking; remember that church we went to last year for Justin and Carol's wedding? What do you think about that for ours?" It was Jonathan, not Stewart and she was so crushed that she almost sobbed into the phone.

Her voice was suddenly wobbly as she answered him, "I think it's a bit ostentatious, all those forty-foot, stained-glass windows and rows upon rows of pews, we'd never come near to filling them. Besides, we're not Baptists."

"I just thought the altar looked regal, but if it's not what you want, we'll keep looking. You feeling all right, you sound tired?"

"I have a slight headache, would you mind if I went to sleep now?" She had to get off the phone; Stewart could be trying to call her right this very minute.

"No, I don't mind. Get some rest, I'll see you tomorrow."

As soon as she hung up the phone, it rang.

"Who were you talking to?" Stewart asked gruffly.

Mallory smiled at the sound of his voice. "Jonathan. He called to tell me he found a church for us."

"Wonderful," he said with absolutely no enthusiasm.

"How was your flight?"

"Long, bumpy, crowded. I always book two seats in first class so I can spread out and get some work done, but this time a stewardess felt it was her obligation to keep me company with her mindless drivel. I am seriously thinking that it's time I got my own plane."

She felt a sudden pang of jealousy that was as foreign to her as low-fat cottage cheese would be to a gourmand. "She was probably just lonely."

"Lonely, my ass. She was husband shopping."

"Are you on the market?" she chided.

There was silence on the other end of the line for half a minute before he answered, "I hadn't really thought about it all that much. What exactly are *your* reasons for wanting to get married?"

"I want to have children. Two, one boy, one girl,

or two boys or two girls."

"I think those are all the possible combinations you can have for two children," he teased.

She laughed and he relaxed against the pillows propped up on the headboard almost three thousand miles away, God, he loved that sound.

"What color underwear did you wear today?" he asked in a low, sexy voice.

"That really vivid lime green set. Neon chartreuse I think it's called."

"I can't picture it. Wear the red tomorrow, that I can picture."

"These bras make me look busty."

"Sweetheart, you *are* busty," he replied and she could hear the pride in his voice.

She yawned and stretched. "I have to turn in now, for some reason, I didn't get a lot of sleep last night and I have a 6:30 surgery tomorrow morning."

"Okay, I'll let you go. I'll call you again tomorrow night. Good night."

"Good night," she whispered.

Regardless of what she said about needing to get some sleep, she wasn't able to fall asleep for several hours. Her mind was all knotted up and her body was actively searching out the warmth of another's as she tossed and turned until finally falling asleep.

She knew the reason they lost the patient the next morning was not because she was tired. It had been a high-risk operation from the very beginning. But the guilt she felt still weighed her down as she went from patient to patient, and then finally drove home. Jonathan had heard about the patient who had died and came over to console her. This was the thing they had in common, they understood these things. It was a forged bond. He brought pamphlets from a travel agency and together they sat on the sofa trying to decide their honeymoon destination.

When the phone rang at ten, she jumped. The phone was on the opposite end of the sofa and since she had become used to Jonathan answering it when he was there, she quickly flopped over him to get to it first. Then she moved all the way back to her side of the sofa before she answered it. "Hello?"

"Hi, sweetheart."

"Mom, I can't talk now, Jonathan's here and we're planning our honeymoon. Can we talk tomorrow?"

He didn't even answer her. He slammed the phone down and cursed a blue streak as he paced back and forth in his hotel suite. The feelings he had were so intense that at first he had a hard time defining them. Anger, incredible anger, caused by jealousy— bitter, raw, jealousy.

The next night when he called, she made sure she was alone.

"I'm really sorry. He came over to console me because I lost a patient and he knew I didn't want to be alone with my thoughts. He's really wonderful that way."

Again, that fierce jealousy, he should have been the one she turned to. He should have been the one to console her. But he could be there for her now, "Oh sweetheart, I'm so sorry. Tell me about it."

He listened as she poured out her heart over the sixty-eight-year-old man whose heart had worn out, and the tender feelings he had for her overwhelmed him. "Honey, I wish I was there to hold you, to tell you it wasn't your fault. I know you did the best you could. These things just happen, even to the best surgeons. I'm sure you're one of the best there is, no one else could have helped him either. A man who neglects his health like that until his golden years can't expect miracles at the eleventh hour."

Somehow, even though he wasn't a doctor, he knew exactly the right things to say and she wiped her tears and smiled into the phone. "Guess where we decided to go on our honeymoon?" she asked cheerfully.

This was not a topic he wished to discuss. But it was slightly better than listening to her cry. "I give, where?"

"Disney World!"

"This was *your* choice?"

"No, not really. I favored one of the Virgin Islands, but he was so keen on it, that I gave in."

"It's your honeymoon, you should go where *you* want."

"Well, it's his too."

"Yeah, but he's the man, he should acquiesce to you."

"Why?"

"Because, that's what men who love their wives, do."

"And how do you know this?"

"I just do. Tell him you want to go to St. John or the wedding's off. Then I'll take you there myself."

"You'd do that too, wouldn't you?"

"Of course I would. I'd sacrifice myself to watch you tan topless on a secluded tropical beach. It would be hard, but I'd force myself to endure it."

"You are so considerate," she teased and they both laughed together.

"I reached for you this morning while I was still asleep. I was very disappointed when I discovered that you weren't in my bed," he whispered into the phone.

She felt an irrepressible surge of sexual energy flow through her at the sound of his words.

"Come visit me," he said. "Get on a plane and come visit me."

"I can't. How would I explain that to Jonathan?"

"Don't. Give him back his ring and just come."

"Stewart, I can't do that."

"Why not? I know you don't love him."

"How do you know that?"

"Because you're falling in love with me."

He was speaking the truth and she knew it, but still she said, "Well, that's the height of conceit."

"It's the truth and you know it."

"It is no such thing."

"Okay, seriously now. Picture this. And I want you to concentrate and think hard. You're in bed. The lights are low. You wake up really aroused and you duck your head under the sheets to gently wake the man sleeping at your side. Your lips search out his manhood and you kiss him. Then as you feel him respond under your lips, you lick him. You lick the entire length of him as he hardens for you. You wrap your mouth around his penis and you kiss it. Then you suck on it and suck on it as you caress his balls. Suddenly he spasms and he comes in your mouth and you take it all in greedily. Then you wipe your mouth on the bed sheet and climb up his body to kiss him. Quick, who is he? Is it me or is it Jonathan?"

"It's you," she whispered, surprise apparent in her voice. "It's definitely you."

"I know. And I can't wait for you to do that for real. You can't marry him Mallory, you know you can't marry him. Tell him, and give him back his ring."

There was a long silence between them. Then Stewart chuckled, "I think I may have to call housekeeping, I think I need a new set of bed linens."

She laughed and said, "I don't believe for a

minute that you're serious, but thanks for making me laugh."

"You need to laugh more. I will never get enough of hearing your delightful little laugh. Good night, sweetheart. If you change your mind about coming to see me, call my assistant, she'll arrange it."

"I can't. You know that I can't."

"No, I don't know that. And neither do you."

She hung up the phone with a soft click and stared at the darkened ceiling. Her mind flitted from thought to thought and when she realized that she was thinking how she'd like to try that sucking on his penis thing, she moaned and curled into her pillow. Why, oh why, had she been the one selected from a handful of physicians on call to do Stewart Ravencross' physical?

Over the next several days, Mallory pined for him. At times, it was even hard to keep her mind on her work. Twice, she even thought about calling his assistant and going to him, but her loyalty to her patients as well as her uncertainty about her feelings stopped her. But by the end of the second week, she knew it was useless. She was in love with him and there was no helping it.

As soon as Stewart got back into town, he called her at her office. He was told that she was having a physical and that she couldn't be reached just then.

"*She's* having a physical, not giving one?" he asked.

"Yes, I think that's what she said. I expect her back around one."

"I'll call back," he growled.

That damned doctor was examining her *again*? Her long, slim legs and smooth thighs were spread wide for *him*? He was furious and everyone in the conference room during his meeting was well aware of it as he snapped at each and every one of them.

He was still in the meeting when his assistant came in and handed him a note. He glanced down and immediately stood up. "We'll do this later," he said as he curtly dismissed them.

He picked up the phone and pressed a button. "Mallory?"

"Stewart, I heard you called."

"Yes, and we need to talk," he said brusquely.

"Yes," she agreed, "and the sooner the better. Can I see you this afternoon?"

"I have meetings for the next two hours, how about I have Tony pick you up and take you to the penthouse?"

"Okay. Can he pick me up here? I have one more appointment."

"A patient *you're* going to see?" he asked tersely.

She turned the phone in her hand and stared at it, puzzled. What was wrong with him? "Yes."

"Fine. I'll have Tony pick you up at four. I'll meet you at the hotel."

"Are you okay? You sound angry."

"I am. We'll talk about it later."

Geez, had he somehow found out about the baby? He couldn't possibly think that this was her fault, could he?

She finished up her work and was waiting in the lobby when Tony pulled up.

"Hello, Miss Mallory," he said as he opened the door for her. "Oh, beggin' your pardon, Dr. Mallory."

"Actually, it's Dr. Greene, but I prefer Miss Mallory," she said as she flashed him a brilliant smile. He beamed as he went around to the driver's side and got in. Mr. Ravencross would be a fool, he thought, if he let this one get away. There was nothing phony or put on about her, she was drop-dead gorgeous and a vast improvement over the society gold diggers he'd seen Stewart entertaining lately.

The doorman rode the elevator to the penthouse with her and the housekeeper met her at the door. Apparently they had all been alerted to her arrival. The man didn't forget a detail, no matter how small.

She was sitting on the sofa reading a magazine when he strode in. He was still angry, she could sense it, see it in the set of his jaw. Nonetheless, he pulled her up out of the deep cushions and into his arms, which went around her, pulling her close—holding her tight. "God, I've missed you," he breathed into her hair.

His hands cradled her face and he lowered his mouth to hers and kissed her long and passionately. He was gentle as he kissed her, sought the textures of her mouth and took the kiss deep. He was kissing her senseless, expertly using his tongue to imprint her taste and she was feeling her response in her very core. Liquid pooled between her legs and fire raced through her veins.

Their lips parted and as they both caught their breath, he stared into her beautiful green eyes. His rubbed his thumb over her kiss-swollen lips. Then he released her and walked over to the window. "I hear you went to the doctor's today."

"Yes," she stammered.

"Dr. Sorbing?" he spat the name out like a filthy word.

"Well, no actually. I saw someone else. A woman colleague from med school."

Instantly the jealous rage fled, replaced by alarm. He turned quickly back to her. "Is something wrong? Are you sick?"

"Well, no, I'm not exactly sick. I'm pregnant."

"What?" he asked with a raised voice, his eyebrows reaching for his hairline.

"I'm going to have a baby."

His eyes narrowed as he looked at her. "Whose?"

"Yours, silly. I haven't been with anyone else."

Relief flooded his face, but also consternation. "How can that be? We always used a condom."

"They aren't foolproof, you know."

"They always have been before." He stomped into the bedroom and retrieved the box of condoms from his nightstand drawer. There were three left. He held them up to the light and that's when he saw the tiny pin marks, four in each one.

"What the hell?" Then he put it all together. "Jillie. Jillie did this. I'd bet my last dollar."

"Who's Jillie?"

"My girlfriend before I met you. She'd been hinting pretty strongly about marriage, but I never thought she'd do this to get me to marry her."

"Well, I guess her plan backfired on *us*," Mallory said as she walked over to the large picture window and looked down on the bustling city.

"You couldn't be that pregnant, we've barely known each other three weeks. What made you go to the doctor to be tested?"

"I missed my period and you can just about set the atomic clock by my cycle, so right away, I knew something was wrong and I had a hunch what it might be. Virgins have a lousy track record for first time exposure; it's some kind of divine justice, I think."

"Well, that settles it. Now you're marrying me. I will not have you marrying another man while you're carrying my baby."

"I am not going to force you to marry me. I know

you don't even want to get married."

"Who said I didn't want to get married?"

"I will not allow you to marry me just because I am with child. I can manage on my own."

"What makes you think I don't want to marry you?"

"If it weren't for the baby, you wouldn't be asking. And that's not how a marriage should start."

"How do you know I wouldn't have asked you anyway?" he said as he put his hand in his jacket pocket and pulled out a tiny blue velvet box. He flipped it open and there on a bed of white velvet, slipped into the ring slot, was a beautiful, pear shaped diamond, sparkling in the late afternoon sun. It was the largest diamond Mallory had ever seen.

"I bought this in Seattle a week ago, our baby was known only to God then."

Tears welled in her eyes as he lifted her chin and gently kissed her mouth. "Mallory Greene, will you do me the honor of becoming my wife and the mother of my *two* children?"

She sobbed her happiness as he placed the ring on her finger, then he handed her his handkerchief to wipe at her streaming tears.

"I love you, Mallory. From the moment you snapped that glove on your hand and squeezed my balls, I think I knew that you were the woman for me." He smiled down at her, "Now if you'd done that digital thing, I might not have fallen so hard or so quickly."

She grinned up at him, "You never did have that or the colonoscopy done, did you?"

"No, my attorneys came through for me, Christmas is coming and they really wanted a nice bonus."

"Jonathan said he'd do it for you at no charge

when I told him that I couldn't marry him because I was in love with you. He said he'd use a pyrotechnic device to illuminate the area."

"Mmm, not a pleasant thought. But I'm glad you told him that you couldn't marry him."

"What about Jillie? What if she's pregnant, too?"

"I think if that were the case, I'd have heard from her by now, after all, you already know that you are and it's been over a month since I was with her."

"You can take the test when you're only nine days along."

"Then I feel it's safe to assume that she's not. But it wouldn't matter, I'm marrying you. It's you that I love. You that I want to spend my life with. You that I want to carry off to St. John."

"St. John? Really?"

"We leave exactly a month from now. So plan your wedding; however you want—big, small, elegant, simple. I don't care as long as you can pull it off within a month. You've got a blank check; so don't alarm your parents. I want you topless on the beach in front of our bungalow on the 26th. Got it?"

"Yes sir! Gosh, I'd better call my mother!"

"Not just yet, we have another matter to discuss first."

"What's that?"

"It's a bedroom matter and we can't talk with all these clothes on," he said indicating his business suit and her hospital garb. He picked her up and carried her into the bedroom, "Now what did I do with that dental floss?" he said as he nuzzled her in the neck.

Garrett shut down his laptop and closed his eyes. What a beautiful love story. Sexy, poignant . . . touching on all the base emotions. And for the first time in his life it had him thinking seriously about his future. Children . . . dogs . . . maybe a cat . . . but definitely Laurel. He knew now that something would always be missing if he didn't have her in his life. Since he'd found that flash drive and started reading her stories, nothing mattered to him as much as she did. Now that he'd met her he was as determined as Stewart Ravencross. *Interesting that Mallory's eyes were green like Laurel's, and that Stewart's were blue like his . . . hmmm.*

Chapter Thirty-eight

Laurel woke and stretched luxuriously. Something was making her happy, deliriously so. When it kicked in that she had a date with Garrett, the impossibly handsome, funny, sexy man from the bike ride yesterday, she shivered from the delight that thought brought. She remembered their moment on the stairs inside Old Baldy when he'd caught her in his arms so effortlessly that she'd felt positively tiny, and then he'd held her in his arms as if he never wanted to let her go.

Their eyes had met and she'd thought he was going to kiss her. She couldn't believe how much she had wanted him to. On one of their earlier rest stops he had offered her some lemon meringue Jelly Bellys. He carried a handful of them in a baggie in a tool bag attached to the handlebars of his bike. She had declined because she already had a Werther's caramel halfway melted in her mouth. But when he'd held her close, tight to his chest, and bent his face to look at her she had smelled the tangy lemon and she had wanted to taste it on his tongue.

Idly, she remembered the chart on the back of the Jelly Belly containers she'd often seen at Costco and wondered what flavor you got if you combined a caramel jelly bean with a lemon one. Maybe tonight, if he kissed her, she'd know.

Another shiver passed through her, setting her shoulders high and making her tense. She needed to get a hold of herself. She knew practically nothing about this man. Other than . . . she brought up her hands and counted out the things she knew: he liked beer, cheeseburgers, and cheesecake. Bought Jelly Bellys by flavor—lemon meringue running neck and neck for popcorn-flavored as his favorites—she remembered he referred to them as "any-flavor-beans," instead of Jelly Bellys, so she knew he was into Harry Potter. He was strong—she could still see him lifting his bike with one big hand and deftly putting it in the slot on the rack as if it weighed next to nothing.

She had stared at his broad back during most of their lunch break, and it was nothing if not impressive and powerful looking. The memory of how his shirt tucked into his shorts and how his waist tapered in before his rounded butt met the bench caused her pulse to thrum. He came off as being self-assured, an über-confident male, yet comfortable in casual clothes, relaxed to the point of being able to straddle a picnic table bench while talking high finance with an insurance man well past his prime. She remembered his piercing ice blue eyes when he'd lifted his sunglasses and met hers, his sooty lashes and radiant smile, his straight white teeth . . . and his laughter as he'd watched her eating his cheesecake. He was sexy, smart, athletic and miraculously unattached. He was perfect.

She thought of the stupid ritual she and the girls had performed the other night, and tilted her head as if to wonder. Then she threw the covers off and reached for the phone. She needed to know if this was how it had happened for them.

Roman answered for Tessa and, as usual, had her dampening her panties with a simple, "Well Laurel, darlin' how are ya doin' ma luv?"

"Uh, fine Roman. Just fine. Tessa home?"

"Ah yes, in the shower washin' off the best part of me. Can I have her call ya back?"

Her knees just about buckled. How the hell did Tessa

manage to keep from falling on her face in front of this man? "Yes. Yes, that would be great. Just great."

"Have ya seen him yet?"

"Seen who?"

"Your man. The one Tessa says will be coming for you. As I came for her . . . now she comes for me." He chuckled at his play on words.

"Uh, that's what I was calling about actually. I met someone. And I have a date tonight."

"Well then, I'm sure she'll want to hear all about it. Do you want some advice from the likes of an old lecher like me?"

"Uh . . . suuure."

"Leave the panties at home. You won't believe how ready you'll be by the end of the evenin'. Ah, here's my darlin' wife now. She's givin' me the look."

Laurel heard some low whispering; more like snarling actually, and then Tessa came on the line. "Ignore him. Apparently he's ready for round two. These Europeans have a thing about mornings, and I can assure you, Sunday mornings are never about church. So what's this I hear, you have a date?"

Laurel told her about the bike ride and how she'd fallen into Garrett's arms, eaten all of his cheesecake, and then agreed to have an Asian salad with him tonight.

"Tomo's at Ocean Isle is nice, so is Osaka Japanese Steakhouse at Shallotte Crossing, but if he's really interested in you he'll take you to P.F. Chang's or someplace like Loyal Thai, maybe even north to Wilmington to Indo-Chine so he can spend more time with you. Tell me everything you know about him, starting with his looks. He's got them right?"

"Oh does he ever . . ."

Half an hour later she was finally off the phone, confidence boosted by Tessa's encouraging words. She knew the phone lines would burn up for the next hour as

Viv and Cat were brought up to speed. But she didn't have time for any more chitchat. She had to figure out what she was going to wear and she had to go for a walk on the beach. She needed to touch base with The Kindred Spirit, and work off some of this jittery anxiety. Gosh, she hadn't had a date in . . . how long had it been? Four years? Five?

Sure, she'd had boyfriends in college, two were even serious. And then after graduation she'd been in a relationship for eight months. She'd just begun seeing an attorney in Georgetown two weeks before her parents died but what might have bloomed fizzled as she spiraled down into a depression no man would have been able to deal with, nonetheless one who hadn't even worked her into the sack yet.

Oh, she liked sex. Liked it very much in fact, as her stories attested. But she wasn't easy with her favors. Things had to go in stages. Getting to know you. Getting to like you. Getting to trust you. All that had to happen before the Getting-under-the-sheets part. So, she wouldn't be heeding Roman's advice, it would be a full-on panties night. That part of her wardrobe she was certain about.

Chapter Thirty-nine

Garrett woke with a muzzy head from staying up so late reading. But he shook it off and went for a long run on the beach. He followed that up with a bowl of pasta tossed with a simple, quick primavera sauce—sans garlic and but loaded with fresh vegetables. He had to be a powerhouse tonight. Although during his run, which gave him time to plan things out, he reasoned that it might be better to just tease her senseless tonight.

He made a few connections via email with old friends, went into Shallotte to do a little shopping at both The Home Depot and Office Depot. Then he dressed for his date with Laurel. He selected a pair of black slacks that he paired with a crisp white Oxford shirt, and matched his braided leather belt to his cordovan loafers. As he slapped on some aftershave, he noted his hair curling at his nape and getting a bit unruly, and made a mental note to get to Cindy at Totally Chic next week.

He opted for the 'vette for two reasons: he really loved putting it through its paces on the long, winding exit ramps off 31, and he thought it might be a good time to hint at his affluence. Women liked men with money. Expensive cars conveyed that admirably. Plus, she'd already seen the Edge.

He never held a woman's bias for moneyed-men against a woman, as he understood the laws of human nature better than most. The rules of engagement, i.e. dating, were simple: men chased women who they divined had all the essentials for mating and producing superior offspring, women tried to attach themselves to men who could protect and provide for said offspring. Tonight he would confirm that she was beautiful with nice tits for nursing should it ever come to that, and she would see that he was big and strong . . . and loaded.

He was ready to pull into her driveway at seven, ready to show her that he could defend her, honor her, afford her, and bed her better than any man competing for her. If men like Mountain Man were posturing and preening for her, this would be a slam-dunk.

Chapter Forty

He rode through the perfectly manicured development, admiring the upscale homes, and thought this could be a nice place to raise a family. He'd never get rid of the beach house, but he'd consider moving south. There were great colleges for kids down here.

He drove down her street and turned into her driveway right on the minute. He got out of the car, jogged up the steps and rang the doorbell. Then waited. Waited some more. Then watched as she walked toward him through the intricately etched sidelight. She was wearing a slinky little dress. She looked adorable.

From his fashion research into new trends, he knew that every woman in the dating pool owned what was called the essential little black dress. Hanging in every woman's closet, the knee-length sheath was designed to be the all-occasion date dress—body flattering, especially when accompanied by form-fitting Spanx, it showed off feminine assets and complimented a woman's form: bust line, waist, hips, legs, they all got a boost. Men loved it, as it was always easy to remove. With only one long zipper down the back, he often had it open and parted, his hands caressing a woman's bare back before she was aware her clothing had been compromised.

The door opened and a smiling Laurel greeted him, "Hi, you're right on time." She stood back to let him in.

Laurel wore what he imagined was Talbot's finest, and it definitely showcased her full breasts, slim waist and slightly rounded hips. He'd already had time to admire her shapely legs while biking; still, his eyes followed her curves to the Barbie Doll-styled heels and to the polished shiny silver anklet around her trim ankle. He wanted to stroke her bare legs. Run his fingers up under her dress. His fingers itched to search out the zipper on her back. He reined back, remembering this was a first date. *Miles to go before we sleep* . . . But damn, getting her out of this dress was going to be one satisfying experience.

"What do you have there?" she asked, her eyes on the small rosemary plant he held in his hands.

"A peace offering—a rosemary plant for the sprig I swiped. A friend of mine, Alessandro, from Florence, Italy recommended this particular variety. It's called Tuscan Blue. It's known for its beautiful blue flowers and upright orientation. As I'm sure you know, rosemary is for remembrance . . . He hefted the plant toward her, "So here's to a memorable dinner."

"Thank you. It's beautiful. I can't wait to see the first blooms." She took it from his hands and walked it through an archway. He followed, listening to her light footsteps on the hardwood flooring to gage the direction she took, then watched as she sat the plant on the longest slab of granite he'd ever seen. That, he knew, had to have cost a fortune.

"Wow, what a beautiful kitchen." The sincerity in his voice was genuine. The kitchen was impressive in that it reminded him of authentic Old World kitchens he'd seen in Europe—French, Italian, German, Swiss—eclectic touches from each were set off by colorful ceramic roosters, wire baskets brimming with onions and peppers, crystal wine servers covered with wrought iron grape vines, a chef-worthy knife block with red handled knives inserted to the hilts. State-of-the-art appliances matched the matte white patina of the cabinets done in the French chateau-style. They were inspired—and purposely distressed to look, well . . . old. Except for the designer Wolfe stove which he knew was commercial quality and the price of a small car. This was a kitchen where someone cooked with a serious passion, and he doubted there was another like it anywhere. He saw the whimsy in the choices she'd made for her canisters, the dishes showing through the glass-fronted cabinets, and the over-sized but easily accessible ceramic platters and bowls that hung from wrought iron hangers on one massive wall.

"Thank you. I consider it my constantly evolving masterpiece, as I do tend to mess it up royally. Broke one of those platters last week," she said as she pointed high on the wall to a series of empty black iron hooks. Had to send for another one from Tuscany. I just hope the old painter from Montelupo is still around to make one just like it. It was so beautiful." The wistfulness in her face touched him. A woman who fell in love with her dishes—something in his chest tightened.

The phone at the end of the counter rang just then, and she walked over to look at the Caller I.D. and broke into a grin. "I have to get this, it'll just take a minute, it's about tee times for my golf group tomorrow. I've been waiting for this call all day. Help yourself, look around."

While Laurel took the call, Garrett strolled into the formal living room. Not usually bored—always one to be content amusing himself, he walked around the room, picking up the odd paperweight and tchotsky. She had some really fine memorabilia.

An article signed by his favorite columnist was under glass in a gold burnished frame on the entrance wall. He was blown over by which article it was—a humorous but deeply thought provoking piece on neutrinos that Charles Krauthammer wrote in 2010. He'd loved that article. Judging by the elaborate custom-made shadow boxed frame, it seemed this woman not only revered this man, but understood his complex thoughts—there was a lot more to her than he thought. So she wasn't all gorgeous hair, sexy body and naughty mind, he thought with an amused smile.

On a built-in bookshelf, he spotted a framed picture of a youthful Laurel sitting behind the wheel of a yellow Firebird convertible—the top down, and a huge grin on her face as she held up a set of keys for the photographer. *Aha! She was the woman on the bridge.* He smiled and shook his head at the chance encounter. At the time, he had been spending every spare moment looking for her.

He turned his head to the opposite wall and his eyes flashed wide as he saw an extensive collection of Tangrams in a lighted triple curio. More sets than he'd ever seen in one place. The ancient puzzle forms were reverently displayed and protected behind glass doors. What were the odds? Only a handful of people in a thousand knew about the Chinese puzzles, and here he'd lucked into an aficionado—he who prided himself on owning a rare edition book of Tangram patterns dating from the early 1800s. The puzzles fascinated him. Her stories fascinated him. And she fascinated him. He was in trouble. And he knew it.

He heard her approach from behind and turned to face her.

She smiled at him as she came alongside, opened a glass panel and stroked the shiny pottery pieces that were on a square of velvet in a place of honor. "A simple game. I'm addicted to these simple little shapes. I can't seem to stop adding new sets as I find them. They're called Tangrams. You try to create patterns using all seven pieces, or *tans*. The trick is that they have to lay flat and not overlap."

He nodded at her concise description. "An impressive collection. I'm familiar with the game, I even have a few old sets myself."

"Really? I thought I was the only odd one collecting

these silly things."

He chucked her under her chin. "Odd? No. Beautiful, vibrant, yes." His long firm fingers wrapped around her jaw and he tilted her head up. Their eyes met and held. He watched as the green of hers darkened and then widened. It was too soon for a kiss. He saw the thought running through the back of her mind. What he was about to do was an after dinner, after date, after depositing-her-at-the-door move. He was about to shock both of them. Because there was no way in hell he could wait.

The only sound was the gentle chiming of a clock in a room down the hall as he stared steadily into her curiously green eyes. He bent and leaned into her, dropping his focus and concentrating on her parted lips. He leaned closer until their breath mingled and he smelled caramel before gently touching his lips to hers. Lightly grazing back and forth he softly pressed his lips to hers until he had covered her lips completely and settled them against her. His body roared from the contact of his thigh against hers. He had no choice but to deepen the kiss, tracing her lips with his tongue before forcing her lips to accommodate his questing mouth and eager tongue.

He fought to keep his leg from encroaching and sliding up the short linen dress to the notch between her thighs. She tasted delightful. So fresh. So lovely. His temperature spiked.

He had to force himself not to back her against the glass case and let his hands and mouth have free reign. Hearing her low murmur he finally broke the kiss. Meeting her eyes and seeing them dazed, he tilted her head the opposite way, and took another, this time allowing his inquisitive lips to liberally savor hers before chasing her timid tongue.

He wanted more than anything to be inside her, hands fisted in her hair, plunging and thrusting deeply into her core with that part of him that was vaguely scented of

Tuscany's finest olive oil these days. But he tempered the kiss, remembering that this was their first, and that she'd only known him two days—whereas it seemed he'd known her for years.

He gently nipped her bottom lip as he moved away, letting her know that there would be more kisses and that he not only intended for her to allow them but that he expected to have his way with her because of them. It was the language of the pack. She'd just had her first lesson.

He let her know by his eyes that he was a demanding and passionate man as he stood and stared into her glazed over eyes. His touch on her cheek and rueful smile showed that he also knew how to be both gentle and fun.

He'd have to read another story tonight just to keep his sanity, because he was not going to break the promise he'd made to himself that he was going to take things slow with her. It was going to kill him, but he would heed his own advice. This game was too important to lose.

He had to use the right strategy and maneuver her at her own pace, not his. And while every cell in his body was screaming to capitalize on the moment, his sensible side was saying wait for the right time and reap untold treasure. This woman, primed and brought to the brink would devastate them both. He couldn't wait to feel the explosions that would pass between them when he finally took her in all the ways he knew she wanted to be taken.

"Ready to go?" he asked, deliberately breaking the mood and reverting to the traditional agenda—back to that of a first date.

When she just stared up at him as if in a trance he had to keep from smiling.

"Dinner?" he prompted and watched with concealed pride as she flinched back to the present.

"Uh, yes. Yes. Ready. Sure I am. Just need to get my wrap." She spun as if she needed to get away from the heat building between them. He needed her to stand down too. His erection was damned near painful.

He followed her to the hallway where she picked up her purse and a stunning peacock-influenced pashmina. It was striking against the black dress as she swirled it around her shoulders and let it settle. She opened the simple black clutch to fish out her keys. He took them from her and locked the door behind them, then handed them back.

He could have kept them. Could have dropped them into the pocket of his cashmere sport coat. But it would have said too much about the control he knew she craved in her men. Too soon, too soon, he kept reiterating to himself. He didn't want to spook her. She was as timid as a rabbit and he didn't want to see her run.

Chapter Forty-one

Laurel shivered with desire as she settled her pashmina over her shoulders. So . . . as to the question of what you got when you paired caramel and lemon? She sure got her answer faster than she could ever have imagined. And now she had to deal with the result: the lemon completely overpowered the caramel. Symbolically, she had just seen this play out. He had devastated her with that kiss. The caramel was no more. She tasted lemon inside her mouth. And she knew that when the taste wore off, she'd have to have more.

When she saw the 'vette she broke into laughter.

"What's so funny?"

"I saw you driving this the other day. Right after that big rainstorm. You passed me when I was coming out of Food Lion. I followed you until you turned on Georgetown."

He took her hand and led her over the pavers to his car.

"And I saw you in your yellow Firebird on the bridge a few days ago. I was running when you got to the top of the bridge. You had the top down and your hair was being whipped around, and you were wearing these huge sunglasses."

She laughed. "So that was you. Hmmm. Small world."

"I think you might have also ridden by me on your bike while I was jogging on the beach one day. I remembered the pretty blonde and the sweet retro-looking bike."

She looked at him and tilted her head to the side, as she recalled the hottie she'd seen running on the beach that day. "Small, small world," she reiterated.

He helped her into the car.

"So where are we going?" she asked after he'd settled her into the passenger seat and walked around and slid into his.

"I wanted to take you to my favorite Thai restaurant, but I forgot they're not open on Sundays." He looked over at her and winked, "So we'll have to do a redo if you don't find tonight too hateful. Meanwhile . . . P.F. Chang's has the *second* best Asian salad—a chopped chicken salad with ginger dressing."

"Oh I love that place! Mmm, they have those wonderful lettuce wraps and my favorite Singapore Street Noodles."

"So that's what you normally get?"

"Oh yeah. They're awesome."

"Then you should try something else. In fact, I think I'm going to insist on it. With me, it's a requirement that you try new delights." He shot her a look that was both stern and suggestive, an eyebrow lifted for her response. How she accepted his control over this would determine how she accepted his dominance in other ways.

He watched as her face reflected her thoughts, considering. She sighed for dramatic effect and mumbled, as a child would, "Okay, but can I have the Great Wall of Chocolate for dessert?"

He smiled and patted her thigh, "Of course you can . . . if you're a good girl and you eat all your dinner." Then he lifted her hand from her lap and kissed each fingertip. Out of the corner of his eye he saw her tiny shudder and he smiled as he replaced her hand. This was the most fun he'd had in a long time.

They rode up Route 31, listening to music shuffling on

his iPod while he put the 'vette through its paces, exceeding the speed limit by thirty miles in some places, and taking the long spiraling exit ramp at what clearly was a dangerous speed for anything other than a low-slung sports car with a proficient driver behind the wheel.

When he zipped into a parking space at The Market Common, near the restaurant, she let out a long slow breath that she hadn't been aware she was holding. He chuckled, gripped her hand briefly then got out to open her door.

They dined on lettuce wraps, the chopped salad with ginger dressing they'd come for, and a Lo Mein Combination dish they shared so she would have no problem earning her dessert. They spoke of hometowns, non-existent siblings, and how being an only child had affected both their lives, as they sat caddy-corner in a generous-sized booth, facing a fountain.

Then Garrett watched, his elbow propped on the table, his chin resting on his open palm, as she devoured The Great Wall of Chocolate. He dipped his own fork into the gooey confection twice, curious to taste the combination of flavors that were putting that look of abject pleasure on her face—a look he hoped to duplicate using her other senses.

When there was only the hint of a smear left on her plate, he took her fork from her and set it down. Using his fingertip he ran his finger through the remains of the chocolate "lava" then dabbed it on her bottom lip. Leaning in, he covered her lips with his and used his tongue to lick off the decadent icing. As he distracted her with a devastating kiss, he ran his fingertips up the inside of her thigh using the barest touch. He stopped short of making the connection to her panties before dragging one lone fingernail back to her knee. It was done so quickly and with such precision that Laurel was momentarily confused as to whether she had imagined the touch that had caused the most delicious shudder. Her pulse was thundering through her core by the time he lifted his lips and his eyes met hers.

"Cold?" he asked playfully as he lifted her pashmina from the booth to her shoulders.

Anything but, she thought. "No," she managed to stammer as he took a charge card from his money clip to pay the bill.

"Thank you for dinner. I am so full," she said when the waiter brought back the sales ticket and his card.

"The first of many I hope," he said as he added the tip and signed the receipt, then looked up at her, "I suppose I should drive back at a slower pace so as not to risk an eruption of that *lava* on my interior."

"Considering my experience with roller coasters, that would be a good call."

He smiled and pulled her up. "Good. I'm not at all willing to drop you at your doorstep yet anyway."

Once they were back on 31, Garrett opened his console and took out a flash drive he'd fished from inside. Then he inserted it into the USB hub for an MP3 player and used the touch screen to select Il Divo.

As the powerful strains of *The Man You Love* filled the car, he looked over at her. The ambient lighting in and under the dash cast her in silhouette but he could still see her wide smile.

"You look happy."

"I am. I love Il Divo. And I can't remember when I've had such a good time with a man."

"Hmmm. What does that mean exactly?"

She laughed as she read his thoughts. "I may have stated that wrong. I actually haven't dated in years. And that was men. Only men," she clarified. "I don't really remember my last date all that well, as my parents had just died and we met mostly just so I could tell him that I needed some time to myself." She took in a big breath then slowly let it out.

Remembering those early days after her parent's death still left her feeling anxious.

"For the last couple years, all the really good times have revolved around my girlfriends. And before you give me that look again, they're all happily married to gorgeous guys."

"Good to know."

He pulled into her driveway, helped her out of the car, and took her keys from her so he could open the door. Then he handed her back her keys, turned her toward him and gripping her forearms lightly he bent and kissed her on her forehead. "I'll call you," he said. Ignoring the knitted brows and her confused expression he turned her and gently nudged her inside before closing the door between them.

He strode back to his car with a jaunty step. *Oh this was so going according to plan.*

Chapter Forty-two

He waited two hours before he punched in her number. It rang five times before she answered. His cell phone didn't broadcast his number so he knew she didn't know who was calling.

"Hello?"

"It's Garrett."

"Oh. Hi."

"I told you I'd call."

She laughed. "I guess I assumed that meant tomorrow or the next day."

"It's fairly safe to say that you shouldn't assume anything about me."

"I guess I'm finding that out."

"I had a good time tonight."

"Yeah me too."

"I want to ask you a question and I want you to answer it honestly. Do you think you can do that?"

"Mmm. Okay. I'll try."

"Have you thought about me spreading your thighs and putting my tongue inside you?"

There was a gasp and then a long silence. Finally he heard her sigh.

"Be honest now," he admonished. "Have you?"

"Yes," she whispered.

"Good. Because that's all I can think about right now."

Again there was silence.

"Just wanted you to know that. Good night."

Laurel was left sitting in her bed, propped against her pillows, staring at her portable phone. *Had he just called and said what she thought she'd heard him say? And then hung up?*

It was many minutes before she replaced the handset, and almost an hour before she slid down onto the soft mattress and pulled the covers over her head in frustration. Every thought revolved around him as her mind walked her through scenario after scenario—all involving her being naked, him being fully clothed and his head settled between her splayed legs.

She finally came to the realization that he had done this on purpose. That he had planned that phone call and her subsequent gnashing of teeth into her 700-count Egyptian cotton pillow cover. That scoundrel!

She tossed the covers off and used the redial feature on her phone to call him back. When he answered she lowered her voice to what she hoped was seductive, and without preamble asked, "Have you thought about me kneeling before you and wrapping my lips around your gloriously hard cock and then sucking it all the way down my throat?"

She was rewarded by a long, drawn out moan.

"Tit for tat," she murmured, satisfied that she'd woken him and put him in the same aroused state she was in.

"Who is this?" he asked.

She was in the process of slamming the phone down but heard his throaty chuckle and lifted it back to her ear.

Her appreciative laughter joined his and then abruptly stopped when she heard him ask, "So . . . what are we going to do about this? You undoubtedly have a sopping wet pussy and I have an erection that could be used as a pile driver."

Taking a deep breath she said, "I think we should

move onto date number two."

"Tell me upfront how many it's going to take until I can feel myself sliding into you?"

She arbitrarily chose a number. "Seven."

He negotiated. "Three."

"Five."

"Four. And breakfast, lunch and dinner tomorrow each count as one."

She laughed with genuine delight and it coiled something in him so tightly that it caused him to shake his head at the sensation.

"The sad thing about that is that I can't meet you tomorrow. I'm playing in a charity golf tournament, and then helping with the silent auction afterward. "

"That is very distressing because sporting this hard-on means that *I* won't even be able to leave the house."

"You started this."

"Just so we're clear, you started this the second you fell down those stairs and into my arms." She had in fact started this, but she'd never know that it had begun with a click of a mouse opening one of her files.

"So what are you doing Friday night?"

"You tell me. What am I doing Friday night?"

"Going with me to the beach concert at Ocean Isle and eating deli sandwiches while we listen to the Craig Woolard Band and watch the sunset. It's the last concert of the season and not to be missed."

"It's a date—date number two, mind you."

"Do you like Italian cold cuts?"

"Love them."

"Beer or wine for after the concert?"

"Wine."

"I'll meet you there at 6:30 so we can get upfront seats."

"Sounds like a plan."

"You'll need to bring a chair and your dancing shoes."

"Dancing shoes?"

"We shag on the asphalt. It's a hoot. And we also line dance."

"I don't dance."

"You don't shag?"

"Only the Austin Powers' version."

"We're waiting for date number six for that, remember?"

"Four—and not one minute later. Do I need to get this in writing?"

"That would be an odd contract to present before a judge."

"We already have an *oral* contract. Binding for *both* parties," he said suggestively.

She thought of Garrett's lips. *There.* She been to Italy and seen The David firsthand. And while the other women on the tour had stared at his butt, she had been mesmerized by his full sensuous lips. Garrett's lips had the same pouty and sculptured quality. The thought of his lips on her anywhere caused liquid heat to flood through her veins. The thought of his tongue . . . well, there was no point in denying herself the pleasure of *that*!

"Alright, four."

"Goodnight Sexy."

"Goodnight Garrett. See you Friday."

"Can't wait. "

They both hung up and sat in their respective beds staring at the opposite wall. Laurel, hardly believing she'd agreed to have sex with a man she'd only seen twice, and Garrett, trying to remember if there was any olive oil left in the bottle in his bathroom.

Friday was a long way away off, Garrett thought, when he woke up at four in the morning with the bed sheets twisted all around him. How the hell was he going to amuse himself until then? He turned on the lamp and walked into the kitchen for some ice water. On his way back he picked up his laptop. If he couldn't have her, he could have one of her stories. He chose the one that had intrigued from the beginning. Who didn't love an innocent? And this one smacked of a fair amount of BDSM judging from the subtitle.

The Rake and the Young Innocent

Alternate title: Bought, Bound and Bared

She sat at the formal table going through the motions of eating, stalling for time as she watched the man across the table eyeing her. She had been so nervous since this afternoon when her Aunt had told her he was coming to dinner. She had hinted that he was coming for much more than the simple fare they were now serving at the ornately carved mahogany table. And now, she somehow had the feeling that he was here solely because of her.

Without lifting her head, she looked around the table at her siblings and her cousins. Margaret, her own sweet cherub of a sister was desperately trying to keep the small pile of riced potatoes on her fork until it reached her mouth. She was five and had only known her mother for three short years before she died. Next to her sat Theodore, her very grown up brother, who was trying to be everybody's keeper. He was nine. He had been sorely affected by their mother's passing. At the end of the table sat Molly, Aunt Patricia's youngest daughter. She was a bit simple or maybe just a little slow at times, but a smiling, cheerful towhead nonetheless.

She was six. On the other side of the table sat George, Aunt Patricia's only son, and the bossiest child she'd ever had the misfortune to meet. He was fifteen. Next to him was Mary, a momma's girl who was rarely more than a few feet away from her mother. She was eight. Then there was Aunt Patricia, newly widowed and burdened with six children, herself included. She was Julia—tall, willowy and curvy with long blonde hair, dewy skin in an unremarkable face, and nineteen just last month.

At the head of the table sat the man her aunt had invited to dinner. The man she had met on only one other occasion. At a wedding, in Dorchester, a long, long time ago when he had been only twenty-five. He was thirty-two now. She couldn't remember whose wedding it was, just that he'd been there and that he'd never lacked for a simpering woman on his arm for even a moment.

He was good looking by any woman's standards, devastatingly handsome by hers. He was rather tall and well formed with hard chiseled looks that made her aware that this man was probably never denied much of anything. And he was wealthy, extremely wealthy. Wealthy beyond compare, her aunt had told her. It was evident in his manner of dress and by the ornately adorned livery of the coachmen that had accompanied his regal black lacquered coach. There was a ducal coat of arms on the door, but she wasn't familiar with the hierarchy of the court, and didn't recognize the crest. It was curious though, a mermaid entwined with a serpent against a clamshell. He had been introduced as the Duke of Thornhill.

She was having a very hard time fathoming why he was here; they hardly ever had visitors, and certainly none of this caliber. And how was it that her aunt even knew this well-bred gentleman?

After dinner the Duke asked Julia to take a walk with him in the orchard. She hesitated, but her aunt encouraged her with a vigorous nod of her head and a pointed look toward the door, so Julia finally took his proffered arm and let him lead her out though the French patio doors.

They walked in silence along the oyster shell path that led to the far end of the orchard. She had heard her Aunt Patricia admonish the other children not to tag along, and to allow the Duke his privacy with her, so she knew she would be all alone in the moonlight with this man who was not much more than a stranger to her. And that in itself was very odd.

As they walked, he gingerly took her hand and then lifted it to his lips. He placed tiny little kisses on each fingertip before turning to face her and looking into her bewildered eyes. She was stunned by his attentions. Things like this simply didn't happen to her.

"You know why I'm here, don't you?"

"No, Your Grace, actually, I do not."

"Your aunt sent for me a week ago. She heard that I am finally in search of a bride. She says she chanced upon you bathing two weeks ago, and she seems to think I will find you suitable. She knows I have very discerning tastes when it comes to women."

"Pray tell, Lord Thornhill, how does she know this?"

"I am not at liberty to say. Just be assured that I trust her word, that is why I am here today."

"Exactly what did she write you about me?"

"She said that you were long of limb with a very sweet nature."

"And that was enough for you to come all

this way?"

"She said other things."

"I wish to know them, sir."

"Are you sure?" he asked as he led her over to a masonry bench in front of a rose arbor.

"Yes."

He gave her a wry smile. "Very well then. I choose not to keep secrets from you, if they are for the telling. She said that you had breasts as luscious and as plump as ripe white-fleshed peaches, and that the tuft of fur that protects your womanhood is so fair and so fine that even standing twenty feet away, your cleft is fully visible."

He chuckled as her hand went to her throat. She blanched and then gasped.

"You asked."

"She would not dare say such a thing!"

"Of course she would. She's saddled with six children and she's completely expended the monies left her. She knows that you are her most valuable asset, and she intended to make certain I would come to inspect the merchandise."

"I am not merchandise!"

"Oh, my dear, how wrong you are. The fact is, that you are. You are a commodity to be bartered to the highest bidder. She knows I can pay the highest price and that I am willing to do so, if I find what I want . . . what I desire." His eyes smoldered as he looked into her face.

"I have a say! She cannot sell me!" She stood and began pacing.

"Madame, if you are to my liking, she already has."

It was then that Julia remembered that her Aunt Patricia had been sequestered in the library with the

Duke for the better part of an hour shortly after his arrival this afternoon. She turned, looked at him, and gasped. Could it be true? Could her aunt have sold her to this man?

Now that she thought about it, it was probably the only viable solution her aunt had been able to come up with after learning of their dismal finances from her late uncle's solicitor last month. Of course! This would solve all her problems! Unload the ugly, undowried niece, and at the same time earn an income to provide for the rest of the family.

In actuality, it was a rather good plan and she should be grateful to her aunt for thinking of it. After all, her own dear siblings would suffer along with her aunt's children if they were to be thrown out of their home, destitute, onto the street. She should be happy to help in any way that she could, but this, not this! Married to this arrogant aristocrat whose only concern for her marriageability was her youthful body.

She moved back to the bench, and as if in a daze, slowly retook her seat. This could not be happening to her. She had been raised as a lady, a proper and respectable lady. One who would have a come out, attend balls, and be courted by proper and respectable gentlemen.

The Duke knelt beside her as she sat on the bench and his fingers gently stroked the side of her long neck. "Your forehead is high and your nose a trifle long. You have nice cheekbones and creamy fair skin, but you are not lovely in face, neither are you homely though. Your looks are just average. Your one outstanding feature is your beautiful pale blonde hair. I do like your over plump lips though. Even though they are not fashionable. I however, shall find many uses for them."

He stood and looked down at her. "You are without a dowry, you have not had a proper coming out or attended a season and you are virtually an unknown living out here in this rural burg as you do. You have no skills other than teaching, child rearing and gardening, although Patricia has done extremely well with training you in the social graces of being a lady. You could do far worse than marrying me—a duke. A duke who can provide for you and your entire family in an elegant and grand style."

"If this is a proposal, it is not one such as I've dreamed of all my life. Being reminded that I am an unlovely maiden with over plump lips, an unknown country goose, dependent on my aunt, with no funds available to secure a husband."

"You are lovely in the ways that I need you to be lovely. I require a special bride, one that pleases me carnally. I venture that once broken, you will suit me quite well."

"Are you asking me to marry you, Your Grace? Your words addle me, sir. I cannot tell whether you approve of me or disapprove of me."

His hand cupped her cheek and as he pulled her to her feet, he leaned in to kiss her. His lips were ardent as they pressed against hers. His other hand moved through her hair as he pulled her close and crushed her mouth under his. His lips covered and moved over hers as his tongue forced its way between her teeth and upon entry, he plundered her mouth until she finally pushed against his chest to separate them. She was woozy from his advance, but it had not been entirely unpleasant, and that surprised her.

"Yes, I am asking you to marry me, if you meet my criteria, that is."

"Criteria?"

"Yes, there are certain conditions that must be met."

"And what might they be?" she was still trembling from his kiss, but trying not to let it show, so she forced herself to be haughty in her reply.

"I must view you first and you must be virginal—no man must have ever penetrated you."

"I assure you sir, that I am virginal. Chaste in fact, except for your kiss. View me? What do you mean by that?" Odd feelings came over her—fear, awareness of his impressive size, and desperation—the longer he spoke the more real this was all becoming.

"I mean I must see you naked first. I must see your breasts and your womanhood and you must prove to my doctor that you are indeed a virgin. I am sorry, but your word just will not do in this matter."

She stood there wondering if she was imagining this whole ridiculous conversation. She shook her head in disbelief as she mumbled, "You expect me to disrobe and allow for your inspection before we are to become betrothed?" She was incredulous with shock. The impropriety of such a request was so foreign that she could not comprehend it in its entirety.

"Yes. In fact, that is why we are here. Your aunt has sent us to this secluded orchard for you to do just that. She has assured us of privacy while you bare yourself to me so I can see if you are as pleasing to the eye as she has told me."

"She would never!" Julia was indignant and shamed to her toes. "Surely, she did not!"

"Madame, I assure you that she did. You are welcome to check with her if you like. She knows it is a condition of my accepting you as my wife. You are to display yourself for me this night, here in the moonlight in this secluded glade."

He bent and kissed her on the neck. It felt warm and tingly and it thrilled her. He continued kissing her neck, trailing light kisses all the way up to her ear where he engaged his tongue in the whorls. Her body was betraying her and she sensed that he was counting on that.

"So, what say you?" he breathed devastating warmth into her ear. "Do you wish to be my bride?"

He was right, she could do a lot worse than this incredibly handsome man who stood before her causing her body to vibrate and sing. His hands caressed her forearms as he kissed her lightly on the lips, then he kissed her eyelids and her nose before clasping her hands in his and gazing into her light blue eyes.

She stared back, mesmerized, looking into his hard, steely, dark blue ones. She simply nodded as if in a spell. She had acquiesced without meaning to.

His lips descended to hers and he greedily feasted on her full, pouty lips, nipping lightly on first one then the other before forcing her tongue to tangle with his. He murmured his pleasure as he kissed alongside her jaw. He felt her lean into him as her knees weakened and he smiled into her hair. When his lips reached her ear he breathed into it again, "Bare your breasts for me, or as I prefer to call them, your titties."

She was shocked by his vulgar words, but strangely, also tantalized by them.

"I . . . I cannot," she whimpered.

"You can," he countered, keeping his eyes on hers as he deftly unbuttoned the line of buttons along the back of her gown. Then he started pulling her gown down over her shoulders. When her lily-white shoulders were bared, he forced the gown even lower, revealing her lace chemise and corset.

Unlacing the bodice, he whispered, "No one is

around, it is just you and I," as he continued to tug on the strings lacing her in. Before she could stop him the tension eased and all was undone. His hands moved the fabric of her gown and corset out of the way. Then he pulled her chemise to her waist, baring her breasts to the night air.

"Sweet Mary Agnes, she was right. Your tits are magnificent," he said as his eyes hungrily devoured her. She stood there in her shame as she watched his eyes rove over her. His face was alight with pleasure, his lips in a wide grin.

"Perfect, perfect—the shape, the size, the nipples. They are absolutely perfect." It was hard not to see the pleasure and lust in his eyes, and even though she was unnerved posing like this in front of him, she was also excited and thrilled by his lavish praise.

His hands reverently cupped her and he gingerly hefted each breast, his fingers groping and kneading as he felt how full and pliant she was. "Like warm, soft clay, molding itself to my hands," he murmured as he stroked her and pinched her. The sensations were new to her. She was flushed with heat and tingling with feelings she had never felt as he continued to stare down at her and fondle her. His thumbs grazed her nipples and she moaned from the intense pleasure he was giving her.

"Ah, responsive, too. I like that very much." He circled her nipples over and over and they budded into tight hard pellets. Then he bent and took a nipple in his mouth and she thought she would die from the heat it sent coursing through her.

"Oh my!" she exclaimed.

"Oh my, is right. These mounds are luscious. They display *very* nicely, very nicely indeed."

He bent to kiss the other breast and she swooned.

He had to catch her about the waist to hold her up as he continued to suckle her.

"Ah, yes," he said as he straightened, never taking his eyes from her chest. "These will do very nicely. Now let's have a look at the rest of you."

"The rest?" she squeaked.

"The rest," he said firmly, looking up from her breasts to meet her eyes. "Your cunt, your womanhood, the juncture between your thighs. I want to see your body and learn all its secrets."

"Sir, I beg of you, surely this can wait for the nuptial night?"

"Surely madam, it cannot. Pull the hem of your gown up to your waist and I will remove your pantaloons." His brusque matter-of-fact manner unnerved her, yet she didn't know how to deny him.

She moved to cover her breasts with the camisole but he grabbed her hand, "Keep those uncovered, I have not yet looked my fill upon them. Now raise your skirts." It was a voice not to be brooked, his ducal voice, one she imagined caused everyone to bow to his demands. Immediately.

Her hands trembled as she inched her gown up from the sides, each hand bunching the satin material. He watched as she revealed her feet, clad in soft but badly worn slippers, her trim ankles encased in white snagged stockings. She hesitated at her knees, but all he had to do was pierce her eyes with his and arch his brow and she continued gathering the folds in her arms. When she finally stood before him with the skirt of her gown completely gathered at her waist, revealing her garters and her pantaloons, he sighed in appreciation.

She stood before him topless, her breasts bared to the night air as she held her dress out of the way so he could strip her of her pantalets. His aim, to view her womanhood, or in his words, "her sweet naked cunt," uttered as he prepared to strip her of her remaining undergarment.

He was excited beyond measure at the sight in front of him. He was as hard as he'd ever been and he could not wait to kneel before her and examine her closely. He stood and took her by the shoulders and gently led her backward so she could lean against the trunk of a huge tree.

"This may take a while, you may need the support," he said as his eyes raked over her breasts again. Then she watched as he knelt in front of her and his hands moved to unfasten the tapes of her pantalets. She held her breath as he undid them and slid them down her thighs, letting them fall below her knees.

She felt his low gasp followed by a long drawn out sigh of wonderment as his breath fluttered the tight curls sparsely covering her. She was tempted to drop the skirts she was holding, but knew that was not the thing to do—already she had divined his one-mindedness about her body. But his perusal there, the knowledge of exactly where his eyes were focused caused her knees to buckle. He gripped her thighs tightly to steady her.

"Do not even think of removing this sight from in front of my eyes by fainting," he murmured as his fingers skimmed the insides of her thighs on their way to their target. His thumbs led the way, gently pushing against the flesh at the top of her thighs to splay her for him.

"Spread your legs further for me," he commanded in a soft whisper. And even though she whimpered, she knew better than to disobey. His fingers groped higher, pushing the flesh apart between her legs.

"Beautiful muff, my love. Show me more, I

want to see it all," he said as he forced her legs even further apart. She looked down to see that he knelt on one knee, wedged between her thighs with his neck crooked so he could view her better. She saw the top of his head angle to the side as he craned his neck to look into the absolute core of her body, and she felt so violated that she sobbed out loud.

"Shhh . . ." he whispered. "It's all right. I'm not going to hurt you. I just want to look. You are incredibly beautiful here, my love. You have the most beautiful cleft I have ever seen. Patricia was right, you are perfect. I will have you as my bride."

He leaned in and kissed her where his fingers had separated her labia and she trembled. She felt herself stiffen under his warm caress and then she involuntarily arched herself to receive another blessing from his lips.

He laughed as he stood, moving close to her so that even if she dropped her skirts, they would still stay up. "You will break in just fine."

His hand caressed her naked thigh as his eyes sought hers, then his fingers found her warm, wet slit and he softly massaged her. "My fingers feel good on you, don't they?" he asked, daring her to lie.

She only nodded as she trembled against him and he chuckled again. He kissed her thoroughly as his fingers explored her, and she didn't know what was delving deeper, his tongue in her mouth or his fingers in her secret place. The sensations he was causing as he kissed her, impaled her, and then bent to suckle a tender, fleshy breast flooded her with a desire she had never known before. Her breath came in hard uneven pants as heat coursed through her veins, she felt lightheaded and in need of something she couldn't name. When she jerked against his finger, drowning it

347

with her hot, sticky juices she cried out with her release.

She felt she was being washed over the edge of a precipice after reaching the summit, and then softly floating down to be caught by a welcoming wave of fluffy cotton. It was like drowning in a warm sea while still being able to breathe. Her body shuddered against his and he kissed her beneath her ear as he whispered, "I promise you that is the first of many, my delectable bride-to-be."

"Was I right?" A voice called out in the still night, and Julia recognized her aunt's voice. She strove desperately to cover herself, but the Duke would not allow it, forcing her hands from her breasts with one hand while keeping her skirts up with his other hand around her waist.

"Yes, you were right. As always," he said to the approaching voice as he indicated the bared breasts with a flourish of one hand. His hip, pressed into hers, secured the gown when he removed his other hand from her waist, "These are magnificent—ripe, full, fleshy and high on her chest. With soft pink nipples I will be the envy of. And this," he cupped her mound, "is every man's dream. Cunt hairs so soft and sheer, it is almost like she is shaven for viewing. You have done well, my love."

My love? Why was he talking to her aunt that way? And why was he allowing her aunt to see her like this? Why was he not covering her? She struggled to free herself, but he held her firmly. The word "nipples" connected in her mind to "envy" and "shaven for viewing" screamed at her, but she couldn't make sense of what they could possibly mean. She continued to try to pull away from him so she could cover herself.

"Now, now, you have a body built for display, do not be self-conscious. While you are not fair of face, you are more than fair of body. Believe me, few women possess such enticing charms in both arenas," he said, his tone mocking.

Her aunt sidled up and took her time surveying her. "Yes, she is first quality. I fear you may not have paid enough for her. Mayhap, we should renegotiate?" she said with a sly smile.

"I've settled enough on you for you and your brood to live comfortably for the rest of your lives, and you know it," he said with a wink. "Accept my thanks for finding me this prize, I shall indeed treasure it. I have the dispensation and the special license with me; we will be wed on the morrow after the doctor has certified her for me. You're sure she is virginal?"

They were talking as if she wasn't even there, yet both sets of eyes were fully on her. She was red with shame but helpless to cover herself.

"I am sure. I have allowed no males, servants or otherwise to be in her presence alone, especially once I discovered her naked in her bath. I knew she was uncommonly formed."

"Good," he said as he ran his fingers through her tight curls, angling his head down to see past the bulk of the wadded gown. "She is an incredible find, I cannot wait until I have the time to play with my new toy and discover all its special secrets." He pulled his hand away and let the gown drop to the ground. Julia visibly relaxed until she remembered that her breasts where still uncovered and both her aunt and now her betrothed's eyes were fixated on them.

Her aunt sauntered over and grabbed a handful of the plump flesh and pinched it together, letting her thumb graze the nipple. "You did well, Your Grace. You will be truly proud on your wedding day."

"That I will," he said as he pulled Julia's camisole

up over the full white mounds with their jutting rose-colored tips. "That I will."

"What are you two talking about and how do you know each other and why do you call her 'your love,'" Julia demanded in her indignation, as she tried to piece her garments back together and to achieve some semblance of order in her appearance. "And why are you allowing him to look upon me like this after all these years of teaching me to be proper and chaste and ladylike?"

The words were issued in a scream as the realization of exactly what had happened here in the openness of this orchard came to her. She was now betrothed to this man. She would be marrying him tomorrow as soon as the doctor vouched for her! Her body would be his to do as he willed and apparently he willed it to be displayed for his eyes. How often, she did not know, but he was obviously paying a great deal for the right to do so as often as he wished.

Her aunt had indeed sold her to this man, this man she knew nothing of, nothing except that his kisses drugged her soul and made her body betray her by relishing the touch of his fingers and mouth.

"You may tell her all you know of me when you are away with her tomorrow, but I would have her know nothing of us until she is far away from here," her aunt said with a stern countenance.

"I understand."

"Come Julia, I will see you to your room where you will be locked in for tonight. It is for your own good. I have come too far in this for anyone to breech you and ruin my arrangement."

Julia was stunned by her aunt's words. Her aunt had plotted in this scheme or whatever it was, and now she, Julia, her once beloved niece, was not even to be trusted until the morrow when a doctor would come and examine her?

"Molly and Meg will sleep with you tonight to insure that you do not harm yourself," she said, the meaning of her words all too clear. "Your maidenhead will provide a roof over the heads of your siblings and half-siblings. They will have new clothing on their backs and ample enough food because of you. Should your maidenhead be breached tonight, they will be orphaned."

Her aunt did not say this in a mean-spirited way, just in a matter-of-fact way, as if the choices were simple—as if this was indeed the last option open to them. She looked tired and sad, but unapproachable. It was obvious that her mind was made up and that nothing Julia could say would sway her.

Her life had been given over. She now belonged to the Duke of Thornhill— body and soul. But sadly, he only seemed interested in her body. She followed her aunt back to the house and up to her bed chamber where her sisters were already in bed waiting for her.

She was surprised when the Duke arrived at nine the next morning to take her to the doctor.

"I thought Dr. Herrington would be coming here," she said.

"You're not seeing Dr. Herrington, you're seeing my doctor. Dr. Lucien Rinaldo. He's traveled from London to examine you for me. He and his nurse have been invited to use Dr. Herrington's offices in town."

"You don't trust anybody do you?" she sneered at him.

"No. Not when it's important. And this is very important."

"Why? Why is it so important that I be a virgin?

You obviously aren't unpracticed."

He laughed uproarishly. "That is, in fact, true. However, I paid for a virgin and a virgin I shall have. I don't really have to explain it to you, but I will. I am thirty-two, never married—in fact, never planned to marry, until my eldest brother died late last year. Now the line must continue with me. I will eventually need an heir. You shall provide me with one when the time comes. When I deem you are ready to bear a child for me, you will do so. Although I would prefer the mother of my children be a virgin on the day I marry her, the legacy of my family requires it to be so. So, I must be assured that no man's prick has found its way between your thighs before mine."

She gasped at his language and he chuckled, "You might as well get used to my language, I don't intend to change it for you." He took her elbow and assisted her onto the carriage block.

The coach pulled up and she saw that six outriders as well as the over-embellished, liveried footmen from yesterday accompanied it, along with the same two drivers she'd seen the day before. Even the tiger, the young man riding on the back, was in full uniform, and from the little she knew of the aristocracy, that was considered a flagrant display of excess. How wealthy was this man she was going to marry anyway?

He handed her up into the carriage and for all outward appearances, it looked like he was a detached gentleman taking her for a Sunday afternoon outing, not the rake she now knew him to be, taking her to *his* doctor to have her inspected because he believed she could be lying to him. And never in her life had she ever wished so much that she had lied and that the good doctor would back her in her lie. But since he was such a good friend of the Duke—that was highly unlikely.

Molly and Meg had been so severely instructed not to let her out of their sight last night, that she was not even left alone to go to the garderobe, so even if she had been able to find something appropriate to use, she wouldn't have had the opportunity to use it to cause her virgin blood to flow. But she had thought about it all night as she tossed around in her sleep.

As soon as the Duke was situated in the carriage beside her, he tapped on the roof and the carriage surged forward.

"Good morning, my dear," he said belatedly, "I trust you slept well?"

"About as well as one could with two youngsters in my bed kicking me all through the night."

"Well, tonight shall be different; I don't kick."

Oh yes, she had that to look forward to. Being bedded by a man she hardly knew. She had hoped one day to find a mate, but she had fancied being able to fall in love before being expected to relinquish her body over to the desires of a rutting husband. That would have made it at least tolerable, she thought.

She didn't know much about the actual act of consummation—her aunt had told her only a little of what to expect. She had advised her to make sure her bladder was emptied before going to the marriage bed if she preferred pleasure to pain, but other than that she was completely unsure as to what to expect. She knew that the male penis would enter her between her legs and that he would pleasure himself in her body until he had coaxed his seed to spill out of him and into her. That was enough to terrify her; she wasn't sure she wanted to know any more of what would be expected of her in the marriage bed.

Her aunt had hugged her this morning and told her to be obedient, that some unpleasantness was to be expected for the grand reward they were all getting. She had told her about the new manor house the Duke had bought for her and the children, and the school the Duke was sending her brother, Theodore, to at the end of the summer. It had warmed her heart when Teddy had come to her this morning after breaking their fast. He had hugged her around her hips and thanked her wholeheartedly for marrying the Duke so he could attend the most prestigious Bolton Arms Academy. All of the girls had new gowns delivered to them early this morning, including her. All the accoutrements had also been provided and she had learned that the Duke was much more than considerate; he was thorough—not neglecting a single detail. Not so much as a hair ribbon was omitted from the new ensembles.

She was wearing her new gown as instructed in the letter that accompanied the gown, the petticoats and all the prerequisite undergarments. He had also provided new leather slippers, a matching pelisse, and a velveteen cloak that was as soft and cool as wild moss in a summer glade. The quality of the materials was impeccable and the workmanship the finest she'd ever seen. If this was a sampling of the luxuries the Duke would bestow on her, mayhap it wouldn't be so bad being yoked to him and occasionally availing him of her sexual favors. She knew that many women had it a lot worse than she would have it. At least she wasn't to be saddled with a toothless man thirty years older than herself with three chins, gout, and pudgy, pasty skin.

She turned to look at the man sitting beside her and realized that he was staring at her. His dark blue eyes were assessing her from the new, pert green velvet hat with the brown-feathered plume all the way down to her new stylish kidskin slippers.

"Proper clothing makes a world of difference on you. Although, don't get too used to it. I expect soon for you to be out of all your clothing for a goodly amount of the time."

She blushed at his words but his husky voice had triggered another response in her that she was completely unfamiliar with, and a seeping warmness crept into her chest and belly. The man was so sure of himself. What must it be like to always get what you wanted whenever you wanted it, she wondered.

"Now that I am really taking a good look at you, I find I may have spoken a little too hastily yesterday. You really are quite charming. Your skin has a wonderful glow and your plumped lips are quite enticing, indeed. Lean over here and kiss me."

"What?"

"Kiss me. It's easy, just press your lips against mine and move them around some."

She sat back against the squabs and shook her head.

"That was not a request, that was a command. And no one disobeys me. I hope you do not have to learn that the hard way. Now do as I say and kiss me."

She looked from his steely hard eyes to his firm lips. Timidly she sat forward and turned toward him. She allowed her body to lean into him until her lips grazed his, then she sat right back.

"If that's the best you can do, we have a lot of work ahead of us," he said before he grabbed her by the shoulders and hauled her onto his lap. She squealed as his lips descended to hers and he kissed her passionately and thoroughly, his tongue quickly breaching her lips and darting inside between her teeth. His tongue repeatedly flicked over hers trying to coax it to retreat with his into his mouth, and finally, he succeeded. He managed to tantalize her tongue into exploring his mouth and it surprised them both. He groaned from the unexpected pleasure and she gasped from embarrassment at her forwardness.

He laughed and pulled away from her, "Do not cower so, your tongue will soon know all the places there is to know on me, the inside of my mouth is just the beginning."

Her insides shuddered at his words. She was shocked not only from the impact of learning that he would be expecting her to use her tongue on other parts of his body, but also from the effect of his kiss. It had called to a place deep down inside her and Lord help her; she wanted another just like it.

The carriage pulled up in front of a short drive and halted at the front door of the local doctor. She knew him well because of her sisters and her brother, but personally, she had never taken sick that she could remember.

A footman opened the carriage door and the Duke stepped down and then turned to lift her out. His hands on her waist instead of on her forearms attested for all who cared to watch that she was allowing him to be quite familiar with her body, and she again blushed at the intimacy his touch afforded.

He set her down beside him and together they walked up the short path to the door. The door opened just as they reached it and the genial old doctor she was familiar with greeted them.

"Your grace," he said falteringly, "allow me to introduce myself. I am Dr. Herrington and I am most humbled that you have chosen my offices for your personal physician to utilize during your visit here."

"Where is dear Lucien?" the Duke asked jovially.

"He is waiting for you in the study with a glass

of sherry."

"Marvelous."

"I will take your betrothed to his nurse."

"Thank you, but I prefer him to meet her while she is still clothed if you don't mind."

And then it all came back to her, what they were here for. Horrified, she realized that soon a strange man would be gazing on her naked body, well, not so much on it as into it. She ducked her head and looked at the hem of her gown as the dread washed over her. If she didn't comply, he would not marry her. Her aunt and the children would be homeless. Teddy would have no academy or university awaiting his arrival with his coat full of tuition money. All would be lost if she did not obey. She remembered her aunt's words. She had known how hard this would be for her. Julia realized she had no choice in this, she was the only one who could save her family from ruin.

The Duke took her arm and led her down a darkened hallway and then with his hand on her lower back, he escorted her into the study. A man stood from behind the desk and smiled at them.

Dear God, he was young! Not a fuddy-duddy old man in his cups as she was hoping. Sweet Jesu, this rakish-looking man with his intelligent eyes would soon be examining her! There!

"Lucien!" the Duke called out. "Good of you to come on such short notice." They clasped each other about the shoulders like the good old school chums that they were, and she saw that the doctor was taller than her soon-to-be husband. When he turned to face her, she saw that he had exotic dark eyes that sparkled with mischief.

"Did I really have a choice?" the man answered with a lopsided grin. "A summons from the Grand Duke of Thornhill is not to be ignored," he said in a put-on lofty voice. "Besides, I wouldn't have missed this opportunity for the world and you know it."

"Julia, this is my dear old friend, Dr. Lucien Rinaldo, doctor to the *ton*. Incredibly smart lad. He found a way to have women eagerly part their thighs for him, and he gets paid for it. Handsomely, I might add. We were roommates at Cambridge. Lucien, this is Julia, my betrothed . . . unless you tell me otherwise," he said with a pointed look in her direction.

The reminder that he thought she could be lying to him pricked her again, but she didn't dwell on it. A nurse came into the room and stood beside the doctor.

"Julia, it is indeed a pleasure to make your acquaintance. This is my nurse, Agnes. She will take you to the examining room and help you to disrobe. The Duke and I will share a sherry and then we'll be with you shortly."

"We'll?" she asked horrified, her wide eyes darting to the Duke's.

"You did not think I would allow another man's eyes to feast on the part that makes you female without me being present did you?" His tone was mocking and somehow she knew that he was enjoying this.

She took a deep breath and said as calmly as she could, "I don't think that would be proper, surely you trust your friend. He is a doctor."

"Proper or not, I will be present for his examination of you." His eyes narrowed as they bored into hers, "No man looks at you outside of my presence," he said and she could hear the anger and determination in his voice.

She knew then that he would not listen to any of her pleas for decency, decorum, or modesty and she turned scarlet with rage and embarrassment.

The doctor picked up a glass of sherry that had already been poured. It sat on the edge of a silver tray beside a crystal decanter. It was filled with a matching light brown liquid. He handed it to her saying, "Here, have a few sips of sherry, it'll calm you down a little."

"I don't want to be calm!" she retorted.

The Duke took the proffered sherry and thrust it into her hand, "Drink it!" he hissed through clenched teeth. Then he turned back for the glass the doctor was offering to him.

She took several small sips as she looked over the rim of the glass trying desperately to think of a way out of what was coming next.

She was still trying to think of something to say, something to let him know she refused to do this, when the nurse suddenly took her arm firmly in hers, and none too gently led her out of the room and down a hallway.

When the nurse had shut the door behind them in the tiny examining room, she gruffly rasped, "Remove everything. Not a stitch is to be left on ya."

"I cannot believe that you expect me to disrobe for two men! It's not proper!"

"One of those men is your doctor, one is soon to be your husband. That's proper enough." She reached over and pulled off Julia's hat, pulling the large hairpin out of her hair as she did so. Her long blonde hair tumbled past her shoulders.

"Now look what you've done!" Julia screamed, suddenly aware that she was practically hysterical and totally foolish to be concerned about her hair when this matron was rapidly divesting her of her clothing.

Garrett put the laptop aside long enough to go to the bathroom and to replenish his wine glass. This was some hot stuff, he said to himself as he watched the tented front of his boxer shorts jounce with each step. This woman, Laurel Ashleigh Leighton, had an incredible way of keeping him hard.

He slid back into the bed, fluffed the pillow at his back and repositioned the laptop. He could not wait to find out what was going to happen to Julia. This story looked like it could easily morph into something with a kinky BDSM theme. He felt his cock grow harder at the thought. Wow, this woman could write! He took a hefty swig and moved the cursor.

Julia fought the nurse as she tried to unbutton her bodice, but clearly she was no match for her, and suddenly she felt her arms grow heavy and useless against Agnes' formidable maneuvers. Within minutes she was standing naked before her in the small room, her clothing locked in an armoire in the corner.

"Here," the nurse said as she thrust a bed sheet at her. "You can wear this 'til they get here, but then they're going to want that off, too." Agnes openly ogled Julia as she opened the sheet and spun it around Julia's body and then tucked it under her arms. "You're a real pretty piece once your clothes is off, I'll give you that. Get up on the table," she said gesturing to the cloth-covered table in the center of the room.

Julia turned and looked at the table for the first time. It was high off the floor. It was padded and covered with an oilcloth. A short stool had been placed at the end of the long table. Attached to all four corners of the table were leather straps and silver clamps with short bindings.

"No! No!" she cried, and then as she saw the nurse advancing on her, her sobs turned piteously low, "no, no, please, no."

The older woman softened slightly, "It's no use fightin', they're gonna do it, ya might as well make the best of it. C'mon, sit yourself up here and let me strap you down. I don't want to hurt you, but my job is to get you ready for them."

"No, no, no," she wailed. "Please, don't let them do this."

"The stuff in the sherry'll be workin' soon and it won't be as bad as you're thinkin'. The doctor's real gentle-like, he won't hurt you none, nor cause you no harm. I been working with him eight years, he's kind."

"But I can't," she whimpered, "I just can't."

"Ya must missus. Your master wants Dr. Rinaldo to show him your maidenhead, and ain't nobody gonna tell the Duke 'no' 'bout nothin'. C'mon, I'll help you. Sit in the middle now. Now lay down." She pushed her until she was prone, her head resting on a small pillow.

"What was in the sherry?"

"Just a little laudanum, it'll make you mellow but I didn't give you enow to knock you out."

"Why not?" That sounded like a pretty good idea right about now.

"Doctor's orders, just give you enow to settle you down and strap you up, otherwise you'll get the megrims."

Right now, she'd rather a case of the megrims than the memory of this. She felt the matron lift each arm and secure it with the strap, then the matron went to the foot of the table and separated her legs and secured each ankle with her foot flat on the table. With each limb, Julia tried to fight her, but every muscle was so heavy she couldn't do much more than flail at her before it was restrained at the edges of the examining table.

Then Agnes pulled the sheet out from under her

and snapped it high into the air letting it slowly waft down on top of her naked body. She walked over to the window and opened the curtains leaving only the sheers closed, flooding the room with bright morning sunlight. "This window faces the rose garden and there's a locked gate at the end, so you don't have to worry about anybody seeing sumpin' they're not supposed to be seein'. But the doctor requires the daylight to see. The doctor and the Duke'll be in shortly, you got no worries ifn' you've been a good girl, if not . . . " she shook her head and shut the door behind her. Then Julia was alone in the room, naked except for the sheet that had settled lightly over her.

I don't have to worry about anybody seeing sumpin' they're not supposed to be seein', she mimicked to herself. Neither of these men was supposed to see her like this! What made them think they had the right? Oh Lordy, what had she gotten herself into? Tears leaked out of her eyes and ran down to the pillow that was propping her head up.

The knob turned, the door creaked on its hinges, and the doctor walked in followed by the Duke, who closed the door firmly behind him. Her eyes met his and she felt sure he was delighted with her palpable fear.

"Julia," the doctor said as he sat down on the stool at the end of the table between her covered, splayed thighs. His voice was very soft and cultured as he continued, "I won't be doing anything that will hurt you. We're just going to take a little look at you. You will feel me touch you from time to time, and I will be inserting a small spreading devise that will enable me to get a better view inside you." The Duke stood over his right shoulder smiling down at her. This was going to be awful. She closed her eyes tightly. How could this be happening to her?

"I'm going to lift the sheet up over your knees now so I can examine you."

She sobbed and struggled against the restraints as he gingerly lifted the sheet over her knees. She felt the cool air of the room on her thighs and genitals and knew she was uncovered, naked in front of their eyes. She tried to move her legs to close off their view, but she couldn't.

The doctor reached up and pushed her knees fully apart and she knew she was now gaping wide for them. Nothing was hidden from their view. She turned her head and stared at the wall and let her tears silently wet her face.

"Jesus Stewart, she's gorgeous!" the doctor whispered, evidently so awed by the sight of her that he couldn't help his outburst.

"I told you she would be. Look at those light blonde curls would you? I've never seen anything like it."

"Me either, such fairness against the pink. Her hairs are so pale that they're almost white."

She turned her head and looked down between her knees and saw the wavy brown curls of the doctor's head. The Duke was bent, peering over the doctor's shoulder. She squeezed her eyes shut and even more tears oozed out.

"Watch as I spread her lips," the doctor said as his fingers touched her. She jumped and squirmed away but his hands went under her, gripped her buttocks and pulled her back down to the very edge of the table saying, "Shhh, it's okay," he crooned and she felt his fingers touch her again then spread her nether lips. "Ahhh, such a pretty, healthy pink vagina."

The Duke looked up at her, as if to reassure her,

"You're showing us your pink vagina, sweetheart and it is truly lovely. You have a delightful little cunt." She squirmed and tried to close her legs but they were too heavy; she couldn't get her muscles to contract. Then the Duke actually seemed to be smiling at her discomfort, and in that moment she hated him for it.

Then he looked down again to where the doctor's hands were installing a small tube, and he addressed his friend, "So, is she?"

"See for yourself," the doctor said and moved slightly out of the way, but she could still feel his fingers on her holding her labial lips apart with the tube partially inserted into her. "She's small inside, but I can see everything's still intact."

The Duke moved into the vacated space and crouched low. She heard the doctor say, "See that thin membrane way up inside? Here, I can touch it with this swab." She felt something enter her and touch her. "That's it, Stewart, that's her hymen or maidenhead as you Highlanders say. It's intact and ready for popping!" he said, sounding very pleased, as if he had just discovered a rare jewel. He pulled the tube out.

"What is this?" The Duke asked, and he bent forward to graze his finger on her. She felt more fingers join his. *My God, now they were both touching her at the same time!*

"That's her first set of lips, this," he said stroking the inside of a velvet fold, "is the second set, where all the love juices come from, she'll get wet for you here and it'll spread to here," he said pointing. "Look, she's getting wet now. See that light milky glaze? It's coating her like a fine, silky patchouli oil—her body's getting ready to mate, making your entry easier and protecting her from being rubbed raw. If you make her come, this is where that lovely woman's essence comes from," he said as ran his finger around the top rim of her vagina.

He inserted his finger inside her, stood and pushed against her mound with his other hand. "If you curl your finger inside her and stroke the front wall of her vagina like this, making steady and firm contact, there is a very special spot where you can make her scream and cause her to flood your hand."

He shoved hard, sending his long finger deep into her core, his palm cupping her. Leaning slightly forward, he pushed against her mons from the outside, flexing his wrist several times with the effort. When she groaned, he stopped and held both hands still. A moment later, Julia's body arched up to meet the downward pressure. She lifted her hips, grinding herself into his hand. All control left her as she cried out and began frantically convulsing against him. Sobbing with shame, she turned her head to the wall as her body betrayed her and swamped his hand.

"See?" he said triumphantly, pulling out his finger and showing him her copious release. A pool of thick creamy slickness coated his palm.

"Nice . . . you do know your way around a woman's cunt. Always wondered where that creamy stuff came from," the Duke said with a chuckle. "I've looked between the legs of many women and never noticed that there were two sets of lips before. I suppose I was more interested in the sweet honey hole."

The doctor smugly smiled at him and began to slowly massage Julia, calming her and forcing her to relax after her powerful orgasm. He was pleased he knew something about women that his friend, the Duke, London's most notorious rake, didn't know. But he was doubly pleased that he was able to bring this beautiful woman to her completion so readily by his more than capable hands.

The Duke elbowed his friend aside to sit on the stool between Julia's parted thighs. He leaned in and kissed Julia on her nether lips, using his tongue he redistributed the musky dew as he licked her slit from top to bottom and back again. She gasped and her eyes opened wide. Both the doctor and the Duke chuckled, then the Duke stood, licking his lips.

"Can't let any of that stuff go to waste, can I?" he said when he saw his friend's amused expression. "She tastes as good as she looks, Luce."

Lucien knew that, as he had just sucked her essence from his fingers. They both stood back and stared at her, at the moist junction between her thighs. "She is lovely isn't she?" the Duke said.

"You've done very well for yourself, Stewart. You've certainly done your family proud."

"Yes. I think everyone will be well pleased."

What in the world were they talking about, she wondered in her lightly fogged head.

"Now, let me see her breasts and I'll check to make sure she has good nipples for nursing your heirs."

"You just want to see her tits."

The doctor laughed. "Yes, I do in fact."

She felt the sheet being pulled completely off of her until she was lying on the table completely naked and open, nothing covering her anywhere, nothing at all.

"Ahhh. Perfect. They are simply perfect," Lucien breathed.

"Here, let me sit her up so you can see their true shape. They are quite full and heavy, yet still high on her chest," the Duke said proudly.

She felt the Duke's hands on her back and shoulders as he lifted her into a seated position, and when she looked up she saw the doctor's eyes deeply searching her own before his hands reached out and cupped her breasts.

"Ahhh. Stewart. You are the luckiest man in the universe. These are marvelous. So soft, yet firm," he bent lower and concentrated his eyes on her nipples, "nipples to entice any man's tongue." He stroked them and pulled on them and then rubbed them back and forth between his fingers. "Look how long they're getting just by my rubbing them, imagine how long they'll get by you suckling them. She'll nurse just fine, both you and the babes will be able to suckle her with abandon."

He kneaded the flesh back and forth and up and down and around in circles on her chest. "Showpieces, these are," the doctor murmured.

"Yes, I know," the Duke said proudly from behind her where he was still propping her up for him.

She turned her head and her eyes met his, and she could see the lust in them. She was on her elbows, her legs splayed; her knees spread wide showing them both every private part of her body. She was still unable to move, unable to retract anything, and unable to keep them from looking at her most private parts. All she could do was sit there and let them look at her to their heart's desire.

The doctor abandoned her breasts and came around the table to stand at the foot of the table. The Duke eased her back down and went to stand beside him and together they stared at her in silence for several long minutes.

Finally she could take their fascinated scrutiny no longer and she whispered, "Please." The doctor bent to pickup the sheet from the floor and covered her with it.

"Thank you, my Lady Thornhill," he said as he

smoothed the sheet in place, then he bent and kissed her on the cheek. Using her soon-to-be title was his way of assuring her that she had passed all of his tests. "I've never enjoyed an examination more."

"Hey! Don't make me jealous here."

What kind of man was she marrying? A man who would allow all these liberties to be taken on her body by this man's eyes and his hands, but now he was objecting to a simple kiss on her cheek? How was she to get along with this man? He was a monster. And so was his friend.

The doctor left the room and the Duke bent over the table to take a nipple into his mouth to suckle it. She sucked in air and cried out in surprise. He continued for many minutes, alternating between breasts and she felt more of that warm liquid collect between her thighs.

When he was finished, he ravaged her lips and she thought she tasted herself in his kiss. Then he stood above her looking down at her and with steel in his eyes as he grated out, "Men may look at you, but remember, *you are mine.*"

He abruptly left the room and the nurse returned to help her dress. *What in the name of Holy Heaven did he mean by that?*

On the carriage ride back to her aunt's house, she vented her anger at his treatment of her. "If I am to be your wife, a lady of the realm, why was I treated so shabbily and so disrespectfully, by you, the doctor, and his nurse? Surely it is obvious to me that you meant to humiliate and shame me beyond what was required to certify my chastity!"

"Madam," he said complacently, "You were a player in this game long before I even knew of you. Dr. Lucien Rinaldo, the Earl of Navona, has been promised an unencumbered view of my betrothed's maidenhead since we were but fourteen years of age. And had he not turned doctor, I would still have been obliged to make sure he had it."

She gasped at his harsh words, and as her hand clutched at her throat. Her eyes met his hard defiant ones, and she knew she would never have a say in anything that concerned her. She was indeed, bought and paid for, and he would never accept her as anything but his sovereign property, over which he had complete and absolute control. Her body belonged to him. He would do with it what he wanted, and she was beginning to suspect that he had plans she was not going to like.

"No need to be shocked. Between friends such as he and I, it is done all the time. What a woman's body is subjected to is just not always something that they are aware of," he said with a sly leer, "she is not always conscious or awake and so is quite often unaware of her husband's proclivities. At least the liberties I have taken with your body have been done with your full knowledge."

"And outraged objections!"

"You might as well learn not to voice them, it will only get me angered and make things harder for you."

"What am I to be? Your lady or your whore?" she said with great vehemence.

He reached out and roughly grabbed her breast through her gown and bodice. She felt the savagery of his possession of it. "I may allow men to feast their eyes on you, but I will never allow them to have you! You are mine! While I will enjoy watching others build their lust for you, I will never let them sate themselves within your body." He squeezed her breast harder and she could feel his fingernails digging into her soft flesh like talons. "And you best never allow that to happen either, my Lady," he sneered at her while making a mockery of the word 'Lady.'

Then, with a slight shove, he removed his hand from her breast and lightly stroked her cheek as he softly whispered, "Your job is to tantalize. To make men openly aware of the wondrous prize I have attained for myself, to make jealousy ride high in the hearts of my cohorts. I wish them all to envy me, my *very lovely Lady Julia.*"

Whoa, this was some hot stuff! Unbelievably hot stuff. Garrett's mind could hardly get around the fact that Laurel, sweet, vibrant, youthful Laurel, had written this. He was about to shoot his release to the other side of the room and he'd not even touched himself yet. These characters . . . they were so real . . . so . . . so like the men he envisioned for the time.

Feudal lords, whose holdings were vast, owned everything in their domain. They were skillful, bloodthirsty fighters who undoubtedly had an immense hunger for sex. After the business of war was shelved for the day, what else did they have to entertain them? Without TV, NASCAR, Football or the NBA, wenching had to be high on the list of things to occupy their dark evenings.

A peer of the realm, by virtue of being in supreme command, had a clear field with his servants, and with the law granting ownership, wives were no more than chattel. When brides handed over their dowries, their bodies were part and parcel. From the day of the betrothal they had no say. If a man had no mores, her destiny was doomed—she couldn't foist her prudishness on him, couldn't insist he behave or even act reasonably. All she could hope to do was endure his attentions whether they be base, demeaning, humiliating, hurtful, or damaging. Wives had no rights; Julia would have been the Duke's to command. If society didn't object, there was no one to answer to. And in a family such as Julia was being absorbed into, if her husband desired to share her, she was powerless to resist. Garrett knew these things had happened way back when, he'd just never read a story depicting it so graphically. He was tired, but still, he was compelled to read on.

As she sat stunned by his venomous revelations, she was told the details about the marriage ceremony they would be having later this afternoon, and about the journey back to his estate near Heather Moorland. It would take three days for them to travel, and on the fourth day, they would again be married. This time it would be a proper Hedonic ceremony honoring his family and their traditions, and this he told her, would be their true handfasting day. The ceremony today was something to appease her aunt because he knew she would not let him take her away without the benefit of marriage and all that it promised her. Their true marriage ceremony would be one in the style of the ancient druids, the pagans, from whom his father's Welsh ancestry was derived.

None of this made a lot of sense to her, but she listened anyway, hoping to understand more of what was expected of her. When he got to the part about their wedding night, her heart sang. She had a reprieve. Since he felt that they were not really and truly married until the second ceremony, they would not be consummating their marriage until that night, five days hence. However, he said, admonishing her severely for her zealous delight, "We will be traveling together in the same coach, sharing the same room at the inns and sleeping in the same bed. And there are other things I expect you to do for me, and one or two

I may do for you if you choose to behave."

The man was so cryptic all the time, why couldn't he just speak plain English? What was in store for her on the road to her new home? The strange light in his eyes hinted to her that he would be pleased, but that she might not. She was quick to note that he seemed to divine a strange sense of pleasure whenever he exerted his power over her, especially when it required her to be humiliated or humbled by him.

The wedding at her aunt's took place in the formal salon, shabby though it was. They both repeated their vows mechanically, she because she was nervous and still caught up in a maelstrom of different emotions, he, because he gave little credence to the validity of this ceremony as this was not his religion.

While they were attending the small reception her aunt had arranged for them, the servants packed all of Julia's possessions and loaded them into the wagon the Duke had instructed his head coachman to purchase. Then Julia said tearful goodbyes to her siblings and cousins. Finally, turning to her aunt, she buckled under the strain.

"I don't know if I can do this," she sobbed in her aunt's arms, "I'm not ready to be a bride or a mother!"

"You are indeed ready to be a bride, my dear," her aunt said as she consoled her. "As for being a mother, I would not worry. I venture it will be quite some time before the Duke allows you to become one."

Julia looked at her with questioning eyes, but her aunt did not elaborate further. As she stroked Julia's overlong blonde hair, she whispered in her niece's ear, "I know one thing for certain; he will not hurt you if you obey him. If you do not though, he has his ways, and they are not pleasant. You will never wear a bruise from his loving though . . . love bites—that I would expect.

Maybe you won't come to mind them. In truth, I envy you. His is quite a virile man and you will be cherished and well loved as his lady bride."

"How do you know all this?" Julia asked.

"He was my first, a long, long time ago. Before I met either of my husbands. He will tell you all when he is ready. Take heed of my advice, if you know what is best for you . . . and for the family you are leaving behind." With that, she gave her a small kiss on each cheek and set her aside.

The Duke of Thornhill bent and took Patricia's hand in his. He raised it to his lips while he focused his stern blue eyes on hers. "You have found me a gem among gems, the prized ruby of the lot. It is that much more rewarding that this gift comes from you, a very special lady of my past. Tell me, do you ever think of me and the times we had?"

"Always," she answered with a small smile. "More often than you would ever imagine," she whispered.

He bent to kiss her on the cheek and Julia swore that she saw his hand stray to cup her bottom before he turned to face his new bride.

"All is in readiness, let's make haste. I would like to make the first inn by midnight."

She was ensconced in the carriage beside him and after many frantic waves to the family she was leaving behind, the caravan pulled through the crumbling front gates and began the long journey to Thornhill Manor.

Many moments later, she looked up to find him staring at her.

"Is something wrong, sir? Do I have mud on my face?"

"No. I was just assessing your looks. It is your overlong hair that draws your face down and focuses such attention to your high forehead. I think when we arrive at Thornhill, that mayhap your new lady's maid should trim the front and allow some wisps to grace your forehead. She could thin away the heavy weight of it with loose layers. It is well past your arse so it could stand some attention."

She blushed at his reference to her bottom.

"I am to have my own lady's maid? I will not have to share her?" she asked.

"Indeed you shall. In fact, you shall have several. You will have all the trappings of being a Duke's lady, save one."

"And may I ask what that might be?"

His eyes bored into hers and he said, "Modesty. You will not be permitted modesty. In fact, for the rest of the ride tonight, I will require that you remove your gown, corset and camisole. You may keep your pantalets and stockings on. For now, I just want to see your titties bounce."

Her eyes went wide and she drew her cloak tighter around herself.

"And I am desperately tired, so please do not argue with me. Simply remove your garments and sit in front of me displaying your breasts."

"Your Grace," she said, "you said yourself that we were not yet man and wife. How can you ask this of me?"

"My Lady, you are mine, one way or the other. I have paid a fortune for you. You are either my slave or my wife, I do not care which, just remove your clothes!"

The anger in his voice was evident and she was afraid to prick his ire any further. She remembered her aunt's words about him not hurting her unless she disobeyed him. Slowly, she unwrapped the cloak and let it fall off her shoulders.

His eyes watched her fingers as she unbuttoned the front of her gown. When she had unbuttoned it well past her waist, she slid it off her shoulders and allowed it to bunch around her middle. She sat looking at him, hoping for some sort of reprieve, but he simply nodded his head at her chest in a silent command for her to continue disrobing.

The corset was tightly laced under her breasts, and it took her a few moments to get the strings untangled so she could loosen the stays and unlace it. Finally, with his help, it was completely unlaced and it fell behind her against the leather seat squabs. The only thing left to remove was the thin cotton chemise, and as she looked into his face, she saw his hunger and knew that if she did not hurry and pull it down, that he would rip it right off of her. It was one of the new ones he had given her, and it was fine and soft against her skin. She did not want him ruining it. Quickly she slid her arms out of the sleeves and let it settle around her midriff. Her breasts were now free, jiggling up and down with the motion of the carriage.

She watched his face as his eyes drank her in. And felt cheap and tawdry like a sailor's whore displaying herself. His eyes darkened with desire. There was something wicked behind his eyes, something evil, but it was also sensual and commanding. She could not help but look down at herself to see what it was he was seeing.

From above, she could not see the sumptuous, curving fullness made round like heavy globes that beckoned to be hefted and cupped. All she saw was the gentle slopes leading down to the pert nipples, the tantalizing pale undersides completely out of her view.

"Pull on your nipples," he commanded.

"Pardon?"

"You heard me. Stop trying to defy me and do as you're told. Use your fingertips and pull on your nipples!"

Afraid the head coachman would hear, and embarrassed that he should know what she was doing in the well-sprung coach, she reluctantly lifted her hands and moved her fingers over her nipples. She grabbed the very tips of her nipples and pulled them out, holding them away from her body.

"No, not like that," he said gruffly. "Pinch them and keep pinching them, pull them and release them, over and over again."

She did as he said and soon she felt a tightening in her groin and a peculiar warmth spreading in her belly.

"Yes, yes," he said, "like that exactly. It's amazing, the color actually changes with your arousal."

Is that what she was feeling? But the thought that she could be lusting for him was preposterous. Yet she continued to tug on the tips of her breasts, making them tingle as she felt her womb tightening.

He sat and watched her play with herself for many minutes before telling her to cup a breast with each hand and to squeeze them together on her chest.

"Now, lick your nipples," he said.

"Your Grace, my tongue will not reach."

"Try it and you will be surprised to learn, that it will," he said with a wicked smile.

She did as he asked and she found that she could just get the very tip of her tongue to touch the tip of her nipple if she held it high enough.

"Now the other," he said, "make them both glisten for me."

Again, she did as he asked, feeling vulgar and ashamed. She was beginning to realize that she was going to hate being his wife if these were the kinds of things he was going to require of her.

"Here," he said as he knelt on the floor between the seats, "let me have a taste."

He took her nipple deeply into his mouth and suckled on it, laving it thoroughly with his tongue while the fingers on his other hand plucked and pulled on the sensitive nub of the other breast. She felt molten desire flow through her veins.

"Nice, nice titties," he breathed into her cleavage as he moved his mouth from one to the other.

She was getting hot everywhere, her blood was flashing through her system like lightning streaking through the sky with each tug of his lips on her.

Suddenly his hand snaked beneath her skirt and up through the edge of her pantalets. She felt his fingers on her thigh. "Spread your thighs," he moaned in a husky voice. When she hesitated and did not do his bidding right away, he barked, "Now!"

Instantly, she let her legs fall open and he pushed her thighs wide apart. His fingers found her moist cleft and they entered her, separating her lips and digging for her tunnel. She felt his fingers inside her, thrusting in and out repeatedly. More than one she was certain. He stopped and withdrew them to tease and stroke her labial lips. His fingers gripped the slick lips and he plucked at them sending hot flashes and spiking waves of fluid though her. Then all too soon, his hand threaded its way out of the folds of her clothing. Both of his hands pulled her skirts up and her pantalets down and off.

His hands roved over her calves and then up her long legs, stroking the sides of her thighs. "You hardly have any hair on your legs, my dear, and what you do have is so fine you can hardly see or feel it, it's so downy." He massaged her firm outer thighs, working his way around to the smooth, soft, inner parts.

"Kick your shoes off and put your feet on the seat squab behind me, as far apart as you can get them." When she didn't immediately respond to him, he reached up and tweaked her nipple hard. "Obey me, dammit!"

She slipped her feet out of her new kidskin slippers and struggled to get them up onto the seat cushion across from her. He grabbed her ankles and placed them as he wished, and she realized that she was as splayed and her womanhood as prominently displayed as it had been in the doctor's office this morning. Fortunately, it was not as well lit now, as the sun was going down and the curtains on the carriage had been drawn for them.

It was as if he had read her mind, for he reached up with one hand, and jerked the curtains aside allowing what was left of the meager daylight to enter and illuminate her.

"So pretty," he said as he watched the tips of his fingers toy with her tiny outer lips. He flicked his fingers back and forth until they opened for him and revealed the thinner, slicker inner lips protecting her wet dark channel. "Your knees," he whispered, "pull them up and hold them. God I loved watching Lucien's eyes eating you up this morning. He wanted you, I know he did."

"And that made you happy?" she breathed harshly; for he was doing something wicked inside that felt wonderful.

"Yes. I was delighted with you. Hold your knees up high."

She did as he asked, because now she wanted to, now she wanted him to touch her and for his eyes to devour her. When his head bent and his lips sought to taste her, she shivered and moaned and he gave a great laugh. He whispered hoarsely against her thigh as he placed a line of kisses alongside it, "I will break you in tonight for you are as lusty as I. "

She threw her head against the seatback in shame as his lips latched onto her and he began in earnest to lick and suck her. His tongue feverishly delved into her tight channel before returning to lave the engorged nub plumping at the top of her slit.

He was very thorough in his explorations. He allowed his tongue free rein, he furled it and thrust it into her cavity, he pointed it and thrust it in as far up inside her as he could get it, he fucked her with his tongue until she thought she would go crazy from the sensations he was causing. When he felt the slight tremors begin and the little contractions building, he moved his mouth up her cleft to the secret cache and suckled on the throbbing nubbin he found there. It pulsated under his lips and she went wild thrusting up against his mouth and using her hands to hold his face tightly against her.

He stayed with her and rode out her orgasm as it rocked through her. But he was careful not to touch the ultra sensitive nub again, once it had finished throbbing and retreated into its hiding place, he would not touch it again. She was too new at this, she would need recovery time and practice before she was capable of multiple climaxes.

He lightly lapped to cleanse her of her milky essence, then gently rubbed his face with its evening stubble along her smooth thighs before he sat back and looked at all the places his tongue had been.

"You are lovely my bride. And you play well; I can't wait for you to get some experience. You are going to be a phenomenal lover. Ahh," he said as he sat back against the bottom of the opposite bench, "What a display piece you are my dear. The best I've ever seen, and I've seen many."

She knew she should be flattered, but somehow being told she was beautiful between her legs was not the same as being told she was beautiful of face. After all, how many people would ever know of this but him?

He helped her arrange her clothing and then they napped for a while as the coach bounced along on its way to the roadhouse.

They arrived at the inn shortly before midnight, as he had desired. His coachman woke the innkeeper and arranged for the innkeeper's wife to prepare a light repast for them to take to their rooms along with a jug of ale for him and a flagon of wine for her.

After they had supped at the small table in their room, he helped her to remove her outer clothing. In the garderobe, she removed the rest and slipped her nightgown over her head.

When she came back into the main part of their room, she timidly walked toward the bed. Passing a series of candlesticks on the beside table, she paused to look at him. He was naked to the waist as he sat in the upholstered chair in the corner. His muscled, bronzed chest fairly glinted in the burnished light. His face was tilted and he was staring at her as if he could see right through her gown. She gasped and turned back to the candles and then looked down at herself. He *could* see right through her gown! Quickly, she scrambled up onto the bed, pulling the coverlet up over her.

He laughed heartily at her rash actions. "Not too hasty my dear, you still have a lesson to learn tonight."

"A lesson?"

"Yes. I told you that on the journey to Thornhill, you would be required to learn three lessons. The first you will learn tonight."

"What lesson is that, sir?"

"The pose of the Druid's Mermaid."

"Druid's Mermaid?"

"Yes, did you not notice the coat of arms on my carriage?"

"Yes, I do remember that. There was a mermaid sitting on a large rock with a serpent coiled behind her in a large fanned clamshell."

"Yes. You represent the mermaid, I represent the serpent and the clamshell is the family and hearth."

"I am the mermaid?"

"Every Duke of Thornhill's bride is the mermaid, every duke is the snake."

"Not very flattering for you is it?"

"No, but it is of you. You must learn to pose as she does. Here, come sit on this stool, it will serve as the rock."

"You are not serious."

"I am more serious than death, Madam. Get yourself over here!" he snapped his fingers and she knew this was a signal not to be ignored.

She slid out of the bed and went to sit on the low ottoman.

"Remove your nightshirt."

"I am wearing nothing beneath sir."

"I am well aware of that. Remove it."

"But we are not yet husband and wife."

"We are by your church and I do not require the blessings of my church to see a woman unclothed. It is getting late and I am tired, do as I say so we can be to bed soon."

When she just sat there, he leaned forward,

grabbed the nightshirt by the collar and ripped it down the front.

Her loud gasp continued to echo in the room long after she had emitted it.

"I told you not to try me tonight. Just do as I say!" He dropped the tattered shirt to the floor leaving her sitting on the ottoman, looking down at the beautiful new cambric gown while wearing only a torn and elegantly embroidered sleeve.

"Now, I hope I have your cooperation, because I am getting most weary of your constant objections to my desires. Now pose as the mermaid for me. Entwine your fingers behind your head and thrust your breasts up and forward."

She squirmed on the bristly horsehair ottoman as she met his eyes. He was tired, she could see it in his eyes, and it would be best not to try his patience anymore. She raised her arms, put her hands behind her head and laced her fingers.

"Good, now sit up straight and force your elbows back so your titties jut up and out."

She made her back ramrod stiff and forced her rib cage out.

"Your elbows should not be facing front, make them point to the far walls."

She forced them further out. She could feel her breasts lift even higher on her chest wall.

"Good, very good. That is the first part. It will be required of you often, so learn it well. Your eyes should not look so angered though, try to feign as if it pleases you to do this."

"That sir, I am sure I will be unable to do!"

"We'll, see. One day, you will do this of your own volition, of that *I* am sure."

"I assure you Your Grace, that I will not!"

"As you say. Time will attest one way or the other. For now, do the second part of the pose."

"What, pray tell, is that?"

He stood and walked around her then he repositioned the ottoman and sat down again in the chair just a foot away.

"You are not a mermaid, mermaids have fins that do not separate. However, you are a woman, and you have legs that do. I bid you to separate them and display yourself. Wide, mind you, this is the position you will assume to show submission. So I must see all."

"Sir," she spat at him, "you are loathsome!"

"Yes, that may indeed be, however, you are mine to do with as I please, and loathsome or not, I please for you to submit fully to me. So part your legs, your feet planted at least as far as your hips and your knees facing the same walls as your elbows."

She stared at him as if she was in a mind-numbing fog until he yelled at her, "Do it!"

She did as he said, opening herself wide to his inspection of her. At that moment she loathed him more than she could imagine loathing anything or anyone.

"That's better. Now one more thing, scoot your arse forward so you are sitting on the very edge of the seat, forcing yourself open even more."

He watched her as she did so, and she saw his eyes flame with appreciation and lust. "Yes, yes, yes. You have it. That is the Druid Mermaid's pose. That is it exactly. You have learned your first lesson well."

He sat back in his chair and lifted his mug of ale from the table beside the chair. He put it to his lips and drank heartily, never once taking his eyes from her. He continued to stare and sip for several long, torturing minutes. Then his eyes moved up her body to her face. "You may need to practice. There will be times that you will be required to sit like this for upwards of an hour."

"I cannot believe you would be so cruel as to require this of your lady."

"Believe it, I will. Many, many times." He stood and put his hand out for her to take. She removed her hands from behind her neck and put one in his and he pulled her to stand against him.

She felt the soft furry tickle and the heated flesh warm her as his chest pressed against her breasts, and for a single moment she was not so inclined to pull away. Then he set her away from him while he continued to look down at her breasts.

"You may retire now," he breathed with some difficulty, "tomorrow night's lesson will require more of you, for I am ready to receive my satisfaction, and it cannot yet be in the conventional way."

Again his cryptic words stymied her, but even without knowing their true meaning, she knew that her second lesson would not bode well for her.

She went over and picked up what was left of her nightshirt and wrapped it around herself before crawling back into the bed.

"You may wear that scrap tonight, but in future, you will come to our bedchamber naked, naked except for your smile."

He smiled benevolently at her, lifted a sardonic brow and nodded. Then he finished his mug of ale before removing the rest of his clothes and sliding in beside her.

She had made sure she was facing the wall and well off to the side of the bed, utilizing only the tiniest portion of space, so that he would not be tempted to accidentally touch her during what promised to be a long night.

Her mind would not let her sleep. Her life had

changed drastically in these last twenty-four hours, and more surprises were in store for her. She had to endure two more nights of his 'lessons' before they would well and truly be married, and then she would have to endure endless nights of his touch. Long nights where he would force himself into her after using her body to tantalize all of his senses. Then he would spill his seed deep inside her. Not for the first time in her life, she wished she had been born male, with a rod and testicles between her legs, instead of the slimy wet slit he seemed so very fond of.

The next day was dreary with rain and the carriage was gloomy with little light seeping in through the streaming rain pelting the windows. Both the Duke and his soon-to-be-duchess felt the depression of the day deep in their bodies, and so slept for a good portion of the long ride. They were almost mired in mud when they finally pulled off the main road and into the yard of a shabby inn.

"I'm sorry for the accommodations," the Duke said to her as he handed her down to his footman, "it was either this or the coach all night and I for one, am in dire need of a change of scenery, be it good or bad."

She tended to agree with him. Her back hurt, her legs were cramped and she desperately needed to find a garderobe. She'd had a sneezing fit a few moments ago and that hadn't helped matters at all.

She followed the innkeeper's wife into the inn while her husband gave his instructions to the coachman. When he joined her a few minutes later, she could tell that he was in no mood for simpering pleasantries.

"We will not be dining in the common room," he barked, looking down into the faces of the short couple who owned the inn, "instead we would like a meal brought to our room, some meat, cheeses, bread and the best wine you have. Also, I should like a hot bath brought to our room immediately, I am afraid my dear lady may be in danger of catching the ague, and that will not do. Bring her plenty of hot tea and I would like you to provide a maid to attend to her needs." He dropped a heavy bag filled with coins into the man's hand and suddenly the pair became frantically agitated in their haste to serve the Duke and to carry out his wishes. Julia thought the desperate woman was going to expire as she made her way toward the kitchen, bumping off of the sturdy oaken timbers that were barely wide enough to accommodate her more than ample frame.

"Well, at least your money buys good service," Julia said snidely as she moved past him to follow the young maid that had been summoned for her.

He leaned down close to her ear and huskily whispered, "My money buys lots of things: grand carriages, ducal mansions . . . winsome brides," he reminded her as he patted her rump as she turned to go up the stairs.

Her mood was somewhat restored after she had been allowed to soak in a hot copper tub set behind the screen in the garderobe area. She noticed that the well-endowed chambermaid, turned temporary lady's maid, was eyeing the Duke with keen regard each time she chanced to look over the screen. She could hear him moving around the room and giving orders to his valet who was out in the hall. Then she heard the door close and a few minutes later as the maid knelt while washing her hair, he sauntered into the small alcove. He eyed her as she sat in the tub, the tops of her breasts barely under the level of the water, the rest of her clearly in view, as the water was clear and still.

She sat helpless as his eyes roved over her. Then she watched as he followed the trail of her soapy hair to the hands of the young maiden kneeling by the tub. She watched as he brazenly assessed the young woman, from the dark brown curls wispy and wet around her face, to her bountiful cleavage displayed almost to the tips as she bent low to dip the small pitcher she was using to rinse the soap. She stood to get Julia's comb and hiked her skirt to her thigh when she lifted one knee from the floor before the other. Her long flounced skirts trailed on the floor covering her dirty bare feet as she crossed the room, swaying her ample hips. She came back and began combing out Julia's hair. Julia saw the Duke's eyes looking up, past her shoulders and knew that they were silently communicating something to each other over her bent head. Then his eyes returned to her face and he asked her if she was feeling any better.

"Yes, thank you, I am. The hot water has taken away the chill that had seeped into my bones."

He continued to look into the depths of the water, and she was unnerved as she felt his probing gaze. The maid poured a final pitcher of water over her head and then held a towel out for her, indicating that she should now stand and step from the tub.

He wasn't taking the hint though. He was standing steadfast waiting for her to exit the tub. She didn't know if she could do it. He'd already seen her naked a few times, but she was by no means used to it—to be naked in front of him with a strange woman also in the room viewing her at the same time—it was somehow unnatural. Not to be done. But what did she know of gentlemen and ladies and their servants? Maybe this was done all the time.

Finally, she crossed her breasts and stood,

turning to face the towel that was open and waiting for her. She thought the maid would wrap it around her but she did not, she simply took the towel and gently dried her. She took her time doing first one limb and then another before wiping at her neck, her chest, her abdomen and lower. She had never had anyone dry her off before. Unaccustomed to having servants like this, she didn't know if the maiden was lingering or just being thorough, but she did know that the Duke was enjoying the show.

Finally a robe was brought to her and she slipped her arms into the long silk sleeves and wrapped the long garment around her, cinching it with a belt.

"There is some dinner for you on the table by the fire. I think I will take a bath now to see if I can get as toasty as you."

The maid moved to leave, but he grabbed her wrist. "You may stay, I have need of your services." The woman blushed a deep red, but she stayed where she was as the Duke began disrobing. Julia, taking that as her dismissal, left the bathing area and sat in a chair by the fire. Idly munching on small chunks of cheese, she wondered at the feelings she was having. She did not like the fact that there was a woman assisting her betrothed with his bath, and from the sounds of things, she wasn't all that sure that getting him clean was the object. She should be feeling relief that there was someone holding his interest instead of her for the time being, but the feelings she was experiencing were more akin to anger and some form of dissatisfaction and unsettlement.

She heard a low groan from him and several high-pitched giggles and squeals from the servant before there was a long, weighty silence. Minutes later, he appeared in front of her in a deep crimson gown of fine satin with his ducal crest embroidered on the pocket. She watched as the chambermaid slipped out of the room behind him, her bodice drenching wet, her dark nipples easily seen through the thin cotton.

"Sounds like you two had fun," she murmured.

"Jealous?" he asked with a crooked smile.

"No, not hardly. You can have her if you like, I really won't care." She wasn't exactly sure she meant it when she said it, but it conveyed the attitude that she wanted to have.

"No. Not tonight. I have plans for you. It is your job to please me now, not hers, although she did make a valiant attempt at it." His hand went to the opening of his robe and he pulled the long cord that held it shut. When it parted she saw his manhood jutting out, proud and long, poking out of a thatch of curling black hair so thick it covered the entire juncture where his thighs met. Hanging slightly below the fleshy pole, was a bulbous sack, covered with its own downy hairs.

So, this was it. This was the male incarnate, the temple of man that women worshipped at, the part of their bodies that ruled their thoughts and determined their futures. As impressive as his was, and she really had no comparison to base it on, it did not seem like such a forceful weapon, capable of overpowering centuries of women, bending them to the will of the man who wielded it. And then she saw it grow larger and redder. It danced up his belly, straightening and jerking—jutting out as if to lead the charge. She could see pulsing blues lines feeding to the tip. The tip that was almost purple now in what seemed like rage. Dear God, this was supposed to fit inside her?

When it finally stopped growing, it was substantial enough to keep his heavy robe from closing.

"Like it?" he asked simply.

She stuttered a reply, "I . . . I suppose it's acceptable."

He sputtered. "Madam, it is far better than acceptable. Some women have called it magnificent."

"Oh."

"Kiss it."

"Pardon?"

"Kiss it."

"You're not serious."

"Oh, indeed I am. I have just bathed so it is very clean. I assure you that the little maid was very thorough with her task. Lean forward and put your lips on it. Now!" he commanded.

She jumped from the suddenness of his loud voice. She watched as he thumbed it down to the level of her lips. She sat forward on the chair and he inched it toward her.

"Just take your lips and kiss the very tip," he urged, his voice softer now as she was in the act of complying.

She pursed her lips tightly and then leaned forward barely grazing it with her lips.

"Again, more sensuously this time, not just a peck."

She did as he asked, careful to kiss it above the little hole she had noticed that was oozing something glistening. She heard his guttural moan at just about the same time she felt his hand on the back of her head, pushing the stiff rod into her face.

"Take it between your lips," he hissed.

"No!"

"Yes! Do as I say!"

"No!"

He forcefully held her mouth open and shoved a good portion of himself into her.

She gagged and tried to push away.

"You can make this easy and we'll be done in a matter of minutes or I'll call the serving wench back, have her do it with you watching, and then require you to do it after her, and I guarantee, instead of minutes, I'll be up to an hour of thrusting into your lovely mouth. Now let me feel those soft puffy lips I bought, treating me properly."

He placed his penis at the edge of her lips and waited for her to kiss it. Tentatively, she did, lingering slightly longer this time.

"Better. Now alternate between kissing it, licking it, and taking it into your mouth and sucking on it. If you want this to be done fast, you could also reach down and gently cup my balls. Gently, mind, they are soft and the most fragile part of a man. Squeeze too hard and what might be ecstasy turns into agony."

She did as he asked, moving her hand slowly down to cup his swaying sacs. If this would make things go faster, she would do this, more of this and less of her mouth would suit her just fine.

But soon, she was surprised to find herself challenged by this strange appendage, trying to coax it into submission to her desires. She found she could make it do things, and she could make him do things by simple touches, wanton licks here, there, and then lower. She could hear him gasp and groan above her and she felt his knees jerk as he fought to stay on his feet.

Mesmerized by the power she seemed to hold over him, she ruthlessly sucked on him as she silkily caressed his scrotum. She suddenly felt him lurch inside her mouth and at about the same time, she felt the warm spurt of something vile fill her mouth. Quickly, she moved to back away but his hard hand was gripping the back of her head, holding her fast to him, not allowing her to disengage herself from his pulsing, throbbing member as it continued to jettison its load against the back of her throat. When he finally released his hold on her head and allowed her to ease off of him, she found she had a mouthful of the most repulsive-tasting stuff she'd ever tasted. She ran for the garderobe and spit into the wastewater still standing in the tub.

"Lesson two, quite solidly learned. You're turning out to be a pretty good student," he called out to her from the other room.

She wiped her mouth out the best she could and then came out to stare at him. "This is something you expect me to do as your wife?"

"Oh most definitely, my dear. I will insist on it."

"I can't believe it. Women actually do this?"

"You just did."

"You made me."

"Usually that's the way it comes about. But some women actually come to enjoy it and even ask to do it. I've had prominent ladies of the *ton* kneel between my legs and suck me off with abandon."

"You're joking!"

"No, I'm not. In fact, even some of the whores prefer that to being poked."

She shook her head in disbelief. "It never even occurred to me that this was done, that a man would stick his penis into a woman's mouth!"

"Men do it whenever they can. As far as I know, they've always done it. On the campaigns, when there are no women around, they even do it to each other."

"Stop!" she said, her hands up, palms out. "I don't want to hear anymore. This is too much. Isn't that the same thing you use to eliminate with?"

He gave her a cocky wide grin. "Well, yes, but not at the same time."

"It must be filthy!" she spat against the back of her hand.

"I just had a bath! You saw me!"

"Ohhh! This is just so disgusting!" She turned her back and walked over to the window to look out at the rain. "What pray tell do you have in mind for lesson three?"

"Would you like to see?" he asked excitedly.

"No! No!" she said as she backed away from him. "I'm sure I'll need at least a day to recover from lesson two."

He chuckled and went over to her. His hand breached the opening of her gown and he found a warm mound of flesh. "You'll like lesson three, I promise you," he said as he slowly turned her to face him. Then he bent low to take her nipple into his mouth. "I promise."

"You promised!" she cried as she scooted off the bed the next evening at their last roadhouse stop. "You said I would like lesson three! Well, you're wrong! I hate it! Hate it! Hate it! You hurt me! My aunt said you wouldn't hurt me if I did as you asked! I have tried hard to do as you've asked! Can I not trust anyone anymore!" She ran crying from the bedroom to the garderobe and sat in the cold bath water that she had used an hour earlier. It helped with the immediate problem but left her shivering and covered with goose flesh.

Fresh from her bath, when her body had been warm from the heated water, he had taken her to the bed, stripped her of her robe and placed her on her hands and knees at the end of the bed. He had gently massaged her bottom with warm oil and indeed, it had felt wonderful . . . until his hand had strayed and developed a particular fondness with her crevice. She had noticed when she had looked over her shoulder at him that he was naked and that his male member was glistening as if it too was coated with the very same oil. But she hadn't made the connection. He was giving her pleasure by using his slick hands on her and she thought she'd come to like Lesson three.

Until without any warning he had plunged himself inside her tight bum, causing her to emit a loud scream. He knew, that because of his rank, despite her echoing screams throughout the roadhouse, that no one would disturb them. Such were the ways between men and women. Women had no rights. No one would dare to interfere with a man taking his pleasure in a woman, no matter how he achieved it.

As she had continued to scream at him and sob, he had grabbed her swaying breasts and roughly squeezed them. He had pulled hard on her nipples, callously pinching the tender tips with his thumb and fingers. All the while he had brutally withdrawn and reentered her, taking great pleasure in her tight puckering hole. When he had finally collapsed on top of her after spending his seed inside her, she'd given one great shattering sob and fainted.

She was conscious now; soaking in a tub of cold water and so sore she was afraid what would happen on the morrow when the food she had eaten tonight had to leave her body. The man was vile! How dare he!

He walked into the small, enclosed room and stared down at her. "I said you'd like it, and I promise you, that you will. It may take several more times for you to get used to my size, but then you will achieve pleasure from this. Lots of women do. Did you not know that this is the place men take their pleasure in when their wives are heavy with child? Or too loose from the births of many?"

"No! Why would I know such things! I know nothing of the ways between a man and a woman. But what I have learned from you, I would gladly forget if I could!"

"It will take time. But I assure you, that men and women have been doing this for many, many years, long before you or I were ever born, and this is the way it is. These are the things they do."

"I do not believe you! I think you are evil, that you practice a strange sort of concupiscence! You desire women in unlawful ways!"

He laughed heartily at her words, "Unlawful you say? Nothing a man requires of his wife, or his betrothed is unlawful. You should be happy that I don't take my pleasure with a woman as others do, with the whip."

She blanched and stared wide-eyed into his smirking face. Good Lord, what kind of monster had her aunt sold her to?

The next afternoon they arrived at Thornhill Manor and Julia was relieved to be settled, but also fearful of the lessons the Duke might have in store for her.

They went through the impressive wrought iron gates of the large estate, and then traveled down a long lane flanked with massive cedars on each size. It was not until they cleared the lane that she was able to see the enormous house that was Thornhill Manor. Surely this could not be her new home. It was a castle, four of the largest houses she'd ever seen combined into one. No wonder this man who was her husband in one faith, and soon to be doubly hers in another, walked as if he owned the universe. It seemed he did.

A scout had ridden ahead so now household servants were lined up on the large curving drive in front of the palatial steps that led to the regal front entrance. There must have been forty of them, all in different uniforms signifying their duties. She turned and looked behind them through the coach window when she heard the sounds of dogs coming to greet their master. The velvet green lawns that surrounded the manor led to ornamental gardens with rows upon rows of trimmed hedges, a fountain in the center of each. The bushes around the foundation were artfully pruned and beautiful flowers bloomed in profusion. Everywhere the eye focused, there was something beautiful growing. She sighed at the magnificence of the setting before her. The landscaping chores alone would keep twenty men busy.

"Like it?" he asked, as he reached for the latch on the carriage door.

"It's lovely, like something out of a fairy tale," she whispered as she watched him stoop down to gather his dogs. It was obvious that they adored him, as he called each one by name and rubbed it behind its ears. How could anyone who loved animals like this be cruel to his wife, she wondered, momentarily allayed of some of her fears.

The Duke's butler welcomed him home and asked for the honor of introducing his soon-to-be bride to the more elevated servants. The Duke simply nodded, and she was introduced to the housekeeper, the upstairs maid, her own ladies maid and her assistants, the cook and the head groomsman. The others were pointed out in the groups they had been arranged in, and then she was following behind the Duke into the grand hall.

She had to bite her tongue in an effort to keep from gasping in awe, and clamp her reticule tight to her chest to keep from spinning around on the polished marble floor to look at the beautifully frescoed ceiling above the huge crystal chandelier. Surely, there was a bevy of servants whose only job was to light and extinguish the hundreds of candles it required each evening.

The Duke was led off to the left through a high archway, and she was quickly escorted up the huge curved staircase. She was a little winded by the time she made it down the long hallway to her room, where she was met by yet another maid. She was admiring the beautiful room when the Duke's valet knocked on the door.

When he was bade to enter, he announced, "The marriage ceremony will be downstairs in the formal ballroom in two hours. The Duke has instructed the household staff to prepare your bath. He requests that Clarisse do your hair. He will arrive shortly with your gown."

She nodded her acquiescence and followed her maid from the antechamber to the bedchamber and then to the bathing chamber.

Each room was grand, opulently decorated, with each designer touch complimenting the overall scheme. The bed was lavishly dressed in rich satin, the bright colors muted by fine lace edging. Everything matched: the shams, the rolled pillows, the tiered bed hangings and the wall hangings. It was sumptuously beautiful. She wanted to hug her arms and spin around in her glee, but the formal setting and the stiff and proper attendance of her servants stifled her.

"Come this way, Madam," directed Clarisse. "Time is getting by us, we must hie, lots to do, lots to do," she said fretfully. Julia soon became aware that there was a significant amount of tension between the maids, caused no doubt, by the fear of not being able to do the Duke's bidding within the Duke's time constraints.

While she was being undressed, the comments that were made confirmed that he definitely had that effect; all the servants lived to please the Duke. Or, more accurately, their aim was not to displease him.

She was naked and in a fragrant tub within minutes. She tried to relax and enjoy the silky hot water surrounding her, but her maids were too intent on their duties, bustling to and fro, to let her enjoy a thorough soak.

She was dried off, swathed in a thick, white robe, and led over to a dressing table, where two women worked on her hair. They trimmed her hair per the Duke's instructions, sent up on a monogrammed note card, while she was bathing. Following his suggestion, Clarisse gave her bangs. It made a remarkable difference in her appearance, as it softened her face and took away the detracting look of her high forehead. The rest of her abundant mass of hair was curled with hot irons and pinned to her head, achieving an intricate coiffure such as she'd never seen before. When they were done with her hair, she looked remarkably different, quite lovely, in fact. Looking in the mirror that was slanted over the dressing table, she was amazed at the difference, and continued to stare at herself. Why, she was actually pretty, she thought.

The style they gave her was a work of art, and the crowning touch was, literally, a crown. A small diamond-studded tiara was tucked into the blonde curls at her temple. Gorgeous diamond earrings were attached to her ear lobes, and then a matching diamond necklace was fastened behind her neck. She felt like a princess in a fairy tale. She could hardly wait to see the dress.

One of the maids left the room and a few minutes

later the Duke accompanied her back. Over her arm she had a voluminous white gown, and Julia could see from where she stood that it was first quality. Made from yards of beautiful, smooth, brilliant white satin it had seed pearls sewn everywhere.

"Ohhh, it's lovely," she said as they entered the room.

The maid shook it out and draped it on the bed, the long, flowing skirt grazing the thick, lush carpet. That's when she saw that it was slit up the middle of the skirt, all the way from the waist to the hem. The opening at the waist a good four inches wide at the top, cutaway to two feet or better at the bottom. Surely there was an under skirt for it, but she looked around and didn't see any other pieces of fabric except for the tulle veiling for her tiara that Clarisse was holding in her arms.

"Where is the underskirt?" she asked as she looked over at the Duke.

"There is none," he said. "The dress has been specially made to showcase your breasts and your womanhood."

It was then that she looked up toward the bodice and saw that it was scooped out. There were wide satin straps for the shoulders, but there was no material between, until ruched satin resumed from the sides, as a wide empire waist joined to the material of the skirt. Surely her breasts would be completely exposed. She gasped and put her hand over her mouth. He meant for her to wear this atrocious gown to her wedding! He meant for her to show his guests her breasts, her belly and her womanhood! All his odd comments came back to her: *Display piece, showcase, men may look at you, your family will be so proud . . .*

Garrett rubbed his eyes and closed his laptop. Though there were about seventy pages left, that was enough for now. It was seven in the morning and now he felt as if he could finally get some sleep. His laptop was over heating from being in his lap on the bed, and it was covering the part of him that he needed to spend some time with.

He slid the laptop to the floor beside his bed. He contorted his body, so he could push it under the bed to make sure he wouldn't step on it. Then he switched off his light, pushed off the covers, and dug into his nightstand drawer for the lubricant he had bought at CVS.

The vision of Laurel on her knees loving him with her mouth was the one that sent him off, but it was accompanied by many others. As he cleaned himself with a tissue, he wondered what her breasts looked like. When she was describing Julia's, was she actually describing her own? His dick stirred as he recalled some of the passages dealing with Julia's breasts. If not hers, maybe Callie's? Callie was a brunette, so maybe she hadn't patterned her after herself. Mallory was a blonde . . . hmmm. She was a hot one—with fine, pale public hair that Stewart kept getting stuck in his teeth. Garrett ran his tongue over his top lip.

He flicked at his rising dick in frustration and then rolled over onto it to flatten it. He'd read stories about what happened to men who kept jerking off by thrusting into their mattresses, so there was no temptation that he'd ever do that again! The thought of the pictures he'd seen of the malformed and surgically altered penises cooled his ardor. He reached for the water bottle he kept on the nightstand and downed a healthy swig.

He wondered if Laurel knew she had used the name Stewart twice as protagonists in her stories. He was definitely more Stewart Ravencross than Stewart Entitled-to-Everything-in-his-Dukedom-Thornhill, he thought.

No way would he take a woman, especially *there*,

if she were unwilling. He thought of Laurel, naked on her hands and knees at the foot of his bed. But goddamn, he'd certainly do his best to make her willing.

Chapter Forty-three

Laurel had just finished tallying her scorecard when Tessa tapped her on her shoulder. "Hey stranger. I haven't seen you all day. That's the trouble with these tournaments, sometimes we're spread out all over the place!"

They hugged and Laurel told her to wait right there while she turned in her card, "We need to talk girlfriend," she said as she spun away from her.

When Laurel came back, Tessa was talking with two members she didn't know, so she waited for her at one of the buffet tables that had been set up for the event. Nibbling on some fruit slices and cheese squares, she looked out over the course and smiled. What a pretty day! To add to that, she'd played halfway decent she thought, as she took a glass of wine from a tray. Tessa came alongside and took one too.

"Let's go sit on the veranda, I need some shade," Tess said as she filled a small appetizer-sized plate with chocolate covered strawberries and pineapple florets. "Grab some napkins, would ya?"

They sat at a small table and Tessa hunched toward her, her head low. "So . . . tell me about the date, how'd it go? And I want all the highlights."

Laurel told her about the Tuscan Rosemary bush Garret had brought her, how she'd never gotten to Market Common so fast before, adding that Garrett was an exceptional driver, just fast. And how, through the wonderful dinner, they always had something to talk and laugh about.

Then she backtracked and told her about the amazing kiss in her study, adding that he had not bothered to capitalize on it when he had left her at her door . . . much to her chagrin. Both she and Tessa fake pouted.

"But then he did call me, just like he said he would, only a few hours later. He told me he couldn't get me out of his head. He actually told me what he'd been thinking about—and it was some pretty heady stuff." A long drawn out sigh escaped through her lips and she ducked her head to look at her empty plate.

Tessa patted the hand that was fidgeting with the folded napkin on the table. She didn't know when she'd ever seen Laurel this happy—or this nervous. Something was bothering her. She could sense it.

"Well has he asked you out again?"

"Oh yeah. We're going out Friday night. We're going to the concert at Ocean Isle. If you guys are going to be there, I thought it would be nice if we could all sit together like we usually do."

"Laurel, why are you so hesitant? Is there something wrong?"

"Yeah, I like him—too much. It scares me."

Tessa laughed. "Really? That fast, huh?"

Laurel nodded, biting her lip. "How fast was it with you and Roman?"

Tessa sat back and Laurel saw the wistful look on her face as her friend remembered the day she had met Roman. She blinked and looked over at Laurel and answered her question. "Pretty fast. As they say, 'He had me at hello.'"

"Yeah, well . . . looking like he does, I'm not surprised."

"It wasn't so much his look as his manner," Tessa said. "For some reason he set his sights on me, and he was going to have me, no matter what."

"I have that same feeling about Garrett."

"Well that's good then. It's nice to know that a man

wants you. It's empowering."

"He said he meant to have me. We even talked about the time frame when that would happen."

"Really?" She sounded both intrigued and piqued.

"Yeah," Laurel blushed and stammered, "he said he couldn't sleep, kept picturing himself . . . me . . . well it was one hot phone call, I'll tell you that!"

Tessa laughed. "Hmmm . . . he going too fast for you?"

"I don't know. We seem to have a connection and we both want to explore that."

"*He* said that, or you?"

"We both said that. We both feel it. If you must know . . . we agreed we're going to have sex—joked around about it, and even negotiated when. Now we just have to get there."

"And where is that?"

Laurel sensed mothering instincts kicking in and wished she hadn't revealed that last bit to Tess. "Date number four."

There was a long silence where Tessa had to cover Laurel's hand to keep her from shredding the napkin.

"Did you wait that long?" Laurel asked.

Tessa thought about the day she met Roman in St. Thomas, on the morning her cruise ship had docked, being talked into spending the day with him and then saying goodbye in the late afternoon.

She smiled as she remembered that Roman had finagled with the Captain of her ship to be seated alongside her at the Captain's table that night. Then after dinner, after Roman had seen their ship safely out of the harbor, he'd knelt at her feet, lifted her gown and kissed her *there* before literally jumping off the ship and into the harbor pilot's launch. The next day, while she had been sunbathing on deck, he had arrived by helicopter to take her off the ship.

"No, we didn't wait long. Or I should say *he* didn't wait long."

"And look at you now."

Tessa grinned broadly. "When you know what you want, it doesn't make sense to wait. As long as you're sure," she admonished.

Carol came up to their table and smiled at Laurel, "You're on Laurel. It's time for the silent auction now."

"Thanks. I'll be right there."

She turned back to Tessa. "You'll be there Friday night? You'll let me know what you think?"

"Oh, I'll be there all right, we'll all be there. But don't let what any of us thinks influence you. Use your four dates wisely . . . get to know him, get to know how he thinks. How he treats women. With Matt, Philip and Roman, I don't think you'll have to worry about whether he's genuine. If he's not the real deal, they'll know it in a heartbeat."

"They're not going to grill him are they?" There was panic in Laurel's voice. She didn't need three surrogate fathers.

"Not so he'd know," Tessa said as she stood up. "Go. Do the auction. Don't worry about this. Merlin's got it. You just be your sweet, little adorable self." Tessa kissed her on the cheek and left to go look at the auction bid sheets one final time before Laurel announced the winners.

Laurel walked to the microphone and announced that the silent auction would be closing in ten minutes. Walking over to admire some of the paintings displayed by the podium, she mentally began planning the evening ahead. After reading off the names of the winners, she'd gather her clubs, and go home. She'd take a nice hot shower and then attack her garden. The area around the mailbox could use some sprucing up, so could the roses on the side of the house—and she could use some therapy. She was nervous about the idea of having sex. It had been a long dry spell. Despite thinking about it all the time, and being distracted to the point of writing long descriptive passages, sex wasn't actually part of her life. Never really had been, to the degree that she'd wanted it to be. She wondered if Garrett would be the man who could draw her out, make her experience what her heroines got to feel.

As the soft breeze coming off the course fanned her face, she turned and accepted the raft of papers Carol handed her. From the look of the filled up pages, the tournament had been a huge success. She quickly scanned through the sheets to see what the final bid was on her donated topiary. Donating one of her plants was like sending off one of her children—and hoping their new home was nurturing so they'd thrive. Seventy-five dollars. Not bad for something she had babied, watered, fed, and shaped for four years. She looked at the name of the winner. Oh, JoAnn. She grinned. At least she'd be able to go visit it whenever she wanted. JoAnn was a good friend.

Chapter Forty-four

That night, she was sitting in her easy chair watching a rerun of *Uncorked* when she heard the doorbell ring. She wasn't expecting anyone, so she slowly unfolded from the chair and hit pause on the DVR remote. She couldn't see anyone in either side glass panel as she approached the door. She flipped on the outside light and looked out. There didn't appear to be anyone there, but she could see that there was a package on the mat. She could even read the note taped on top. In a bold hand, it read: LAUREL.

She opened the door and looked down the driveway to the street. At the corner she thought she saw the back of Tessa's car as it turned. Bringing the package inside, she closed and locked the door before putting the package on the dining room table. She tore the small envelope off. Inside was a note card, the message written in Tessa's precise hand.

Roman sends this. He says it will drive your young man crazy Friday night. My thoughts are you should wear it with your blue paisley crepe cami over skintight jeans. We have money riding on this. Philip says your guy will last until date number 4, Roman says no way. But he wants to hedge his bet and ensure your cooperation.

Laurel smiled and tore at the wrapping. What were those crazy fools up to now? She probably shouldn't have been so open with Tess today. Garrett might not like her telling everyone about their progressive "dating" plans. She opened the box and fished through the tissue until she pulled out a tiny lacy bra. She held it up by the straps. It was all straps. It had no cups. Absolutely none. What exactly was the point, she wondered as she walked with it swinging in front of her over to her bedroom.

Curious, she took off her sweatshirt and bra, and put the cupless wonder on. Oh my. It had a purpose. It definitely did. While no part of her nipple was covered, in fact, most of both breasts were bare, there was enough material underneath to hike her up and jut her out. She helped the bra along by running her fingers around the inner edges and pulling the fleshy parts of her breasts forward through each opening. The effect was as if she had gripped each breast at her chest wall with both hands and hefted them up. Wow, what a difference. Everything was front and center, pushed together and just asking for trouble. She kind of liked it.

She went to her closet and got out the blue paisley camisole Tessa had mentioned. She slipped it on. Gadzooks, she couldn't wear this . . . like that! She turned this way and then that way, looking at herself in the full length-mirror. Well . . . maybe . . . hmmm. Maybe not. Hmmmm. The fabric constantly grazing her nipples shrunk them into hard, tight buds, making them clear little points, poking their way out, like tiny spotlights. While it appeared she was braless under her flimsy top, she knew that only a Barbie doll jutted out like this. Not even a twenty-year-old was perky enough to defy gravity like this—not without some silicon enhancement. She smiled and posed in front of the mirror. She couldn't get over the difference. She looked like she could pose for Playboy. She knew she had nice breasts, just not quite this nice. Still . . .

She pranced around the house admiring herself in every shiny surface, and enjoyed the exposed feeling the bra gave her, despite being technically covered up. She was decent except for those steely bullets out front. She walked over to the box the bra had come in and reread the note. Could she do this? Hell the worst part would be Roman. He would know. He would stare. He would smirk. He would chide her all night. She would be hot and bothered, agitated. And Garrett would get wind of it. God, Roman sure knew his way around this arousal stuff. She was already randy. She liked how she looked in this get up. She picked up the box and took it into the kitchen to throw out.

Scrunching up the tissue she discovered something lumpy in the paper. She dug it out. It was a little cellophane package advertising 500 Polybands in bold primary colors. What the hell? She turned the small package over in her hand. On the back was a tiny post-it.

In the event you're not ready to poke someone's eye out, you can use these bands around the tips to get you started. But don't leave them on for too long, twenty-thirty minutes tops. Tess.

P.S. I've got money riding on this, too. Garrett must succumb before the 4th date!

These guys were crazy! Where did they come up with these ideas? Of course, Philip, the former porn star of the group, knew all the insider tricks. To have been a fly on the wall at their dinner tonight . . . while they were discussing her. And Garrett. And apparently her boobies.

She looked down at her matched set. No, she had no need for the bands. At least not tonight. She threw the package in her whatnot drawer. She kept the card from Tess and threw away the box. Then she walked back to the den and hit the button to take the TV off pause. As she watched the movie, she idly stroked her pebbled tips. The problem was going to be keeping herself from wanting to do this while she there, next to Garrett, at the concert.

She didn't know if she should be pitting Roman and Tess against Philip and Viv in this contest involving Garrett's willpower, especially if it caused her to lose all of hers.

The things idle minds found to bet on.

Chapter Forty-five

Garrett put his professor's hat on and answered some emails, clarified assignments for those too lazy to read the syllabus, and fended off a coed, who with her flagrant double entendres was being more than obvious. She included a picture of herself in a bikini that was no larger than two slash lines as her signature attachment.

But this was one bailiwick he was never going to fall into, as he had always felt that parents didn't save money for twenty years to provide him with fodder for his loins. Now . . . a master's level student, who wasn't one of his, or one who wasn't on daddy's tab, might be a whole other matter, but since going strictly online, the issue hardly ever came up anymore. That last thought caused him to chuckle. He came up plenty, just not for his desperate students.

He responded to Miss Barely-there-bikini:

Unfortunately, Ms. Greene, the "issue" has never come up where students are concerned. And as I am rarely able to do the deed with pictures alone and you are 1800 miles away, I would suggest you read the material. You could use your talents to secure a tutor. But isn't the idea of you going to college and getting a degree, so you won't have to rely on bartering your body and self esteem for an income?

He reread what he'd written and decided he'd been

411

too harsh. Then as he was in the process of deleting it, line by line, he changed his mind and hit the undo button. Nah, this wasn't her first overture, time to flay her open at little and make her think. He wasn't doing her any favors otherwise. If nothing else maybe he could teach her that some men appreciated a woman's mind.

He read several papers, correcting and editing in the Track Changes mode until midnight, then put everything away to go collapse on his bed.

Never one to dream lightly, his body tensed and reacted to what his mind saw and now as he drifted into a deep sleep, he saw himself climbing a ladder, getting up on a roof and installing a series of motion-detecting cameras.

He saw himself mumbling as he worked, and defining the word stalker in his mind—someone who watches with the intent of owning, possessing, or capturing someone or their image—because he was up on her neighbor's roof. He hears a door open and sees Laurel come out of her house. He watches as she walks around to the side deck on her house. Now she is fifteen feet away and almost straight down from where he's crouched. In one swift move, she takes off an oversized shirt and suddenly she is topless, wearing only a tiny bikini bottom!

She is softly tanned, her fair skin glowing golden . . . everywhere. Her perfect tight little breasts are lightly tanned too. He flattens against the roofline so as not to be seen.

Then she's watering the flowers on her inner patio using a Mary-Mary-Quite-Contrary watering can with painted flowers all over it. She looks cute, innocent and so sexy at the same time that he is completely bowled over . . . to the point he's worried he's going to tumble off the roof. His erection is jutting into a ridge created by the shingles he's resting on, and because of it, he realizes his breathing is harsh. It's loud to his ears. He's afraid she might hear him and look up. He bites back a groan and wills his body to be still . . . to stop humping the roof.

As he watches her watering the plants, he realizes that he *is* a stalker, and that she's definitely something he wants to own—to possess. When a tiny yellow butterfly flutters to the crest of her breast and lands there, she lets out a delightful laugh. The look on her face is so sensual, so enchanting, that she takes his breath away.

He envisions himself standing behind her, cupping her breasts, drawing in her essence as he presses his face into her hair and nuzzles the back of her neck. He imagines that he's nudging his cock between the globes of her ass and that his penis expands to fill the space, plus some. In his mind, he pulls the elastic of her bottom down to just below her cheeks and slides himself between her thighs, strokes her lovingly, then bends her over the low brick wall and plunges inside. It is all he can do to keep from leaping off the roof on top of her.

She goes back inside to refill the can and he inches back to the ladder and quickly climbs down. He stows the ladder under the neighbor's deck and leaves. His mission accomplished. Now he can view her whenever he wants.

The next day, he watches her from his laptop as she comes out onto her deck dressed in jean shorts, a fluorescent bright yellow T-shirt, and tennis shoes. On the back of her T-shirt it says Sunset Cyclists. Minutes later, from the webcam angled at her garage, he watches as she loads the bike onto a bike rack on her SUV. As the garage door closes he Googles the bike club's website and discovers that they're spending the day at Bald Head, riding over on the ferry, and then biking around the island before having lunch at Ebb and Flo's.

This could be the perfect time to meet her face-to-face without her suspecting anything. And what a wonderful way to test their chemistry. He can't wait to get close enough to smell her and to drink in the scent of her. He scrambles to get ready and sees himself riding the ferry and spending the afternoon at the bar at Ebb and Flo's. She is nowhere to be found. She must have changed her mind.

He sees her on her patio reading mail. She opens a letter and stares, her eyes wide. He sees her stifle a scream before she starts sobbing. Curious, he investigates when she goes out. He's good with electronics; he's bypassed her alarm and used a scanner to duplicate her garage sequence on the remote he's fabricated. Searching her drawers, he finds a handful of letters from a stalker. Who the hell is this? She's his! He discovers she has a gun in her nightstand drawer and he murmurs, "Good girl." He reads her certificate for completing the course for carrying a concealed weapon. "A very good girl."

He takes his time looking around, noting everything in her room. Smelling her essence, touching her things—her lamp, her light switch, her window, her door . . . her pillow. He checks the Caller I.D. log on her phone. He already has her number.

Then he's back home, sitting at his dining room table, using his laptop, when there's a distinctive ding notifying him that one of the cameras has been activated. He looks over at the clock, 1:23 in the morning—a bit late for her to be up and outside.

He switches screens and sees a man, dressed all in black using a glasscutter to break into the French door leading into her kitchen. He grabs his cell phone and scrolls to her name, selects her number, preset with #67 inserted to block her Caller I.D., and hits the green button.

"C'mon! C'mon, pick up!" he says as he hears the phone ringing through both his phone and his laptop. Finally, he hears a groggy, "Hello?"

"Laurel! Don't ask questions, just listen. A man just broke into your house; he's on his way to your bedroom from the kitchen. Get your gun out and get your hand ready to use the touch lamp, but wait until he opens the door before turning on the light. You don't want him to see you first, and don't turn it all the way on; you don't want the sudden brightness to blind you. Do you hear him? He's in the house now."

"Yes, I hear someone. Who is this?"

"Never mind that now, the important thing is that you're ready when he opens that door. Is the safety off?"

"Yes." God love her, he could picture her shivering just from the timbre of her voice.

"Point it midway in the door frame. As soon as he steps inside, shoot. Don't hesitate."

"He's getting closer!" She was keeping her voice low, but there was no doubting the panic in it.

"Take a deep breath. Remember you've trained for this. You can do it. Double tap, chest first to be sure you hit him, then a little higher for the head. Don't let yourself get excited, stay calm and use all the bullets if he makes it into the room."

"He's coming. He's here!" The last was a low desperate whisper, "Oh God."

He heard the phone clatter and then two loud pops followed by a scream. Thankfully, hers.

"Laurel? Laurel? Laurel! Are you alright?"

An eternity later he heard her mumble, "Yeah."

"Where is he?"

"On the floor."

"Turn the light on all the way and see what he's doing. But keep your gun ready."

"I'm scared."

"You can do this, honey. Get up slowly, lean over the bed. See if he's still alive. If he is, shoot him again."

Another eternity.

"He looks dead."

"You need to be sure. Hold the gun on him, check his pulse, grab his hand or foot."

"I can't."

"Then shoot him in the head again."

"No, I'll check his pulse." Followed by a loud sob.

"He's dead?"

"Mmmm." Huge wracking sobs.

"Honey, listen to me and do exactly as I say. I want you to hang up the phone, and then dial 911. Tell them you shot an intruder. Then call the gate; they can have someone there in just a few minutes. Go open the front door and wait outside. Got that?"

"Yes. Hang up, dial 911, then call the gate," she repeated.

"Do it now."

"Who are you, how did you know . . ."

"Let's just say I'm your protector. I can't tell you who I am just yet. But I care for you, very, very much. Now do what I say. You were a good girl, a very good girl. I'm so proud of you."

"I want to know who this is! And who is this man I just killed. Tell me!"

At a time like this he didn't know how he could develop such frissons of heat from those soft-spoken, yet commanding words. But develop them he did as his heart bloomed with his love for her.

"Who are you?"

"Do as I say, and do it now." He hung up. Mentally, it was the hardest thing he'd ever done, leaving her alone at a time like this.

He'd blocked the call from her Caller I.D. but even so, the police might still be able to retrieve it. And after she told her story, they would certainly make every effort to do just that. He had to get away, just in case. His cell phone was in the name of one of his many LLCs, so they probably couldn't trace it to him personally until morning, but no sense waiting.

The screen on his laptop had put itself to sleep while he was on the phone with her. He touched the space bar and woke it. Clicked through the series of cameras, he'd installed. He saw the French door, wide open and the circle of glass on top of a shrub. He closed his eyes and took in several deep breaths. He clicked on the one hidden in her bedroom light fixture—the scrolly art deco one he'd scraped his hand on while installing. He saw her bed, empty except for the blood that spattered the tousled cream-colored sheets. He used the controls on the screen to pan the room and saw the body lying at the foot of the bed. He zoomed in and saw his own face staring back at him.

Garrett jolted up out of the first truly terrifying nightmare he'd had as an adult. He'd killed the stalker and the stalker was he.

He shook his head and looked around trying to get his bearings. He was safe. He was alive. He was an idiot. And he wanted to call Laurel just to hear her voice. He looked at the clock. It was 4:20. He was pretty damned sure she wouldn't appreciate his call right now.

What the hell did that dream mean, he thought, as he got up to pee and to hang his head under some running water to stop the pounding.

He wasn't a stalker. He wasn't. He just couldn't tell her how he knew her. It would take away any chance he had of wooing her with prescient carnal knowledge and guaranteeing his suit. If he told her now, he would gain nothing and probably lose the chance to even continue seeing her. Guilt weighed on his conscience as he replayed their day on Bald Head and their date the evening after. No, he couldn't let on. Not yet. But he would. Hopefully, before he had another dream like that last one.

It was ten minutes later, as he was pouring a cup

of coffee from the pot he'd made, when he recognized the Sting song that was going through his head. "O can't you see, you belong to me . . . Every breath you take . . . Every move you make . . . Every bond you break . . . Every step you take . . . I'll be watching you." *Great, the stalker song—his subconscious had picked this as the tune to play over and over in his head.* He leaned forward and banged his head against the custom cabinet door.

Chapter Forty-six

On Wednesday he called and left a message on Laurel's voice mail asking if there was anything he could bring to the concert Friday night. He missed her return call and listened to her message saying not to bother bringing anything, that she was making sandwiches and bringing brownies and lemonade. She ended with, "Can't wait to see you . . . you've been on my mind . . . a lot." He replayed the message at least ten times.

By Thursday morning he just had to see her—or her house, her bike, her car . . . something to connect her to him, if just for a moment. He needed to be assured this was all real, that she really was in his life now. It smacked of stalker, but he didn't care. He was like a junkie on withdrawal. He had to see her.

He called the pro shop for Panther's Run and arranged to take a lesson from one of the pros while playing the course. They played the back nine first, so they didn't get to Laurel's house until after two. As they got closer, he was beginning to have trouble concentrating on his game.

After they had both hit from the tee and returned to the cart to approach the fairway, the pro leaned toward him and lowered his voice. "The lady in that house," he said as he nodded with his chin toward Laurel's back deck, "she is the cutest little thing, and once, my cousin got a real show."

Garrett's body tensed on the seat. An image of Laurel in full stripper mode, with twirling boa flashed and hung suspended in front of his eyes. He blinked and managed to say, "Pardon?"

"She tans on her deck topless sometimes. My cousin, Jeremy, is the bug guy for the house next door. From the upstairs attic storage room there's a window that looks down on her deck, right where she sunbathes. He says she's luscious. He just got a new cell phone with a camera, says he's gonna get a picture next time. Oh look, she's in her backyard now. Take a gander—she's mighty fine, don't cha think?"

The pro pulled up just a few feet from the out of bounds marker and the rosemary bush. Garrett hopped out the moment the cart stopped and made a beeline for her, stalking through the rough grass as the pro called after him, "Hey, where ya goin'? You can't go on private property!"

Laurel looked up when he was a few feet away, her eyes wide with surprise. When she recognized who he was, she beamed with delight and stood, hands on hips, mocking him. "Garrett, you didn't hit out of bounds again just to steal more of my rosemary?"

He smiled back, closed the distance between them, and with his hands gripping her elbows, he effortlessly lifted her over the newly dug hole that was between them.

"No," he said looking down into her flushed face. "I'm here for a kiss to tide me over until date number two. I'm suffering. I miss you." He ducked his head and took her lips with his as his arms went around her shoulders and pulled her to his chest. Long and thorough, he mated his lips to hers, tasting and absorbing her flavor. When he discovered the caramel melting in her mouth, he skillfully flipped it off her tongue and sucked it into his mouth.

"Mmm," he said as he reached down and swiped a finger across her lower lip, catching a smear of caramel. He licked the dab off his finger. "Mark my place, I'll be back for more Friday night." He fished in his pocket for the bag of lemon Jelly Bellys and fed her two of them, murmuring, "Even exchange." Then he dropped his hands, steadied her, turned and headed back to the cart, smiling and sucking on the Werther's he'd stolen.

As he climbed back into the cart, with steel in his voice, he said, "She's mine. Don't touch. And tell your cousin I'll break his fucking neck if he looks at her again."

"Uh, yes sir. Uh . . . I suppose we're done sir?"

"We've got a few more holes to go. You think you can stop shaking enough to work with me on my irons?"

Chapter Forty-seven

Garrett called while Laurel was stirring the batter for the brownies. She picked up the phone and tucked it under her chin as she continued to blend the ingredients. She sensed that it could be Garrett, but oddly, the number was blocked from her Caller I.D.

"Hello?"

"Hi there." Yes, it was Garrett—his voice soft, low, and seductive.

"Am I disturbing something?"

"No, not at all. Just making brownies."

"From scratch?"

"Of course. No other way."

"With nuts?"

"Both ways. Roman likes them, Philip doesn't."

"These are the friends I'll be meeting?"

"Yup."

"We only had one date and I have to meet your friends? Do I worry you so?"

"No. Why would you say that?"

"Well if I'm not worrying you, then surely I'm not putting enough effort into this."

She laughed. He literally felt his knees give out and he had to lean against the counter. He loved that sound.

"You'll like my friends. Don't sweat it. We're going to have a great time. I guarantee it."

"I know how you can absolutely positively guarantee it," he murmured.

"Four. The magic number is four, we agreed."

"You know we could have already had number four by now if you hadn't been so busy this week."

"Yeah," she sounded wistful. Then bounced back nice and cheery, "But it couldn't be helped. Commitments you know."

"What kinds of things do you commit to?" Again that soft sexy drawl. And a blatant innuendo.

She had to smother her gasp. *Oh my, this was heady stuff.* "Well, the Garden Club took a tour of my garden yesterday, so that was pretty stressful."

"I've seen your garden. You had nothing to worry about."

"Well, I had to feed them, too."

"Hmmm. Okay. What else?"

"I had a charity luncheon on Monday, then an oyster dig on Tuesday—"

"You dug oysters?"

"Well, not the way you're thinking. I dig them out of the trash. Behind the restaurant. With Cat. Sometimes with Tess. Viv doesn't like to do it so much anymore."

"Uh . . . I think you and dumpster diving is going to take a little more explaining."

"We collect them for the Oyster Recycling Program. There are a few restaurants in Calabash that save them for us. When they have enough we haul 'em away, take them to Varnamtown, where they are loaded onto a boat to get taken out to be recycled in the ocean."

"Ahh. I thought you had a penchant for them . . . which I saw as promising."

That silky, chiding voice—did the man never stop? "No, not all that fond of them actually."

"As causes go, I figured you as more of a

turtle follower."

"Oh, I do that, too! In fact, I have a nest assigned to me that I have to check on after the concert. We're patrolling it constantly 'cause it's about to hatch. I thought maybe you might want to walk down with me."

"Sure. A walk on the beach in the moonlight, a pretty girl on my arm, what's not to like?"

She giggled and he vowed he would coax more of those amazing sounds from her.

"But, here's the thing. Since, we're changing locations, doing two totally different things. I'm afraid it's going to have to count as two dates."

She could practically hear him smiling. "You're a determined fellow."

"Yes, I am."

"Well, then I'll see you tomorrow."

"I'll meet you there, then take you from the concert to the nest . . . and then I'll take you home." There was a lot implied by the way he drew out the word home.

"Uh, alright." She noted that whose home hadn't been established. It sounded like the most tentative of answers. But they both knew that she'd just said yes.

Chapter Forty-eight

Midway through *Pink Cadillac*, Garrett thought his eyes were going to fall out of his head. He felt like a high school jock. He hadn't been able to take his eyes from Laurel's chest since he'd met her and her friends in the museum parking lot two hours ago. And he was pretty sure he wasn't the only man caught gaping.

From the moment he'd stepped up to her in the parking lot, shook hands with her friends, and kissed her cheek, he hadn't been able to focus on anything other than those two weighty mounds gently lifting and swaying under her filmy top. With each step she took the full globes surged high on her chest, firm and resilient, yet jiggling delightfully, and making his hands itch to caress her. Several times he'd had to force his hands to his sides while his fingers drummed impatiently on the chair he'd been carrying.

He wanted nothing more than to pinch the peaked nipples that were prominently outlined and oh so obviously broadcasting the high-tipped targets to lively, comely breasts. She wore tight capris that showed off her slim legs and dainty feet. She was on a petite frame, but she was built—she filled out her allotted five-foot-two with curves a man longed to caress. It was all he could do to force himself to keep focused on her face. She was stunning. And he was a goner—something the man named Roman had picked up on right away.

Roman had taken a large picnic basket from the trunk of a gold Lexus and handed it to Garrett. "Here, this should help," and Garrett flushed with the knowledge that this man was reading him like a neon sign.

Through the introductions and prerequisite man banter, he'd been okay. He'd turned his chest toward each man he spoke to, effectively diminishing her effect on him and easing the muscles in his groin. He'd read about Matt's various enterprises, knew Philip from his banking reputation, and saw a kindred spirit in Roman. On the walk over to the concert stage, he discovered that he and Roman were both unsocial renegades, running with the pack only when it was unavoidable—preferring one-on-one interaction with a lovely lady and a small, close-knit circle of friends. The fact that he had been included in this tight little gathering was not overlooked. But it was like a man dating a woman with three godfathers. Garrett had to turn on the charm and allay each one's fears in turn.

Through dinner, eaten in low-slung beach chairs, he'd gotten to know them and they'd gotten to know him. He watched each man, learning things about them by the way they treated their wives, by the way they sat and chatted, by their confident repose and easy mannerisms. That they adored their wives was readily apparent. Roman eyed Tess so openly and with such blatantly sensual eyes that even he could feel the charge in the air. Philip, with an easy grace, leaned into Viv and whispered against her neck, sending secret messages that colored her neck, her throat, her cheeks—plans for later, no doubt. And Matt, sitting next to him, snagged Cat as she returned from talking to friends, and settled her in his lap for enthusiastic kisses that promised more of the same.

Now Laurel was shimmying and shaking, cha-cha-cha-ing and twirling to *Pink Cadillac* as she and a slew of men and women did the Tush Push not ten feet from where he sat, trying to master his erection and back it down. *My God, why wasn't she wearing a bra?*

Roman leaned forward from three seats away and called out to him, "Poetry in motion." He didn't know whether to bust the scoundrel's lip or laugh with him. But it was pretty obvious that he wasn't the only man gaping at the woman line dancing on the asphalt. Well, he couldn't take them all on.

When Laurel returned to her seat laughing and panting, he leaned over and nuzzled her temple, "Why aren't you wearing a bra?"

She reached behind her and snapped the elastic. "Oh, but I am."

He cocked his brow. "This I have to see."

She smiled at him coyly. Too coyly.

He stood, "C'mon, let's go check out that turtle nest."

She looked up at him, an innocent look on her face, "But the concert's not over yet."

"It is for us. Get your things." He pulled her up, folded their chairs and shook hands with the men. Then he leaned down to whisper something in Tessa's ear. He saw Roman tense and his smile widened because of it. Tessa laughed and turned to Cat and whispered in her ear. Viv was next to get the message. They all laughed, raised their Solo cups and promised to take all the picnic items with them when they left.

Garrett hoisted the chairs onto his shoulder by the straps and took her hand.

"What did you say to Tessa?" she asked.

"I told her the truth."

"Which is?"

"That we were going to have sex on the beach."

They were walking toward his truck, hidden between two vehicles when she turned to face him. "We still have two more dates to go."

"No, after we get to the nest, date number five will be history."

"How do you figure?"

He counted on his fingers, "Bald Head, Chang's, dessert at your house yesterday, the concert, the walk on the beach."

"Dessert at my house? Yesterday?"

"Yes, don't you remember? We dined al fresco; I was treated to a marvelous caramel treat. By all rights, we should be having sex right here. Right now. And believe me, I want to."

With his free hand he reached up to cup her, to heft her heavy left breast. She moaned. He bent and took the peak into his mouth, sucking and tugging both her and the fabric between his lips, worrying the nipple with his tongue. She gasped. His hand dropped and slid under her shirt. He felt the elastic band under her breasts, and slowly ran one lone finger under it, from right to left and then back again. She held her breath. He slid his hand up to her shoulder and fingered the strap there, rubbing the skin under it in tiny circles with his thumb, up and down and over her shoulder. She sighed. Then he trailed his fingertips over her breast, caressing her flesh and tugging the sides of her breasts more fully away from the elastic circling them, bringing her breasts impossibly forward. He inched toward each nipple, but did not give her the satisfaction of even a light graze by a fingernail. She sobbed and leaned her head against this chest in supplication.

"Enough double, triple, and quadruple dating. You've been teasing me all night. Exposing yourself in a way you knew would entice. You drove me crazy and clearly you meant to. It's payback time."

He took her nipple between this thumb and forefinger and pinched it lightly as he took her lips with his, taking possession of her warm glossed lips and eager tongue. It was a thorough kiss, sampling and testing at first, and escalating with the increased pressure he was using to pinch her nipple. When he was pinching it as hard as he dared, he ended the kiss.

"I want you Laurel. I want you in the worst way, well . . . maybe not the *worst* way, but certainly a universally accepted one. Let's get a blanket, go find that nest and make love on the beach. Just you, me, and the turtles."

His hand slid to her waist and he lightly squeezed it. "If you're not sure I have no scruples, I'll convince you right here. " His hand slid to the fly on her capris and he skillfully undid the single button with a quick flick. His fingers found her zipper, tugged on the tab, "I'll make you so horny right here that we won't get much further than this parking lot and my truck."

She looked up into his dark, intense eyes, glinting in the meager moonlight. Hers, he could see were filled with stars, and it was the first time that expression had ever made sense to him. But there she was, a woman with stars in her eyes—for him.

"What do you say?" The zipper inched down.

"Well, I really do need to check that nest tonight."

He smiled, pulled her zipper back up and spun her around toward his truck. His hand grazed her ass. "Those eggs better not hatch tonight. I don't want an audience while I'm learning your body's naughty little secrets."

Chapter Forty-nine

Laurel couldn't get her mind around the fact that she had just consented to have sex with this man that she'd known less than a week. Good God, she hadn't had sex involving another person in . . . forever. All the old insecurities came crashing home—was he going to like her body, would he be able to make her respond, or would she climb and climb, only to be left shaking with want and not be able to be satisfied? And of course, the mother of all fears, if she let him "go all the way" now, what would he think of her later? Would he lose interest after he'd had her?

He looked over at her, ran a finger down her cheek and cocked a brow, "What are you thinking? You look lost in your thoughts," he said as he drove down 179 toward Sunset Beach.

No way was she going to voice her insecurities, he didn't need to know that she was intimidated by him, by his size, by his manner, by his gorgeous profile and windblown mop of sexy hair. She improvised, "I'm wondering if the nest is going to hold off or if we're going to have a boil tonight."

His eyes flew wide and he turned to her with shock, "You eat them? I thought you were working to protect them!"

She shook her head in wonder. Here was a very intelligent man, a local on the island, how was it people knew so little about the turtles right outside their beachfront doors? She sighed in exasperation and began her spiel.

"It's called a boil because it looks like a pot boiling over and it's caused by the eggs cracking and shifting as the turtles climb over each other to get out of the nest, or crawl as it's called, which is essentially a big hole in the sand that the eggs have been buried in. The eggs can hatch up to three days before hatchlings emerge because they have to absorb all the nutrients from inside the shell through their navel in order to have food to sustain them for the long swim. When the boil is about to begin, the sand gets grainy and dark and actually looks like coffee or tea granules shifting. *We* don't eat the hatchlings; in fact, we spend a lot of time and effort keeping foxes, feral cats, and ghost crabs from eating them. The turtle patrol has been watching this particular crawl for several nights now. After the hatchlings are released, the nest is opened by patrol members who are certified to count the unhatched or unfertilized eggs. An average nest has 100-125 hatchings whose sex is largely determined by the temperature of the sand. I'm surprised you don't know all this."

"I didn't know all that, but I still do my part. When I'm running on the beach, if I see any large holes, I fill them in so the hatchlings can't get trapped in them; I have motion sensors on all my outside lights, some I even turn off until the hatching season is over; I close my blinds at night, and I donate so the turtle patrol can buy the tape and webbing used to keep people away. I appreciate people like you being so dedicated, but it's just not my thing . . . too much hovering and waiting."

"Well I appreciate you walking down to the nest with me. This is one of the last crawls of the season, so we're monitoring it very closely. I just have to check in before eleven."

"So we have plenty of time," Garrett said as he pulled into a spot marked in the pavement at the end of Main Street, just past the 40ᵗʰ Street Access.

"How far down is it?"

"Not too far, about half a mile or so."

He smiled and leaned in to kiss her lightly on the lips. "Do we need anything other than water and a blanket? Maybe a condom or two?" he asked with a wicked grin.

"Garrett . . . I'm not sure I'm ready."

He ran a finger down her cheek. "That's my job, sweetheart, to get you ready. Hey," he said, serious now, his eyes focused solely and intently on hers, "if it doesn't happen tonight for whatever reason, that's okay. But let's not let it screw this up. We've got more than high passion going for us here—we can fuck anytime. But we can't have our first time again—so it has to be special, no anxiety, no regrets. I want you, don't ever doubt that, but you also have to want me, for this to work."

"That's just it, I do want you. But I'm afraid of the chase ending if we do this too soon."

"Trust me babe, you're not getting rid of me that easily. Whether we do this thing tonight or not, I'm coming back for more. How about we take the pressure off and I leave these here?" He took two foil packets out of his pants pocket and placed them on the console between them.

She looked down at them, then back up at him. "No, we'd better take them. Life has a strange way of turning out for people who don't plan ahead." She smiled and kissed him quickly on the lips. "But you know . . . if we use one of these you have to bring it back here."

His left brow arched in question, "And that would be because . . ."

"Like plastic trash bags, turtles think condoms and balloons are its favorite food. It's not pretty what happens when they get in their digestive system. Two-hundred-year-old turtles that have survived countless hurricanes, Asians trying to grind them up for aphrodisiacs, and merchants offering insane amounts of money to make combs, brushes and barrettes, often succumb from mistaking a plastic bag for a jellyfish."

"Well then, should I have the opportunity to don one, or both of these," he said as he replaced them in his pocket, "I promise to dispose of them properly." He picked up her hand and softly kissed each knuckle, then he sucked her baby finger into his mouth and smiled around it when she gasped. He slowly brought his head up so that her finger slid away from his mouth in achingly unhurried increments. "That is, should the opportunity arise."

He stayed long enough to see her eyes glaze over before opening his door and coming around to get hers. With a blanket draped over his arm and a bottle of water in his hand, he helped her down from the truck.

"Do you have one for me?" she asked as she saw the water bottle.

"Sweetheart, we may not fuck, but we are definitely going to share some spit. I think we can share the water bottle."

"Are you always so—"

"Yes."

Chapter Fifty

Garrett took Laurel's hand and led her down the boardwalk to the beach. There was no one in sight, not on the long access over the dunes, not on the wide stretch of beach. They kicked off their sandals at the dune line then strolled, lost in their thoughts as they watched the waves crashing on the shore. Out in the distance there was a cruise ship from one of the casinos moving along the horizon. It was a beautiful night, the stars shining bright against an inky sky.

As they headed toward Bird Island he asked, "Did you know that there was a shipwreck on the coast in 1664, 1785, and again in 1860, where there was only one survivor?"

"Well that wasn't all that unusual back then was it?"

"The interesting thing, was that in each incidence, the sole survivor was named Hugh Williams."

"Really? What an odd coincidence," she said.

"And what have we learned from this?"

"Don't get on a ship with a man named Hugh Williams?"

He threw back his head and laughed. "Yes, precisely right. Most people say don't get on a ship if you're Hugh Williams."

"Is that a true story?"

"So I've read. I like to study shipwrecks. It's especially fascinating to study the ones around the lower Keys."

"Do you dive?"

"I have, but not for some time. I don't seem to have time for hobbies like I used to. Other than gardening, what are your hobbies, what do you like to do with your free time? You don't work do you?" He made an attempt to get her to open up about her writing.

"No, I don't have a job anymore. I just play golf, cook, and ride my bike. And lately, I've been doing a lot of volunteering."

So we're not there yet. She's not ready to share that part of her life. He took another stab at it. "I would have more time for things like diving and scuba if I quit teaching, there's so much reading and writing with that—it takes a lot of time."

"Yeah, it must. But surely you enjoy it, shaping young, questing minds."

He snorted and thought of the student he'd emailed a few days ago, the one using a picture of herself in a provocative bikini as her signature line. "So far this semester I've had three female students offer to send me topless pictures of themselves, so they're questing all right. But their quest has nothing to do with learning the material I assign. They want the grades but they don't want to work for them."

"How do you handle that?"

"I decline of course," he said with a wicked grin. Using their connected hands, he pulled her close. There was just enough moonlight coming off the water to light up her face. God she was lovely.

"I don't want to see their breasts. I just want to see yours."

Her eyes flashed with interest, but there was also a hint of fear in them. "C'mon, you've teased me all night. Show me this sexy bra you picked out to wear for me."

He touched his lips to hers then dropped the blanket and bottle in the sand so he could wrap his arms around her. His hands slid up her back, stroking her lightly until his fingertips grazed the nape of her neck and he sprang the latch on her barrette, letting her hair billow free. He tucked the fancy clip into her front pocket then dug his fingers into the flying tresses. He held her head with both hands as he kissed her, massaging her lips with his. The raging need he'd been fighting all night took hold and he deepened the kiss.

She tasted the tang of lemon on his tongue from the jellybeans he'd been sucking. She used her tongue to savor it, mating it with his while he lit little fires in her with his hands, his lips, and his low groans.

She put her hands against his chest and pushed away until they were forced to separate. He looked down at her questioningly.

She crossed her hands at her waist and whipped off her top.

He had known what he'd see, but he was not prepared for the effect. *This was hot. Unbelievably hot.* It devastated him. This was so much more arousing than if she'd been completely topless. The way her ample breasts were squeezed through the tight openings, the way it made her jut out, the way her nipples were displayed, it bordered on vulgar—it was tits on a shelf and he loved it. His groan was carried on the wind and he had to blink wide to keep taking her in. Her pink tipped nipples were drawing tight from the breeze, the aureoles plumping from his heated gaze. The smooth, even texture of her skin a delight to behold in the pale cool light.

"Jesus, Laurel. Your breasts are amazing. So beautiful." His hands cupped her, hefted her, kneaded and squeezed her. Testing the firmness, trying to collect them in his hands, he was overwhelmed with the need to satisfy primal needs welling in him. He'd never had a particular fondness for pushing a woman's breasts together to make a valley between to slake himself there, but damned if he didn't want to do it to Laurel. He wanted to kiss each nipple with the tip of his creaming penis—instead, he took her with his lips, closed them around the hard buds and sucked. She heaved a heartfelt sigh as if she'd been holding it in for years, and let her head fall back exposing her throat. The moonlight shone on her long neck and her lightly sun-freckled chest.

As he moved from one breast to the other and back again, he whispered, "Where did you get this little bit of confection?" he snapped the elastic of the bra.

"From Roman," she breathed.

He abruptly stopped the attention he was lavishing on her and stepped back. "What?"

"His and Tessa's idea actually. Some kind of bet they had with Philip."

He brought his hand up to cup her chin and his thumbs grazed over her lips. "Expound please."

"I told her about the four-date thing. She told Roman. Roman thought it'd be fun to tempt you beyond bearing. This is what he came up with."

He looked down at her and his hand followed his eyes to thumb at both of her nipples. "While I appreciate his efforts on my behalf, I'd rather our 'courtship,' for lack of another word, be solo. What we do, what we say, be ours, and ours alone." His voice lowered, "There are things I plan on doing to you, that I don't want anyone else to know about. Things I don't want shared. Is that going to be a problem?"

"Well they do have this bet . . ."

"What?"

"Roman bet Philip that we'd do the deed tonight." She motioned to the bra, circling her fingers, "This was supposed to put the odds in his favor."

"Oh it did. It most certainly did." He pinched her nipple—hard. Then the other. And back again. "It did." He took a long nipple between each thumb and forefinger and tugged her toward him.

"Let's open up that blanket. Then later, you can get me Roman's address. I think I know how I want to dispose of the condoms I'm going to use tonight."

He released her long enough to flutter the blanket in the air and settle it on the sand. He pulled her down with him, and rolled her onto her back. Hovering over her, he stroked her neck and snapped the strap on her shoulder. "Let's leave this little marvel on, but everything else has to go. I want to look at you. Then I want to lick, suck, and kiss every single inch of your body. When you're ready, really ready, I want you to invite me inside you." He took her lips and crushed them under his.

His hands moved to her waistband and before she had time to think, he was lifting her and pulling her capris down her legs, and over her ankles and bare feet. "Nice panties, did Roman pick these out, too?" he fingered the elastic lace waistband of her boyshort panties.

She could tell by his tone that he wasn't pleased with the idea of Roman selecting her lingerie. The idea that he could be jealous warmed her. She wanted him to be possessive. Needed him to be possessive. It was the kind of emotion that fueled her fantasies and drove her wild. God, to be owned by this man she thought, as his lips lavished kisses on her breasts, belly and throat.

She shook her head no.

He was gentle and thorough. Not one inch was spared his attention as he exposed flesh, ran tantalizing fingers up and down her legs, her thighs, her torso. When the tiny scrap covering her mons was pulled down to mid-thigh, she sobbed at the overwhelming sensation created by being displayed for him, framed for him, in the crosshairs of moonlight. She could hardly stand to look at his face as his penetrating gaze drank her in as if memorizing her. She was hotly embarrassed as he carefully inspected her, examined secret folds, and toyed with tight curls. He was so openly gazing, his eyes avidly lingering that she finally realized with shock, that he was purposely building an element of shame in her. She moaned with her desire, and felt the floodgates open, coating her. When he removed her panties, tossed them aside, drew her knees up high and parted them wide, she sobbed. Placing her feet in the sand, as wide as they would go, he tucked his head between her legs and took in the view while his fingers probed at her.

"I wish there was a full moon. I'd love to see more of your sweet pussy than this light allows. I suppose, I'll just have to get to know you by using one of my other senses." He ducked his head and his lips kissed all around her mons as he told her how much he appreciated her bikini wax. His thumbs pulled her labia lips apart and he kissed her heated, slick flesh. She moaned and cried out his name.

Her hands clasped his head holding him to her. He reached up and untangled her fingers from his hair and repositioned her hands. Silently, he admonished her with his heated gaze and lifted brow. He tucked her hands flat, under her hips so that he used them to his advantage and lifted her higher. She sobbed her pleasure as she realized he was using her to make herself more vulnerable, more exposed.

She felt herself flooding again and he moaned enthusiastically, his mouth devouring her. His tongue came into play next, licking and lapping at her tender, plumping lips and running up and down her velvety slit, stopping intermittently to thrust at her opening. She was sobbing now and clutching her hands into the blanket under her bottom.

He drilled her with the tip of his skilled tongue, twisting it inside her and then using the flat to oscillate like a vibrator. She screamed his name.

"What? Is there something you want? Something I'm not giving you?" he asked, and the huskiness of his voice was enough to thoroughly wet her again.

"Yes," she panted.

"Well, what is it?" he asked, feigning the voice of patience. "Tell me."

"There, I need you there."

"Where? Here?" he asked as he kissed her opening.

"Higher," she moaned.

"Here?" he sucked on a labial lip.

"Aarrgh!"

"Maybe here?" He latched onto her straining clit and sucked. Every nerve went white hot as she fractured and screamed out her release. Pulsing and throbbing against his tongue he milked her contracting nub with his firm lips as tremor after tremor went through her. She sobbed as she flailed her head from side to side, "Oh, Garrett, Garrett, Garrett . . . Oh God."

Her use of his name at the height of her passion caused a raging tide of need to surge through him.

With a final sucking kiss, he released her and climbed up her body to see her face. Her dazed expression and limpid eyes warmed his soul. Leaning on one elbow, he shoved two fingers inside her and began thrusting, assuring that the heel of his hand met her clit full on, tight to her mons, with each pass. She groaned and arched to meet him. He pulsed his hand against her, using a fast paced rhythm to reawaken her nerve endings. "Am I invited inside?" He buried his face in her breasts and rooted for a nipple. Finding one, he tugged at it with the edges of his teeth.

"Yes! God yes!"

"Say it."

"I invite you. Come inside me, please."

"Be crude, you know what I want to hear. And use my name."

"Fuck me, Garrett. Please, please fuck me!"

"Again," he insisted as he pummeled her with his hand, shoving his fingers up inside her.

"Fuck me! Garrett . . . aaah, please, please . . ." her

voice trailed off to a whimper, "please, fuck me."

He lifted off her, leaving her heaving her hips pulsing the air, while he undid his belt and whipped it out of the loops. He unzipped and pulled his pants down past his hips then fished for a condom. Using his teeth he tore the packet, spit it aside and with one hand rolled the condom down his thick, heavy erection. Using his belt, strapped across her midsection, he pinned her down. Fists at her hips, wrapped tightly around the belt, he held her still, kept her immobile for him. He wanted to hit her clit like a jackhammer.

He positioned himself and sank into her, stretching her and filling her completely. She cried out her pleasure and moaned. He took a moment to savor their joining, to absorb the wonder of being inside this incredibly beautiful woman. Then he began fucking her, hard and fast. The pace punishing.

"Oh God, oh God, please don't stop. Don't stop!"

"Not until you get there," he said between clenched teeth, reassuring her. "Not until you give me what's mine. Give it to me, baby," he coaxed. And she did.

Sobbing his name and calling to her God, she keened and trembled inside and out, her release flooding her and sending arcing white sparks jangling through every nerve. She saw prisms of light flash on the insides of her lids as she careened out of her body and floated on a rolling wave of pleasure.

Her vagina, clenching like a fist around him, sent him over the edge as he gritted his teeth and threw back his head. "Fuck! Fuck! Fuck! Ahhh," he hissed as his release washed through him and took his breath from him. He rode out on a tsunami of bliss before returning to his senses and collapsing with his face against her neck. He sighed her name and breathed in her floral fragrance. He kissed behind her ear, the hollow of her throat, her sternum . . . the tips of her breasts.

When she could manage it, she whispered, "Thank you. *That* was amazing." She idly stroked his back through his shirt, feeling his rippling muscles relax.

"Hmmmm . . . the pleasure was all mine."

"I think not."

"Why Miss Laurel, are you telling me you had a good time on your fourth date?"

"That is an gross understatement. I had the best time. I can't get over how you knew exactly how to . . . well everything."

"I aim to please."

"I have never experienced anything like that. Didn't even know I was capable of multiple orgasms. I've dreamed about climaxing like that," she shook her head, "never thought I could though . . ."

"Well, let's see if we can make all your dreams come true," he said as he thrust into her again. He was still hard, hard enough to go again.

They heard a dog bark in the distance, and then voices being carried on the wind before he was able to make the next thrust. They both looked over and panicked. About three hundred yards away, they could faintly make out a man and a woman walking a dog in the gray mist by the water.

"Shit!" he said as he leveraged off of her. He removed the condom, tied it in a knot and stuffed it into his pants pocket. He stood and zipped up while he found her top, billowing in the sand a few yards away. He rethreaded and buckled his belt, then held out his hand so she could stand to arrange her clothing. He scooped up her panties and quickly pocketed them.

She frowned at him good-naturedly. "Souvenir?"

"I won't need a memento to remember tonight. But maybe I should send them to Roman as proof," he said with a grin. He bent and picked up the foil wrapper and took a long slug from the water bottle. She patiently waited then took her turn.

"I think we'd better check out that nest now, before I'm late checking in."

He shook out the blanket and folded it. Then he took her hand and lifted it to his lips. "Remind me to thank Roman for that bra. I hope he had a hefty bet."

Laurel laughed. "Knowing him and Philip, he probably did."

Chapter Fifty-one

The nest was secure, but it was showing signs of boiling. Laurel pointed out the differences in the texture of the sand and showed him how the nest was slightly depressed within the hole. "There are eggs underneath that have hatched, and soon the hatchlings are going to be making their way to the top and spilling out onto the beach."

"So what's the next step?"

"Sound the alarm, get some shovels, build a French corridor, monitor the ghost crabs, shoo away the foxes . . . things like that."

"Hmmm. What can I do to help?"

"I left my cell phone in my purse in the truck. I need to call this in."

"Tonight?"

"I know how all this is done, but this is my first time seeing a nest begin to boil without Carmel being around. It's too important to wait. Anything can happen. I need to call Carmel and the others."

"Okay, I'll go get the phone."

"Great, leave me here alone with the feral foxes."

He chucked her under her chin. "I'll run. All out, for you."

She smiled and tugged on his belt buckle. "I noticed you took your belt off and used it to hold me down. Why?"

"I didn't want you to get away."

"No, really. Tell me."

"Sometimes I like to use a form of restraint. One day I may like to tie your hands together, or lash you to a bed frame . . . tonight I just didn't want you to move. I wanted to hit that button of yours relentlessly. With absolutely no mercy." He ran a finger down her nose.

Her eyes flew wide and he saw the flash of interest in them. "Would that have been a problem if I'd bound your hands together?"

She met his gaze. It was clear she didn't know how to answer that question. She just blinked, eyes wide.

"We'll never do anything you don't want to do, Laurel. But I've been known to kink things up a bit. I'm hoping you're open-minded enough to consider some of them."

He heard the breath whoosh out of her lungs, saw the heat, saw the rosiness flush her face.

"Anyway, we can talk. But I want you to know I have big plans for you." He bent and kissed her on the lips, passing her one of his lemon jellybeans in the process. "Be right back."

She watched him jog away until she could hardly see him against the dark sky as she sucked on the jellybeans. An outrageously good-looking man, running with an easy grace, his strength and masculinity in perfect symmetry with the majesty of the roaring ocean. She rubbed her well-loved lips as she recalled every single thing he had done to her. She took a deep, cleansing breath. Even if the nest didn't boil tonight, this was going to be a very memorable night. She realized with a huge grin, that she was happy, deliriously happy, and thrilled about getting to know this exciting man.

Chapter Fifty-two

Hours later, Garrett stood beside Roman, hands in his pockets, watching Laurel and Tessa, on their hands and knees guiding a woefully disoriented straggler on its way through the corridor they had helped dig.

Eighteen people had shown up when the call had gone out, arriving within minutes with shovels and cameras, walking toward them in the dark like a ragtag regiment. Using only moonlight, they had all pitched in to make the corridor to the sea, smoothing out the humps in the sand as they went. It was low tide when they'd started so it had been a noble undertaking, but the tide was coming in now and taking some of their hard work with it, as well as helping to launch a hundred and nineteen hatchlings.

Garrett had to admit it had been touching to see the little flippers so hard at work, and impressive, considering it was the first time they'd ever been used. A few of the baby turtles managed to flip themselves over and had to be righted, but most made it down the chute that had been prepared without incident, and being swept up by the waves to avid clapping. He noticed that many people were moved to tears, oohing and aahing over the adorable new loggerheads.

"I'm impressed. This is quite a passionate group of supporters. What is it, three or four o'clock?" Garrett asked.

"Don't know. Left my watch on the nightstand. And she'll kill me if I light up my phone to check," Roman murmured.

"Yeah, well . . . speaking of grand passion," Garrett took Laurel's underwear from his pocket and shoved it at him. "Did you need proof for your bet?" he asked with more than a touch of irritation.

Roman chuckled. "If I go home with that in my pocket, I'll be bunking with you. No, no proof is necessary." He emphasized the last word and because of his brogue it came out as *necessorry,* and Garrett was reminded that Roman had left his life on the sea to be here with the woman he loved. Still, he didn't like the idea of this man having a say in Laurel's sex life.

"I don't cotton to the idea of you picking out my girl's underwear."

"Your girl, is she?" Roman said as he turned to look at Garrett with a slightly elevated brow, his distinctive shock of white among the thick black tresses giving him a regal, authoritative mien.

"She is now."

"Good. Then I expect my job is done."

"And what job was that?" Garrett asked with a frown.

"Getting her launched. We've had a helluva time of it, she's refused all our fix-ups two years runnin'."

"Hmmph," Garrett muttered, pleased at that.

"That's a fine girl you're getting. Don't hurt her." The steel in his voice was unmistakable.

"Well, just so you know, the special bra was not necessary."

"Maybe not for you," he said with a wicked smile, "but she needed the confidence. Did you not appreciate the advantage of foregone foreplay?" This time his smile was bland.

"I can provide whatever she needs in that department."

"Glad to hear it, because I suspect you will have a handful *in that department.*"

447

Tessa and Laurel sidled up, "What are you two talking about?" Tessa asked. They were both rubbing their arms briskly. Now that the excitement was over, they were feeling the late night chill.

Roman gathered Tessa in his arms and tucked her chin under his as he held her close and wrapped his sweater around them both.

"We were just remarking on the lovely sight you two were providing us, you on your hands and knees, your bottoms in the air. Very inviting indeed," Roman whispered against Tessa's ear.

"Roman!" Tessa hissed, and slapped at the hands that were snaking around to rub her jean-clad bottom.

"Let's go home," he said, "I'm suddenly inspired."

He put his hand out to Garrett, "Welcome to the Bewitched, Befuddled, and Beguiled. You may not know it now, but I assure you that after tonight, your life will never be the same again."

Garrett took his hand and shook it. "Oh don't I know it. I've already accepted it."

"Good, because we're all very fond of Laurel, and would not tolerate a player." This was simply godfather number one asserting himself, Garrett told himself as he watched Roman kiss Laurel on the cheek and whisper something in her ear.

Garrett was surprised when Tessa grabbed his shoulders and hugged him, but didn't miss Roman's upraised brows and look of annoyance at the gesture.

When he and Laurel got back to his truck, Garrett asked her what Roman had whispered to her.

He watched her face flush in the meager dash lights, but she didn't open her mouth, kept it in a firm line.

"Out with it. I want to know what he said." They were not going to start this relationship with her keeping secrets, too. The fact that he was, was bad enough.

"He said, 'If you're interested in a man, you're supposed to let him into your panties, no' let him have them.'" The fact that she had imitated his brogue down to his use of no' instead of not, endeared her to him even more.

He laughed heartily as he put the key in the ignition.

"Let's go back to my place so I can see if I can acquire the other piece to the matched set."

"I'm tired Garrett, and really dirty."

"Then I'll wash you, and let you sleep first." He was not leaving her now. Their bond was too tenuous; he had to capitalize on this magical time—he'd shown her he could be masterful and supportive, now he needed her to see that he could be caring, gentle . . . loving even.

She didn't say anything for a few seconds. Then she asked, "Does that include washing my hair?"

"Most definitely."

"Can you do all that at my place instead? I'm very particular about my hair products."

He took her hand in his and kissed the back of it. "Your wish is my command. Just get me through the security gates."

She smiled. "I have the code."

"Then let's go get ready for bed."

She was asleep, leaning against the door of his truck before he'd pulled off the bridge.

Chapter Fifty-three

He marveled at her master bath, so feminine yet simple and functional. Most of the women he knew cluttered their countertops and bathtub rims with soap dishes, brushes, sponges, and all manner of cosmetic marvels. She had one bottle of shampoo, one bottle of conditioner and one bottle of shower gel. There were no cosmetics in sight; the counter held a nickel-plated hand towel holder and a pump bottle of Trader Joe's Lavender hand soap.

He was a minimalist, and he liked knowing that she was, too. "Towels?" he asked as he led her into the shower alcove. She pointed to a cabinet in the corner beside the double sinks, and he took out two bath sheets that complimented the dark teal and cream décor.

He turned on the shower and began removing her clothes, first her shirt . . . he bent and kissed each nipple lightly. Then her capris . . . he kissed her above her pubic hair. He lifted her out of her heeled sandals, then as he stood, he grazed his hands up the back of her legs, stroking her ankles, her calves, the backs of her knees, and finally her thighs. His hands met in the center of her back where he unhooked her bra. He drew off the shoulder straps and gently tugged toward him so that her breasts fell out of the lacy elastic edges of the cups. He frowned at the red circles encompassing the base of each breast.

"Mmmm, looks like this might not have been very

comfortable," he murmured as his fingertips stroked the red creases.

She looked down and flushed. "No tighter than a corset or a bustier really."

"You own corsets and bustiers?"

There was a hopeful glint in his eyes and she had to laugh. "Of course. Why wouldn't I?"

"I got the impression from Roman that you didn't even date."

"I haven't since my parents died. But I like to keep up with the current fashions, and I like to look nice, even if it's just for me."

"Believe me, you look nice. Very, very nice." He allowed his fingertips to coast along the tops of her breasts, his thumbs to lightly flick the tips.

"C'mon, let's get you under the water before you collapse on me." He led her to the arched opening of the tiled-in stall and dropped her hand. "You get under the spray, I'll be right in."

She heard his sandals clunk on the floor followed by his belt pinging against the tiles. Then he was standing behind her, his warm hands pulling her back to his chest. She felt his chest hairs on her back and his erection pressing into her buttocks. He reached over and grabbed the shower gel and began using it on her front. Gentle hands filled with suds circled and caressed as he washed and massaged her. His big hands cupped her breasts, splayed over her belly, and rubbed briskly at her triangle of curls.

"Spread your legs," he commanded.

And she did.

One hand dove between and cleansed her from the front while the other smoothed soap over her ass and into the hollow. She moaned and threw her head back, resting it on his shoulder.

"If you keep making noises like that, I'm going to

find it very hard to honor my promise to clean you and tuck you in."

"What if I want more than to be cleaned and tucked in?"

"I could consider that. I suppose we could renegotiate."

"What did you have in mind?"

"That's a hard question to answer, but thoughts of you on your hands and knees, wiggling that cute ass back and forth as you cajoled that last hatching to the water, come to mind."

She gasped and then moaned when he brought his hand down and smacked her playfully on her right cheek. "I think I could find taking you from the rear extremely pleasurable. The view of your pussy as I slide inside you might unman me though," he groaned as he slid a finger into her slick warmth.

She moaned and met the thrusts of his finger as it pushed inside her.

He grabbed his penis and placed it lengthwise along the crack of her ass so he could hold her flush to him, then he breathed into her neck and kissed the tender skin behind her ear. "But first, I have to wash your hair, so put your head under the spray."

He pushed her forward and the water cascaded over them both. He poured some shampoo into his palm then smoothed it into her hair. Expert fingers massaged and gathered the long tresses. He enjoyed piling and squeezing the suds through her honey blonde hair. Over and over again, he collected the soapy curls and then watched the white froth cascade down her back. Finally, he rinsed her hair, repeated the process with the conditioner, then he rinsed it again.

"My turn," he said as he turned her to face him. "You don't get to touch though. Not this time. You just get to watch."

As she turned, she saw him naked for the first time

and was delighted by what she saw. An impressive broad chest with dark wet curls fanning over sculpted pecs, strong muscular arms, and a long corded neck that flexed as he turned his head to search out the soap. She let her eyes drop and followed the darkening trail. His erection, bouncing in the spray, could have kissed his navel if she'd pushed it forward. Tall and thick, it called to her primitive urges and she moved her hand to touch it.

She was barely able to graze her fingertips along the crest before he slapped her hand. "Uh uh. No touching, remember? You just get to look."

He rubbed soap on his chest, over his arms and around his neck. His skin was tanned and smooth, pale where bathing trunks would be, but otherwise an even soft burnished gold. With lathered hands he reached down and cupped his balls from underneath, washed them thoroughly and then palmed his penis with more of the gel. His long fingers, with their impossibly clean white nails looked capable and sensuous as he stroked the long length. He knew exactly what he was doing to her with this unabashed display. The sight of this classically handsome, extremely virile man suggestively touching himself in front of her made her throat dry, and the area between her legs wet. When he was satisfied that he was clean, he turned around and handed her the bottle. "You could do my back if you'd like."

She took the bottle from him and poured a liberal amount of soap into her hand. Then she took her time running it up and down and back and forth along his wide shoulders and expansive back. "You have a great body," she murmured, and then let her hand explore lower.

"Aaahh," he breathed out. "No fair," he hissed as her hand caressed each globe, separating one from the other and squeezing the firm muscles of his ass.

"Nice," she whispered, "very nice butt. I could do this all night."

He turned and said, "Well, unfortunately for me, the night is about gone, and I promised you sleep."

As he faced her, his erection slid right into her hand. She smiled and clasped it. He groaned.

"Look what I found."

He covered her hand and gently removed it. "I said no touching."

"It wasn't my fault, you put it there, right in my hand."

He reached up and turned off the shower. "I want to put it someplace else right now." He took her hand and walked her out of the shower, grabbed both towels and used one to wrap around his waist. He opened the other one and began drying her, starting with her hair. "Are you looking at me?" she asked from under the towel.

"Yes, I most definitely am."

"Well stop."

"No way. You are beautiful. Your whole body is lovely."

He dried her quickly, top to bottom, then wrapped her in a fresh towel and walked her over to the mirror over the sinks. "What shall I do about your hair? Do you want me to blow dry it?"

"No. I'll just comb it." She opened a drawer and took out a wide-toothed comb.

"Let me," he said and he took it from her.

For several minutes they stood staring at each other in the mirror as he drew the comb through her shoulder length hair, separating the strands and tingling her scalp. She stared at the outline of his chest and arms, wanting more than anything to be able to run her hands through the sprinkling of crisp hairs. She looked forward to when she would be given leave to delineate the broad muscles with her fingertips and to pluck at his nipples. Her eyes met his several times and lingered, feeling the heat, sensing the hunger. His dark expressive brows arched and one brow lifted in warning when she succumbed to temptation and reached behind her to drag her fingernails up his powerfully built thighs.

He put the comb on the counter and turned her to face him, then he bent and put his arms under her knees and lifted her off her feet. He carried her effortlessly to the bed and whipped the covers down with the hand supporting her knees. With great care he placed her in the middle of the bed then climbed in beside her, kissed her lightly on the nose, and resolutely turned her away from him.

"Big plans for you in the morning. Rest now. Get some sleep." He kissed the back of her neck and pulled her to him, wrapping his leg over one of hers.

"I have to go to the Shallotte Farmers Market in the morning. I promised some friends I'd come see their booth."

"You're going to have to start saying no to everyone except me for a while. If we start on the list of things I want to do to you, we won't be done until 2020, so we can't afford any distractions," he murmured against her ear.

"Tell me what you want to do to me."

"It's 4:30, get some sleep. I'll give you a sample in the morning." He kissed her neck again and breathed in the delightful fragrance of her shampoo.

She fell asleep cradled in his arms. It took him a while longer to nod off. He didn't want to waste the time he had with her by sleeping it away. But his mind finally gave in to the fatigue.

Chapter Fifty-four

He woke first, or more precisely, the appendage he affectionately called Spear woke first. Proud and pointed in the right direction, his penis nestled between her thighs, nudging her opening and calling attention to a significant problem.

"Mmmm," she moaned in her sleep, moving her curved bottom to accommodate him.

"Morning," he breathed into her ear as his fingers worked to make her slick for him.

"Who is this?" she asked and waited for his response. It came in the form of a slap to her rear. She giggled. He thrust and filled her.

After the shock of the initial impact she groaned, "Uhhh! mmm, ahhhh. . . . ."

"Music to my ears," he said as he inched back, gripped her hips and dove in again.

Writhing together on the bed, he ground into her while his hands loved her bottom—each round cheek lovingly kneaded, scratched, pinched—until she couldn't hold still. She heaved her bottom so furiously back against him that he had to wrap his hands under her, splayed over her navel to keep them fused together.

When he felt her lower her hips to the bed to find relief for her neglected clit, he brought his hands down from her belly to gently cup her. He used the pads of three fingers to press against the top of her needy cleft. It took four steady depressions of his flattened fingers pressing against her mons before she cried out and spent. He added to the slaughter of her senses by lightly pinching her swollen nub and sending her over the edge with his name screaming into her pillow.

He gave her a few moments to process her orgasm, let it settle and weigh into her brain before he knelt behind her, lifted her to her knees and went for his. The bed shook from the ferocity of his thrusts, as he gave her no quarter and slammed into her, claiming her—driven by a demon weeks in the making as he'd read her stories late into the night.

His release was upon him before he was ready, causing his body to harden, his jaw to firm, his arms to pull her tight against his groin with each full thrust. He fought against the tide and momentarily held her to him as if frozen in place, no further exertion necessary or possible as his head fell back and he damned near howled with the want of her.

He took a deep breath and resumed his pummeling. As his body thrummed and his penis pulsed inside her with each taking thrust, he became aware of her arching, keening, and now reaching for her own elusive climax. With monumental control, he forced himself back from the edge he was so precariously balanced on and brought one of his hands around from her hip to her backside. Sightless now, with his own scattered senses, eyes squeezed tight from the effort, he felt her ass, forced his fingers down the smooth valley and widened the cleavage with his thumb. He pressed it into her tightly puckered opening, gently breeching the rim. She screamed and bucked and as her sphincter muscles milked his thumb, he let himself join her in the abyss. His jaw clenched, and he hissed through his teeth with each spurt that left him.

As he floated back from the state of euphoria he'd been transported to, he could hear the echoes of her screams joined with his heavy pants. The fading nonsensical rants of, "Christ! Laurel . . . Laurel . . . Nnngh!" had run through his head like a mantra and even now, with his lips on her back, he heard them. He was stunned. He'd blanked out, lost consciousness and fell into an oblivion so deep inside his body that he'd heard his pulse beat, visualized each pump of his heart as it had worked to revive him. Experiencing his own version of *Fantastic Voyage*, he had careened off walls of pleasure so intense he couldn't find the energy to lift himself off the woman he'd flattened under him.

She was the first to speak. "You still alive? I can't even feel you breathing."

His lips grazed her shoulder blade. "Alive . . . just not breathing yet," he muttered.

She turned her head and smiled. He managed to move his hand, run his fingers down her cheek.

A minute passed and he tucked a strand of hair behind her ear as he asked, "Did we ever discuss the topic of birth control?"

She snorted and smiled. "Not that I recall."

"Tell me you're more responsible than I am."

"I'm more responsible than you are."

"Thank God. I'm sorry. Can't think what came over me. So we don't need the condoms?" There was a decidedly cheerful lift to his voice when he asked the question.

"It wouldn't hurt to do both."

"I'll try to do better. In the meantime . . ." he pulled out of her and lifted himself off the bed. "Let's use the shower head to rinse you out. Could be fun," he added with a wiggle of his expressive brows.

"I'll do it," she said as she slid off the bed and made her way to the bathroom. He sensed she needed some private time and grabbed one of the towels he'd tossed on the floor last night. "I'll go take a shower in the guest bath. Then I'll take you to the Farmers Market, if that's okay?"

She smiled, dreamy-eyed, and simply nodded as she

closed the door between them.

He shook his head in wonder. How had he lost control like that? How had he forgotten to protect her? And how the hell was he managing to stand? Never would he have thought his body capable of sensations that intense, that . . . devastating. An infant could have crawled along the hallway faster than he could put one foot in front of the other. *Dear God, what was this woman doing to him?* But he had to smile. He'd rocked her world. If he closed his eyes, and shut everything else out, he could feel her last orgasm pulsing around his thumb and latching onto his penis.

He'd have to tell her that he was going away for a few days. Not that he couldn't avoid the trip back to Baltimore if he wanted to, but he needed to put some distance between them now—he needed her to want. Last week she'd called the shots. This week, he would be the one to pull away, leaving her hungry and wanting more . . . keeping her on edge.

As he stepped into the shower he looked down. Talk about wanting more. Spear was clamoring for attention again and he doubted that Laurel kept olive oil in her guest bath.

Chapter Fifty-five

He watched as Laurel raved over her friends' booth. He'd been introduced to both Eileen and Carol, and then stood back as she fawned over their hand-made fleece comforters and aprons, quilts, sports paraphernalia and jackets. Gathering her purchases, she led him over to a booth proclaiming herbs by Shelton Farms.

"Meg has the best herbs. I could use some more basil, and she usually has five or six types."

"What's your favorite?" he asked.

"Sweet Genovese."

"Hmmph, mine too," he teased.

She laughed and smiled brilliantly up at him. "Why don't I believe that?"

"Because you're not that gullible?" he bent and kissed her lightly on the lips.

He'd just had her not two hours ago, and not in a token way. Mind-blowing sex is the only way he could describe it. And he desperately wanted her again.

They strolled from canopy to canopy, enjoying the warm summer day and the delights of the market. When they walked up to a display of beaded jewelry, he listened to the lady describe how she had made the collection of necklaces and bracelets that were shimmering in the sunlight. "I use genuine Swarovski crystals and real gold beading. The clasps are gold or silver, depending on the design. Try one on," she encouraged Laurel. But Laurel smiled at her and declined.

As she walked away, Garrett spotted a tiny silver turtle in one of the charm boxes. He waited until Laurel was out of earshot.

"Can you make an anklet for her using this," he held up the tiny turtle, "and some clear crystals so she can wear it with anything?"

"Sure."

"Can you do it now?"

"Uh yeah. Be about sixty bucks."

"Good." He pealed off a hundred dollar bill and handed it to her. "We'll be back for it."

"Take me about twenty minutes."

"That'll be fine." He moved to join Laurel who was asking an artist about his metal sculpture.

She looked over her shoulder at him. "Oh, there you are. Isn't this ladybug cute?"

"If you say so."

"I say so."

He looked over at the man behind the table. "We'll take it." He handed over a fifty and the man handed him back a twenty."

She turned back to him, "I have money."

He smiled down at her. "So do I."

She frowned. "I don't want you spending your money on me."

"I can afford it."

"So can I."

"Look, let's not fight over this." He picked up the bags containing the ladybug lawn ornament, her herbs, and the quilted items from her friends' booth, and moved her along, whispering over her shoulder, "Be gracious, or I'll have to spank you for your bad manners when we get home."

He saw her shudder and smiled. The next table was

homemade jellies and jams, and they both picked out two that they liked. Then they walked down to the river and to the dock and admired the view. He couldn't remember a time when he was so relaxed, so focused on doing absolutely nothing but strolling along a lazy river.

When it was time to leave, he walked her by the beaded jewelry table. The beaming woman stood and handed him a small bag along with his change. He put the money in his pocket and took the small bag from her as Laurel stared at him, a questioning look in her eyes.

"A memento," he whispered as he drew the tiny anklet out of the bag to show her. He knelt at her feet and attached it to her ankle. As he stood, his fingertips ran up her leg stopping mid-thigh where the hem of her short ruffled skirt began. He looked down at her and noticed she had suspiciously wet eyes.

"That is so sweet."

"I wanted you to remember your first boil."

"Is that what you wanted me to remember about last night?"

"That, and a few other things. But I'm not worried about you remembering those."

"Why not?"

"Because I plan on doing them over and over again so you don't forget. Many, many times." He bent and kissed her, thoroughly. The women watching at the nearby tables opened their eyes wide and sighed at the romantic gesture.

He broke away and whispered, "Ready to go?"

"Yes."

"Good. How about some lunch?"

"Okay. What did you have in mind?"

"How about the Inlet View? We can get a bite to eat and a glass of wine."

"Sounds wonderful."

He took her hand in his, kissed her knuckles, and led

her back to his truck. As she was getting in, she turned her ankle to admire her new anklet. She crooked her finger at him, a seductive smile on her face. "This deserves a reward." She clasped his cheeks between her hands and kissed him. "It's beautiful, thank you."

"You're welcome. I'm glad you like it."

He closed her door and got in on the driver's side. "Now, just so you know, I'm buying lunch. And if you argue, I'm going to stop on the way back and paddle you."

She blinked her eyes wide. Would he? Would he really do that? And why did that thought not distress her? Not in the slightest.

Chapter Fifty-six

Driving along 179 through Shallotte, Garrett looked over at Laurel and his eyes met hers. Sea blue met summer green as his eyes burned with desire. "Slip off your panties," he said. "Then put them in the glove box. It's unlocked."

Her eyes went round and she opened her mouth to protest.

"No, no arguments," he said. "Just do it."

He focused on the road, mentally ticking off the seconds and waiting. So many things counted on her doing his bidding right now. If she didn't do as he asked, he'd lose ground he might never recover. He'd lose the upper hand he was trying to establish as the dominant male she needed. Her fantasies, as he knew them, required this type of control. Would she relinquish it? He couldn't remember the last time his nerves had been frazzled like this.

He forced himself to hold his breath in and not breathe out a long sigh of relief when she put both of her hands under her gauzy skirt and slowly tugged off a pair of baby blue panties. He watched trepidation flash over her face as she opened his glove box and tucked them on top of his owner's manual. With a finalizing click, she shut the hinged door with her tiny shred of dignity inside. He quirked his lips in a smile he hid from her.

Nothing was said, no mention was made of her state of undress as he lifted her from the seat of the truck to the pavement outside the restaurant. Her skirt was short enough that he was not about to allow her to climb the stairs with others present, so he slowed their pace to allow a group to go before them.

He took her hand and watched her face as she took each step. He knew that the thought of her pussy, open to the air, with her thighs widely parting with each step, completely exposing her, affected her in many ways. She'd be wet by the time they were seated. She'd be soaked by the time they got back to the truck.

Seated at an outside table enjoying what was perhaps the best view in Brunswick County, Garrett watched Laurel dip a corner of each forkful of lettuce into a cup of ranch dressing.

"So, Special K and yogurt for breakfast, salad for lunch . . . one would get the idea you were dieting."

"Perpetually. Isn't every woman under forty?"

"What happens at forty?"

"We give up, let the powers that be run amuck."

"Hmmm, maybe I shouldn't get too attached."

"Maybe you shouldn't." She looked at him over the rim of her wine glass.

"I think it might already be too late," he whispered, and ran a finger down her arm. He watched her shiver, flush . . . and flutter her eyes at his husky words.

He took a bite of his club sandwich. Nibbled on sweet potato fries. Met her eyes. Raised his sexy slash of a brow. "You're facing the inlet, why don't you consider relaxing your thighs a little? Your knees are working overtime."

"Is that an order?"

Oh God, now she was asking to be topped. She might not know it, but that was exactly what she was doing. His penis leapt.

"Yes."

He watched as her thighs parted slightly. His breath

hitched. He watched her face flush crimson. He decided to change the subject. Give her a few moments to adjust, accept . . . revel in her awakening sexuality.

"I have to fly back to Baltimore this week for a few days. Can I get on your dance card for the weekend?"

She nodded as she looked over at him, and while she was trying to appear nonchalant, he could see the desire flaming in her eyes. He stared into her face and read the signs. He had the distinct feeling that she was going under. Fighting a battle with the lust growing inside her and rapidly losing. The timing was going to be rushed if he didn't slow her down.

He took the wine glass from her hand and took a sip, then placed it back on the table. He leaned in and kissed her, his fingertips running over the smooth skin above her knee.

"Ready to leave?"

"Yes," she whispered.

He motioned for the check, and when the waitress returned he handed her a fifty-dollar bill without even looking at the ticket. "We're in a hurry," he said and gave her his megawatt smile as he pulled Laurel up from the chair. Laurel had noted that his amazing good looks, coupled with his extraordinary presence, tended to make the female population skittish and self-conscious. The cute little waitress was no exception, and she actually tripped on her own sneaker-clad feet. Garrett reached out and gripped her arm, righting her before she fell on her face.

"Easy," he murmured, like a rider would calm his horse, and the full power of his aura washed over Laurel. The waitress was mesmerized, and Laurel was sure that if she hadn't been with Garrett, the restaurant would have had one less server for the rest of the afternoon. Except that she seemed very young. And Garrett had said he was exceptionally careful about that.

The restaurant was getting crowded now. People

were hanging around the stairs on each level and also on the landing, so he wasn't about to take her down by the stairs. He walked her to the elevator and pushed the button.

When the door closed and they were the only ones inside, he pulled her to him, kissed her on the lips, and with her in front of him and both facing the door, he pulled her skirt up to caress her bare ass. Her loud moan fueled his erection as his fingers explored lower and found her wet— delightfully, wickedly, and incredibly wet. He was kissing the side of her neck and intimately touching her when they reached the bottom level, but he managed to pull her skirt back into place before the doors opened.

He smirked at her, enjoying her dazed expression, then took her hand and led her to the truck. He had thoughtfully parked on the marina side, and had also backed in, so that now they were hidden from view on the passenger side of his truck. He looked down at her beautiful face as he lifted her onto the seat, leaving her legs hanging over the edge. Keeping his eyes concentrated on hers, he parted her knees and inserted his hand between her thighs. Worked it slowly to the apex, tugged at the moist curls he found there. With deft fingers he explored her as he leaned in to kiss her with a desperate and needy tongue. Her moan joined his as he thrust two fingers inside her. After a few suggestive stabs he withdrew them, brought them to his mouth and sucked them clean, his eyes never leaving hers. She let out a long low moan, and her eyes closed. He ran his damp fingers down her cheek and saw her eyes flutter open. He closed her legs and eased them around front so he could close the door.

He went around to the driver's side, got in, and started the truck.

"We're not going to make it home, Laurel. I'm going to find a place to pull over and take you. When we get to the main road, I want you to pull your skirt up and let me watch you play with yourself until I can find a place where

I can fuck you."

Her eyes popped wide. He was afraid he might have blown it, that he'd cooled her ardor with his crude pronouncement. But then she surprised him as he pulled off Piggott Road, by shifting on the seat and raising her skirt. He was hard as a pike; he felt precum wet his briefs. If he watched her toy with herself, he'd be no good to her. He'd be unmanned before he could get inside her.

He turned left onto Brick Landing Road and found a pull off just past Goose Creek Road. He followed an overgrown dirt road that didn't look as if it got much use, as it led back into the woods. He followed it for a hundred yards, then nosed his truck off to the side into a small clearing.

She turned to face him and the lust he saw on her face spiked his temperature. God she was hot. And so uninhibited. He groaned as she turned to him, one knee cocked, showing him that her fingers were doing what he had instructed. He looked at where her dainty hands were rubbing and foraging. Even in the shadowed interior of the truck he could see her fingers glistening from her juices.

"God, Laurel, you are so hot. So beautiful. Lovely." He leaned in and kissed her, plunging his tongue inside her mouth and claiming her. He kissed her long and deep, mating his tongue with hers as his hand wrapped around her neck and he held her face to his. His other hand went to her waist and delved under her knit sweater, hiking her bra up and shoving the lacy blue cups aside to expose her nipples. His fingers drew on the tips, tugging and twisting. He died a new death with each one of her cries, then whipped off her sweater, tossing it onto the back seat.

She protested when his lips left hers, but was instantly appeased when they found her hard, long tips and suckled.

"Garrett . . . I can't wait. I need you."

"You'll have to wait. I want to see you before I fuck you. I want to watch your fingers play with your sweet cunt," he whispered between her breasts. Then he bit down lightly and stretched out her nipple, grazing it with his teeth. She keened and sobbed. "Please Garrett . . . I need you to fuck me. Now."

"Soon baby," he breathed against the long column of her throat as she arched her back against the door of the truck. He had turned her to him and he was leaning over the console fondling her, pinching her, and tugging on her long, needy nipples. The sounds of her breath catching with each escalating touch were causing his penis to strain and jump against his zipper. He had to get some relief.

"Show me," he said. "Show me your pussy. Spread your legs wide and let me look at you. I want to see that secret place where I'm going to be fucking you." She sobbed and leaned her head back against the window. She hesitated only a moment before she opened her thighs wide for him.

He hissed his pleasure as his eyes took her in. "Wider, spread your knees wide. As far as they'll go."

He took each of her hands, damp from her arousal, and placed them on her knees and then urged her to push them wide for him. The truck was filled with her essence, and his blood heated with her intoxicating scent as he stared at her womanhood, now fully displayed for him. He tore his gaze away from her sopping wet slit and looked into her face, saw her eyes filled with lust. Saw that she was going under.

"You are so beautiful. Your pussy, so lovely." His eyes left hers and he watched as more pearly liquid leaked from her tiny, flared opening. He knew his words pleased her and that she was as aroused as she could stand it right now. He knew he was. He leaned in and put a finger inside her vagina and watched as he moved it in and out of her. He joined it with another. Then another. He shoved them all home and she screamed with pleasure.

He looked up at her, saw her half-lidded eyes, her slack mouth, her shallow breathing. He ran his hands over her breasts, her fullness popped out under the confines of her bra strap, her nipples pebbled and tight. He reached up and pinched one with his free hand, hard. "I'm going to fuck you now. Is that what you want?"

"Please," she whimpered. "Please."

"Okay baby. Just give me a moment." He undid his belt, pulled down his zipper and pulled his erection free. It stood tall, grazing the steering wheel. With his left hand he reached down beside his seat and powered the seat all the way back. Then he reclined it partway. He took a condom out of his pocket, tore the foil and rolled it down onto an angry looking, purple-veined erection any man would be proud of.

"C'mere you," he said as he reached for her and lifted her from her seat and placed her on his lap.

Once she was settled, he held her head between his hands and kissed her thoroughly, thrusting his tongue in and out of her mouth in the same fashion that he was going to be thrusting his penis into her vagina. He tugged on both nipples until she was frantic, then he lifted her and easily impaled her.

She sobbed and cried out, then immediately took her due, riding him as if she were running a race, and eclipsing his capacity for restraining her. She was fucking him like a banshee and nothing he murmured against her neck slowed her pace.

Afraid she'd either break his penis or get so wound up she'd lose her climax, he gripped her ass and took control, taking her from an agitated state that accomplished little, to a rhythmic rhapsody that drove her higher. Her breathing slowed, her sighs bloomed and expanded her chest as she hissed her pleasure. He smiled as he looked into her face, at her tightly closed eyes, her lips turned in and clasped together.

It did his heart good to know that in moments like

this, he owned this amazing woman. He alternated lifting her, jamming her down onto his penis and feeding every inch of his straining cock into her as completely as he could, with holding her still and grinding against her.

He could not remember when he had wanted a woman as he wanted this one. He heard her breath hitch, saw her chest flush, and then he felt her insides quiver as she rose and slammed back down onto him. He lifted up from the seat, changed his angle and probed at her g-spot. He wasn't sure he'd found it until she screamed a fierce string of obscenities. He relished her shudder, her screams, and her out of control spasms as she dug her nails into his shoulders and let everything career away. The floodgates came, she drenched him. Then she cried, cried so hard she soaked his shirt within a matter of seconds.

He held her as she unwound from her release. He stroked her back under her sweater as she sobbed with something primal fighting its way out of her. He knew what she was going through, knew she was experiencing a cleansing like no other. Knew she had to come out on the other side of this all right for them to continue.

G-spot climaxes were devastating on both a physical and emotional level. He knew they moved through a woman's body like tiny scrubbing bubbles, collecting unresolved emotions and intensifying them before dispelling them. They could purge her in a way that left her ready to deal with what life dealt next. One of his girlfriends had equated them with a massage times twenty. They had awesome power . . . that sometimes backfired. He hoped this hadn't been one of them.

Her shame had to be quelled, tamed, and reckoned with. She had to know everything they did was acceptable, allowed—kinky maybe, but permissible and sanctioned—at least by him. Oh God, she was so needy, he thought, as he held her to him. And what man didn't long to be needed?

He needed her now. But he could wait. This was

about her. He had olive oil at home, he reminded himself, and a very experienced fist.

She surprised him a minute later.

Chapter Fifty-seven

Unwrapping from his arms and climbing off his lap, she slid back into her seat and fixed her clothing. As he removed the condom he was surprised to see her open her door and get out. At first, he thought she needed to use the woods for a personal matter, but instead she came around to his door and opened it. He was fighting to tuck himself back inside his pants when her hand stayed him.

"Don't," was all she said as she kissed him. He kissed her back, pleased with her recovery, and then double pleased when he felt her hand encircle him and begin a tried and true up and down motion. Her hand was so soft, her fist so small and tentative that at first he wasn't sure she'd be able to bring him off this way. Then her fingers loosened, became like a maestro's as she played his lengthening "keyboard."

He sighed and let his head sink back to the headrest. She pressed the button on the side bolster and lowered the seat to its last setting. Then she pressed the lever on the seat back until he was fully reclining. Her fingers never stopped their slow torture. Her hand dove into his pants to seek out and to gently caress his balls. He moaned his pleasure as she manipulated and cupped him, stroked and felt him. He closed his eyes and allowed her to work her magic. By now, she'd established a goal and he aimed to see her meet it.

From the open door he could hear the sounds of bees buzzing and lawnmowers running in the distance. If she hadn't been fingering his balls and tugging on his dick so expertly, he thought he might have been able to drift into sleep. He felt her shift and then he felt her lips on him and all thoughts of a leisurely nap in the sunshine while she jerked him off vaporized. Spear jerked to attention and searched out the cavernous warmth of her mouth. Her deep-throated moan, the reflex of taking him past her uvula, established her as being seasoned in the art of fellatio and he praised the gods with nonsensical babble. He was big, he knew that, but she had no trouble taking him to the back of her throat and sucking. And sucking. He was giddy with unabashed joy and greedy for more of the same. He thrust up, she took what he offered . . . and sucked. She literally went down on him as he opened his eyes and watched her head vigorously nodding into his crotch. She sucked, she licked, she kissed, and as she did all this she continued to caress his heavy sac. He felt as if his head was going to blow from the pressure, every muscle in his body tightened, and then with one final tug with her wrapped lips she sucked the life out of him. He discovered that in addition to sucking, kissing and licking, she also swallowed. There wasn't a happier man in the universe at that moment. And by his long heartfelt groan he conveyed it.

Her head rested in his lap and he idly stroked her hair as he wavered in and out of lingering bliss. "Oh that was special. Very special. Remarkably special," he murmured, lifting his head to meet her eyes.

She smiled up at him with a smug smile.

"You've had some experience with that," he whispered, still trying to get his bearings.

"Some. It's what you do when you aren't sure whether you want your date to fuck you, but he's hell bent that he is."

"Well I'm surprised you have *any* experience with fucking if that was your first salvo. I don't know any man who would turn that down. And I am somewhat pleased that you allowed me to fuck you before offering me that truly amazing alternative."

She took the handful of tissues he handed her from inside the console. Wiped her lips and under her eyes, then disappeared from view as she ducked around the door and closed it. He watched her over the hood as she walked around the truck and got back in her seat.

"I need a nap," he moaned and she laughed delightfully.

"This was my first inside a vehicle experience," she boasted and beamed at him. "I really had a good time."

"I know," he said with a grin. "I was there."

She waggled her brows, "You sure were. I wouldn't mind doing that again sometime." He heard the hesitancy in her voice, and something else . . . the contrition of a submissive being forward enough to voice her desires?

He sat up and adjusted his seat and his clothing. Looked in the rearview mirror and ran long fingers through the tousled strands of his dark chestnut hair.

He reached over and wrapped his hand around her neck and brought her head to his. He kissed her hungrily. "I wouldn't mind doing that again sometime either. But I have a whole playbook I want to run through before we start doing reruns. As an aside, I like car sex too, just not in the 'vette. My back can't handle that."

"This was so wicked," she said with big grin, and he had to laugh out loud when she hugged herself and shivered with happiness.

"C'mon," he said, "buckle up. I'd better get us out of here before we have a *Dueling Banjo's* scene."

"That was a pretty amazing duet. I once heard that it was spontaneous. That Ronnie Cox, the actor was just strumming his banjo when a hillbilly boy started playing his, and then it just went from there."

"That's an urban legend. In fact, the original composer, Arthur Smith, sued for credit and royalties and won. It's a great piece of music though."

"How do you know these things?"

"I know a lot of useless things. For instance, do you know who Judith, Rachael, Argine, and Polas are?"

"No, never met 'em."

"Oh, I'm sure you have. They're the queens of hearts, diamonds, clubs, and spades. Their husbands, Charlemagne, Caesar, Alexander, and David are the kings. And their knaves are LaHire, Hector, Lancelot, and Ogier. LaHire and Ogier are the one-eyed Jacks."

"Hmm. Not so useless."

"Okay, try this. What's the name of the numbness you get when your foot or your hand goes to sleep?"

"It has a name?"

"It does. In English, *everything* has a name. It's called obdormition."

"Okay, that's pretty useless."

"And would you happen to know what a mumpsimus is?"

"You're kidding."

"Everything has a name . . . a mumpsimus is something I try never to be."

"What is it?"

"Someone who keeps making the same mistake over and over again despite being corrected."

"Okay, I cede, you *do* know some useless stuff. You should go on Jeopardy."

"Not much for making a fool out of myself on TV. But back to dueling banjos, they have dueling pianos at Broadway, you want to go sometime?" he asked.

"Sure, but what I'd really like to do at Broadway is see the WonderWorks upside down house."

"Really? I've been looking for someone to go with me to see that."

"Well, when we're finished with that playbook of

yours, we should venture out. See the sights."

He laughed hilariously as he pulled out onto the main road.

"You're very good for a man's ego, you know that?"

"That's because you're very good. Period."

"I aim to please."

"Well, you're a crack shot. I'll tell you that."

"Hmmm, is there a double entendre there, Miss Laurel?"

She flushed as she remembered his fingers, his thumb especially . . . in her crack. "That was all pretty new to me," she said in a soft voice.

He smiled over at her, "I know."

He patted her thigh. "I think we're going to have a lot of surprises for each other."

"Do you really have to go to Baltimore this week?"

Aha, the trap is sprung, he thought. *And she just fell in.*

"If I don't go this week, it'll make a lot more work for me later. This is the time of the year I plan my investments through the holidays. There will be a lot of people in town this week that I need to talk to. It will make my life so much easier to see them all in one place, at a trade conference."

"Oh. I forgot. You're a broker."

"No, not really. I have partners from time to time, but for the most part, I only manage my own portfolio. I buy and sell, speculate and move money around on a daily basis. So there's a lot to keep track of."

"I see."

Oh, he had her good. Next she'd be asking when he'd be back.

"So, when will you be back?"

"I'm targeting Thursday night. But the meetings could go as long as Friday. I'll call you when I get back to the beach."

"Okay," there was a moment as doubt registered in her eyes, and then she forcibly brightened. All the way back to her house she talked non-stop about her friends, Cat, Viv, and Tess.

He walked her to the door, carrying her purchases from the farmer's market. He told her he'd have to go, as he had a golf lesson scheduled with a private trainer. He could have cancelled it with a phone call, but his game plan was to keep her off balance, to make her yearn for more. He helped her inside and kissed her hungrily.

She smiled up at him and told him to travel safe, then reached up and brought his head down for another kiss.

"You get all your work done, then come back and we'll play some more, big guy," she said seductively and then capped it off with a wink worthy of Lauren Bacall.

He laughed and kissed her forehead, then stepped away. It was at that moment that he realized he was going to miss the hell out her. But no way was he going to let her know that.

So it was with great chagrin that he arrived back in Sunset Beach on Friday to find she was not available to him. He couldn't find her anywhere. And she wasn't returning any of his calls.

Chapter Fifty-eight

"I don't know, Viv. It was odd—everything was perfect one minute—then bam, he was different somehow. I suddenly had this feeling he was playing me. On the way back to the house, he backed off rather abruptly and I got the distinct impression that he was afraid of me getting too involved." Laurel and Viv were animatedly gesturing as they sat in wet bathing suits under an umbrella at a table at the Ocean Ridge pool. Tessa, lost in her cell phone, was texting Roman and seemed oblivious to their conversation.

"Did you feel as if he was trying to tell you that all his time wasn't going to be spent with you? Did you feel like he was stringing you along for the sex?"

"I *did* get the feeling I was being patronized . . . I guess. I don't know. I just can't explain it. I felt wonderful and at ease with him one minute, then off kilter the next. Like I didn't matter all that much to him. Which didn't make sense, because no one has that kind of sex without being invested. It was the most amazing sex, you just wouldn't believe. So hot!"

Tessa stopped texting long enough to look over at Viv, and they shared a secret smile.

"You think he might be seeing other women?" Viv asked.

"Well, we only had that one week, really. Maybe he already had a girlfriend and after our fun and games, he knew he had to back off."

"So you think he's a player?"

"You know, he could be . . ." Laurel paused and tapped her fingers on her lips, remembering something. Remembering when he'd forgotten to use a condom. No player worth his salt would ever take a chance like that. There was more here.

"So he didn't set up another date? That surprises me. From the way that guy looked at you Friday night, I thought for sure he was a goner. What was the last thing he said to you about getting together?"

"That he'd call me."

Tessa sat silent listening to the whole exchange, her eyes going from one to the other above her flying fingers, assessing. She put her phone down and broke in, "Well, he won't be able to get you. You are not going to sit home and wait for him to call. No way. Two can play that game."

"What game?" Laurel asked as she turned to face Tessa.

"I'm not sure. It's either the make-her-work-for-it-game, or some kind of I'm-the-one-in-control-of-this, you-just-be-ready-when-I call game. Either way, you're not playing it," she said emphatically.

"I'm not?" Laurel asked.

"She's right," Viv said. "You're not."

"Okay, so what do I do?" Laurel trusted these women; each one had landed a very difficult and powerful man. Collectively, they were the wise counsel she had called on since her mother's death.

"You go away," Tessa said.

"Go away!"

"Yeah, let's go to Charleston, just you and me. Roman's parking ships for a harbor pilot whose kid is having surgery. He won't be back for a week. We could leave on Thursday and come back on Sunday—do some shopping, take a house tour. There's this nautical art gallery that sent me a catalogue I'd like to check out. Roman has a birthday coming up and I want to surprise him with something for his den."

The idea of going to Charleston was very tempting. She knew she and Tess would have a marvelous time. But the thought that she might miss Garrett's call didn't sit well with her. "What if he calls?" she asked in a timid voice.

"See? Look what he's done to you already! He will call. Count on it. And when he finds out that you aren't going to just sit at home until he's ready to make another move, maybe he'll appreciate you more."

"Yeah, you've got to put him in his place. You don't need a man who walks all over you."

"Well . . . you're right about that. I'm not looking for a man who wants to control me." Except that she was. She thought about the time she'd spent in the truck with him, in the woods. His words, husky and commanding, came back to her. *Show me your pussy. Spread your legs wide and let me look at you. I want to see that secret place where I'm going to be fucking you.* Her head swam with desire; she felt moisture pooling and coating her. She did want a man who controlled her. One who made her feel as Garrett had made her feel . . . sexy, desired, beautiful . . . and so wicked, so delightfully wicked.

"If you want him to be interested in you for more than sex, you can't be at his beck and call." Viv added. "He's wisely given you some space, take it. Show him you function perfectly well without him."

"What you say makes sense. And I certainly can't fault either of you for your tactics. After all, ya'll are wearin' the rings. So I guess Charleston it is."

"Wonderful!" Tess said as she gathered her things. "I'm going to run over to Island Classic and get something to wear."

"Wait a minute, you're going shopping to buy clothes, so you'll have them to wear, while you're shopping for clothes?" Laurel asked.

"Well, you saw *Pretty Woman*. They treat you better in the shops when you're already wearing the latest thing."

Laurel shook her head and waved her off. As an afterthought she called out to her, "Since this was your idea, you're driving, *and* booking the room."

Tessa came back to bend and kiss her on the cheek, "No problem. I'll pick you up Thursday at ten and we'll go to lunch at High Cotton. Ooooh, we're going to have soooo much fun." She squeezed Laurel's shoulders and ran off to the ladies room to get out of her wet suit.

"She's a trip," Laurel muttered.

"She's gonna run you ragged."

Laurel smiled over at Viv. "Why don't you come, too?"

"No, you two do up the town. Besides, I told Cat I'd help her with that bike-a-thon she's putting together. In fact, I'm supposed to meet her to map out the route right now."

"Well, thanks for coming to swim with me," Laurel said as she stood to give her friend a hug.

"Wouldn't have missed the chance to see how things were going with that young hunk of yours." She reached up and ran her fingertips down Laurel's cheek and tucked a long blonde strand that was lifting in the breeze behind her ear.

Her mother used to do that, in the exact same way, and she had to blink away the tears at the thought.

"You're a beautiful, smart woman. He'd be a damned fool not to want you, and to want you for keeps. But you never can tell these days what's motivating a man. Just make sure you don't let on about the lottery winnings or you'll never know if he wants you for who you are instead of what you have."

"I think he has money, too."

"Honey, very few people have the kind of money you have. Your 'godfathers' would be very upset with you if you let a man walk away with any."

"I know, they've coached me. The six of you are like my family now. I listen, I pay attention, and I watch. I'm being a good girl."

Viv smiled. "I suspect Garrett thinks otherwise. Just remember, if it's meant to be, it'll all work out in the end. You and Tess have a good time in Charleston. Relax and have some fun, and don't let Tessa talk you into doing any Jell-o shots."

"Yes, *Mother*," Laurel said, and with great affection, hugged Viv tight to her chest. She really did feel as if she had three mothers in the dear friends her mother had befriended in the short time her parents had lived here. And the godfathers that came along with them? Well Garrett had better not be a player . . . that's all she had to say about that.

Chapter Fifty-nine

Garrett was beginning to get pretty ticked off. He'd expected to get home, get unpacked, and showered before heading over to pick up Laurel. He thought he'd take her to dinner, maybe go to Broadway and walk around—see that upside down house she'd talked about. Then take her home and fuck her brains out. He felt as if he'd had a hard on from the moment he'd left her at her door last Saturday.

Friday had come and gone without a return phone call, so he'd driven to the park on Georgetown Road with his bike on the bike rack. From there, he'd biked into the Ocean Ridge development and then over to her neighborhood. He had hopes of seeing her or her truck on the road or parked at one of the golf courses. With ear buds in his ears and wires dangling down into a pocket, he rode around the development looking for her SUV and pretending to sing to an energetic soundtrack. It made people think you weren't paying attention when you were so visibly distracted, but he was only giving a cursory amount of focus to the music, he was looking for signs of Laurel. But there were none.

Now here it was Saturday at four, and she still hadn't called him back. He'd driven over to Ocean Ridge twice. Rang the bell and waited before walking around the house in hopes that she'd be working in her garden. He was tempted to call her friends. Find out where the hell she was.

By seven he was pissed. He grabbed his cell phone

and punched in Paul's number. He waited while it rang and thought, how lame was this? Calling his private detective to find his girlfriend . . . *what was she doing to him?*

When Paul answered, he explained the situation and braced for the sarcasm.

"You mean you lost her already?" he wasn't even trying to keep the smile out of his voice.

"I haven't lost her. We've just had a miscue of some sort. I want to know where she is. Can't you do that thing you do with charge cards and cell phones and let me know where the hell she is?"

"I can. It'll take some time . . ."

"Just do it and get back to me, would ya?" The impatience was hard to disguise.

"I'll see what I can do. You sound like you could use a drink."

"I could use several. Let me know what you find," he said and ended the call. He paced the living area, running his fingers through thick strands that had grooves from how many times he'd done this. *Where was she? Why hadn't she stayed at home and waited for his call?*

At that moment he realized what he'd done. And how she'd reacted—clearly, in a way he hadn't expected she would. And he had to smile in spite of himself. He snorted. She was a stronger woman than he'd thought. Stronger, smarter . . . and probably one hell of a chess player.

He shook his head. Hell, it seemed he needed her more than she needed him. She'd made a stand . . . sent him her statement in the form of doorbell resounding through an empty house. *Fuck.* He was in love with the woman.

He didn't know exactly when it had happened. Whether reading her stories had predisposed him to falling for her, or whether she was just that amazing and seemingly custom-made for him. But he physically hurt right now because he didn't know where she was. Didn't have the assurances that she was safe.

Games aside, he wanted this woman. Wanted to be the man she turned to when she needed to be satisfied, pleasured . . . taken to glorious heights. He groaned as he thought of her lips wrapped around his cock, her eager enthusiasm, her wicked and contented smile afterward. He groaned again.

He was pouring his second Patron, anxious for the bite of the hundred percent agave to calm his nerves, when his cell phone rang. He picked up his phone and saw that it was Paul.

"Where is she?" he asked.

"Geez. Give me a minute will ya?"

"Do you know where she is?"

"She's in Charleston. Just left a place called 82 Queen. Spent $128, so it's not likely she's on her own."

The flash of heat that coursed through him that she could be with another man matched that of the Patron he held in his hand. With great care he placed it on the counter. This was not the time to drink.

"What else do you have?" he asked with forced calm.

"A pre-approval went through Thursday afternoon for a suite at HarbourView Inn. Charges at three top-line dress stores . . . looks like she's spent close to three grand."

"Can you call the hotel and find out who she's with?"

"Not this kind of hotel. I could get someone there in the morning to tempt housekeeping."

"That'll be too late. I'm leaving now."

"You have it bad don't you?"

"I don't know what I have," he said gruffly. "Any chance of a room number?" He looked at his watch. It was 8:30; it would be close to midnight when he got there.

"I'll do what I can. I have a friend in Mount Pleasant. Sometimes there's a valet ticket with the car with the room number . . ."

"She may not have taken her car. The garage doors

are solid so I couldn't tell if her SUV or Firebird were in there or not."

"I'll see what I can do. I'll call you on the road if I get something."

"Thanks."

"Hey, don't drive too fast. South Carolina Troopers don't bribe easily."

"Hmmph! I'll try to remember that."

He closed his phone and tossed some things into an overnight duffle. Threw his laptop in the case and hefted it on his shoulder. Checked for his wallet and his phone charger. He looked at the full glass of Patron on the counter. Took a hefty swig and enjoyed the shudder. Then he grabbed his keys and ran out the door, locking it behind him.

He wanted to take the Corvette, but since he didn't know what he was up against, he took the Edge. Loaded with his favorite music, and just gassed up, he backed it out and drove down Main Street, and then off the island. Did she go alone, he wondered. If not, who was she with? While several unsettling scenarios ran through his mind, he comforted himself with the fact that, whoever he was, he was soon going to be minus teeth and sporting some well-placed bruises.

At 10:53 his phone rang. "Third floor, waterfront, southeast corner. Can't get in to get a room number, this is from my spotter. Says he thinks it's two women, but he can't be sure."

Ah, Tessa or Viv, he'd just bet. His money was on Tess though. He remembered Roman saying he was heading to Bermuda this week.

"And guess what else?"

"Don't bait me."

"You better be nice to me or I'll consider offering my services to her."

"What's that supposed to mean?"

"Your lady love is rich. Very rich. Unless I'm mistaken, she can buy and sell you."

"What are you talking about?"

"She won the lottery. Literally. Thirty-six million."

Garrett almost drove off the road. He drew in a deep breath and held the wheel steady. "You're sure about this?" He'd seen evidence of prosperity, but not that much.

"Umm hmm, just about the time her parents died. She struck it rich but she refused the photo-op. She doesn't advertise it. It's in her tax file though. Had to dig deep to get that. Just came through a few minutes ago."

"Well, that is a surprise. But just for the record, she can't buy and sell me."

"Then you're not paying me enough."

"Send me a bill. Include what would be a fair bonus."

"Now you're talkin'."

"Thank you, Paul," he said and hung up. He sped down 17 taking in all he'd just discovered—processing it and wondering how it impacted him. Finally, he realized that it didn't.

So she had money. So did he. The only way it changed things is that at one time, he thought she might have become dependent on him because of his situation. Now it seemed she'd always be independent. And if they married, he would never allow her to merge her money with his. No woman was going to contribute to his support. He smiled as he drove; no wonder she hadn't seemed impressed with his Corvette or his new Edge. This woman could own a fleet of Testarossas. He amended that to *his* woman. Because he had no doubt that by morning she'd be his again.

At 11:45, he pulled up to the HarbourView Inn, grabbed his duffle bag and computer case and handed the sleepy valet his keys.

"Miss Laurel Leighton and Mrs. Tessa Byrnes back from 82 Queen yet?"

"Got back an hour ago sir."

He handed the man a fifty and walked into the hotel. He managed to get a room on the same floor, two doors down from the room Laurel and Tess were in. He tossed his stuff on the bed, washed his face, ran his electric razor over his face, and brushed his teeth.

He grabbed his room key and strolled down the hall, and then he knocked firmly on the door of the corner suite.

The door opened without hesitation and he saw a smiling Tessa staring back at him.

"C'mon in," she said breezily, "looks like I pegged you right."

Laurel was just coming out of the bathroom. Dressed in blue silk pj's she was an adorable sight.

"Garrett, what are you doing here?"

"It occurred to me that I might have been a bit ambivalent about planning our date this weekend."

"Oh?"

"Yes. I should have mentioned that I had planned," he quickly looked at this watch, "a midnight walk on the battery in the lovely city of Charleston."

"Did you now?"

"Well, not initially. But as I drove south, the idea cemented itself in my mind. If you're free, I'd love for you to accompany me."

"I'm in my pajamas."

He looked at her and raised a sardonic brow. "You can remove them, or I can. But I assure you, it will delay our walk greatly if you leave it up to me."

"Garrett, maybe she doesn't want to go for a walk right now," Tessa said.

"Tessa, either she takes a walk with me, or you take one by yourself and I'm sure Roman would not be happy about that. I am going to talk to Laurel privately one way or the other. Either we go or you go. I do have a room down the hall, you're welcome to use that."

Tessa stood, hands on hips and looked over at Laurel. "Laurel, what do you want?"

They both just stared at each other. The emotions of the last few hours had drained him and she could see he was tired. And quite frankly, so was she. It would be better to get this over with.

"We know how this is going to end," she said.

"I hope to God you figure that to be in my bed."

She gave him a tiny sideways smile. "Well, actually I hadn't. But now that you mention it . . .."

"Laurel," Tess began.

"Tess, have you never seen two star-crossed lovers trying to work things out? Surely it wasn't all wine and roses for you and Roman," Garrett said.

Tessa smiled at the memories that thought evoked. "No . . . no, it wasn't."

"Let me take Laurel with me. Just to my room. In thirty minutes you can check on her. If at any time she wants to leave, she can. I only want to talk to her, to apologize for my not making my intentions for this weekend more definite."

"Sounds fair, don't you think, Tess?" Laurel asked wistfully.

Tess shook her head. "Look at her, she's already in a sexual coma for God's sake. How do you men do this?"

Garrett grinned. "She is, isn't she?" he said as he stepped forward, took her hand and led her out the door. "Don't wait breakfast for us."

"I'm still going to check on her."

"That may delay things. But I'm nothing if not a patient man," he said as he closed the door behind them.

He could hear Tessa's laughter all the way down the hall. He had to smile at her audacity.

At the door to his room, he lifted Laurel into his arms.

He opened the door and carried her inside, letting the door close softly against his foot.

Chapter Sixty

He stood her beside the huge four-poster bed and ran his fingers through her loose curls, tipped her head back to look into her sultry green eyes. There was something else there though; fire, and she let him know where it came from.

"Before you fog my brain with all that sexy mambo you have going on, you should know that I'm angry at you. You trivialized *us*. You caused me to have emotions that tore me up inside for days. I won't have anybody treating me like a woman who can't see through these types of machinations, who doesn't know how to stand up for herself. The sex aside, I do fine for myself . . . for the most part."

He took her frantically waving hand and brought it to her side, stroking the thumb as he held it in place. "I know you do. And I'm sorry. You may not believe this, but I had good intentions—the very best of intentions."

"Oh, this I'd like to hear."

He took a big breath and dove in. "I was trying to exert my control over you. In a purely physical way. The way a dominant might to ensure that the woman he's with obeys."

She gasped and her head jerked back. Then she simply stared. You could hear the ocean outside the window in the silence that grew, as her wide, curiously bright eyes met his. "So . . . you're a Dom?" he saw the interest in her eyes.

"I am whatever you need me to be. I want this

relationship to work. I'll be whatever you tell me to be. In the few encounters we've had, I sensed submissiveness in you, it was calling to me and I wanted to channel it. So I was trying to set myself up as a master of sorts, for you . . . only clearly I didn't go about it the right way."

He watched as desire flared in her eyes. Oh, she was intrigued all right.

He continued, still stroking her thumb and gazing into her eyes. She had no makeup on and she looked lovely, her skin so smooth, so fresh, he wanted to kiss it all. And why did she bother with eye makeup, her lashes were naturally sooty-looking around her wide, bright eyes.

"To do the roles properly, they have to eclipse into our every day lives. I guess the idea that I could sit you on a shelf and come back for you later, on my own time schedule, didn't work its way into your overall thinking."

"No. It did not." She removed her thumb from his caress and walked over to the window facing the waterfront.

It was dark, few lights shone but you could make out the water churning its way to the coast in the distance.

"Garrett, I was very upset the day you left, and every day after. It's hard for a woman not knowing, not being sure of her man."

"Am I your man?" he asked softly, coming up to stand behind her, about to put his hands on her shoulders when she turned to face him.

"You are currently the only man I am fucking, so, yeah, I'd say you're my man. Now whether that grants me exclusive rights, that's hard to say. But it works both ways, as you don't have them either at this point." She turned back to the window.

"I don't?" he asked as he ran his fingertips up her arm and stroked the back of her neck. Confidence filling him again, he smiled. *She thought of him as her man.*

"From a strictly health-based issue, we need to talk

about this—especially if you plan on foregoing condoms. Emotionally? Well, I can only commit to one person at a time. And they get my full attention."

"They?"

"Okay, by they, I mean he."

"Good to know. Although for the record, I'm not opposed to the other scenario as long as I can watch or be included."

She looked into the glass and gave him a wry smile, "Let's just settle our current issues, okay?'

"I would love to. What do I need to say or do to make that happen? You want a calendar with the date nights blocked out?"

"No. I just want to know we aren't going to play games with each other. I need true feelings, honest emotions . . . I want to see where this can lead, but only if it's genuine. And if you find you aren't interested anymore, I want you to tell me. I don't need the high drama of finding you with another woman."

"I had the high drama of thinking I was coming here to find you with another man," he whispered close to her ear, his hand sliding on the smooth, cool silk over her belly as he pressed her back against him. She groaned and he let out a sigh of relief. *They had this. They would always have this.*

She snickered and brought him back to the present. "Humph! Not likely. I haven't had a lot of experience, but I've had enough to know that nobody plays my body like you do. I go from hot and bothered to a fevered pitch in nanoseconds when you touch me. And nobody can make me step away from myself and completely let loose. I've done things with you . . . gosh, I blush to think."

He met her eyes in the reflection of the dark glass. And for the first time he realized how good they looked together.

"Well, I think the most important thing to establish, is

. . . will you do them again?" he asked as he bent and kissed her on her neck.

"Yes," she breathed.

"Good." He unbuttoned the first two buttons of her pajama top and brushed his fingertips along her collarbone. "I guess before we get started, it might be prudent for you to call Tessa and let her know I'm not abusing you . . . yet," he added with a wicked gleam in his eye.

He walked over to the nightstand, picked up the phone, punched in the prefix and then Tessa's room number, and handed the phone to Laurel. He listened as she talked to her friend, assuring her that everything was going to be fine, telling her that she would be staying with Garrett in his room and going home with him tomorrow. Garrett interrupted with a raised finger to say, "Tuesday . . . that is if it's all right with you."

She nodded and gave him a big smile. A moment later she offered him the phone, "She wants to talk to you."

He groaned and reluctantly took the phone Laurel was handing him.

"Yes, Tess?"

"I just want to make sure you understand that this girl is not to be trifled with. If your feelings are not real, if you have any doubt about being able to make something of this, something lasting . . . then end it now. Because I can assure you that Roman, Matt, and Philip, hold her in high regard, and will come down on you hard if you hurt her again."

"Technically, I didn't hurt her this time. She came to the erroneous conclusion on her own that I was not interested in her other than physically."

"It was not on her own. You were being manipulative."

He paused for a long moment and took a deep breath. "All right, I'll grant you that one."

He heard her chuckle. "Good for you, you're a big boy, owning up to your transgressions. Now, no more games.

She's been through a lot. She doesn't need a love affair to bring her down."

"Tess, I promise . . . I will not hurt her. I'm vested in this. Truly. But believe me," he said in a sultry voice, "there are going to be some games." He winked at Laurel.

"Well, mmm . . . that's very nice to hear. Good night, Garrett."

"Good night, Tess."

He hung up the phone and walked back to Laurel. "Mambo sexy, huh?"

She nodded and finished unbuttoning her pajama top.

When he saw the tiny lacy bra under it, he frowned. "You wear a bra to bed?"

"Not usually, but sometimes. I like to think of it as working against gravity for my dotage."

"Okay, we'll leave it on," he said as he used his index finger to hook the scalloped lace edging then pulled it down to expose her right breast.

"I only need one to play with right now anyway."

He tugged her to him by using his fingers, inserted under the cinched strap between her breasts, ducked his head and kissed her hungrily, his skilled tongue doing incredible things inside her mouth.

Desire unfurled in her belly as a finger of his left hand traced its way down from her neck to her collarbone and then grazed the top of her breast. His finger circled it, then his hand lifted it more fully from the cup holding it prisoner, and he lightly plucked at the heavy fullness on the underside. He was careful not to touch the tip. She moaned and whispered, "Please . . . it's been so long."

He lifted his head from where he'd been kissing her lips, nibbling at them and sucking on them.

"Please what? What do you want me to do for you?"

"My breasts . . . your mouth . . ."

"Lick, suck, bite?" he asked, as his thumb and

fingertip found the tip and lightly pinched it.

"Aaaah . . . I'm not sure . . ."

"Let's try a little of each, shall we?"

Just the thought that his lips were moving in the direction of her breast had her gasping. When he flicked the tip back and forth with his tongue, closed his lips over it and tugged, she sagged in his arms. He nibbled on the lengthening tip and tugged with his teeth drawing it out further, and she cried out his name and gripped his arms to keep from falling.

He released her nipple and looked up at her with slumberous eyes. "I'm not about to let you fall, baby. But maybe this will help hold you up." He unbuckled his belt and whipped it from his belt loops. It made a whirring and snapping sound. It made her jump.

He smiled at her reaction, then took both of her hands and held them above her head. He cupped them around the back of the bed support, forcing her to overlap her fingers behind the tall post. When she was gripping the column of the four-poster bed the way he wanted her to, he stepped back.

He threaded his leather belt through his hands as he watched her—admired her. Then he leaned in to kiss her forehead.

"I'm going to bind your wrists to the bed post and then I'm going to make love to your body. And you're going to stand there and take it . . . every lick, every kiss, every bite. When you're trembling with need, I'm going fuck you . . . and if you're a good girl, I'll let you come. Now if none of this appeals to you, I'd mention it now before I get too involved. Are you going to be okay with this?"

She was nodding her head before he could finish the question. He chuckled. "I thought you might be." He reached up and wrapped his belt between her hands and then circled both her wrists and the pole until he could fasten the belt with the buckle.

When he saw she was bound properly, he stood back and admired his handiwork. The woman tied up in front of him was trembling with need. His own body was hardening and he was getting impossibly heavy in his groin. His erection was a painful ridge inside his jeans. He squeezed it lengthwise and let out a groan as his head fell back and his eyes closed.

When he opened them he looked at her and said, "See what you do to me, see what the sight of you restrained does to me? Laurel, you are so fucking beautiful, I can hardly stand it."

She felt her womb contract and then the flow collect and dampen her panties. She squirmed and panted as he focused on her joined hands, the loose blonde hair grazing her shoulders and the one sweet breast poking out of her bra cup. Her midriff was bare, the long silky pajama bottoms she still wore, slung dangerously low on her hips. The same ones she was desperately trying to pull off with her bare feet.

He couldn't hold back the smile. "Stop fidgeting. You can rest assured that I will be taking them off. Everything is going to come off, except your bra. As I promised . . . you can keep that on. He walked over and bared the other nipple, this one by lifting the cup over it. He openly examined her, raising both brows and giving her a smug smile. "I can't decide which way I like to display your breasts better."

She flushed and creamed herself even more, wondering what she looked like, trussed for his perverse pleasure—unable to cover herself, unable to do anything but watch this incredibly handsome man have his wicked way with her. She fought to keep from looking at herself in the mirror over the dresser on the other side of the room. But then gave in and looked. The way she was posed was sinful . . . lewd . . . objectifying . . . and hot—unbelievably hot.

He took her head between his hands and kissed her

hard, delving his tongue deep. "I love how you taste. I can taste caramel on your tongue. It drives me wild. What flavor will I find when I taste you here?" he whispered, lightly stroking her mons through the silk. "Maybe I should shove a few Werther's up there and then try to fish them out with my tongue."

Her knees buckled and only the belt around her wrists kept her from falling. He cupped her genitalia until she got her legs back under her. He loved seeing her so aroused. Loved the look on her face as rapture overtook her and her eyelids fluttered closed.

He leaned in and began kissing her right breast, working toward the nipple as his talented fingers plucked at the nipple of her left one. Her throaty moans, devastating shivers, and arching hips were a testament to the heady desire moving through her body that was making her soft and ready for him.

His lips found her nipple, sucked . . . tugged. He heard her gasp and knew he couldn't hold her back much longer. His kissed his way down her cleavage to her navel where he sucked and tongued her. He followed the slanted line of her pajamas, kissing and using his teeth to inch them down, one side, and then the other. When they fell past her hips, the weight of them took them to the floor and she was all but bare. Skimpy lacy underwear, a scrap of material he felt sure would fit in a lipstick tube, and a bra hiding nothing were all she wore. He looked up at her, drinking in the sight of this beautiful woman displayed so provocatively for him. He couldn't stand the pressure of his erection fighting to stand tall in his pants any longer.

He stood and unzipped while he looked into her eyes. In a husky voice he said, "I want you to see what you do to me. What the sight of you displayed like this does to me."

He pulled out his penis and showed her its impressive length, its thick girth. He wrapped a fist around it and pumped to show her the wetness she had caused to ooze from him and to pool at the tip.

She let out a groan that ended with a needy whimper. "I want that. In me."

"You're gonna get this. In you. But not yet."

She sobbed and begged . . . "Please . . . please Garrett. I need you."

He stood in front of her and held her face between his hands. His erection grazed her hip and he felt her turn toward it, felt the trail of moisture it left with each uncontrollable jerk. He was on fire, harder than he'd ever been and just as needy as she was. As he kissed her lightly on the lips, her chin and her forehead, he whispered, "Soon, baby, soon."

He slid slowly down her body, grazing her with his fingertips as he dropped to the floor in front of her. He kissed every inch of her underwear, starting from the top and working his way to the tiny cotton triangle between her legs. She shifted to meet his lips and sobbed his name over and over again. He murmured his delight; bestowing lingering kisses where her thighs met her legs. "Mmm, you smell so good, baby. I can't wait to taste you."

Using his teeth, he slowly dragged her panties down her thighs. Saw them glide to her ankles. Waited as she stepped out and kicked them across the floor. Then he concentrated on the lightly furred blonde thatch between her legs.

"Mmm, such a pretty golden brown, you must be a real blonde. Oh my, what a sweet wet slit." His thumbs spread her and dipped into the silky moisture.

She keened and opened herself to him, her head thrashing back and forth. "God Garrett, I can't take it anymore!"

"I know baby," he crooned, then leaned in and circled her clit with his tongue. He dabbed at it. Flicked it mercilessly. When he felt the convulsions begin he sucked it in. Felt her thighs tremble and shifted her legs to his shoulders. Heard her hiss, followed by a long low moan, and knew she was toppling over the precipice. As her release took her, he kept a steady tug on her clit while his practiced fingers impaled her. He finger fucked her and sucked her first orgasm out of her, then he ground his light beard like a buzz saw against her pubes. Felt her milking the fingers he was shoving into her vagina. He removed her legs from his shoulders; stood and dropped his pants, and kicked them aside to begin working on the third one.

Wrapping his arms under her thighs, he lifted her in his arms, held her suspended high enough to take the pressure off her arms. He gripped an ass cheek in each large hand and held her to him as he probed her with his penis, finding her valley of nirvana, slick, hot and welcoming as he shoved into her over and over again. He lifted from his knees to get the angle he wanted and thought he might have to pay for a new bed as the poster she was tied to creaked and the wood threatened to split with each forceful thrust. He felt her quicken and he sped up. Heard her scream and covered it with his mouth. Then nothing else registered as they both shattered. He drove home one final time, holding her tight to him and spilling his seed deep inside her.

When he could move, he slid out of her and dropped her feet to the carpet. Then he reached up and unbuckled his belt. He kissed her neck as he unwound it, dropping it to the floor with a loud thud.

He lifted her up, placed her gently onto the foot of the bed, laid her back, and massaged her wrists. He bent and kissed them tenderly, sucking at the soft, fragile skin. Then he kissed her on the lips. "I can now attest to the fact that your orgasms taste delicious," he said as he assessed her face. She still looked otherworldly. "You all right?"

"I am perfect," she purred, "I feel like I just had the best sex there could be."

He smiled, "Well, that's quite a compliment, so I'll take it."

She reached up to wrap her arms around his neck and kissed him. "I don't know how you do it, but you push all the right buttons. And at just the right moment. Although I was begging for it sooner, you made me wait. How do you know how to do that?"

"It's called delayed gratification. It's a major element in Tantric sex. And it works especially well with women who are on the naughty side," he said with a grin, as he ran a finger down her nose.

"Am I on the naughty side?"

"Oh, you most definitely are. Here, let's get this off; you're getting lines all over your pretty breasts." He unsnapped her bra from the front and peeled it off. "Better?"

She nodded. He tugged off his shirt and snuggled her into his chest.

They held each other and relaxed, enjoying the afterglow of some awesomely hot sex. Then Garrett got up to get them each some water before pulling up the covers and tucking them under the sheets and throwing on the thick comforter.

He pulled her to his chest and stroked her back as he rubbed his lips along her temple. "So you're okay with staying here with me until Tuesday?"

"Sure. I don't have to be back at any special time."

"Good. I want to spend some time with you." He looked down at her upturned face. "And not all of it in bed."

"Technically, we weren't in bed."

"Okay, I amend that to, not all of it in the bedroom."

"You've been known to utilize vehicles."

"Let me start over. I want to get to know you, in a non-sexual way."

"We won't have sex?"

"I didn't say that. We *will* have sex. And we will eat,

and walk, and talk. Sex is important, but so are other things. Besides Spear has to have time to regroup."

"Spear?"

He lifted the covers and pointed to his recovering and already randy penis. "Laurel meet Spearman, Spear for short."

"I believe we've met. In fact, we're intimately acquainted. I think he's regrouped."

"He's going to have to wait for morning, I need some sleep."

"It is morning."

He looked over at the clock. It was 2:30. "Sleep with me. I'm the one who needs to regroup. Loving you is exhausting."

"Are you saying you love me?"

"There is that distinct possibility. Let's just say, I'm working on it. How about you?"

"I'm pretty much in the done-deal range. But I could use more time to process it."

"Hmmm, me too. Hence . . . three days in Charleston. Go to sleep." He smacked her on the rump.

She huffed, "I thought we were regrouping."

He laughed and turned her so he could hold her in his arms, her back to his front. "Only you would think of a smack to your butt as a call-to-arms."

Chapter Sixty-one

They slept late, had a nice leisurely breakfast at the hotel, ducked into a few shops and were now walking arm-in-arm along the battery, smiling, laughing, and feeding flavored Jelly Bellys to each other. Originally, the idea had been for an inspired run around the battery, so they had dressed casually, she in black lotus capris with a matching garden print Branwyn top and Keds, him in surfer shorts and a crew-neck tee with running shoes. But after a full breakfast, the idea of walking had seemed to appeal more.

"Tell me about your first sexual experience," he said.

"You mean first kiss? First feel up?"

"No, first he-got-to-home base."

"Oh, *that*. No great shakes there, I often wish we hadn't left the movie."

"That bad?"

"Yeah, I think I would much rather have seen the end of *The Pianist*."

"I gather he didn't make you come? What was the matter, didn't he prepare you?"

"To be honest, it wasn't all his fault. When I realized I didn't really want this guy to be my first, I did the time-honored remedy and went down on him, hoping for a reprieve. And that went all right, but then not ten minutes later, he's ready again and this time he's not going for the diversionary tactic—he wants the real deal. He kind of shamed me into it.

"Told me I'd led him on all evening, did things to get him all wound up. He thought the blowjob was foreplay, whereas I thought it was the alternative. He kept kissing me and touching me in all the right places, and he called on my sense of fair play. I acquiesced. I mean, I *was* curious. But I sure wished I'd waited. He wasn't the one. I liked him, and he told me I was beautiful, and I loved hearing how much he wanted me. Actually, I was thrilled that he wanted me so badly that it seemed his penis couldn't get enough. And he seemed so damned determined to have me. He was older, more experienced. I was kind of in his thrall I guess you could say, amazed by his knowledge of a woman's body."

"But yet he didn't pleasure you?"

"No. I loved the kissing and the fondling. But when it came down to it, it really was more about him than about me. I understood that, he was my boyfriend and I wanted to please him."

"Submissive tendencies even then," he said, running a finger down her nose. "You're a born submissive, you know that?" He kissed her thoroughly, letting his tongue play leisurely with hers. "Could he have tied you up?"

"No. That would have really scared me back then."

They were at the end of a walkway. They turned and continued down an oyster shell path. "How often have you been having sex up to now?"

"You know that it's been several years since I've been with someone."

"Yes, but surely you diddle yourself . . . do things . . . "

There was a long pause while she blushed crimson. She hesitated before saying, "I do. I admit it. But I'm not sure I'm ready to talk to you about my love affair with the middle finger of my right hand."

He laughed, squeezed her hand then brought the aforementioned finger to his lips and kissed it. "I'm right handed too, but it takes more than a finger for me."

They walked in silence for a few minutes then she asked, "How about you? Your first sexual adventure, what was it like?"

He heaved out a huge sigh as if he wasn't certain he should tell the tale. Then he jumped in, "The first time I became really aware of the power of lust, I had just turned fourteen. I was beginning to find out the things that worked for me when I found myself captive to an event that would forever be responsible for sending huge volumes of heated blood to my penis whenever I recalled it, often so quickly that I felt I would swoon from the sudden jolt. Just hearing the word basement is still enough to flood my loins and bring on the tingly realm of headiness, nearly twenty years later.

"Although my school chums were friendly, I was not often included in anything unless it required money. Early on, I'd been tagged the guy who always had a spare buck on him, which was odd as all I was doing was pocketing my lunch money and waiting until I got home to make a sandwich before anyone came home. But eighty cents a day plus my allowance added up quickly back then.

"I was putting my books in my locker when Tom Rainey bumped my shoulder, 'Hey, you wanna see some titties, real ones?'

"I remember I looked at him askance, I can still feel my eyebrow cocked. This was a strange question coming from an even stranger kid. This is how I remember the conversation:

"'Seriously, come with me. Joe's gonna have a show,' he said.

"'I don't want to see Joe's titties,' I said.

"'Not his, you twit, his sister's. He's putting on the show, but she's the one providing the goods. Costs ya a dollar and you can look all you want.'

"'You're joking. Isn't his sister Margie? She's only twelve.'

"'Yeah, but she's got nice tits already.'

"'And she wants to show them off?'

"'Hell, I don't know. All I know is that Joe's taking a dollar from each of us for a look, a long look as he tells it. You comin' or not?'

"'Sure, I got a dollar I'm not usin', I'm in.'

" Then get yourself over to Joe's basement as soon as you get off the bus. He's gotta do this before his parents get home from work.'

"As I sat on the bus, I tried to remember Margie, what she looked like, how she walked, how she talked. But honestly, I hadn't paid much attention to her. The last time I'd seen her she was a bit on the chunky side and had freckles all over her. I really wasn't all that interested. She attended the private Catholic school on the other side of town because she had won the mandated scholarship they gave to the underprivileged, so I hadn't seen her in a year or two. I decided I'd better go, otherwise they'd probably start calling me a queer or something if they thought I wasn't interested in looking at girls' tits.

"I got off at the bus stop by Joe's house and was met at the door by Joe, who snickered and took my dollar before letting me in. I was told to go down to the basement and wait with the others. I sat on the lumpy rec room sofa next to four other guys I recognized but hardly knew. As it was February, in Maryland, the basement was damp and cold. We sat with our hands in our laps pretty much twiddling our thumbs until the bright fluorescent overhead lights were turned off by an upstairs switch. Then Joe came barreling down the stairs, switched on the table lamp by a recliner and popped into a seat. 'We're ready!' he called out and two minutes later I heard someone coming down the stairs.

"It took her forever to get down the steps and then another eternity for her to walk to the front of the room and turn to face us. I looked at her chest. She was wearing a white blouse with a round collar and it was buttoned up tight, right up against her throat. Through her shirt you could tell that she filled out her bra. She was taller than the last time I'd seen her, and still on the heavy side.

"'Go on, you know what you gotta do,' Joe said, with a wave of his hand in the direction of her chest.

"I looked at her face and could see where tears had dried on her cheeks. Her lips trembled. And God help me, knowing that she didn't want to do this made it all that much hotter. I remember feeling ashamed for thinking that, and for not putting a stop to this.

"She just stood there as if frozen in place until her brother yelled at her,
'Unbutton your shirt and take off your brassiere. You agreed.'

"After a few seconds her fingers moved to the top button. I knew from the way her fingers shook that if she had agreed, it had to have been for a reason. But I didn't care. Just like the others, I wanted to see her tits, even if she didn't want to show them to me. It was my first experience with peer pressure, and it was stronger than I'd imagined. Even knowing right from wrong, I was captivated.

"All around me everyone's breathing changed as each button was undone and we could see her pale skin and her white no-nonsense bra. There were eight of us, including her brother, and we all held our breath as Margie slowly unbuttoned the last button. When I saw her pale creamy skin, freckled all over, and her pointy white bra with the full cups, I felt my cock grow and move against my hands that were folded in my lap. When her brother stood and pulled the sleeves down her arms and took the shirt from her, my breath hitched. I think everyone else's did, too. I heard someone cough and wheeze.

"'Now the brassiere. Just unhook it and let it fall to the floor.'

"Her dark blue eyes suddenly looked defiant and she

stared at her brother with hatred in her tear-filled eyes.

"He was unaffected. 'Do you want me to tell, because I will. You know I will.'

"I knew without a doubt then that she was being coerced. I wondered what he had on her that would cause her to do this? Her hands reached behind her and she unsnapped her bra and I no longer cared that he was extorting her. I wanted to see her breasts. I wanted to see her nipples.

"The bra straps slid down her arms and fell to the floor and then I saw them. Everyone saw them. Full, round mounds, covered with tiny freckles topped with peach-colored nipples jutting out proudly even as she stood with her head down, ashamed. It couldn't have been more than ten seconds before I came. I bit the inside of my cheek to keep my secret from being known, even as the damp spot on my lap bloomed. The others followed, not at all embarrassed by the sounds they were making. It seemed the only one in the room who hadn't come was Joe. He reached out and cupped her breast, and then he bent to take one of her nipples into his mouth. I think I came again; I was never sure about that part. But I thought that I might have. We watched him fondle her as she keened in misery and then he unzipped his pants and dropped them.

" 'Get on your knees and suck me,' he yelled.

" 'No,' she whimpered and shook her head back and forth.

"'Do as I say! If you don't . . .'

"I watched as he pushed her to her knees and forced her mouth open before shoving his dick inside. She began to suck on him and between sobs, I heard her pleading with him to let her stop.

"I couldn't stand it anymore; she obviously did not want this, not one part of it, even though it appeared this wasn't an entirely new thing for her.

"I jumped up and pushed him away from her then

I drew my fist back and smashed it into his face. His arms flailed and he fell backward landing on the matted shag carpeting. He was out or at least he appeared to be.

"'What's he got on you? Why are you doing this?' I demanded, looking Margie in the eye, trying real hard not to look at her breasts anymore.

"When she didn't answer, just remained on her knees shaking, I screamed, 'Why? Tell me!'

"She answered in a low voice, 'I owe him money. I stole money while I was babysitting and they found out. I had to return it before they told my parents. Joe loaned me the money. But now nobody wants me to babysit and I don't have a way to pay him back. He says I have to do this until I do.'

"'How much do you owe him?'

"'Twenty dollars.'

"I reached into my front pocket and took out a wad of bills. I counted out twenty dollars and threw them down by her knees. I spoke through a haze of anger; my words unbelievably harsh even to my ears. 'Don't ever do that again unless it's something you want to do.'

"I spun around and ran up the stairs. But the damage had been done. Pleated skirts, white starched shirts, knee-highs, basements, and yes, even freckles—formally abhorred, sent blood surging to my cock. And the idea of a woman on her knees servicing me in front of others while she sobbed became my all-time number one fantasy.

"In high school, if I could get a girl to gag so that tears ran down her face I would come almost instantly. And in college I once asked a girlfriend to wear one of those school uniform get ups you can buy in the adult stores for a Halloween costume party.

"So there you have it. My first sexual completion. Not proud of it for a number of reasons. When I saw that Margie didn't want to do it, I should have manned up for her. I gave my hard earned money to her and she didn't even appreciate it, she never even thanked me, and then I had to sneak into the house so my mom couldn't see I'd wet my pants. All-in-all, it was not my finest hour."

They walked in silence for a few minutes. Neither knowing quite what to say after that.

"So, if I get topless, get on my knees and deep throat you until I'm crying, you'll give me twenty dollars?"

"Sweetheart, if you'll do all that, I'll give you *a thousand* dollars."

"Good to know. Next time I'm short on funds . . ."

He grabbed her by the waist and pulled her to him, nuzzling her hair as he smiled, "Actually I'm pretty much over that one, girls in college try so hard to please, and as I'm fairly well endowed, it usually played out in my favor anyway. Actually, it got a bit tiresome . . ."

She reached over and swatted him on the arm.

"Uh huh, yeah. Sure it did."

He laughed and pulled her close. "Okay, make it two thousand."

There was silence for a few seconds so he stopped and turned her to face him. They were on a bike path now that ran along the coast. "Hey, what's this? I was just joking, don't get mad."

"I'm not mad. But I do need to have a conversation with you about money."

He looked at her askance. *What was this about?* It wouldn't be the first time a girlfriend had needed to ask him for money, but Laurel couldn't possibly be one of them. Although she *was* here in Charleston longer than she'd planned to be. But he'd seen Tessa drag all of Laurel's stuff over from her room before leaving this morning, her purse included. Yet, she hadn't bought anything in any of the shops they'd been in, maybe she needed some cash. "Money conversations are always awkward, just spit it out, do you need some cash until we get back?"

"Oh no. Hell, no."

"Well, what's the problem then?"

"No problem really. Just something you should know."

"Okay, then tell me." *Ah, he had an inkling what she was going to tell him and knowing it wasn't public knowledge, and that she probably didn't share this information with others, he burst with pride.*

"My dad won the lottery right after he died, the drawing was the day after actually. I found the ticket in his wallet a few days after the funeral. I almost didn't bother checking it. He never even knew."

He feigned surprise, "Wow, what a shame that he never knew. How much are we talking about?"

"Thirty-six million plus. I invested most of it so it's a lot more now, seventy some."

He whistled. She must have phenomenal investing instincts. "Geez," he said, stunned. He wondered if she would let him look at her portfolio.

There was silence for a few moments then she asked, "So are we both multi-millionaires?"

"Ummhmm. Yup. Self-made on my end."

"Don't be a snob."

More silence.

"Why do you seem mad?" she asked.

"I'm not mad, my perceptions are just skewed, that's all." *And my estimates of her total wealth were considerably off.*

"Meaning?"

"Meaning . . . hell I don't know."

"This shouldn't affect us . . . I mean . . ."

"See?" he said as he smiled over at her. "Weird, huh?"

"It shouldn't be weird."

"No, the fact that you have more money than I do

shouldn't be weird. But it is."

"Why?"

"I don't know why. I guess because every woman I've ever dated made less and had less. I don't think my money was the reason they were drawn to me, but I always had to be careful not to let them know how *much* money I had. I never wanted it to be a factor in our relationship."

"I don't want it to be in ours either. That's why I told you." They made their way down some steps to a small sandy beach.

"Money equates to power and I'm kind of traditional in my thinking."

"Meaning?"

"The man should have the power, or at least the majority of it. I know, I know, it's sexist and not the way things are these days. But I like the male dominant role. And I like the female as submissive . . . somewhat submissive anyway."

"We can still be like that. So I have money? You have money. Neither of us flaunts it. It doesn't have to be an issue."

He turned and pulled her close, tucking her head under his chin, "No, it doesn't have to be an issue. I'll just have to work harder I suppose . . ."

"It's not a contest!"

"The hell it's not. I've got my pride here."

"How much are we talking?"

"You're about thirty ahead of me if I were to liquidate right now. But give me a few more years and I just might catch up and blow by you."

"Well then why don't we just wait and see. If we're still together in five years then we can declare a winner."

He took her hand and shook it, "You're on. But I will call foul if I see you sneaking a peak at what I'm circling in the *Journal*."

"Okay, first one to billionaire has to buy lunch."

"In Paris."

"Via the QE2."

"In the Presidential Stateroom."

"With the bathtub full of Mumm's."

"Speaking of, I could use a drink."

"You buyin'?"

He laughed, "Don't I always?"

"That's because you're the man. You dominate. You have the power."

"Stop sucking up."

"What about your offer, for the two grand? Change your mind?"

"Now that I know you don't need the money, I'll guess I'll have to come up with another incentive."

"You must be pretty awesome in the world of finance to have done as well as you have without much of a stake. Got any insights I could use?"

"Sweetheart, it sounds like whoever you've got managing your accounts is doing a pretty fine job."

"I manage everything myself. But sometimes I get advice. I'd love to hear some of your strategy."

"Ahh . . . no longer interested in body of mine, now she is wanting my investing secrets," he said in a Boris Badenov accent.

"Boris from Bullwinkle?"

"You pass test. Okay, I give you my secret," he said, staying in character. "Sin. That is the secret. Is good Natasha."

"Sin?"

"Yes. Big pay off with sin."

"Elucidate."

He smiled and went back to his normal voice. "The vices pay off—consistently, year after year—smoking, drinking, gambling, sex . . . and the easiest way to get them all . . . the Internet. Cigarette manufacturing is up 12 percent. So that's Philip Morris International, Lorillard Inc., and the

Altria Group. The fund was up four and a half percent last year when everything else was sliding down. According to *Morningstar,* it ranked in the top three percent. Alcoholic beverages are up six percent. Gaming is down though, as the casinos are struggling under heavy debt loads.

"Vice Fund, the only fund consisting of 'sin' stocks, is rebounding in a lagging market, and would be showing a substantial return if not for the gaming segment. And sex toys for the baby boomers . . . through the roof. There's a book out that makes for interesting reading, it's called, *Investing in Vice: The Recession-proof Portfolio of Booze, Bets, and Butts.*

"So if you're looking for deep-value stocks—"

"I thought tobacco was an industry going out of business?" she interrupted.

"Not in the international markets. It's growing in emerging markets. In other parts of the world people are smoking more, not less. And they're going to the premium brands. Philip Morris is in a great position. The dividend is paying steadily at five percent, and they have enough cash to buy back shares. Due to the advertising laws, the company doesn't have to spend a fortune remaking itself over and over again. R & D is at a minimum with an acceptable and consistent product, and distribution lines have long been established for them. It's a nice presence globally, and growing markets like Brazil will make it a cash machine for investors in the coming years."

"So much to consider," she said with a confusing shake of her head.

"Yes there is. It's a full-time job for me. The research never ends."

"So what have you been reading about lately?"

"You know, if you keep pumping me, I'm going to have to ask for a consulting fee."

"And what might that be?"

"Hmmm . . . pumping you back?"

"I think I can handle the tariff. Give me an idea of what you delved into at your conference last week."

"Hmmm. Okay, here goes. The highlights: sustainability of the dollar vs. rapid fluxes; hope surrounding the Chinese economy; iPad stocks and the companies who provide components . . . like Polypore, in North Carolina—they make the filters and separators for use in lithium batteries; flash point techniques; falling home values; convectional solar units; photovoltaic generators; bio techs; GENCO and cancer; you name it . . . someone brought it up.

"You know, analysts predict that by 2013 alternative energy numbers will be in the 13 billion dollar range. That could translate to an enormous return if you were to pick the right start up company.

"I subscribe to over 40 newsletters. One of my favorites is *Gold Stock Advisor*; I have 14 percent of my portfolio in gold. I'm just waiting for the next period of stagnation to buy into Kinross or Kiska, or Full Metal Minerals.

"And then of course, there's warnings of a bond bubble brewing. You really have to stay on top of things, and you have to be able to react quickly. I made a fortune when BHP Billiton failed to take over the Potash Corporation, a Canadian fertilizer company—the largest in the Saskatchewan Province. Due to the failed takeover, the jump was 26 percent. You never see rates of return that high. It's the international markets that play well in this game if you understand them. The first few years I was doing this, I was up all night following the Asian markets, just trying to get a handle on how things worked. A real trial by fire. Lost my ass a few times.

"So . . . in my professor's voice, let me sum this up for you: you can't always be bullish because Wall Street says so. Sometimes the way to make money is to go against the tide."

She laughed at his serious professor voice. "Do you

know what the difference between an ostrich and a Wall Street analyst is?" she asked.

"No, what is it?" he asked, smiling down at her.

"An ostrich occasionally takes its head out of the sand."

He threw his head back and laughed. He took her hand and kissed it. "Enough Investing 101. Although why I'm teaching you, when you're out earning me quite handily, I'll never know. But I'm ready to collect my fee."

"The pumping one?"

"Yes, precisely."

"I guess I'd better pay up."

"Now you're talking. C'mon, I'll race you back to the hotel," he said, "at least that's something I can still beat you at." He took off, quickly distancing them, enjoying the brief sprint. At a bridge overpass, he leaned against the bricks and waited for her to catch up.

"Good thing you're loaded," he said, "'Cause you're never gonna get the gold that way." He tugged on her ponytail and fell into a jog beside her. "You wanna go see if we can rent *The Pianist*? You can see the ending, and while Brody's doing his thing," he mimicked playing the piano, "I can do mine . . ." He waggled his eyebrows up and down and lolled his tongue in and out of his mouth.

She burst out laughing and kept at it until she had tears leaking down her cheeks and they had to stop jogging. They turned their jog into a brisk walk and crossed the streets heading back toward the hotel.

"I adore you," he murmured.

"How do I know you're not just saying that because of my money?"

He laughed. "Do you know how ridiculous that sounds?"

"Sounded pretty ridiculous coming from you, too."

"Really?"

"Yeah, women don't need men with lots of money."

"No? What do they need then?"

"A nice big cock."

"Mine's probably not the biggest money can buy . . ."

"How much do they go for, are they sold by the inch or buy the pound?"

"Square foot."

"You wish."

"And the balls are optional. But I should advise you, the cock is not operational without them. It's sort of a forced option."

"Okay, I'll take two and make them nice and sweaty."

"I believe I have that exact model in stock."

"Good. I don't have time to place an order as I have an urgent, pressing need."

"We guarantee optimum performance at the critical time and service with a smile. Our latest model even has a replay feature if you know how to use it."

"Oh, I'll figure out how to use it. Remember, I've had some experience with that particular feature. Geesh, men who can't be satisfied . . . what's up with that?"

"At least with me, you can be assured of *your* satisfaction . . . over and over again. That I can promise you."

"You are so much fun to be with Garrett," she said, slowing her pace and forcing him to slow his. "I like talking to you."

"Ditto, baby."

Chapter Sixty-two

When they got back to the room Garrett got them each a bottle of water, and as they chugged the much-needed elixir, he toed off his shoes, not once taking his eyes off her.

His shirt was the next to go, and although sweat was running in erratic rivulets through the mat of his chest hair, she thought he was the sexiest thing alive. There apparently was some strict discipline imbued in his lifestyle—those abs, those shoulders—only came from strenuous exercise. He hadn't shaved this morning and the cast of his dark shadow made him even more appealing. Combined with his dark expressive eyebrows and fully lashed cornflower-blue eyes, he was devastating.

He put his water bottle down and walked over to where she stood, eyeing him as hungrily as he was her. He took her water from her, and blindly placed it on the dresser beside her, while with his other hand, he gathered the hem and tugged her tight tank top off. It had a built in shelf bra, so when it came off she was topless.

He was radiant; full of raw energy and the lust darkening his eyes made her feel pretty . . . desired . . . sexy.

"Mmmm," he said as he cupped her breast, hefting it and running his thumb over the tip until she moaned for him. "You are so beautiful. I am one lucky guy, to be here with you, in this room, taking off your clothes."

"I'm all sweaty."

"I noticed. Me too. C'mon, let's have a shower. They have a removable shower head, and I'm in the mood for some water play." He knelt and removed her yoga togs and panties as one, kissed her belly, then the line where her curls began, and finally her upper thighs. He unlaced her tennis shoes, and tugged each one off while she used his shoulder for support, and then he pulled off her half socks. He stood, took her hand, kissed it, and walked her into the bathroom.

If she didn't know better she would have sworn the water she'd been drinking was drugged. She was euphoric, but lacking the limber grace she was proud of, as she meekly dragged her feet, and went into the bathroom with this sexy, over-the-top, gift to women. She stood naked, as if in a daze, while he adjusted the temperature and the spray, and then came back to lift her high in his arms to carry her under the pounding spray.

As hotel bathrooms went, this one was pretty upscale—roomy and tiled throughout. It had a small alcove that closed them off from the world, promising privacy and comfort, and tremendous water pressure from state-of-the-art shower fixtures. He squirted some shower gel in his palms and turned her to face him. Soap-coated hands massaged her collarbone and shoulders. Her arms were next and they were lovingly soaped and caressed down to the fingertips. More gel was added, and both breasts were gathered up, brought together, and the nipples firmly tugged until the tips slid silkily from his fingertips. Her belly was next, and he held his hand over her womb causing it to clench.

He soaped her mons then used his knee to force her thighs apart. Cupping her, he massaged the area between her legs, letting his fingers slip into her momentarily. Her low *hum* charged his senses and sent his libido into overdrive. "Sorry, can't linger here . . . , " he murmured, "not now."

She writhed beneath his hand.

"Sorry, baby. I've got to wash you before we play."

With sure hands he lathered every slick inch of her skin. Using military precision, he covered all areas in a progressive pattern of quadrants, working from top to bottom—and paying an inordinate amount of attention to her firm buttocks and shapely, long legs—before he finally turned her and put her hands on the wall. She shivered even though the water was far from chilly. He chuckled and stood to kiss the back of her neck as he caressed her breasts. He sent pleasure racing and pulsing as his hand stroked her sleek curves. A smile tugged at the corner of his lips when he felt her tremble.

Slowly, he turned her back to face him. He tossed a roguish glance in the direction of her undulating hips and whispered, "That's one of the things I love about you, you're so sensual, so charged . . . it's like you detonate when I touch you. You can hardly flatter a man's ego more."

He lathered both hands as he looked down into her uptilted face. With gelled hands, he threaded his hands through her hair, gripped her head, and brought her face to his. Forcefully, he took her mouth as his hands worked her hair into a frothy lather, careful to keep her head tipped back so he could ravage her mouth without drowning her in the process.

He tasted her moan and smiled against her lips as he recognized the coconut flavor of the Jelly Bellys he'd fed her earlier. He thrust his tongue deeper, savoring her essence, running it over her teeth, and expertly tonguing her inner lips and cheeks.

Oh, she knew what he was doing. She'd read about this. He was using those expert touches; those lingering kisses, those thick-tongued and bone-melting forays to literally leave his mark. Like the hunter, he'd chosen his prey, and now he was saturating her with his powerful, intensifying aphrodisiac. What teenagers referred to as swapping spit, was his literal goal. He was transferring male hormones from his mouth to hers, virile secretions that rendered women incapable of saying no and assuring a willing partner. He was ramping up her desire to a fevered pitch, and he damned well knew it. While his hands continued their magic, causing her scalp to tingle, his mouth plundered and took. Over and over again, he rained down frenzied kisses as he adjusted the angle, the depth, the force of his tongue. Just as she was about to put her hands to his shoulders to pull him closer, to force her tongue into his mouth, he dropped his hands, took the showerhead attached to a hose from the wall bracket, and fell to his knees at her feet.

While the showerhead began pulsing and spewing warm jets of water directly at her clit, spiking her desire and sending a fizzy warmth through her veins, he used his fingers to spread her lips, to open her wide to the streaking sensations, as he steadily aimed the stream at the pink little bud that was unfurling and blossoming.

His penis jumped with each sob and his heart swelled with each protracted groan, as he focused his eyes on her and watched her squirm—watched this most breathtakingly beautiful and intoxicating woman ripple with her building release. He was ready to catch her when her legs failed her, the showerhead already released from his grasp. He saw her haze of satiation, heard her strangled scream as he propped her up with his hands wrapped around her thighs. Foraging in her nest of tight curls, he rooted for the pearl he'd been playing with, then wrapped his lips around it and tugged.

The wail that came out of her echoed off the walls, and if he hadn't known any better, he would have thought a wounded animal had joined them in the shower. But no, it was her . . . her head thrown back, her throat elongated, while she keened to the heavens, as if the pleasure was too much for her to bear. He sucked harder and felt her buck violently. Her hands slid off his shoulders, and she would have fallen to the floor if he hadn't caught her. Boneless, she collapsed in his arms, sobbing and babbling a language he likened to Gaelic, then she went limp in his arms and passed out. He kissed her temple, smoothed her hair, and held her tight until she came back to him, her eyes fluttering in the mist.

"You okay?" The beguiling wickedness of his smile could almost be taken for boasting. He knew exactly what he'd done to her, knew it might be many minutes before she returned to her senses, having come nearly undone in his arms.

Her insides were still jittering and her groans throttling back when she sighed, "I have never been this okay. I could die now and feel as if I have enjoyed the best this world has to offer."

"That is the ultimate compliment. Thank you," he breathed, his forehead pressed to hers.

"No, thank you," she said and she lifted a hand to graze his stubbled cheek.

"Do you speak another language?"

"Not that I know of."

"I wish I had recorded what you said, it sounded Gaelic, like a beautiful mystical chant. If I didn't know better I'd think you were outside your body just before you fainted."

"I don't remember talking." She immediately thought of Merlin and wondered if her subconscious was thanking him for bringing this man into her life.

He reached behind them and found the showerhead and used the nozzle on the side to stem the flow of the water. They sat, her in his lap, exchanging little nipping kisses until he saw the gooseflesh on her arms.

"You're cold. Let's get you toweled off."

"But you . . . I haven't washed you yet."

"Plenty of opportunity later." He lifted her, grabbed a towel from the rack on the corner wall and wrapped it around her. Then he turned her toward the door and swatted her ass. "Give me a minute and I'll join you." He turned the shower back on and quickly washed.

When he strolled into the bedroom, she was in bed, under the covers, shivering. Although dry, his skin was still steamy from his hot shower, so he slid in beside her and drew her close. She murmured her approval in his ear.

"You've got thirty minutes to take a nap then I'm going to wake you with my penis in either your mouth or your vagina. Take your pick."

She looked up at him in shock, then blinked and managed a smile. She turned in his arms, with her back to his front, wiggled her ass against his erection, and whispered over her shoulder, "Isn't there a third option?"

He groaned as his arm snaked around her waist and pulled her close. "There is indeed. And if you don't behave, there'll be no nap."

Chapter Sixty-three

They slept for three hours. And woke hungry—both for different reasons. Being the gentleman, he acquiesced to her and called room service.

While they were waiting, he slaked his hunger by turning her nerves into paths of fire, kissing her from temple to toe and then stopping halfway to draw concentric number 8s with his tongue on her inner thighs. He made the tactical error of kissing up her body backward and unwittingly placing his penis within her reach. His body roared when she grabbed it and with single-minded purpose, worked him into a lust-filled frenzy with her hands, her lips and her tongue. He managed to flatten his tongue and keep it pressed against her clit while she sent surging lust through his loins and heat arrowing through his dick, as she licked and sucked her way to taking the upper hand and wresting control from him. Before he was aware she was even in a position to do it, she flipped him onto his back and within minutes had him impaling her.

The sensation of her shoving him up into her, taking him deep as she rode him, was incredible. He watched her play rodeo girl, as she sucked in her breath and hissed, then whimpered, "Yes, yes, yes," when she shortened her strokes and leaned over him like a jockey. He knew this shortened the length of her vagina, and he used the new angle to his advantage by thrusting and curling his abs in an attempt to touch the Holy Grail—her g-spot. It was clear he was giving her intense pleasure when she begged him, "Oh God, touch it, touch it, just touch it, there, there!" and sent them both careening into an orgasm that he felt to his core.

He came to his senses, feeling her stroking his very relaxed penis and murmuring, "This is as soft as kid leather. So smooth, silky . . . soft." She bent and kissed the head. He didn't remember her dismounting, but there she was lying on her side stroking him.

"You're hitting a horse with a dead stick," he muttered.

She laughed. "As malapropisms go, that one's pretty accurate. But I'm not interested in anything more than being very appreciative. You were amazing."

"I'm afraid all the credit goes to you for this one. You were poetry in motion. You rode beautifully. You didn't sacrifice form for speed. You were radiant . . . glorious. You were definitely in your element, you were one with the beast."

"Spearman?" she asked.

He chuckled, "Yes, Spearman. Although right now he most certainly is not reminiscent of either."

There was a discrete knock on the door and he groaned. "Hop up baby, I've got to get my robe. Sustenance is here. In the nick of time I might add. You've sapped my strength and turned Spearman into Gumby. I'm going to need some serious time to regroup," he sat up, ran his fingers through his hair and barked. "Coming!" at the door when there was another knock.

"Not likely," she sang as she leaped off the bed and ran for the bathroom.

They sat propped against the headboard eating cheeseburgers and fries, drinking champagne and sharing a big slice of cheesecake. It was the identical meal they'd had on Bald Head, if you substituted the beer for champagne.

"I can't believe I once thought you were a vegetarian,"

he said. And instantly realized his mistake. She didn't know he had access to her computer files, the ones that held her recipes that he'd noted were all meatless.

She frowned at him, "Why did you think that?"

"Oh just something Charlene said, she said she's always worried about finding a place for you to get a salad on the rides." As lies went, it wasn't his best. But the fact that he had come up with it so fast, had to count for something.

"Oh, I didn't know that. I do usually eat salads for lunch. I mean, if you're going to go to all the trouble to exercise like that, you really should capitalize on it. I guess I'd better talk to her. I don't want her worrying about accommodating me like that."

"I'm sure she doesn't mind. And what restaurant doesn't offer a salad these days?"

"You're right. But clearly, as you can see, no vegetarian here." She waved what was left of her burger in the air. "But Tess is. Drives Roman crazy sometimes. If he orders a steak, he usually slices off a portion for me. Says he can't see how someone can make a whole meal out of salad."

Whew. He'd sidestepped that one. He'd better be more careful what he revealed. And speaking of revealing, he started making plans for later in the night. Laurel had said she wanted to take a long hot soak in the tub after dinner. She'd brought a book to read and was complaining that she hadn't even opened the cover. He told her there was a baseball game on cable he wanted to watch so she wouldn't feel she had to entertain him 24-7.

So, after dinner, he got her bath ready, and after she had settled into the tub, he brought her a glass of champagne. As he closed the door behind him to keep the steam in, he smiled at the woman who was chin deep in bubbles, bobbling a paperback and sipping from a tall flute filled with Möet.

Something warmed in his chest at the sight, and he knew he never wanted this woman to be anyone's but his.

He leaned against the door to watch her for a few minutes then topped off her glass before leaving her alone with her book.

She settled back into bed, snuggled up against the fluffy pillows nearly forty minutes later. Smelling like honeysuckles and gardenias, her nose still in the book, he smiled over at her. Then he leaned in to give her a kiss.

"Good book?"

"Yeah."

"Well, it's a lousy game."

"Oh, I'm sorry."

"I'm not. I wanted to play with you instead anyway."

When she looked over at him and smiled that sweet coy smile she had, he murmured, "No, keep reading. I can do this without you."

Before she knew what was up, he had shifted the covers off her, moved to the bottom of the bed and maneuvered his way between her legs. Then he lifted her cute little Gilligan and O'Malley nightshirt up until his target was in sight. And he settled in to play.

A minute later, she dropped her book to the bed. He grinned, then went back to what he had been doing. As he held her open to his gaze, thumbing her lips and smoothing her moisture over them, he was thinking of the story she'd written about Callie, Rand and Clint. What little girl doesn't want her Daddy's approval?

The scars of Callie's emotional relationship had left a young woman in dire need of approval. Knowing she was desired hadn't been enough; she had needed to know she was cherished for her beauty in areas no one usually talked about. He didn't know Laurel's story but doubted it paralleled Callie's. While he knew some of her secrets, he didn't know them all. But the ones he did know, he could act on.

While his thumbs held her open and he gazed at her

with heated eyes, she squirmed and attempted to close her legs. Finally, she leaned up on her elbows, "What are you doing?"

"Admiring you. And from the way you're creaming up for me, it's really turning you on."

She arched a brow. "You think telling me that I'm 'lovely, smooth, silky, and as soft as rose petals,' down there, is turning me on?"

"Something sure is," he said with a huge grin.

"For God's sake Garrett, you're examining me like my doctor would!"

"Well, you must really like your doctor examining you then," he said as her slick coating ran over his thumb. He had never in his life seen a woman get this wet.

Her face flushed crimson, but she didn't say a word.

He raised the stakes. He bent her legs, put her feet flat on the bed, and pushed on her ankles until her knees were propped up.

So she wasn't ready to cop to wanting this yet. He pressed her, "Have I misread your body? Tell me what you want. Is this off limits, me being down here, looking at you?" he asked with a wave of his hand in the area of her genitals.

"Lord no! I like you being down there. I'm actually dying for you to kiss, lick, suck, or fuck me with your tongue . . . Please, just for a minute, if you could . . . put your mouth on me . . . If you could just . . ." her breath was snatched away as his mouth lowered and he bent to the task he'd had foremost in his mind since before he'd met her. He marveled at the woman spread before him, at her complete surrender to the passion that was now overwhelming her. He fought to hold back a chuckle as he continued to pleasure her with his tongue. Psychology be damned—did any man ever understand a woman? Despite all his foreknowledge, he was still learning her in stages.

All indications were that she absolutely loved what

he was doing to her, and that she couldn't get enough, as her legs tossed back and forth, her heels dragging on the sheets as she opened her legs and used her fingers to open herself wide for him.

"Yes, Yes!" she screamed.

God. was she ever hot, he thought as she dug her fingers into his hair and pulled him closer. Incendiary was more the word, he realized, as under his lips she bucked, thrust, and wailed through one of the most intense oral orgasms he'd ever been privy to.

Her uncontrolled keening did something to him, unlocked an emotion he didn't know he had. That desire to please her above all else. To love her and lave her until she came to the conclusion that there was no other man in the world for her, no other man who could complete her like this. He shoved his tongue deep inside her and went for round two.

With his tongue flattened, he rubbed hard against her, pressing and holding and then vibrating as he moved his head back and forth impossibly fast, increasing the downward pressure. Then his fingers speared into her as his tongue circled, pressed, circled, pressed, then sucked. He knew the second she rose to the edge and teetered off. She exploded, crying out her joyful release. Her labia swelled and rippled against his tongue, pulsing with an erratic rhythm. Her vagina went into convulsions and clenched around his fingers. Her whole body trembled long after her head slumped to the side of her pillow. She had ridden the wave of ecstasy and she was spent. She was female Gumby, and he was nothing, if not proud of himself.

By the time he'd taken her up and brought her down two more times, he had a whole new emotion churning in his gut for her. She was thoughtful, sincere, caring and knowledgeable, with a quicksilver fuse to multi orgasms that excited the hell out of him—she was perfect.

He climbed up her body and leaned over her, his hands braced beside her head. He positioned himself, then thrust. The dazed look in her eyes, the slumberous look of a woman well sated, and the welcoming lips of a woman starved for the taste of him, caused him to outpace his control and speed to his release. He knew he didn't have to concern himself with her, he could be as selfish as he chose—and he damn well was. His body surrendered to the ultimate pleasure of taking, his powerful orgasm rendering him helpless as he shuddered through the moment of crisis. He came out on the other side weakened and in total awe of the woman who lay beneath him.

He wasn't sure how long they lay entwined, dozing, but it was the sound of ice melting and shifting in his glass by the bedside that woke him. Her eyes fluttered open when he shifted to look at her.

"Hi," she whispered. "What timezz it?" she said in her sleepy, sexy voice.

"Three forty."

"I um . . . should tell you something," she said, and as she looked uncomfortable and nervous. He shifted to the side, for what he hoped would be a conversation leading to her confessing her passion for writing erotic stories. Her face was flushed, and not just from her body's reaction to her earlier orgasms—she gave every sign of being embarrassed. He waited for her to continue, and merely lifted a brow to indicate he was listening.

"I umm . . . well sometimes I . . . well, I fantasize. There I've said it."

"You're going to have to expound, I'm afraid I don't understand." When, in actuality, he knew all too well what she was trying to say.

"I lose myself in fantasies sometimes. I kind of become someone else. And I just wanted you to know, my imagination takes me into another woman's mind, and when

531

it's she who wants to be splayed for your ardent perusal, down there, it doesn't necessarily mean that I do. I really get into my character's heads and I hunger for what they want so desperately, that the need can become frantic if I let myself go. But that doesn't mean that *I'm* that way. What I'm trying to say, is that my sexual needs are uniquely my own. But while you're trying to figure them out with me, from time to time, some demon lady will take over and demand the strangest things. Like a while ago. So figuring out what I want and what she wants may be confusing."

"It will be my pleasure to please you both. And I take direction well, so don't ever hesitate to tell me what you or your lady friend want."

"Right now, my imaginary friend would like to see how well you accept pleasure—with or without an equalizing payoff." Her fingers danced over his reviving member as her tongue circled her lips as if doing warm up exercises. Reaching between his legs, she caressed his sac and made him moan. "Does that please you? Me touching you like this, in the middle of the night?"

His answer was to lift the covers up in invitation. "I can't wait to live out all your naughty little fantasies," he breathed as she slid down his body to latch onto him. Like a live wire his penis jumped as her exquisite lips tugged and ignited every nerve ending.

Dissolving into a sea of boneless lust, his hips undulated and he thrust his penis into her warmth as the primal intensity built. His desperate, plangent cries filled the room and sent his heart halfway up his throat when his release hit him, and he poured into her.

They slept like coon dogs after the hunt, nestled together, snoring slightly and all but dead to the world. Even the sun streaming in through the break in the drapes didn't rouse them. It was only when housekeeping knocked on their door at eleven that they untangled their limbs and faced the morning.

Chapter Sixty-four

They enjoyed a full breakfast at the hotel before heading out on the town. They took a carriage ride they enjoyed so much that they took it again. They walked and talked and looked at art, and visited church cemeteries, where they stood hand-in-hand, imagining life as it was for the townspeople in the late 1800s.

It was hot, so they were happy to find reasons to go inside for ice cream, whipped lattes, and a variety of elegantly designed pastries. He found a reason to kiss her at every street corner, and they laughed and teased each other. He bought her earrings she oohed over, and shoes she said she couldn't live without. She bought him a book that she thought all his students should read. He returned the favor. Then they sat in the shade under a tree in a park by the water, while he thumbed through *Nickel and Dimed, On Not Getting by in America,* and she became engrossed in *Graceful Submission.*

When the noticeable change in activity signaled the approaching dinner hour, he pulled her to her feet and led her back to the hotel.

"I have some work I have to do on the computer in the morning, so I'll leave it up to you when we leave. We can even stay an extra night or two if you'd like."

She smiled at him and shook her head, "I'd love to, but I can't. I've committed myself to a few projects for the community and I wouldn't feel right not showing up to help out."

"What is it this time?"

"I've arranged for a young couple to help educate parents and grandparents on the dangers of cube-shaped ponytail holders. Their daughter, Joy, was hurt very badly when she fell with one in her ponytail. The sharp edges act as a wedge, and on impact, crack the skull. She was in a coma for a long time and then she had to completely relearn how to use her motor skills. Those things are the fifth contributing factor for head injuries in girls under 14, yet they still sell them. So I'm helping Light of Joy Awareness get the message out.

"You sure do a lot for one woman."

"All of the homeowners at Ocean Ridge do. We like to make a difference. Ocean Ridge Charities Association donates handcrafted dolls for Lower Cape Fear Hospice and Life Care Center, and we recently donated $10,000 to support a family alcove. We do a lot for Brunswick Family Assistance and are a major sponsor for First Tee. The Rotary Club meets at Tamer's Restaurant for breakfasts on Fridays, and it seems the charity golf tournaments never end. It's a great community. The giving is spontaneous and heartfelt, which is a wonderful thing."

"Don't you ever get tempted to just write out a check and cover it all yourself?"

"It's the community effort that counts. It's what makes us friends, neighbors, a support group. Everyone needs to do his or her part. It's the giving and the volunteering that enriches. If I just sent a big check it would negate all that. Plus, it would out me. People would treat me differently if they knew how much money I had. The only ones who know are Tess, Viv and Cat—and their husbands, of course. In fact, they all advise me from time to time."

"Aha! So that's how you do it. One corporate raider,

one world-class investor, one ex CEO of the largest bank in the south . . . no wonder . . . and here I thought you were prescient or something."

"Well, everybody needs help figuring out where to put their money."

"This changes our bet. You're cheating. I'm surprised at you. I'll bet you're even getting inside information."

"No! I would never break the law."

He bent and kissed her on the cheek. "No, I don't believe you would."

He held the hotel door for her and watched her ass sway in the short-layered cotton skirt. He'd been itching to put his hands under it all day.

"I'd like to see you in those new shoes."

"I don't have anything to wear with heels."

"Did I say I wanted you to wear anything else?" he asked with a sideways smirk.

"You're not getting away with room service on our last night here," she said emphatically.

"So you want dinner on the town, huh?"

"No, just not in the room."

"Okay, let's rest for a bit then get ready and I'll take you anywhere you want to go."

"That sounds lovely."

"Is there someplace special you'd like to go, because we should make reservations."

"I want to go where I can see the water."

He opened the door to their room and followed her inside.

She turned and stroked his cheek, lovingly smoothed his eyebrows with her thumbs, then kissed him. "Surprise me. Meanwhile, I'm taking my new book and getting in the tub."

He ran his finger along her arm. "I'm all for you doing research on submissives," he whispered into her ear, then turned her and swatted her bottom.

When the door closed behind her, he booted up his computer and while he waited, he dialed the concierge. He was going to need some help with this. He wanted a nice place for them to eat, something that had a view of a marina, and someplace where he could hold her in his arms while he danced with her. As long as he liked.

Chapter Sixty-five

Two hours later there was a knock on their door and a well-dressed man informed them that their driver was waiting out front.

Laurel was putting her new earrings on. "Where are we going that we need a car? I thought you drove your truck here?"

He walked over to stand behind her, then put his hands on her shoulders. He kissed the side of her neck. "Yes, I brought my truck, but tonight I'd like to have a drink or two, maybe some wine . . . I'll let somebody else chauffeur us around. Plus, I don't know this city very well. This way I won't get lost."

"Oh." She stood back, and he admired her in the new V-neck shutter tucked dress he'd had delivered from the dress shop the concierge had recommended. It had been hanging from one of the bedposts when she'd come out of the steamy bathroom, and he had delighted in her reaction. It matched her new coral pumps perfectly. It should. He'd paid the personal shopper to go back to the store they'd bought them in, find the exact same pair of shoes, and match them to a size 6 dress.

"You are stunning. I can hardly believe that it's I who gets the honor of showing you off."

"Oh Garrett, you know exactly what to say to sweep a girl off her feet. But you look stunning too."

He'd had the hotel arrange a tux and all the accoutrements, and he was resplendent in black and white.

"There's nothing I wouldn't do for you, Laurel, so a little dressing up is no big deal." He took her hand, "C'mon, our chariot awaits."

Every head in the lobby turned as they made their way to the front door. People on the sidewalk stopped to watch as the extremely handsome man in the formal tux lifted the incredibly beautiful woman in the stunning dress into the lighted carriage.

She felt like Cinderella going to a ball—without the midnight curfew, she hoped.

"I can't believe you did this . . . this is wonderful."

"The best is yet to be," he murmured as he settled beside her and kissed her lightly on the lips, mindful of her perfectly glossed and glittering lips. People on the sidewalk clapped as they kissed.

"We're creating a spectacle," she said as she pulled back and her eyes met his. In his black tux, with the brilliant white shirt, his eyes were bluer, his impossibly full, thick lashes even sootier, and his lips, now with a tiny gleam of her glitter on them, were starkly sculpted against the dark shadows of the carriage, yet so inviting . . . so soft . . . so warm.

"In Charleston, it's all about setting the scene and being seen. Enjoy it."

He kissed her again and then wrapped his arm around her shoulders as the carriage lurched forward.

They drank in the sights of the city as the carriage lumbered through the old streets, turning this way and that, going through a maze of traffic until they turned off and followed the sounds coming from the harbor. Minutes later, they pulled up in front of a series of boat slips.

In front of the one Garrett was leading her to, was a small launch, and out in the distance a sailboat waited, lit up with white lights like it was Christmas.

"That's where we're having dinner?"

He smiled at her. "Room service of a different kind."

"I can't believe you went to all this trouble," she said as she was handed down a short wooden ladder to an officer in dress whites. Her grin was mesmerizing.

"Trouble? It's no trouble making you happy." He turned around and climbed down the stairs then turned back and retook her hand. He bent close and kissed the side of her neck as he added, "As I will demonstrate with an eager appendage a little later."

She flushed and he chuckled. Then he grabbed her around the waist and led her to the floating dock and the launch.

They rode the launch to the impressive sailboat moored in the harbor, and were welcomed aboard by the Captain and his four-man crew. A tour followed, and they were led around the ship to the dining area, where a silver champagne bucket stood beside an elegant table facing the shoreline. The lights of the city twinkled against the backdrop of the inky sky, as water lapped against the side of the ship.

As they sipped champagne from chilled glasses and dined on Marinated Shrimp, Caramelized Onion Tartlets and Seviche, they heard the engines turning over and felt the ship begin to glide through the water.

"Where are we going?" she asked.

"Just up the coast, past Isle of Palms."

"This is nice," she said and leaned back in her chair to gaze out over the water.

"Yes, it is. But I am discovering that anything I do with you is nice."

A server cleared their appetizer plates and brought them each a cup of Wild Rice Soup. That was followed by a Grouper Salad.

"I hope they don't bring anything else. I'm getting full," she moaned, rubbing her tummy.

But soon a pasta dish was put on the table and a server was heaping Bow-tie Pasta with Country Ham and Snow Peas with Asparagus on the pristine white china dishes that were resting on silver filigreed chargers. Accompanied by Rio Grande Roast Pork, and a Spicy Compote of Mango and Apricot, it was a meal she knew that the chef must have gone into a panic over, when told to prepare it with just a few hour's notice. For that reason, and that reason alone, she managed a few bites of each.

"No more! Or I will waddle off this boat," she protested when the chef began to set up a station to make Strawberry Cream Crepes.

Garrett waved him off telling him that there was absolutely no way either of them could eat another bite. With a polite bow and a knowing smile, his team whisked everything away.

A plate with tiny heart-shaped pieces of Hummingbird Cake was sent out along with a coffee tray and two snifters of Grand Marnier.

They took their coffee cups to a cushioned banquet where they could sit side by side under the stars, enjoying the coastline passing by.

When the musicians showed up and started playing soft, lilting strands of familiar love songs, Garrett put aside their cups, stood, and asked her to dance. She put her hand in his and he pulled her up. He held her in his arms and moved her expertly around the polished wooden deck, stopping with regular frequency to kiss her and to whisper how beautiful she looked in the moonlight as they danced to Eric Clapton's, *Wonderful Tonight*.

When fireworks were lit off the bow, she turned to him in astonishment, her mouth agape. "You are never going to be a billionaire this way," she said. He laughed and held her close, and breathed in the fragrance of her hair.

"No one's ever given me fireworks before," she breathed, spellbound, and unable to do anything but look up at the colorful display.

"That's interesting, because I've never given anyone fireworks before. But they sure do cap the night, don't they?" he said as a brilliant cascade rained down and left them suddenly in the dark. The fairy lights all around the ship had been set to go off at the same time, and now it was eerily dark. Seconds later, rope lighting lit the floor, and the steps leading both fore and aft.

A steward came out of the darkness and brought a silver lantern, which he handed to Garrett. "Will there be anything else this evening, sir?"

"No. Thank you, everything was perfect. Accolades to one and all."

"There is a fully stocked bar in the stateroom and a button on the phone should you need anything else. Good evening sir," he turned to Laurel and included her, "Madam."

When he had disappeared into the darkness, she turned to him and asked, "We're staying here, onboard ship?"

He smiled down at her. "Yes. While we were clomping along in the carriage the hotel staff packed us up and brought our luggage here. We're actually heading back home, we'll dock at Coquina Harbor in the morning."

"Oh Garrett," she sighed and her eyes sparkled with unabashed joy. She leaned up and kissed him.

"What about your truck?"

"A service is driving it back for me. It'll be there at the marina when we dock."

"Garrett, this must have taken you hours to plan. Thank you." She leaned up to kiss him on the cheek.

"I wish I could take credit, but it was all arranged by the concierge, all I did was call him, give him a limit, and hand over my charge card."

"What was the limit?"

"You don't want to know. But it was worth it, every penny."

"This was truly special. I can't believe you did all this."

"I wanted to show you a magical time, and I wanted to dance with you under the stars. Now, I want to take you below and show you an even better time."

"Well if you hadn't fed me to the gills, that might have been possible, but I'm too full to move."

"We have all night."

"I hope they didn't forget my book," she said wistfully.

He laughed. "You get to read about a woman experiencing the adoration of her Dom, and I get an economy lesson? How is that fair?"

It was her turn to laugh. "Show me the way to our bedroom and once I get my nice loose night shirt on, and get these beautiful but tortuous shoes off, I'll read you a few chapters."

"That's a deal." He grabbed a brandy snifter and handed it to her. Then he took the plate of heart-shaped cakes. "Fortification for later. If there are paddles and floggers involved I'm going to need a lot of cake."

She turned back for the other snifter, "If there are paddles and floggers involved, I'm going to need more brandy."

He laughed as he led her to their stateroom, and grinned when he saw her face light up as she admired the opulence. Done in the style of the 30s and 40s, it was over-the-top, down to the polished silver cigarette case monogrammed *Zelda* lying on the sofa table. As she slowly turned and cooed over the chandeliers, the mirrors over the bed, the lush polished wood, his heart swelled. She was so beautiful. And as uninitiated as he was in the ways of the haute-monde . . . she could easily own three ships like this, yet here she was, enchanted with having the use of this luxurious vessel for just one night.

If he'd doubted it before, he could doubt it no longer. He loved this woman—more than life itself.

He'd heard people say that—*more than life itself*— but never really knew what it meant. But he knew now. If this ship went down tonight, he would die trying to save her. For life without her wouldn't be worth living. She was his reason for breathing.

She stopped turning in a circles and stared at him. "You okay?"

He took both glasses from her and placed them on a table. "I'm fine. You just blew me away there for a minute. You are the loveliest thing I've ever seen."

"Oh, I doubt that!"

"Don't," he said as he spun her toward the bed. "Here, let me help you out of that dress. I'm anxious for you to read me a bedtime story." He was immediately reminded of *her* bedtime stories, and thought it might be a good time to let her know he appreciated good erotica. "Nothing like a well-told naughty tale. Read by a ravishing woman, this is going to be a real treat."

He began undressing her. "If you could read the book naked . . . that would make it all the better."

She lifted her arms and began removing the studs from his shirt. "Only if you're naked too."

Five minutes later they were propped up in bed, Laurel braced against Garrett's shoulder as she read to him while sipping brandy. Ten minutes later, she was fast asleep. An hour later he was still holding her and watching her sleep.

He could finally understand why Jack had been so determined to see Rose safe when the Titanic sank. Jack knew that if he'd tried to save his own life, that there was a chance he'd survive and that Rose wouldn't. That would be no life at all for him. He kissed Laurel's hair and settled her on the pillow. If he couldn't have Laurel in his life, he might as well go on deck and jump off the ship now.

Chapter Sixty-six

There was a gray fog moving past the porthole and just a glimmer of light bouncing back from the ship's lights reflecting off the water. Garrett leaned up to check the alarm clock on the nightstand 5:47. Almost dawn, but not quite. He was wide awake.

He looked down at the sleeping angel in his arms. With her blonde curls fanning the pillow, her rosy cheeks flushed, and her lips slack in an expression of trust and contentment, she looked like something divine. Celestial appearances aside, his body was awake, due to other aspects of her. Her rounded bottom was tucked snuggly into his groin and it was giving his penis a fit. Hard and innocently eager, as only a wakening penis can be, he had to consciously strain to hold back from nudging into her sexy little slit and taking her.

He moved her hair aside and kissed the back of her neck. She purred. He kissed his way to her earlobe and licked. She moaned. He blew a breath into her ear and drew the tip of his tongue around the whirl, and she pushed back against him.

Slowly he brought his hand around her waist, skimmed her torso and caressed her soft warm breast. From those soft, pursed lips she let out a sigh so enticing that he had to fight the urge to flip her over and taste her.

His fingers found her aureole smooth and velvety, the nub barely puckered. He gently stroked it back and forth until it became hard and needy under his fingers, then he lightly tugged and listened, as her breathing changed and her legs moved restlessly under the covers. She arched her back and thrust her bottom against him. As invitations went, it was pretty blatant, and Spearman was not about to decline a request to the world of heavenly delights.

Garrett took his time, moving his hand over her belly and stroking through her curls before separating her lips and inserting a finger inside her. His Laurel, was there ever a time she wasn't wet? It did a man good to feel a woman's want-you-so-much proof, especially like this, when he could just tip his hips and slide right into her.

He removed his finger with the intention of replacing it with two, but her mournful moan of disapproval decided his dilemma. He spread the precum over the head of his penis and placed it at her opening, then with slow, incremental shifts of his body, entered her fully. When he was totally encompassed inside her, he stilled so she could feel his dick pulsing and reacting to her tight, warm sheath. He could do this for a long, long time, but clearly Spearman wanted to explore . . . probe . . . thrust—feel the heat, feel the friction. His erection was awake and wanted to play.

He kissed along her neck and shoulder and listened to the sweet sounds of welcome coming from deep in her throat as her hips flexed and the muscles in her vagina clamped around him.

Slowly he moved. A long, slow withdrawal followed a smooth dominating reentry. More languorous and unhurried strokes followed until he finally set a rhythm that was designed for maximum friction, a power glide that thrust to the hilt then reversed itself to drag the sensations out until they both became frenzied with the repetition. He groaned against her and she pushed back to him, pulling one knee toward her chest so he could grasp her hip and angle in deeper. He heard her moans, her whimpers and her panting gasps, then he heard the sound he'd been dying to hear, a low shriek followed by, " Oh God, I'm coming, coming, coming," and then she did. He actually felt the release of liquid flow over him and coat the underside of his penis as he ground into her and erupted into the velvet fist that was milking him. Her name, a wild benediction, was repeated over and over again into her shoulder, as his mouth opened and closed over her skin, until the force of his virtual death from orgasm actually caused him to rear up and bite her. He didn't remember anything after that. Only came to when Laurel slid off him, laughing that she had to pee.

When she came back a few minutes later, she snuggled into his chest and smiled up at him. He managed to open his eyes and focus. God she was beautiful. And sexy. And sweet.

"I think I bit you."

"Yes, I think you did."

"Did I hurt you?"

She looked over her shoulder, "Nah, some nice teeth marks though."

"Really?" he was surprised. He'd never bitten anyone before. But then he'd never had an orgasm like that one. Building soft and sweet and exploding into a nuclear holocaust.

"That was nice," she murmured and kissed him on the chin."

"Nice is an understatement. That was phenomenal." He bent and kissed her on the tip of her nose. "For you too, I hope."

"Oh yeah. Problem is . . . now I'm energized while you look . . . well you look . . ."

"Well loved?" he prompted.

"Sleepy? Out for the count?"

"Believe me, I feel like it."

"I want to go on deck and watch the sunrise," she

said, shifting to sit cross-legged on the bed.

Her perkiness was going to be the death of him, more so than the orgasm that had catapulted him out of his body a few minutes ago. He groaned. "Okay . . . just give me a minute."

He tossed off the covers, made two attempts to sit up and finally sat with his legs over the side of the bed before walking toward the bathroom.

"If this is what sex does to guys, why do they want to do it all the time?" she asked as she scrambled into her underwear then put on the fleecy robe she'd found in a closet.

"Feels good at the time. Feels good every moment *up* to the time . . . already feels good thinking about the *next* time," he said with a wolfish grin as he disappeared behind the door. She noticed that he didn't bother closing it and wondered if that was a man thing, not minding anyone watching them pee. She supposed you had to get used to it. Girls were the only ones who usually had stalls, so maybe they *were* used to it.

She opened the door to go into the stateroom, and discovered a silver cart had been set up. There was coffee and a tray of assorted croissants. She grabbed a chocolate croissant and poured a cup of coffee from a pot that had a tag that said Hazelnut Regular. She walked upstairs and stood at the rail. A minute later Garrett joined her, in his own robe with his own mug of coffee. As she sipped and munched, she thought, did it get any better than this? Great sex, fresh hot coffee, rich chocolate, and a beautiful sunrise dawning with a man she was coming to love, standing beside her.

Chapter Sixty-seven

They arrived in Little River while they were eating an elaborate lunch, and, neither in a hurry to get anywhere, they sat on deck nibbling and watching the people and their dogs run around the marina. Theirs was by far the largest ship, so they got plenty of stares from both the boat owners working on their boats, and the tourists out for a stroll along the waterfront on a bright sunny day.

The crew helped them load Garrett's truck, that had arrived during the night, and after thanking everyone for their magical evening, Garrett surreptiously handed out generous tips. Then they were on their way home.

Laurel was surprised when Garrett pulled over after turning off Route 17. He put on his blinker and eased into Vereen Gardens. He followed the road to the end where there was a parking lot near the water.

"Why are we here?" Laurel asked.

"Two reasons," Garrett said as he parked, then turned to her, his arm on her seat back, his fingers play with her ponytail. "One, I'm not ready to leave you at your door yet. I know you have things to do, and so do I, but I know I will miss you as soon as I leave you. And second, we need to talk. About us."

"Us?"

"Us."

"What about us?" she asked.

"That's what I'm hoping to define." He brushed her cheek with the back of his hand. "I'm falling for you Laurel, and it's a big thing for me as I've never cared for a woman like this. Never. I'm not the love 'em and leave 'em type, but I've never been the take-her-home-to-meet-momma type either."

"Well, for my part, you know that can't happen." She said with a touch of irony.

"Okay, poor choice of words. What I meant to say is that what we have here," he motioned with his hand first to her then to him, "between us, is growing into something that might be of a more permanent nature."

"You're being so formal. We're in a relationship. I get it."

"Well, there are rules for relationships, aren't there?"

"Yes, yes there are."

"Well, let's do mine first, then we'll do yours."

She smiled over at him and said, "Okay."

"We agree we're exclusive. I don't see anyone else, and neither do you. This way when I travel up north or you travel someplace with your friends, we don't have to worry." He gave her a pointed look and she nodded.

"Just so we're absolutely clear, no one touches you but me, got it?"

She grinned from ear to ear. He really was new to all this. "Got it. Ditto you."

"Ditto me. And while I don't expect either of us to give the other a play-by-play of their day, we should share the significant things, the way couples do. Right?"

"Sure. We're a couple. I get that."

"I want to know where you are."

Her eyes went wide at that.

"I don't mean every second, but if you're going to Charleston for a few days, I expect you to tell me. I don't want to have to wonder where you are and if you're safe. So even if we're not seeing each other every day, we should at least spend a few minutes talking."

"Garrett, you don't have to go over all this. I'm sure that if we're not fighting, we'll spend lots of time on the phone. Probably more than you'll want."

He ran his finger down the length of her nose, "I'll always want to talk to you."

"You say that now . . ."

"I don't think there's such a thing as getting too much of you. I'm falling for you, and I hope you feel the same way about me."

"I think I may be slightly ahead of you. I may have already fallen. And I'm sitting here trying to figure out if I've survived the fall. It's why I had to leave, why I couldn't stay around waiting for your call. I'd already invested too much."

"You need to trust me."

"I do trust you."

"I'm not sure you do. And I need you to. I need that very badly."

"I trust you."

"Prove it."

"How?"

"You know I'd never hurt you, right?"

"Yes."

"From time to time I'm going to ask you to do some things, some you'll want to do, and others you won't." His voice got husky, "I want you to do them anyway."

"Because I trust you?"

"Yes. Because you trust me."

"What is it you want me to do?" she asked, skeptically.

"I want you to take your top off."

"You're serious?"

"Yes."

She was wearing a white halter-styled top over

yellow capris. He had watched her dress this morning. She wasn't wearing a bra.

She looked around and didn't see any other cars.

"There's no one around," he whispered.

"What if someone comes?"

"Trust me," he said and looked her in the eyes. "Trust me."

She hesitated, then unbuttoned the strap behind her neck and let the top fall to her waist.

He blinked momentarily and inhaled deeply, then opened his eyes fully to look at her.

Her breasts were almost white in the bright sunlight, her nipples pink. Her skin was creamy and her neck was dusted with tiny freckles. She was lovely. The sight of her was doing amazing things to him. He saw part of the bite mark on her shoulder and went instantly hard. Spearman was pleased that he had marked her.

"Take the top off completely and give it to me."

Slowly, she did as he asked, unbuttoning her top at the waist and pulling it off, then handing it to him, her eyes never leaving his. He could see that her breathing had accelerated, and that her lips were parted and she was panting.

He tossed it onto the back seat. She watched it land there, out of reach.

"You have lovely breasts. 36Cs?" he asked.

"Yes. Good guess."

"An *educated* guess, Miss Leighton. My hands are quite experienced. I've held many breasts in my hands. Squeezed, stroked, caressed, even slapped them."

"Slapped?" her eyes went wide. He registered her shock and had to keep from smiling.

"Sometimes you have to do what the lady wants whether you understand where her desires are coming from or not."

"Would you slap mine?"

"Do you want me to?"

"No."

"Then I won't. I won't hurt you Laurel, I told you that."

He got out of the truck, closed his door and came over to hers. He opened it and offered his hand to help her out.

"What? You want me to get out of the truck?"

"Trust me," he said in a low, gravely voice. And holding his hand out to her he waited. His eyes bounced from her eyes to her chest, and then back again.

"Somebody might see . . ."

"Trust me."

She scooted off the seat, sparing a quick glance at her top on the back seat. She timidly took his hand and stepped down. He closed the door and locked the truck.

She jerked when she heard the locks click. Somehow locking it, knowing she had no place to run for shelter, made it all that much worse. Or better? She had to admit she was unbelievably turned on, excited in a way she'd never explored, except through her naughty heroines. The road noises she hadn't heard before pricked her ears. She was aware of every sound now and she strained to hear the sound of gravel crunching on the road, knowing it would signal someone's approach.

Garrett clutched her hand tightly in his and led her around the truck to a wooden walkway.

"This fronts the waterway," she said with hesitation in her voice.

"Yes, it does."

"I don't think I can do this Garrett."

"Yes you can. Trust me. Do you trust me?"

She looked over at his face. He was looking at her chest, but then he raised his slumberous eyes to hers. "Well do you?"

"Yes," she breathed. "Yes."

"Good," he said and led her around a small cove and then off the decking onto a hiking trail. "Walk with me."

They walked through the woods, his hand holding hers, her topless and him staring at the sight she made. Seeing her like this, her naked breasts heaving against the backdrop of the forest, had quite the effect on him. It was primitive. Timeless. She was his Isolde. He was her Tristan. She was flushed with embarrassment, but aroused. It was highly erotic. He was a tad embarrassed for her, and the effect was staggering.

He wondered what she was thinking, how she was processing all this. He was pretty certain she was soaking her britches. They continued to walk along the path, going deeper into the woods.

"What if we come across someone?"

"We say hi and continue on."

"We what?"

"We say hi, and we keep going."

"You want someone to see me like this?"

"Not particularly. But *I* want to see you like this. *I* want to walk in the woods with you where I can see your breasts in all their naked glory. I am only focused on what *I* want right now. Not what you want. Or what another hiker wants, or doesn't want. This is what *I* want and I am enjoying myself immensely." He pulled her along after him and after a few moments, he spun her and leaned her up against the trunk of a big oak tree.

"This is hot. You, me, in the woods . . . you like this," His head ducked and he began making love to her breasts with his lips, tongue, fingertips, teeth. He sucked, nibbled, kissed, licked and mercilessly toyed with her pebbled nipples until they were distended, hard, and needy. She thrashed her head back and forth on the tree trunk. "Garrett, please." The yearning so intense . . . his teasing touches producing the desired result. She begged. "Please . . . please . . ."

"Please what baby?"

"Please make me come."

"You want to come?" His self-assured smirk spiked her pleasure.

"Yes!" she demanded. "You can humiliate me, shame me, force me to beg, but you damn well better deliver," she breathed as her hand closed over him and squeezed.

His fingers undid the button on her capris and he pulled them to her knees, he slid himself down and took her panties to her thighs. He sat back on his heels and looked up at her radiant face. "You look so hot, so unbelievably hot. I want to fuck you so badly." Questing lips fed on her, sending pulses surging through her body. His kisses were warm and thorough, very thorough, his tongue darting boldly into hidden crevasses, thrilling her even more.

He looked up and smiled at her, his salacious eyes causing a pleasant riff of awareness to ignite and blaze through her. She was out in the open, in the great outdoors— all but naked. It was primal, uncivilized, and it was so fucking hot. That he somehow knew how this was affecting her was suffusing her with pleasure too. He was a partner in her pleasure, and at that moment she trusted him with her soul. The slavish control he had over her devastated her senses. In this moment, she was his. She belonged to him.

He stood, took her wrists and pinned them together with one hand over her head, against the rough bark of the tree, as if reminding her where they were, and how dangerous and wild this was. He kissed her, diving deep with his tongue, snaking it all around, making sure she knew without a doubt where his mouth had just been. All the while, his free hand played over her body, fingers tugged roughly on nipples too hard to bear, and his hand squeezed one breast, then the other as he kissed her, his tongue now coaxing hers into a strenuous workout. When he left her lips to begin kissing her neck, her throat, her collarbone, she whimpered, "Garrett, please . . . please. I need you."

"Soon baby," he breathed against her neck, as his hand parted her thighs and two fingers filled her. "Soon," he whispered again.

When she was practically climbing up his hand he broke away and stepped back. He walked backward until he was several feet away. "You look amazing. You have magnificent tits, and the most beautiful cleft." He was using the same words she had used in her story about Julia. He wondered if she would recognize them. Julia and her duke had been in an orchard . . . they were in the woods. Julia had been propped against a tree . . . and so was she. Would her mind make the connection to her fantasy?

He thought it might, as her eyes went glassy and pleasure suffused her from head to toe as she trembled with urgent, wanton need. He watched as a fever of hunger washed over her, he fed it as he stood before her unbuttoning and unzipping his pants. He pulled out his erection, pumped it twice, showed her the evidence of his desire wetting the tip. "Is this what you want?"

"Yes," she breathed.

"Then this is what you shall have."

He strode back to her, stripped her of pants and panties, and then used her pants as a buffer between her and the tree as he braced her against it. He gripped a buttock in each hand, lifted her legs high and impaled her. She clasped him around his neck and began to ride him feverishly, but soon became frustrated because she didn't have the strength to continue. He shifted his hands to her lower back to protect her from the force of his ardent thrusts as he lifted her from him and then slammed her back down, over and over again. With powerful arms he seated and unseated himself as she fought to stay with him.

He kissed her chest and sucked on her nipples as she cried out and he thrust harder. She almost toppled him over when she used her hands on his shoulders to drive herself onto him as she started to come. She keened into his neck and sobbed, "I just can't get it."

"Yes, you can baby," he said and gripped her buttocks tight. He lifted her and practically dropped her down onto him as he jammed a finger into her ass. She jerked and every muscled tightened just before she found her release and she spasmed out of control. "Gotcha." He whispered in her hair as he felt every tingle, every shiver, every rhythmical clutch of her vagina as she climaxed, not once, not twice, but three times.

"Would you be thinkin' it'd be my turn soon?" he asked with a touch of humor as she panted in his ear. He took her to the ground, and on a floor of pine needles he plowed into her, ejaculating almost immediately into her honeyed center. "I love you, Laurel," he breathed as the wave crashed over him and took him.

She looked up into dazed eyes. He looked down into eyes bright with tears.

"You love me?" she asked.

"Yes. You trusted me," he said.

"Yes."

"You won't let anyone else fuck you?"

"No."

"Then we're good." He lifted himself off of her and stood. After he put himself back together, he put his hand down and helped her to stand. He helped her into her panties and mangled pants and then smacked her butt. "Okay, trailblazer, lead the way."

"What about my top?"

"You didn't have one getting here as I recall."

"But what if . . . I mean there could be a ranger or something."

"You'd pretty much make his day."

But he understood that needs changed, horny and hot,

things seemed somehow acceptable, less over the top—sated and in a normal state of mind, self-consciousness slipped back in charge. He pulled a bandana from his back pocket. "I was saving this to blindfold you with, but I suppose you can use it to cover those luscious mounds of yours, but *only* if we hear someone coming, understand?"

"Yes sir."

"Kiss me,"

She took his face in her hands and kissed him hungrily. Then stepped back and bit her lip. "How was that?"

"As topless wenches go, you'll do. You'll do quite well."

He pretended to maul her breasts and then began walking her backwards through the woods. He watched her tits shake and jiggle as he coached her to step over branches and lifted her over logs.

"I'd love to take you to Fantasy Fest in Key West one day. I'd paint your breasts like daisies, leaving the tips bare for everyone to see."

She just about swooned at the thought of being naked except for body paint in front of so many people. That festival drew thousands, tens of thousands. "Would you really like that?" She wasn't sure she would—in her fantasy world she'd eat it up, but in the real world, she knew she'd be afraid, nervous, self-conscious.

"I love you naked, Laurel, and I wouldn't be ashamed to show you off. But it seems to me that if you're on edge about the occasional hiker, maybe that's not such a good plan." God, he'd die if she really wanted to show her body off to strangers. She was his. He didn't want to share her. He just wanted to make her happy.

"You're right, it's probably not something I could ever really do. But I love playing these games with you, thinking about it and actually envisioning it." She stopped walking and held his face in her hands, "I love you, Garrett. You are an amazing man."

He caressed her naked breasts as he looked down into her face. "You make loving you easy, so easy. I love you like this. Topless for me, just for me." He bent and kissed each breast then bound them in the bandana. "One day, you'll walk completely naked in the woods with me."

"Will you be naked too?"

"No."

"Why not?"

"That's just not the way it is in most fantasies."

"Yours or mine?"

"You tell me."

"Hmmm. Now that I think about it, you're right, the man's always dressed. Why is that?"

"Maybe, because in your fantasies you want to be submissive to a man. And that's how you show it. You let him strip you of your clothes and then you let him do what he wants. Walking naked out in the open with a man gives him possession of you. You become his. His to do with as he pleases."

"That's how it was with us. You did as you pleased with me."

"Yes. That I did."

There was a long silence as she turned to face front, and they walked back to the truck. As he was lifting her into the truck she looked into his face and said, "I trust you, Garrett."

"Good, because I'm going to keep pushing you."

"I think I'll be fine with that."

"No complaints then, next time when you're totally naked, with a butt plug in your ass."

"Whoa, whoa."

He smiled, "Just testing the boundaries. So I suppose, we'll end up somewhere in between."

"God, I hope so."

He bent and kissed her. "You're so much fun to tease."

"Sometimes I'm not sure you're teasing."

"Sometimes, I'm not."

Chapter Sixty-eight

Friday, they both cleared their schedules for a day of fun. It promised to be a glorious day on the beach, and as they'd both been busy on Wednesday and Thursday, they hadn't seen each other since returning from Charleston.

Garrett picked Laurel up at seven, then after a quick run to get flat bagels from the Bagel Dock, they went to Garrett's beach house for breakfast.

After unloading all the groceries she had packed, and getting a quick tour of the house, Laurel found her way around his kitchen and made her special wake-me-up fruit smoothie. Made with fresh strawberries, pineapple, fat-free milk, and the scrapings from a fresh vanilla bean, it, along with a bagel, gave them the energy to spend the morning kayaking through the marshes and along the Intracoastal.

After cooling showers and reciprocating oral sex, they'd had a mid-morning nap and then a lazy lunch on his deck. A long walk on the beach was next, and then Laurel talked Garrett into letting her plant some flowers in the front beds. So it was off to the nursery. While she lovingly planted the impatiens and jasmine plants they'd bought at Shady Oaks, he refreshed her with mimosas.

They talked while they worked, and Garrett was treated to a mini-dissertation on damselflies and dragonflies. He'd never known the differences between the two, and was surprised there were so many varieties. He was impressed when she rattled off a few names, and pointed out a red skimmer on a blade of grass, saying its favorite foods were flies, midges, gnats and mosquitoes, adding that we should bow to them. And then he laughed when she did.

For dinner, Garrett offered to run over to the mainland for Chinese food and more champagne. They'd been leisurely sipping mimosas from big acrylic wine glasses, and when she asked for a refill, he'd discovered that they'd used the whole bottle.

Laurel was reading her book about the submissive Grace, and marveling at how one could so quickly be eased into the submissive lifestyle, for the right person. She had just finished a steamy scene, and could not imagine delving into another interlude right now, so she decided to check her email. It had been two days since she'd checked it. She'd brought her laptop this morning, but Garrett had kept her so busy, she hadn't had time to even turn it on.

She discovered she had left her wireless mouse on her desk at home, and got up to open Garrett's laptop case to get his, as they both preferred working with a wireless mouse rather than using a keyboard mouse. She unzipped a compartment looking for it and pulled out a small baggie instead. There was something red in it.

She shook the bag, and her eyes went wide with shock. It looked like her missing flash drive. She couldn't believe it at first, figuring that it couldn't possibly be hers, but it looked just like hers. Even the Ziploc with the blue and yellow stripe that turns green when zipped looked like the kind she used. She found the mouse, plugged the receiver in, booted up her laptop, then plugged the flash drive into the USB port. As soon as she opened the file, which now bore the name Laurel instead of just Backup, she knew.

Dread filled her chest as panic took over. She scanned the file titles. They were all so familiar to her. She cringed as she read the file names, recalling the story each held. He'd read these. He'd read her most private thoughts. He knew her secrets—her dirty fantasies and dark secrets. Her core began to tremble. Her hands and feet felt numb. Tears welled in her eyes. And she was filled with shame. Horrified with what he knew about her. Humiliation filled her. Then anger built. Her temperature rose and her heartbeat accelerated at an alarming rate. Her head began to throb. She rubbed her fingers over her eyebrows, back and forth, back and forth. Agitated and tense, as the anger built, it grew like a mushroom cloud until she felt ready to explode from it. Her heart, pumping like a sledgehammer with each fresh surge of blood, was loud in her ears. She felt as if she could drown in the sound.

He'd known from the beginning. *He* was the one who had found it that day. And all this time, he'd satisfied his own prurient nature, reading about hers, delving into every single private thought she'd had about sex and how she wanted to do it, have it done to her, with her . . . . *My God.* Tied, bound, gagged, exposed, shamed. She stood there humiliated beyond believing. And trembling with rage. Images came unbidden—her strapped naked to the bedpost in Charleston, walking topless in the woods at Vereen Gardens, without her panties at the Inlet View . . . and then her skirt lifted, by him, in the elevator!

She began to pace. So he'd searched her out, found a nice little sex toy, an eager and willing slut to play with. And while he touched, caressed, fondled, and shamed her, all the time he had been laughing at her, giving her what he knew she wanted, but was afraid to ask for.

She thought of the way he teased her, kept her from coming, making her beg for release. Oh, he must have loved that. Dangling the carrot, then taking it away, dangling it again, and finally using his power to control her by making her come at his command. That bastard! She slammed the top down on her laptop, jerked the flash drive out, belatedly realizing it wasn't the proper way to remove the devise, and cursed. Well, what did it matter if she lost all her files again, she had backups. Backups! Knowing him, he'd have her file on his hard drive. Damn him!

She woke his computer and systematically deleted her files, then trashed everything that was in his recycling bin. She was never going to have her thoughts all to herself again if he had his own backup system. And most assuredly, he did. Probably had his stuff in the clouds somewhere. She huffed. Well, nothing could be done about that.

She grabbed her shoulder bag, tossed in her laptop and slung the strap over her head settling it between her breasts. She took a look around and saw the empty baggie sitting by his laptop. He'd know as soon as he saw it, that she'd found out *his* secret. But it would be too late. By the time he got back, she'd be gone.

As she ran down the steps she realized she could pass him if she ran along the street, and she couldn't face him now. But she wanted to have the satisfaction of him returning to an empty house, seeing the empty bag by his laptop, and realizing she had discovered his deceitfulness.

She turned around and went back through the house to go down the stairs that led to the beach. Her nerves were on edge, every muscle taut with anger, but she could feel a calming force drawing her to the west end of the island and toward the Kindred Spirit.

Chapter Sixty-nine

When Garrett returned to the house five minutes later, he instantly sensed that something was off. He called out to Laurel, and when she didn't answer, he put down his packages and walked through the house calling her name.

When he'd checked every room on every floor, he went back to the great room and then to the kitchen to see if she'd left a note. There was nothing on the kitchen counter. He walked over to the side table by the phone where he kept a notepad—nothing there. He stood hands on hips and turned in a slow circle, and that's when he saw it. The empty baggie. *Shit!*

In two quick strides he was at his laptop. The flash drive was missing. He woke his computer. His fingers flew. Her files were missing. And the recycling file had been dumped. Oh God, she knew. And clearly, she wasn't happy about it!

He raced to the front door but then realized he'd have seen her if she'd left by the street side. He ran for the back door, grabbing his binoculars from the bookshelf as he went. Once on the deck, he scanned the beach. Heading west was a fluff of blonde hair. He brought the lenses up to his eyes and focused on her. There she was, marching at a brisk pace, her hands moving ardently with each stride. *Oh, she was pissed.*

He took a minute to kick off his loafers and tie on his Asics Gel running shoes. If she didn't start running, he could catch her. She had her purse, he'd noted, and of course she would have taken her MacBook.

He ran down the back stairs, leaping down the last three and ran down the decking to the beach.

As he ran, he tried to figure out what to say. He should have told her. He should not have tried to capitalize on the intimate knowledge of her sensual mind, once things had heated up with them emotionally. He'd been an ass, and now he could see, as the blonde bobbing head in front of him continued moving in a steady line down the beach, that she was going to be a tenacious fighter.

He caught up close to her at the 4th Street access. She turned when she heard someone running, faced back and began an all-out sprint, when she saw it was him. Dusk was settling and there were only a handful people on the beach, as it was the dinner hour, so she had a clear field. But she didn't have the power he had, or the stamina to sustain her for a long distance at a full run.

He managed to come along side but she wouldn't listen to his pleas to stop and talk. He finally gave up asking and tackled her to the sand. He eased her fall, taking the brunt of it as he landed on his side and then rolled with her until she ended up under him, the center of his body notched into the core of hers, their legs entwined. He levered himself to his elbows and looked into her anguished face.

"Don't touch me!" she screamed.

"Damn it, we're going to talk—every emotion you can't handle right now—let it out. Tell me what a snake I am. Yell and scream at me if you need to. But you're going to talk to me!"

"You used me!"

"You wanted me to use you!" he said returning fire with fire. Then he softened his voice and stroked her cheek with the back of his fingers. "You loved everything we did," he stared down at her, "every kinky thing. Admit it. You know you enjoyed it—immensely. And so did I."

"You found my flash drive! You had all my private thoughts right at your fingertips. That's despicable!"

"Maybe. So I had a cheat sheet. But I had no choice. I was trying to find you so I could return the flash drive to you. Inconveniently, you did not attach a name or phone number to it. I had no choice but to open the files. I spent almost a month trying to track you down just from clues I divined from your stories, and from your entries on Quicken. You don't know how many times I went to that Food Lion, trying to figure out if each woman getting out of her car and walking into the store could be you. It was your article on flowerboxes and flowering chives that finally led me to you. I played a lot of courses looking for those damn green and yellow boxes." Their eyes met, hers still fired up.

"I lost it at Food Lion?" she spat out, disbelief in her tone.

"Yeah. I found it on the asphalt in the cart return area."

She pushed against his chest. "Get off me."

When he didn't move, she hissed, "Get off me now or I'll scream."

There were people close enough to come to her rescue, and he didn't see how getting arrested was going to help the situation. He lifted himself up and offered her his hand. She ignored it and got to her feet by herself.

She brushed off the back of her jeans, and then forced him to back up as her finger jabbed into his chest. "I don't have a problem with you finding it, not even with reading what was on it. But I *do* have a problem with you not telling me. And an even bigger one with you stalking me . . . pretending to get to know me when you already knew a lot more about me than anyone on the planet. You didn't even tell me when we talked, shared our lives . . . talked about everything that mattered . . . you could have told me!" She was hissing and sobbing between words, the pitch of her voice rising to compensate.

Now she was deadly serious as she fought to control her trembling chin. "I want you to leave me alone. I never want to see you again. Ever!"

She spun on her heel and he watched her walk away.

"Laurel! Please! I was going to tell you. I was waiting for the right time. Laurel, please don't go!" he shouted. "Let me drive you home at least!"

She ignored him and continued up the beach, turning toward the Ocean Ridge Club house and walking diagonally up the beach toward it.

He watched her cross the empty parking lot, stomp the sand from her shoes, and use her coded card to go inside. He stood staring, trying to figure out which floor she was on, and what she was doing. But he knew. He knew she was on the floor in the foyer, crying her heart out. And at that moment he would have bought ten houses in Ocean Ridge just to have the access card to get in there so he could hold her, and wipe away her tears.

He stood, watching the multi-leveled clubhouse, seeing all the lights on in the windows, but not seeing her. He stood for what seemed like hours, then he saw what he recognized as Roman's car pull into the parking lot on the street side. He saw Tess get out on one side and Roman on the other. Then they both disappeared inside the house. Fifteen minutes later, he saw Roman carrying Laurel to the car and placing her on the back seat. Tessa slid in from the opposite side and Roman closed the door. Then he got in the car and they drove away.

As simple as that, she was out of his life. And he was Jack, drowning in the frigid waters of the Atlantic.

Chapter Seventy

Roman and Tess took Laurel to their house after they'd heard the story, as Roman was certain that Garrett would come looking for her. One look at Laurel, huddled in Tessa's arms, and he knew she wouldn't be able to deal with him right now. So while Laurel poured her heart out, and Tess consoled, he poured wine—copious amounts of it.

When Laurel finally fell asleep, he carried her to the guestroom. While Tess removed her jeans and tear-drenched shirt, he went to get one of his t-shirts for her.

Then he left her to Tess and got their own bed ready. He knew as soon as Tessa climbed in that she would go off on Garrett, and he didn't want to miss his fiery bride's tirade. Sex after one of her explosions was earth shattering. He was about to capitalize on the poor schmuck's piss poor sense of timing. Because he was dead certain that Garrett was planning on telling her, that he was just doing what any man would do, and prolonging a good thing for as long as he could.

"That man! He should have his balls pinched with pliers. How could he do such a thing to such a sweet young girl."

"From the gist of her story, she's not so sweet and innocent. Writin' erotica . . . wait 'til Philip gets a load of this."

"Oh, by now he knows. She called Viv and Cat from

the clubhouse and left messages that they both returned about an hour ago. We've agreed to take shifts keeping that bastard away from her."

"Are ya sure that's the best ting?" his heavy brogue completely obliterated the h in thing, but she found it endearing and mimicked him.

"Aye. I tink it's the best ting."

"Dooo ya now?"

She laughed. "Yes. She doesn't want anything to do with him and I promised we'd keep him away."

"For how long?"

"As long as it takes."

"As long as what takes?" he asked.

"As long as it takes for her to realize she can't live without him."

"Ahh, like you not bein' able to live without me."

She smiled over at him. "I did miss you while you were gone."

"Well, lass, let me see if I can make it up to you . . . show you how much my randy self missed you, too." He used the remote to dim the lights then covered her body with his.

"What if Laurel hears us?"

"As she and Garrett were hot and heavy, I'm thinkin' she'll recognize the sounds, and know I'm not truly killin' you—just doin' the tiny death thing."

"La petite mort," she corrected.

"Yeah, tiny death, just like I said." He shushed her next comment by capturing her mouth under his.

Chapter Seventy-one

Garrett knew there was no way he could get to her tonight. Judging from the way Roman and Tess had closed ranks around her, it could be days before he'd be able to see her and talk some sense into her.

But time would be his ally, of this he was certain. Once she had time to think things through, she'd come around. Because it really was a stupid fight. After all, they loved each other, right? How could her discovering his perfidy change that?

But knowing that didn't ease the panic, or take away the gut wrenching fear that he might have fucked up the best thing that had ever happened to him.

He walked slowly back to the beach house. He forced himself to put one foot in front of the other to climb the steps that led up to the deck. Then he locked himself in and paced. At the front window he looked outside at the flowerbeds he'd helped her install just this afternoon. Was it really less than four hours since they'd laughed at the antics of the red skimmer, and he'd learned more than he ever wanted to know about damselflies and dragonflies?

As he stood staring out at the street disappearing in the dark, he faced up to the problem. He'd screwed up. And now it was up to him to make amends. He walked over to his computer, tapped the space bar and brought it to life. He went online and ordered flowers, dozens and dozen of flowers.

Bulbs, arrangements, dish gardens. Everything beautiful that he thought she'd smile at, he ordered and keyed in her address for it to be shipped.

Then he went to Mozy.com and had his backups downloaded. He felt a little relieved to have her files back in place on his desktop. In an effort to be close, he opened one of her stories and began reading.

It was one of her historicals, which he thought she did rather well, considering he only read contemporary fiction because he pretty much hated historicals. It was a story about *Primae Noctus* or Law of the First Night. In France it was called *droit du seigneur* or The Lord's Right.

It was an eye-popping story about ritual defloration, where newly wed Scottish brides had to spend the first night of the nuptials with the English nobleman governing the fiefdom. The *culagium*, a required fee the lord could opt to collect, to forego being physical with the new bride, was so steep few bridegrooms could afford it.

In reading the story, he learned that once upon a time, even the clergy exercised the right of first night for granting permission to marry. Needless to say, it was a jaw-dropping story, as Laurel told of a young Scottish lass of the clan Macintosh, who after surrendering her virginity to the Earl of Kilmarncok, was not released. After taking his rights of first night, he decided he wanted her for all his nights, and refused her husband's demands to release her to him. He ended up petitioning the Bishop for an annulment and in so doing, battling with most of his clan, so he could marry her himself.

In his wildest imaginings, he would never have thought a rape scene would have aroused him so. But Laurel had managed to weave the story in such a way that the reader got a foreshadowing of the epic love story that would soon follow.

The Earl's subsequent nights of lovemaking to the

beautiful Brianna fueled his ardor, and over the next two days, Garrett found himself back on the "sauce," appropriately named Extra Virgin Olive Oil.

Of course Brianna ended up with child, and a marriage was facilitated, due to the laws of primogeniture, which regarded the rights of a first-born child of the nobility as sacrosanct.

In a happily-ever-after scenario, the Earl provided the disenchanted bridegroom with a new wife, one sturdier and more capable of being his helpmate than his own fair and delicate Brianna . . . who remarkably bore the Earl twin sons without so much more than a sneeze.

He had laughed at her ending, as she had wrapped it all up as a fairytale cum fable with its own moral to the story: Thou shall not covet the promised hand.

At 1:15, he stood, heaved a big sigh, tossed out the untouched Chinese food, and made his way to bed.

He was going to win her back. He had no choice. He couldn't live this way after knowing how wonderful the alternative was.

He woke up at 3:55, and wrote his own short story, *The Things I Love About You*. By 9:05 he had proofed it a dozen times, printed it, and taken it to the post office to mail.

The Things I Love About You

I love how your neck smells when I nibble on it.
I love the arch of your foot and how it feels to caress it.
I love how you give me a wicked smile then dive
under the covers.
I love how your breath hitches when I kiss you
behind your ear.
I love how you entice and remove your clothes
ever so slowly.

Flash Drive

I love how you let my eyes linger as long as they
are inclined to.
I love how you flutter, hiss, tremble, and call out my name.
I love how your psyche works—naughty being the first
word that comes to mind.
I love how you look when you sleep, like God's
angel on Earth.
I love how you stand, hand-on-hip, in high heels and a
mini skirt—confident and sexy.
I love how you keep losing your panties, while I find them
in the strangest places.
I love how you taste. Everywhere.
I love everything about your breasts. Everything.
I love that you like to suck my penis. And swallow.
I love that you trust me. In all things.
I love how we thrust together as if we are of one mind.
One body. One soul. But many climaxes.
I love you.
And I am very sorry.
Please forgive me.

Garrett

Chapter Seventy-two

Laurel woke as if in a fog, and pretty much stayed that way as she went through her morning routine, making the guest bed, brushing her teeth and showering by rote. The heaviness in her heart was downright painful at times, and the tears, well . . . no matter what she did or Tessa said, they just kept coming.

A cheery breakfast on Tessa's back deck with both Viv and Cat patting her hand didn't help. Nothing helped. She was miserable and afraid to go home.

Sometime during the night, in one of her anxiety-filled spates of wakefulness, she had forced herself to relive the events of the past weeks. Dredging through the banter, the looks, smiles and laughter, and the sex. If for no reason other than to accept the things that had seemed so perfect at the time, that now seemed too perfect to believe were real. She had been a fool. When she thought of the things they did together, she burst out in fresh tears. She had been too trusting. And that hurt the most. Yes, she supposed she had a penchant for humiliation, but not this way. Never this way.

It took two days to get her home, and then she tugged on everyone's arms when they tried to leave her.

When they found the note the local florist had tucked in the door, Viv put it in her pocket saying, "At least he sent flowers—the universal form of apology. I'll call and take care of this for you."

Laurel hung on Tessa's shoulders. She was still in her pj's.

"Laurel, you're going to be fine. It's just going to take a little time. Do some normal things—pay some bills, make a big pot of spaghetti sauce, do some weeding in the garden. Do what you normally do." Tess tucked a curl behind Laurel's ear and wiped a damp cheek.

"Except don't drink any wine, not a drop," Cat said.

"We'll be back later to take you for a walk on the beach and then out to dinner. The guys are playing poker, so it'll just be us. So take a shower and get dressed. You have to eat."

"I can't. It hurts to swallow. Nothing goes down."

"I know, baby," said Viv. "We'll try some soup."

"Try not to take a nap, so you'll sleep tonight, okay?" Tessa admonished. "Trust me, things will look better soon. Just get over the next few days. Things will look brighter. Remember, you're not the only one to go through this. It's almost a right of passage."

"I just feel so stupid."

"You didn't do anything wrong. Stop beating yourself up over it."

"I miss him," she whimpered, and then began crying all over again.

Tess pulled her close and whispered in her ear. "I know baby, I know. They wrap themselves around our hearts so quickly. Go dig a hole, burn off some of that angst. Why don't you start working on that pond you were thinking about?"

" 'kay," Laurel said with a sniff. 'You guys go, I'll be all right." She sniffed again. "But it's going to be a big pond."

They all laughed, hugged her again and quickly made their way back to the car before the waterworks began again.

As they got in the car, Viv snarled, "We oughta go find that jerk and call him out."

"As we speak . . . ," Tessa said with a sardonic smile.

When the vanload of flowers arrived, Laurel held up long enough to help the deliveryman get them all on the terrace. Then she broke down and cried until she fell asleep. When she woke in the afternoon, she began rationalizing from his perspective. Because it seemed he really did love her. Maybe she was making too big a thing out of him keeping the knowledge of her flash drive's whereabouts a secret from her.

When clouds covered the sky and a steady drizzle of rain cloaked everything outside her windows and sent the golfers running for their carts, she called Tess and told her she wasn't up for going out. She promised she'd eat some soup and make a grilled cheese and ham sandwich.

Then she went out in the rain and potted her new bulbs and planted her new plants, getting soaked to the skin but having a resurgence of life as sensation starting coming back to her in the form of the stinging rain.

Chapter Seventy-three

Garrett was sitting at the table checking his email when he heard three doors slam. He walked over to the window and stared down. His head jerked as he recognized Matt, Roman, and Philip. All three were bent over the trunk of a Lexus. They were taking things out, but from his angle, he couldn't see what. He remembered their warnings about not hurting their little girl under pain of death. He had to admit, he was a little unnerved as he tuned back to get his cell phone to tuck into his pocket.

He heard them clomping up the steps, then the bell rang.

He opened the door to three frowning men.

"Ya fucked up man," Philip said as he pushed his way inside. He was carrying a big pizza box.

"Big time," added Matt, as he strolled in behind Philip, nearly pushing Garrett aside. He swung a big bottle of Jack Daniels by the neck.

"Bloody royally," Roman muttered as he followed the first two, a case of Guinness gripped by his fingers in the cardboard slot.

Garrett shut the door behind them and shook his head. He knew he was in for it, but damned if he was going to go down without a fight. "What the hell was I supposed to say? I read your kink? That I wanted to play with you? And don't tell me that any one of you would have let the opportunity pass."

Roman let out a big sigh. "No, you've a point there. But I might h' found a way while she was screaming with the big 'O' ta mention what ya found."

Matt plopped himself down on an oversized leather ottoman. "So how'd this happen? How'd you get yourself in this fix?"

Garrett rubbed the back of his neck with one hand and took the shot of Jack Philip handed him with the other. He slid onto one end of the sofa with a big sigh. "You ever read any of her stories?" he asked the group in general.

Each man, in turn shook his head.

"Didn't know she wrote any," Roman said with a grin, "but I'm happy to oblige and read a few."

"Oh, that would get me in her good graces for sure," Garrett said with a fair amount of sarcasm. "Let's just say they had me on edge for weeks, until I finally tracked her down. And I admit, I was in no small hurry to bed the woman. But honestly, I wasn't in this just for the sex. I like the woman, liked her from the start."

He stood and paced the room. "Hell, who am I kidding? I love the woman. And I want her back."

Roman smiled and lifted his glass to him, "Well, curiously, that's why we're here. With the blessing of our wives, I might add."

"Hell, I just wanted to meet her and let her gradually get to know me the way I knew her. I just ran out of time," Garrett said.

"And was it worth it, doin' it that way?"

"God yes. To hear her . . . never mind. Let's just say it's never been better."

"Then you probably want more?" This from Philip.

"Lots more."

"How much more?" Matt chimed in.

"What do you mean by that? How much more is

there?" Garrett said as he thrust long fingers into his hair.

All three raised their left hands and pointed to their wedding bands.

"Yeah, there is that," he said with a snort. "And you really think she'll listen to me long enough for me to ask?"

"We have an idea. Go put your running shoes on."

Twenty-five minutes later he was bent over, hands on knees puffing into the wind. The Kindred Spirit Mailbox stood before him, stalwart and comforting as he gathered his breath and his thoughts.

Dear K.S.
While not meaning to, I managed to screw up the best thing that ever happened to me. Long story short . . . I found something, tried to return it, but then didn't when I finally managed to discover who it belonged to.

People meet in unconventional ways. We all run in different circles so I doubt I would have met her if not for her lost flash drive. I'm sorry I stalked her, but she unbalanced me, and I thought I needed the special edge I had to guarantee my suit. I couldn't take the chance that I wouldn't win her. So like any good gambler I used the advantage I had.

I think I fell a little in love with her long before I met her in Southport, and was desperately in love with her before the day was through.

She was meant for me. I know that more than I know my name. It wasn't an accident she lost her flash drive, and it wasn't a coincidence that I was the one to find it. It was God, smiling down on both of us and giving us the miracle we were both waiting for. I love her and I want her for all time.

If she could find it in her heart to forgive me, I would like to ask her to become my wife. To marry me—here on this beautiful beach.

Chapter Seventy-four

With tears in her eyes, Laurel got off the bench and went back to the mailbox. She replaced the notebook, knowing full well she'd be back tomorrow to copy Garrett's beautiful message to the Kindred Spirit.

"We hung around ... in case you needed us," mumbled Cat.

"You okay?" this from Viv. Tess looked anxious; she was fidgeting with the long sash of her dress. "Are things better now?"

They all looked so disappointed that she wanted to burst out laughing.

She addressed each woman's comment, giving each one a stern look in turn. "I'll always need you. And yes, I'm okay." She let out a big breath and met Tessa's eyes, "And things are much better. This is the second letter I read from him today."

Tess looked at her quizzically, "I know he sent flowers, I didn't know about a letter arriving."

Laurel shrugged. "It came in the mail yesterday, I just read it today." She shrugged sheepishly, "I forgot to check the box until this morning."

They all stared at her then Cat said, "So, what did he write?"

Laurel took in a huge breath and beamed at them. "He wants me to marry him."

"And . . ." Viv asked.

"I think I might like to do that."

All three women clasped a hand to their throats and as one, ran to hug her.

When the tears had died down again, Laurel said, "I suppose I should try to find him."

"He's gone. He told the guys that he needed some space, that he wanted to have some time to believe that you were still his. We don't know where he is."

"Then I'll just have to leave him a message in the notebook and hope he comes back to see if I answered him."

She turned back to the mailbox, dug out the notebook and found a pen. She had just written "Garrett . . ." and was collecting her thoughts, when she heard Cat whistle a loud catcall through her teeth. She looked up and saw the girls looking down the beach.

Three tall men in black suits with crisp white shirts were walking down the beach toward them. The breeze was fluttering their jackets open and rifling their hair. They were walking in sync, taking the same even strides, and she was immediately reminded of the way Il Divo came on stage, their commanding presence captivating everyone. Roman, Philip and Matt were smiling, their eyes on their brides.

"It seems your husbands are making their way down the beach."

All three women turned to face her, eyes glowing.

"Must have finished golfing," Tessa said innocently.

"Maybe they found Garrett," Cat murmured, clearly pleased about something.

"Why are they so dressed up?" Laurel asked.

As they neared, Laurel called to Roman, "What are you doing here?"

"We're best men."

"Best men?" Laurel asked, confused.

"Yeah, for the wedding."

"Wedding?" Laurel asked. She looked over at Tess, Cat and Viv. And noticed that they were all wearing filmy, long summer dresses.

"Don't tell me you were gonna say no?" said Roman. "After all your caterwauling, I thought for sure you'd accept Garrett's proposal."

"I haven't seen him. I thought he went off someplace after writing this."

"Look at the date."

She looked down at the notebook at Garrett's entry and noted the date. "This was written yesterday," she breathed out. "But I just read it, just now."

"You were supposed to come here yesterday to read this," Matt said.

Tessa spoke up. "It rained yesterday, so we couldn't bring her. We," she waved her hand at Viv and Cat, "decided to skip the first part and just bring her here today. We knew she'd say yes."

Laurel gasped. "What?"

"Well, you just said you wanted to marry him."

"Not today!"

"Why not today?"

"Uh, no reason I guess." Then her eyes lit with humor as she met Philip's, and pointed her finger at him. "Except you said I couldn't marry anyone without a pre-nup."

Philip tapped the inside pocket of his suit coat. "Got it."

Laurel jerked back in surprise. "You all were in on this?"

"Well, somebody had to get you two back together. The two of you were doing an abysmal job of ironing this out on your own."

"So, you ready to get married?" Roman asked as he came over and hugged her around the shoulders.

She looked down at her clothes, "I'm not really dressed for it."

"At least we managed to convince her to wear capris instead of the cut-offs she had on," Viv said, adding, "it was the best we could do."

"Judging by the way Garrett looked last time I saw him, I'm pretty sure he'd marry you if you were dressed as Ronald McDonald," Matt said.

"Look, here he comes!" Philip said, and pointed out toward the horizon.

They watched as a helicopter flew low across the water toward them, settling in the sand close to the jetty.

As the blades slowed, two men jumped out—Garrett and a man with a clerical collar. They walked, their arms swinging and looking stately and unassailable, striding up the beach.

As they approached, Garrett's wide smile faltered as he saw the way she was dressed. The disappointment in his eyes was palpable. She saw him square his shoulders and brace himself as if expecting a hard blow.

He stopped when he stood three feet away. "But you came back," he whispered.

"Actually, I never left. It seems I was supposed to have read this yesterday," she lifted the notebook and waved her hand at the page it was open to. "It was raining in the afternoon so we didn't make it here. I just now read your message."

"Oh . . . hmmmm. Awkward. So . . . would you have come back?"

She looked up into his beautiful face, a face that was now frowning and registering fear.

She saw panic cross his features and quickly allayed his worries. "Yes, I would have come back. But I'm only doing this once, so I want to hear the words . . . you have you ask me in person."

Garrett slid to his knee so fast she had to blink.

And as if he'd done this a thousand times, he one handedly snapped open a small black box and took her hand in his. "Laurel, I love you. Will you marry me?"

"Yes," she smiled down at him. "Yes!"

He took the ring from the box and placed it on her finger, then kissed it.

The most beautiful brilliant cut diamond winked back at her. Marquis-cut diamonds formed petals around the impressive center. She knew instantly that the flower setting had been created especially for her, as baguette-shaped rubies with details etched and set in gold to resemble her flash drive were inset into the band. It was stunning.

He stood, wrapped his arms around her, and brought her close for a lingering kiss. As he broke away, she thought she saw his eyes glistening.

"I was so afraid I'd lost you," he said. "So afraid you'd never even see me again."

"Well, I was angry. But then I realized, you were right, this was the way we were destined to meet, and I know that you would have told me eventually about my flash drive. I love you so much that I can't stay mad."

"Thank God," he breathed into her hair. "And speaking of God, this is Pastor McKeran. He's ready to marry us."

"But I look like a beach bum!"

"I'd marry you if you wore yoga pants, clam diggers, overalls, a wet suit, or absolutely nothing at all . . ." he said as he kissed her on the lips and enjoyed her deepening blush.

"I favor the last one," Roman said, and everyone laughed.

"C'mon," Garrett said, pulling some papers from his inside coat pocket. "I have the license, the reverend," he said, indicating the pastor, "the best men. You've got your best women . . . what more do we need?"

She smiled and took his hand. He led her down the

beach toward the water and everyone followed.

"I don't have any vows prepared," she said.

"Just say you love me and that you'll always be mine. That's all I need to hear."

"We haven't talked about a lot of things . . . like children."

"Do you want some?"

She nodded.

"Then I'll have a fine time gettin' you with them. Lord knows we already have the godparents to spoil them."

"How about your mother, wouldn't she want to be here?"

"You give her a grandchild and I think I'll be forgiven. Anything else?"

"Where will we live?"

"I think between the two of us we can afford any place on the planet. So you choose, but I'd prefer not to have to learn a new language, or eat bugs."

"You really do love me."

"Oh, yes. I really do love you." He took her arm and turned her to face the pastor. "Come, be my bride. In front of our friends and the Kindred Spirit, become my wife."

They were married on the beach as the three couples stood behind them, each husband gripping his wife around the waist. When it was time to kiss the bride, each man kissed his bride. After many hugs, Garrett swooped Laurel up into his arms and carried her to the helicopter.

"Where are we going?"

"We're going to a place where we can play and I can show you how much I love you."

After he settled her into her seat and buckled himself in, he signaled the pilot, and they lifted up into the air. She waved to her friends on the beach, and thought of her parents, and how happy they'd be for her. She'd married the man of her dreams. And the man of her fantasies.

They landed at the Ocean Isle Airport, and he told her she had two hours to get her passport and pack before they would be returning to get on a private jet to head for their honeymoon destination.

"Where are we going?" she asked, as he walked her to his truck, "I need to know what to pack."

He stood with her by the passenger door, holding it open for her. "Were going to Zihuatanejo. And don't bother packing very much. The idea is for us spend a lot of time naked."

"Zihuatanejo?"

"The final scene, *Shawshank Redemption*, remember?"

"Oh, isn't that in Mexico?"

"Southern Mexico, on the Pacific side, on a half-moon bay. Zihuatanejo's an Indian word, meaning place of beautiful women. With you there, the name will be more fact than legend. I wanted to take you to a secluded paradise. This one came to mind."

"I sure wasn't when it happened, but now I am so happy that I lost that flash drive."

"We had to have missed each other by only a few minutes. I tried so hard to find you. I practically memorized every entry in Quicken. Every Sunday, I sat in my car in front of Seaside United Methodist Church trying to figure out if you'd be there that week, and at which service."

"I don't go as regularly as I should."

"I figured that out from the frequency of the checks. I took the time I spent sitting there thanking God that I was the one who found your flash drive. Had someone else found it, we would probably never have met." He kissed the tip of her nose and saw her eyes close at the thought. "And somebody else would be stocking up on olive oil."

They laughed and he kissed her passionately, before

helping her inside the truck.

"So why was it in a baggie?" he asked as he started the truck and drove down Four-Mile Road.

"We live in an area that's all marshes and swamps, and there are bridges everywhere. I thought if I ran off the road, at least it would be in something that was waterproof. So . . . why didn't you just bring it to me when you figured out it was mine?"

"Oh, and how would that have gone? 'Hi, I'm Garrett, and I know that you dream about being married to a man who loves showing your pussy to his brothers, and that you would be perfectly fine with marrying a business man who takes you on business trips, just so he can drag you to a gynecologist in every city, so he can watch them examine you, or that you'd have no qualms if your husband, who was overseas fighting for our country, sent you a surrogate husband to keep you entertained. Just how would that have gone?"

"I see your point."

"Once I found out who you were, I knew I wanted to get to know you. And not just from what was on your flash drive. I was already halfway in love with you by that time. Actually being with you, talking with you, making love and having kinky sex with you, iced it—it took me all the way there. I love you so much, Laurel. I want to spend all my days and nights fulfilling each and every fantasy that comes into that pretty little head of yours. I want to hold you in my arms when we're exhausted from our efforts. And one day I want to make a baby or two with you. I'm so glad you're mine, Laurel. By marrying me, you make all *my* dreams come true. And I promise, I'll take you to a convention of OBGYNs if that's what you want. I want to make you happy above all else."

When she didn't say anything, just looked up at his face with tears in her eyes, he sweetened the pot. "For our honeymoon, I'm taking you to someplace tropical. We'll find a nice nude beach and I'll insist you get an all over tan . . ."

"Will you be naked, too?"

"Is that how your story goes?"

"Maybe."

"I'll follow whatever script you come up with as long as it means you'll say yes to always being with me."

"Yes." She leaned over and kissed his cheek. "Did you read the one about the Rakehell Society and the stable lass?"

"Sweetheart," he murmured as he pulled up to the stoplight, then pressed his lips against her neck as he nibbled his way back to her ear, "I read them all. Over and over and over again. If we need to do something on a horse, I'll go buy one." His hand slipped under her shirt and skimmed her midriff.

"No, no horse. But feel free to take me someplace where you can mount me and ride me hard."

"It'd be my pleasure. Hmmm . . . I suppose since I'm chartering the plane, we can afford to take some time to consummate our marriage."

In the driveway, he lifted her off the seat and carried her to house.

"You'll have to carry me through the garage," she said with a giggle, "I don't have my key, just the code for the garage door." They did not make it far into the house. As soon as he used the button on the wall to close the garage door he carried her through the connecting door and deposited her on the first soft piece of furniture he came to.

The bolster on the leather sofa served as a fine place to bend her over and let his "stallion" play.

Twenty minutes later, the gang showed up with cake and champagne, and they were toasted and congratulated over and over again, as Garrett was welcomed into the fold. Ribald jokes ensued, and advice from the men was offered, while the girls helped Laurel pack.

Then the truck was loaded, and Garrett phoned the pilot that they were on their way.

Chapter Seventy-five

Laurel was nervous, scared, and excited. She tended to over think things, and Garrett was trying to coax her down to the beach. She'd gone shy on him, and he was frustrated that she seemed ashamed of what she called her "over-the-top highly perverted issues." She was upset that she wasn't more normal in her sexual preferences. For two days she'd been so disgusted with herself that she hadn't allowed herself to free her mind and just play.

She was wearing the absolute tiniest bikini. The top was a narrow bandeau, gathered in the center with a jeweled clasp. The bottom the lowest rise bikini imaginable, he doubted there was much more than two inches of fabric covering her mound. There really wasn't all that much more to remove, he thought with a grin as he led her away from the pool area.

"We don't get to choose our erotic fantasies, Laurel. The things that zing you and make your body thrum with pleasure are triggered by nuances you have little say over. Say you're a fifteen-year-old boy, and a girl in a short pleated skirt with knee-high socks smiles at you, or your best friend's mother flashes her cleavage when she stoops down to pick up something. So ten years later, a girl in a school uniform makes your staff swell and salute the heavens, an older woman wearing a low-cut blouse makes your fingers twitch. So while I love the way things are, we both know that you need more. So let's do this, shall we? Let's explore one of your fantasies again—the sex on the beach one. They named a drink after it, so you know you can't be the only one who has this fantasy. And this is the perfect place for it. No one knows us here. No one."

He took her hand, kissed it, and gently pulled her down the steps leading to the beach. Then he walked alongside her, her hand gripped in his until they were out of sight of the hotel.

When they were on the other side of a secluded cove, in the shade of a single curving coconut palm, he stopped and turned her to face him. He took her face between his hands and kissed her thoroughly, their tongues meshing and seeking, their breathing accelerating and becoming harsh with desire. He stopped kissing her and stared into her languorous green eyes. She knew he could see into the depths where her dark passions churned with want . . . need.

"Right here, right now, I'm going to eat your pussy. With the seagulls and pelicans as an audience, I'm going to taste you as you come."

He smiled as he watched her face and neck flush, her teeth sink into her bottom lip, and he listened as her breathing changed. He turned her so she wasn't facing the bright sun, and then aligned himself so he stood in front of her before dropping to his knees. He kissed her navel and then followed it down until his lips met her tiny spandex bikini bottom, before hooking it with his thumbs and pulling it down past her knees. When she was bare from the waist down, he brusquely gripped her hips and took her hard with his mouth.

After rooting relentlessly through the curls of her tiny little friction patch, and finding her deliciously wet, he smiled up at her and said, "I am delighted with your new flavor. The banana tang of your sunscreen mixed with your musky dew is intoxicating. We should patent it."

He ducked his head and used his thumbs to hold her cleft open as the flat of his tongue lapped at her greedily. He delved lower to capture the juices she was bathing herself with, and he leisurely spread her essence along her slit, before returning to the swollen nub that was begging his attention.

His lips sought her clit, coaxed it to fully emerge, then sucked it artfully away from her body, gently tugging and releasing—feeling it throb as she shuddered and came. He softly milked her with his lips until she collapsed onto his shoulder.

After she had recovered, he stood, keeping his arms wrapped around her and holding her up. Then he bent and pulled up her bathing suit bottom . . . stroked her belly and nuzzled her neck. He stepped back, pulled the stretchy triangle that covered one of her breasts aside and kissed the hard tip.

"You are so responsive. I love that. Absolutely love that," he whispered as he suckled hard on the tip then released it with an audible pop.

"That was marvelous," she breathed, her eyes finally fluttering open.

"You were marvelous. So free. So beautiful. What a sexy woman you are. You please me so much. You'll never know how much." He kissed her deeply, his hands delving into her thick curls, holding her head to him. Ending the kiss, he looked down into her sweet, innocent face, her green eyes sparkling in the sun. "Here, let's cover this up. Don't want my sweet titties getting sunburned. I have plans for them later."

She smiled up at him. "I am so lucky I found you."

"Hey, hey, give credit where credit is due. It was *I* who found you. The best day of my life was the day you lost that flash drive."

"It felt like the worst day of mine at the time."

"It just goes to show you, you never know how things

are going to play out."

"Speaking of play," she said as she took his hand and began dragging him down to the surf, "let's play Atlantis now."

"How do we do that?"

"We do it underwater."

"We do what underwater?"

"Oil well," she said with a sly smile. "You spurt, I collect."

"Ah, oil well, one of my favorite games." He grabbed her to him, untied her top and tossed it up on the beach before he walked her into the surf. As the water reached their waists, he spun her around and for the second time that afternoon, pulled her bikini bottom down past her ass. His followed, falling to his ankles, that were quickly being buried in the sand. His fingers searched her, finding her still slick. He bent her over his arm and thrust inside and they both sighed from the intense pleasure of being one with the other.

"I can come in ten thrusts," he murmured against the back of her neck.

"I can come in six," she replied.

He pulled on her nipple, elongating it. "Four."

"One," she breathed.

He pulled out and plunged home. She shattered in his arms and as she clenched around him, he pumped twice before emptying his seed deep inside her. He cried out her name against the back of her neck and wrapped both arms around her waist, as he pulled her tightly to him. "I love you, Laurel. Jesus, how I love you."

The smile on her face as she looked over her shoulder was all he needed. A wave lifted them then swamped them and they laughed as they both scrambled for their bathing suits.

Walking up the beach, hand-in-hand, Garrett spotted a group of men headed in their direction.

He wished she had her top on, as he no longer wanted to even pretend he wanted to share the view. Their big grins as they came closer made him want to punch somebody. But as he looked over at her, at her head ducked in shyness and saw the telltale flush of lust creeping up her chest to her throat, he realized he couldn't deny her this.

Ironically, he knew that she thought he was allowing this because it was something he wanted. In reality, he was doing this solely for her. Because he knew this was what she needed, what *she* wanted. Like Callie, she needed approval, praise of her body, affirmation that she was beautiful. But if she didn't believe that this was what *he* wanted, that he actually desired to have other men to see her like this, he knew she wouldn't have been able to let herself go and allow it.

"Yowza!" one hollered.

"Oh baby!" another murmured.

"Great tits. Man you are one lucky dude."

"Don't I know it," Garrett said as he pulled Laurel to him. Despite the fact that it was killing him, he gave them a few more moments to gawk, and then he stooped and picked up her top. He handed it to her and she let it dangle from her fingertips, the string dragging and leaving a faint line in the sand as they continued walking back up the beach and away from the gaping men. They were heading back toward the hotel and he was afraid he might have started something neither of them would be able to handle.

"Did you enjoy showing your tits off to those men?" he asked as he took her hand in his.

"Yes," she breathed out then sighed deeply. "I love this. And you. I love that you want to show me off."

He groaned. Yes, he'd created the proverbial monster. "And I love that you want to please me."

"I always will."

"Then let's go back to the room. I'd like a shower, a

nap and a wake-up fuck before dinner."

"Oh yes! And I think I'm ready to start writing again, I have a new idea for another short story."

He groaned, rolled his eyes, and sighed. "I hope I can keep up with you."

She made no move to replace her top and he cringed as they walked into the pool area and over to their chairs where she bent to pick up her cover-up. Five men and six women stopped what they were doing to ogle her. She smiled at him as she slipped her tiny robe on and closed the placket covering her breasts. "This wasn't so bad. Maybe next year we can go to Jamaica, to the all nude beaches."

He groaned. He wasn't crazy about sharing her breasts with a handful of strangers, even though she thought that he was. If she thought he wanted to show her off completely—she was saying she was game for that, too. What was he going to do with this woman who wanted to spend her life pleasing him, doing everything his heart desired? He was going to love her, that's what. And he was going to make her happy . . . if it killed him.

Chapter Seventy-six

Garrett finished the online chat he was having with a clinical sex psychologist. He'd sketched out a little about Laurel's history, her writings, and described her very active libido and imagination. Now he was finding out what it all might mean in a sexual sense.

It wasn't like him to discuss something so revealing and intimate in a chat room with a doctor he didn't know, but he'd been vague in so many areas including their identities. Laurel'd been spurred on by their experience on the beach yesterday and now he needed to know how to proceed; she wanted more, he could sense it, but he didn't want things blowing up on him. He didn't want her to be unfulfilled, but he also didn't want her to be scared or intimidated. Or truly ashamed of herself afterward.

He had the means to accommodate her, in every way, and the necessary experience in most types of sexual encounters. Exhibitionism was new to him, however; he'd never run into a woman who got off on it. Until now.

"It may not have be an actual display that she needs to fulfill her fantasies," the doctor wrote.

"What do you mean exactly?" Garrett typed back.

"The allusion of her fantasy may be enough. Have you thought about using a blindfold and doing some playacting? Maybe you can be the stranger she fantasizes about."

A spark lit and Garrett grinned wide. His fingers flew

over the keys. "You mean pretend there's another man with me when there's not?"

"Sure. It really only matters what's in her head, not who's in the room. How good are you at make-believe?"

"I'm pretty damned good," Garrett replied, recalling some of the antics he'd been involved with in college.

"Well you've got nothing to lose and a whole new sexual realm to gain. She sounds hot. I'd go for it."

"Oh, she's hot all right. Her heady, over-the-top sexuality is what initially turned me on about her. Because of her writing, I knew I had to search her out and find her. And she hasn't disappointed."

"Well I'm glad you managed to find her, it sounds like this delightful woman needed to be run to ground and appreciated. And she actually fantasizes about being some man's trophy . . . naked arm candy . . . wow, she must be something. Good luck with your sex play."

"Thanks! You've been a big help."

"Anytime. Wouldn't mind an update on your progress. Dr. Jay."

Garrett sat staring at his computer until the flashing screen saver came on. He pulled the flash drive out of his pocket and rubbed it, fond thoughts making him smile.

He had just enough time to scan one of her files before she was finished with her pedicure and massage. He concentrated on a short story that he'd already read, one that had initially led him to the conclusion her sexual psyche included voyeurism as well as exhibitionism. It was a scenario that could easily be adapted to the beach. And since they were on this island far from home, where they both were unknowns, it would be a perfect place to try it out. It would be important for her to know that she'd never see this stranger again—that there wouldn't be a chance she'd ever run into him. She'd need to be assured that there'd be no repercussions for her indiscretion. Ever. A blindfold would be perfect. He took a bandana off one of her hats and tucked it into their beach bag.

When she got back to the room forty minutes later, she was droopy-eyed from the relaxing massage. He made her drink a glass of water, and then he gently undressed her and tucked her between the sheets for a quick nap.

He climbed in behind her and pulled her tight to his chest, and as she slept, he played out the scenario in his head. When she woke half an hour later, he was ready—more than ready.

"Since it's our last day, how about a walk on the beach? I hear there's a nice little cove on the backside of the island, about two miles from here, you up for a hike?"

"Sure," she said as she sat and stretched her arms high. Her naked breasts enticed him, but he adamantly faced away from her. He had to stick to the plan. They were leaving tomorrow; he wouldn't have this kind of chance again 'til who-knows-when.

While he slipped into his suit, he smiled to himself. It was his good fortune that during the getting-to-know-you stage, he hadn't told her about his quirky ability to throw his voice. It was uncanny, but without ever having had any special training, he was able to alter his voice and project it. So he was fairly certain that he could *audibly* bring another man into their secluded little inlet. It was a beautiful sunny afternoon and he hoped that none of the other guests had the idea of visiting this particular spot.

Forty minutes later, he smiled at Laurel as she stood beside him, topless, with her bikini bottom pulled down to the tops of her thighs, showing her freshly-shaven pussy to a total stranger. Or so she believed.

Knowing how powerful the brain was, so powerful that often a sensual person with a detailed imagination could bring themselves to climax using just that supreme sex organ alone, he catered to hers.

After opening a blanket and securing their things, he stood her at the water's edge and removed her top. Then he used it along with the bandana to blindfold her. And after a few minutes of telling her how lovely she looked, he invented a man walking on the beach toward them.

At first, she panicked, but he calmed her and told her he couldn't wait to see the man's reaction to her lovely naked breasts, and he even turned her in the direction he told her he was coming from. Her breathing hitched and her nipples hardened. Her lips parted and her tongue darted out to moisten them. She was beginning to go under and it was sexy as all get out watching her. His penis jumped and begged to get out to play.

He knew that if he could get her into the fantasy, get her to believe everything around her was real, that she'd be incredibly, insatiably aroused. He'd done it himself, many times—eyes closed visualizing super models wearing skimpy Victoria's Secret underwear baring it all for him, the hunky photographer . . . being the overly-endowed pile driver in a porn movie . . . the hero football player on a bus with all the Debbie Does Dallas cheerleaders. Yes, the mind was a terrible thing to waste.

Now he was helping Laurel, convincing her that her deepest, darkest fantasies were actually being played out right now on this lonely section of beach.

He was creating her fantasy, and along with it, a secret he'd have to keep. She could never know of his unique ability to throw his voice. And she could never know that he'd actually never consider sharing her with another man.

He looked at her standing there, her perfect breasts being thrust out for the approaching stranger. "He's almost here. He's young, looks like he's out for a jog. He's slowing down now that he sees you. Shaking his head in disbelief. Now smiling. Grinning. Pull your bottom down to your knees and show him your pussy before he walks past."

She immediately did as he asked, and the fact that she had obeyed him—unconditionally, that she had done whatever he had asked, no matter how demeaning, was such a turn on. He shivered from the desire coursing through him as he stared at her sun-kissed breasts, her nipples tightly pulled into hard peaks from knowing she was being exposed.

Blindfolded, she stood regal and proud as if she was fully clothed, instead of her breasts being bared and her genitals being blatantly exposed. Her vivid orange bikini bottom, pulled down to her knees, charmingly set off her sweet bare mound. There was no doubt that this woman was uncovered in a place that should be hidden from strangers, and because of it, her breathing was labored, her hands at her side fidgety. Garrett had no doubt that if his hand was between her thighs that it would be drenched.

He placed his words, thickly accented with a brogue, five feet in front of her. "Doo ya mind so much if I have a taste of 'er?"

He watched her face and neck flush, her teeth sink into her bottom lip, and her breath gasp. He smiled and answered as himself. "Help yourself, you're sure to be delighted with her flavor."

He, as the stranger, quietly moved from her side to stand in front of her before dropping to his knees. Brusquely, as he imagined a young horny Scot would, he gripped her hips and took her hard with his mouth. He used the flat of his tongue roughly, so she wouldn't know it was really him, and lapped at her greedily, disguising his touches by being purposely rough and crude. His tongue delved deep into her vagina, madly and wildly sampling her.

Well-placed moans summoned from deep in the stranger's throat vibrated through her, and comments from him, as Garrett, had her breath wheezing like a banshee. He lifted his mouth and boldly fingered her slit then thrust two fingers, twisted together for luck, into her. As if using a socket wrench, he flipped them back and forth.

"You look so hot Laurel, letting another man eat you while I watch. God look at him finger-fucking you. This is amazing . . . so fucking hot."

He couldn't disappoint her, not now that she was reveling in the attention she was getting from this "other" man. He had to do his part, play his part, but all he really wanted now was to finish what he'd started. He wanted to fuck her so badly.

"He's looking at your pussy baby, and lovin' your pretty little clit with his fingers."

He leaned in and wrapped his lips around her tight pearly little nub and sucked. At the same time he stretched his fingers deep inside her, scissoring them with each upward thrust. She fractured, spending against his lips and keening to the wind-driven clouds high above them.

After a few seconds, he, as the stranger, made a show of pulling up her bikini bottom and handing her back to Garrett and then "disappearing."

She recovered in Garrett's arms and as he slipped a Listerine strip into his mouth, he slowly removed the blindfold.

She looked around, blinked, and sighed. "Where did he go?"

"Up into the dunes."

He smiled at her and gathered her into his arms, his lips kissing the side of her neck. "Do you have any idea how happy you make me?"

She beamed up at him. "I think it works both ways. Were you really okay with that?" she asked, waving her hand where she'd just been pleasured, a delightful blush coloring her already sun-pinkened cheeks.

"It's all good, baby. It's all about your pleasure. And I want you to have it all baby, whatever you need, I want you to have it." He took her hand and dragged her over to the blanket and lowered her down to it. "My turn now."

He whipped off his bathing suit and covered her, his lips latching onto a pebbled nipple as he settled between her hips. He sucked hard then used his teeth to tug on it. Reveling in her soft gasp. He hitched her leg over his hip and rolled so she ended up on top of him. "Climb on baby and put me inside you. I am so ready for you."

And he was, as she soon found out. She gripped him, pulled and jerked his thick length to the music of his agonized low groans. Then brought him up to slide between her slick lips and into her welcoming warmth.

He stretched her to an escalating fullness with each upward push, grinding his pelvis against her and hitting all the right places. "Shit, baby . . . I can't stand this. It's too good, too fucking good. God I love this. And you. I love you. Too fucking much. Ohhh."

Their eyes met, both irises reflecting the brilliant sun and looking luminous and dazed.

"God, what you do to me," he groaned as he gripped her hips and thrust high, leveraging them both off the blanket. She shuddered and sighed as her body ignited with her orgasm. It washed through her, purging her of all sensation but the zinging heat flushing through her. He was filling her, stretching her divinely, and holding her to him as if she was all that mattered in his world.

He retreated, and his warm hands held her as he entered her again and again, increasing to a punishing pace while he held her fast to him. Staccato breaths expanded his chest and fueled him for more of the same, until he shouted her name and found his release. Accompanying his moans of, "Laurel, Laurel, Laurel," was a litany of swear words strung together that didn't begin to complete a single coherent thought.

The adoring wonder in his eyes matched hers as he

shuttered, sighed and came back to the living. As the reality of what they'd been doing, and where, came to him, he barked out a carefree laugh, deep and throaty and completely exhilarating. He was the happiest he could ever remember being, and he was madly and thoroughly in love with this sweaty and sated woman stuck to his chest.

"Wow," was all she could say.

He bent and kissed her, his tongue claiming her mouth.

"Mmm . . . your mouthwash lasts a long time."

He buried his chuckle in her belly as he blew kisses against it to cool her. Then he lifted her into his arms and stood, a miraculous feat considering he'd just destroyed his stamina. He carried her with him into the surf and while she floated in his arms, he nuzzled her ear and breathed, "Will you marry me?"

"What?" she wasn't sure she'd heard him right.

"I asked you if you would marry me." He was looking down into her face as he turned her in circles in the water, her hair streaming out, behind her making her look like a beautiful mermaid. "Would you marry me again? On every anniversary would you marry me again?"

"Yes. Yes. Yes!" Her eyes shone with tears.

He lifted her high in his arms and kissed her. "Oh, the naughty games I'm going to play with you Mrs. Grayson."

"Mmmm," she said as she reached down to cup his balls, "How long do I have to wait?" Her lips curved into a sexy pout.

"At least until we get back to the room, I see a catamaran heading into the inlet."

"Do you think they can see us?"

"I believe those are binoculars glinting in the sun."

"Are you making that up?"

"Stand up and see."

As soon as she did they heard the men on the sailboat

clap and holler. Laurel quickly ducked back into the water and Garrett chuckled, "What's the matter? Changed your mind about going topless?"

She stood and turned around to face him, brazenly she placed her hands behind her head and posed for him. "These belong to you now, it's up to you to decide if you want to share the view."

Cinching his hands around her waist, he ran them up her torso until he had a breast circled in each hand. "Let them find their own, these are mine."

Laurel looked into his face and he noticed her eyes were damp and not from the ocean. "Laurel, what's wrong?"

"I'm glad you said let them find their own. This was fun. And I like that I got it out of my system. But if it's okay with you, I don't think I want to take my clothes off for other men anymore."

He spun her around and held her tight to his chest. "Baby, it's more than okay! It's actually what I would prefer, too."

He kissed her softly, murmuring against her lips how much he loved her, how much he adored her, and how much he loved her. And that he would always treasure her and the memories of their wild and crazy honeymoon.

Epilogue

When they got back home and began combining their things, Laurel started cleaning out closets to make room for Garrett's clothes. At the top of one guest closet she found her baby scrapbook. It had been years since she'd thumbed through it, so she sat on the guestroom bed and opened it.

She smiled as she looked at all the pictures of her as a baby, dressed up for an Easter parade as a bunny, in a tiny tutu for ballet classes, in an even tinier outfit for gymnastics . . . all the way up to pictures of her in cap and gown at her college graduation. She rubbed the tips of her fingers over the faces of her beaming parents.

Then she flipped back to close the book and it opened to the page of her birth announcement. At the top of a page was a faded matchbook. She lifted the book to stare at it closer. It was from the liquor store she and her dad used to go to when they went to the races, The Starting Gate. She put the album back on her lap to open the flap. She gasped when she saw the handwritten note scrawled around the inside edge of the matchbook.

"Our baby conceived. Sept, 19th 1983. Won $2,000 in the tri-fecta! Her name will be Laurel, named after this town.

Flash Drive

When Garrett came into the room and saw her crying, he sat down beside her. She showed him what she'd found.

"That's pretty interesting, because that same racetrack is the reason I'm so well off today."

"Really?"

"Yeah. I had carefully researched a stock; it was my first big investment. I finally jumped in and bought it and the next week it sunk. I lost nearly everything but I did manage to recoup $5,000. I was driving around kind of lost, wondering if I should give up, when I was led to the track. I'd never been one to play the horses, knew virtually nothing about the sport really. Then in the fifth race, there was this horse named "Try Again." I figured what the hell, five grand wasn't enough to set up an investment career anyway, so I put it all on the horse. And won 180 grand. The next day, I started investing with a fresh and cautious mindset, and after that I picked up a few investors and things went from there. I never went back to the track. But I've always felt that the town of Laurel was the reason I'm wealthy now."

Laurel ran her fingers over the matchbook. "I'm named Laurel, and it's where I was conceived. You live there; it was there you made your fortune—"

"I was conceived there too. My parents went to a family reunion and stayed at the Holiday Inn on 179."

"Wow . . . that's a lot of coincidences."

He took her hand, "Baby, where you're concerned, there are no coincidences. This is the way God planned everything; it all fits as it's supposed to . . . you . . . me . . . and whatever comes of our union."

"I think we'd better use protection when we go to clean out your house in Laurel next week."

"You think a thin sliver of latex is going to stop God if he wants my sperm to find your egg? Sweetheart, if you're

608

not ready, we'd better abstain."

"Yeah, like that's going to happen." She rolled her eyes.

He patted her knee then squeezed it lightly. "I can go by myself . . ."

The doorbell rang.

On his way to the door, he took a few lemon Jelly Bellys from the silver bowl in the foyer and popped them in his mouth. The intricately engraved bowl had been a wedding gift from Roman and Tess, and Laurel kept it full of Werther's and lemon jellybeans.

He came back with a long white box.

"Someone send flowers?" she asked.

"Not hardly. It's addressed to me. And it's from Ireland."

He pulled off tape, ran his thumb along the sealed edge and lifted the lid. Nestled inside cotton batting was a walking stick. He lifted it out and they both stared at it. There was an intricate carving of a wizard at the crook, his long hair scrolling down the sides of the cane. "Looks like one of my grandfather's."

He fished in the box for a note and found one. He read it aloud. "Made this for you and your bride, my boy. Now get busy, I'm getting on in years and would like to meet my grandchildren before I die. Grandfather Merlin Grayson."

"Your grandfather's name is Merlin?" Laurel asked, her eyes agape.

"Yup. Sure is. What a lovely gesture," he said as he admired the intricately engraved artwork. "This looks a bit like him, too. I should take you to Ireland to visit him. He'd adore you."

Merlin . . . the wizard man in the tree at Sea Trail that had brought Cat, Tessa, and Viv their true loves. Merlin . . . who they had chanted to at the cemetery just up the street. Merlin . . . who had made sure her lost flash drive was in a safe place.

"I'd like that. I'd like that a lot."

"About that other matter . . ."

"Yes?"

"When we go to Laurel, let's tempt fate. I'm ready if you are. I mean, we will have nine months to prepare, you know."

She laughed and pulled him down to the bed with her. "Surely, we don't have to wait until next week."

The End

Note to Readers:

For those of you who would like to finish reading *The Rake and the Young Innocent*, please go to my website for instructions on how to download the story for free. I hope you have enjoyed this book. I would love to hear from you. Feedback, both positive and critical, is very important to me. Thank you for buying my book.

Jack DeGroot
www.jacquelinedegroot.com

If you enjoyed this book, check out *The Widows of Sea Trail* trilogy—the stories of Catalina, Tessa, and Vivian as they find true love with Matt, Roman, and Philip.

About the Author

Jacqueline DeGroot lives in Sunset Beach, North Carolina with her husband Bill. When she takes a break from writing, they enjoy riding bicycles, walking on the beach, lounging at the pool, and making plans to take off in their "vintage" RV. She started reading romance novels when she was a teenager and still has her beloved collection of Emilie Loring and Georgette Heyer books. She read her first erotic novel when she was fifteen and kept it hidden in a box in her closet. Thankfully, she doesn't have to keep that collection hidden anymore. She loves to hear from readers and has a website you can visit at www.jacquelinedegroot.com

CPSIA information can be obtained at www.ICGtesting.com
Printed in the USA
BVOW011627140612

292702BV00002B/1/P